WHAT IT TAKES TO KILL A BULL MOOSE

WHAT IT TAKES TO KILL A BULL MOOSE

A POLITICAL THRILLER

BULL MOOSE
BOOK 1

MICHAEL FEDOR

Edited by
THEA NEWELL

Edited by
JOSHUA M. COFFEY

EPOCH
EDGE PRESS

Copyright © 2024 by Michael Fedor

All rights reserved.

Published by Epoch Edge Press, 2024

ISBN: 979-8-9899213-1-7 Hardcover

ISBN: 979-8-9899213-2-4 Paperback

First Edition: June 2024

Cover Design by Michael Fedor

No part of this book may be reproduced in any form or by any electronic or mechanical means, including information storage and retrieval systems, without written permission from the author, except for the use of brief quotations in a book review.

For requests to distribute, reproduce, to use portions of this copyrighted material, or to schedule its author for media interviews, email bookrights@michaelfedorbooks.com or call 717.745.7224.

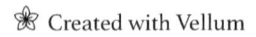

❧ Created with Vellum

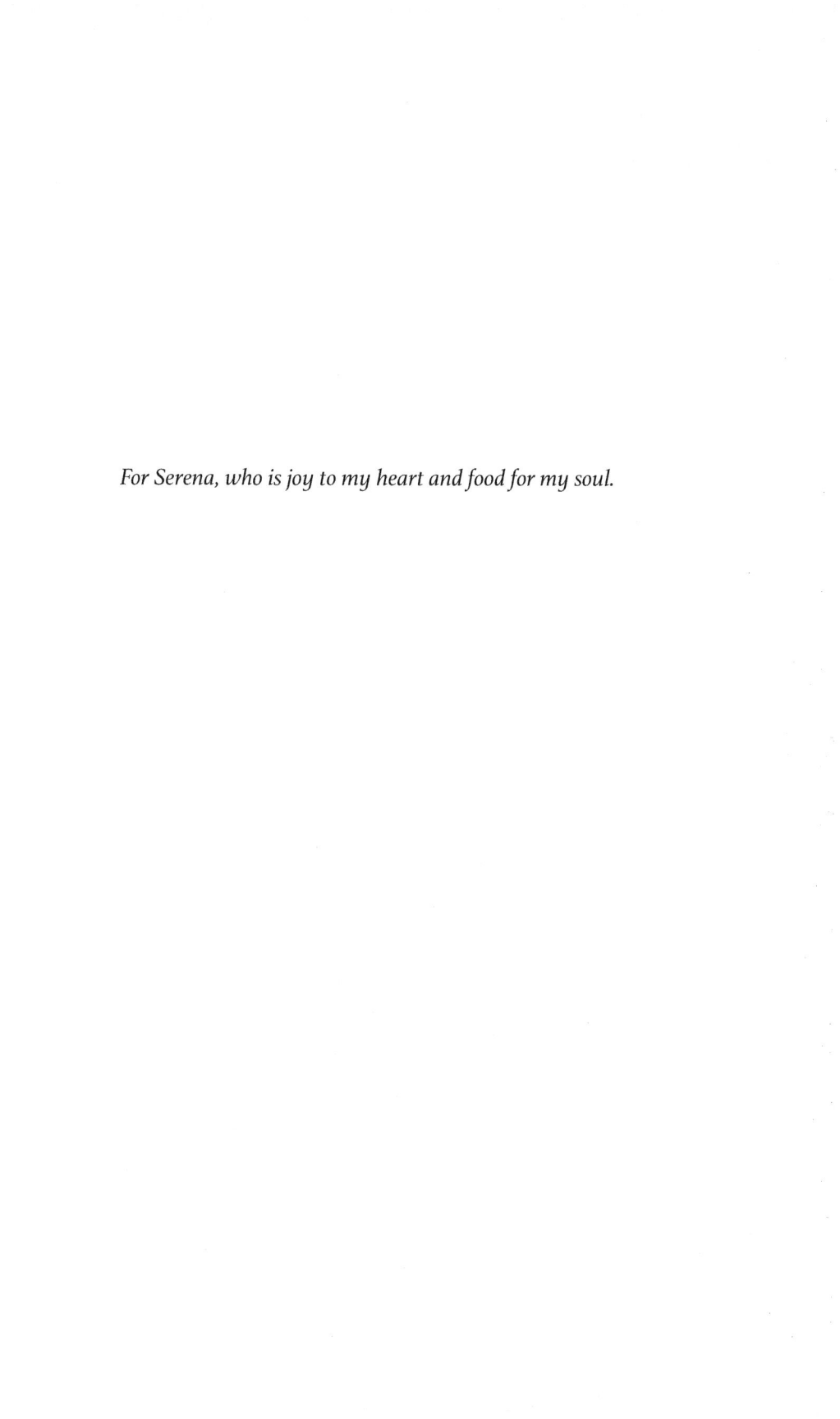

For Serena, who is joy to my heart and food for my soul.

"Friends, I shall have to ask you to be as quiet as possible. I do not know whether you fully understand that I have been shot, but it takes more than that to kill a Bull Moose."

— FORMER PRESIDENT THEODORE ROOSEVELT

Opening remarks at a campaign rally in Milwaukee, Wisconsin, October 14, 1912. President Roosevelt spoke for an additional 50 minutes before seeking medical attention. He spent two days in the hospital recovering from the bullet, which was never removed from his chest. A rolled-up copy of a speech and a steel glasses case slowed the point-blank assassin's bullet to a non-lethal speed as it entered his chest.

CONTENTS

Foreword   xiii

PART I

CHAPTER 1   3
Close Encounter

CHAPTER 2   7
The Proposal

CHAPTER 3   21
The Devil You Know

CHAPTER 4   38
Invisible Man

CHAPTER 5   43
Decisions, Decisions

CHAPTER 6   68
A Bold Approach

CHAPTER 7   77
Juniper Models
"Piper Files Historic Bid for Both Party Nominations."   77

CHAPTER 8   81
Reboot

CHAPTER 9   97
Sparks

PART II

CHAPTER 10   111
Objects Are Closer Than They Appear

CHAPTER 11   122
Change the Rules, Change the Game

CHAPTER 12   133
The Secret Southern Summit

CHAPTER 13   150
Duty Calls

CHAPTER 14   156
Declaration of War

CHAPTER 15   164
Diagnosis

CHAPTER 16 — *Perceptions* — 166

CHAPTER 17 — *Death and Resurrection* — 169

PART III

CHAPTER 18 — *Misled* — 179

CHAPTER 19 — *Save America* — 188

CHAPTER 20 — *The Ticket* — 199

CHAPTER 21 — *Cursed Revelations* — 206

CHAPTER 22 — *Former Friend* — 220

CHAPTER 23 — *A Meeting Off the Record* — 227

CHAPTER 24 — *Broken Promises* — 233

CHAPTER 25 — *Conventioneers* — 251

PART IV

CHAPTER 26 — *The Golden Four* — 279

CHAPTER 27 — *Surprise Patient* — 284

CHAPTER 28 — *Enemies Domestic* — 290

CHAPTER 29 — *Bad to Worse* — 295

CHAPTER 30 — *The Curse of Knowledge* — 308

CHAPTER 31 — *Ghosts* — 314

Election Day: 61 days. Early voting: Begins in the first states in just over two weeks. — 314

CHAPTER 32 — *Aftermath* — 331

CHAPTER 33 — *River of Doubt* — 345

CHAPTER 34	354
Damnatio Memoriae	
CHAPTER 35	358
Rest in Peace	

PART V

CHAPTER 36	369
Trouble in Athens	
October 1: 38 days until Election Day	369
CHAPTER 37	383
Election War Games	
CHAPTER 38	394
A Traditional Stolen Election	
CHAPTER 39	402
Francis Scott Key	
CHAPTER 40	411
Successionist	
CHAPTER 41	418
Seeds of Revolution	
Acknowledgments	429
About the Author	431
Also by Michael Fedor	433

FOREWORD

In November 2004, after George W. Bush's reelection, I sat down to write a book. It was my third year teaching at a central Pennsylvania high school. My American literature curriculum was full of founding documents, nonfiction examples of dissent, Nathaniel Hawthorne, Mark Twain, Ray Bradbury, and Arthur Miller. I ended the class by showing my students the brilliant movie *Dr. Strangelove* from 1963.

I'll confess: the book was not good. It was a 100,000-word diatribe of complaints and grievances. The characters were weak, and the writing committed the main sin I coached my 11th graders about in their writing—show me, don't tell me what's happening.

The incomplete work, *Bull Moose*, was tucked in a three-ring binder in my basement for the better part of twelve years until the 2016 election. I watched as many of the book's themes unfolded during that national election—candidates few people truly loved and a candidate willing to toss aside every norm in order to shock, awe, and win.

I started rewriting the novel in 2016. I took an online class in self-publishing and added a shocking ending in which the sitting president refused to accept the election results. I wrote about an Arab

Spring-style revolution that attempted to force the president from office. Our family expanded that year with the birth of our third child. The pregnancy had a cataclysmic conclusion that nearly took the lives of my wife and our newborn son. I set the project aside to focus on my family.

On January 6, 2021, I saw my novel unfolding in real time on the news. I wondered if I was onto something with this story. Was I offering a warning or just an entertaining, true-to-life tale that was as shocking as it was likely to come true?

When I lost a position I loved in 2023 due to downsizing, I was given the gift of time to see the project through once and for all. I discovered Thomas Umstattd, Jr. and his incredible Novel Marketing podcast and AuthorMedia.com. I finally had the impetus and a strategy to get the 20-year project across the finish line.

That is how the world of Bull Moose was born — a new world of political intrigue set in 2038 and beyond in America. Now, the story includes a sentient A.I. named Ziggy and a time when America's dominance is not a given.

The protagonist of the story is former Senator Jackson Piper. His story begins in *The Senate Deception* and continues in *What It Takes to Kill a Bull Moose*. Disillusioned by the politics of destruction and the pursuit of power for power's sake, Jackson is humiliated by a defeat. He goes into a self-imposed exile with his family in the mountains of Colorado to reinvent himself and hide from the forces of corruption that cost him further pursuit of his dreams.

The antagonist of Book 1 is President Russell Warner. After revealing a ruthless side in *The Senate Deception*, Warner is back wreaking havoc on the nation with a national agenda lacking moral scruples or solutions to lift a nation sinking fast in a new age where American supremacy has faded. Warner will do anything to stay in power, potentially even rigging his reelection. Warner is about to face two forces he did not count on standing in his way - that do-gooder Jackson Piper back with a vengeance and the Curse of Tippecanoe. That is, if you believe in curses.

This is a thrilling, page-turner of a tale. The story is complex, with several subplots around the 2044 presidential election. I wrote this book in part for the segment of readers who are ready for a reinvention of American politics. One that takes us beyond our binary answers to every problem, the limiting two-party system, and for folks who feel left behind or rightly outraged by just how unworthy of this great nation the stormy present has become.

But make no mistake, I'm retired from politics. This is meant to be a great story that makes the reader think that perhaps there are other ways out of our mess. I hope you enjoy the read!

-Michael

Disclaimer

This novel is a work of fiction. Names, characters, businesses, places, events, locales, and incidents are either the products of the author's imagination or used in a fictitious manner. Any resemblance to actual persons, living or dead, or actual events is purely coincidental.

The use of real brand names, trademarks, or specific commercial locations is for storytelling purposes only and is not intended to imply any affiliation with or endorsement by these entities. These brands and locations are used fictitiously and should not be viewed as an accurate representation of the products, services, or locations involved.

While real places may be mentioned, their depiction in this story is a product of the author's imagination and is used to provide a sense of realism and familiarity. These descriptions are not intended to reflect the current state, reputation, or characteristics of these places.

Readers should note that this story is intended for entertainment purposes only and should not be used as a source of factual reference about any brands, locations, or historical events mentioned within.

Awards

What It Takes to Kill a Bull Moose (Bull Moose Book 1) by Michael Fedor is the recipient of the following awards:

2024 International Firebird Book Award Winner
Political Thriller (Speak Up Talk Radio)
2024 International Firebird Book Award Winner
Speculative Fiction (Speak Up Talk Radio)

PART I

1

CLOSE ENCOUNTER

The second Jackson Piper raised the rifle to his shoulder, he regretted it.

The sudden shift in weight, which he had not thought through, caused the precariously placed tree stand to buckle ever so slightly fifteen feet above the forest floor.

The tree stand, placed by a friend who was a professor at the University of Denver, had held his two-hundred-forty-pound frame valiantly for well over four hours. However, now he had caused the poorly secured strap to slip, loosening its hold on the smooth bark of the birch tree. Luckily, Jackson did not fall fifteen feet to the forest floor. But the cacophony of branches, brass rifle shells, and his half-eaten turkey sandwich falling to the earth from the near disaster sent his 900-pound intended target running for safety.

Jackson lifted the scope to his right eye quickly enough to see the jagged antler rack of the mature bull moose disappear like a ghost into a thick aspen grove. It was remarkable how quickly and silently this half-ton beast could move a five-foot-wide antler rack through the dense forests of northwest Colorado.

"Fuck!" said Piper loudly so that every forest creature in his vicinity knew his frustration. "I should have known better than to trust the placement of a tree stand to a *fucking* English professor."

Piper had a habit of talking to himself aloud when he was frustrated or angry.

A red fox squirrel emerged from a nearby rotting tree stump and darted for the half-eaten turkey sandwich, the one Jackson's wife Catherine had so thoughtfully prepared for him the night before his final chance to score a bull moose before the end of rifle season.

"Hey! You thief!" The fox squirrel paused for a moment, staring up at Piper. It was almost as if the furry creature had understood. "Oh, hell! Go ahead now. Lord knows you probably need the calories more than I do."

The squirrel snatched up the sandwich and disappeared into the autumn undergrowth.

Feeling insecure about the status of the tree stand, Jackson Piper unloaded the .308 Winchester, which had been his father's rifle, secured the weapon across his back with its sling, and began carefully descending the tree to the leaf-covered earth below.

It was a warm afternoon for Colorado in mid-October – almost 60 degrees. All this climbing was making Piper sweat under the leaf-print, safety-orange coat. When his size 14 shoe reached the ground, he removed his baseball cap, looked up to where he had just been sitting, and ran his large hands through his thick, brown beard. It now included obvious signs of grey, which he stared at with disappointment in the mirror each morning.

"That would have been one hell of a fall," said Piper aloud.

Suddenly, Piper heard a very low, raspy grunt behind him. He turned his head slowly; standing not twenty feet from him was the very same moose he had scared a moment ago. It had circled back for a curious, closer look at this strange-smelling creature formerly in the tree, now standing alone on the ground.

The bull moose was mysterious in its body language, terrifying in its sheer size and scale, and as beautiful a creation as any designed by God. Standing this close, ten miles or more from any manmade structure, Jackson wondered why he had worked so hard for two years to try to kill one. Moose meat was not a delicacy he cared to try. Perhaps it was the romantic thought of a majestic trophy over the fireplace...

His wandering thoughts and admiration for the beast were jolted back to reality when the creature stirred.

The moose began to shake its head, wiggling the heavy dewlap that dangled from its furry chin. Its thick antlers contained two monstrous, hand-like paddles that blew the branches and leaves around it. It looked at Piper with one eye, ears forward, then back. Forward, then back.

"You're trying to figure out if I'm friend or foe, aren't you fella?" Piper asked nervously. Moose hunting was not supposed to involve being this close to an irritated bull. Piper had hunted and killed plenty of squirrels as a tween with his now-deceased grandfather. He had shot six whitetail bucks, more turkey and grouse than he could count during twenty or so years hunting with his father. This animal was something entirely different.

The moose turned his head and stomped his front feet, creating a powerful thump that indeed shook the earth under Piper's overpriced boots.

The moose let out a grumbling growl. It sounded bear-like. It was horrifying to hear it this close.

"Listen, fella, how about you just head south, and I'll go north back to my truck," Piper said, trying to negotiate like he had in his days in the U.S. Senate and House. "We can forget I ever came into your woods to try to kill you, ok?"

Another low, rumbling growl, louder and longer. Piper's arm hair stood on end.

He decided it was time to try to load the rifle in case he had to fight his way out of there. Never taking his eyes off the espresso-colored mammoth, Jackson reached into his pocket for one of the three rounds he had unloaded from the gun. He slowly swept the rifle from the position on his back to hold the weapon in his left hand. He reached for the steel ball at the end of the bolt with his right hand, slid it slowly back to expose the magazine, and placed the cartridge into the chamber. He firmly pushed the action forward.

Jackson did not flip on the safety.

All this movement was unnerving to the moose, and it started to pace, frustrated that Piper was not running away. Jackson raised the rifle to his shoulder and attempted to align the tip of the rifle with the chest of the bull without looking through the scope. He opened both eyes to try to get his bearings, and that is when he made eye contact with the beast.

In those eyes, he saw not fear but certainty. He saw not panic but determination. He saw power, courage, and innocence.

Piper slowly lowered the rifle. He flipped on the gun's safety with his thumb. When he did, the bull moose raised its awesome head and straightened its front legs, like he was standing at attention. The moose bellowed; the sound was deafening this close. Piper did not look away.

Then, the moose turned with an air of simultaneous respect and dismissal and disappeared again into the thick Aspen grove.

Jackson Piper, the former junior U.S. Senator of Pennsylvania and four-term Congressman, stood alone in the warm autumn forest, vanquished by a stronger foe for the second time in four years.

2

THE PROPOSAL

Two weeks had passed since Jackson Piper's encounter in the Colorado wilderness. Tonight, he was safely back at home preparing dinner for the guests. It was a dream home situated on a rural lake in the Rocky Mountains, close enough to the hustle and bustle of Denver not to feel so isolated but remote enough to provide privacy for a man running away from an embarrassing defeat. Jackson and Catherine were trying to start over where they felt less judged and scrutinized at every turn than in their former home in Pittsburgh, Pennsylvania.

Jackson Piper had relinquished the title of Senator for professor; he taught part-time at the University of Denver and was part of a law firm specializing in state government affairs downtown. Luckily, because of his once meteoric national profile, Jackson Piper's name associated with the firm was nearly all the work they required of him. He was permitted to be highly selective about his clients and projects. These days, it was mainly site redevelopment at the request of the State of Colorado.

Dr. Catherine Piper was the primary reason they landed so softly after his election loss four years earlier. She was an accomplished and highly sought-after oncologist. Her research into simulated intelligence-assisted gene editing therapies put her on the map as someone thrusting the world closer to a cure for cancer's scourge.

"Hey, Jack! Should I pull these potatoes out of the oven?" Catherine called to her husband on the back patio. He was huddled over a sizzling grill and well-bundled for the wind off the lake on a late October evening. "How close are we to dinner time?"

Not accounting for the heels of his worn, pointed-toe cowboy boots, Jackson stood at 6 foot, 5 inches. He rubbed the smoke from his grey-blue eyes with thick but soft hands.

Jackson bellowed back through the screen door, "Yes, go ahead!" He flipped the steaks over the glowing red coals. His heavy carmine and grey flannel shirt was impeccably pressed and tucked into his thick brown denim jeans. He wore a heavy black down vest, zipped up over his barrel chest, his full beard with shades of hickory, pecan, cinnamon, and silver gently rubbing the collar as he looked down over prime cuts of beef.

It had been over a year since he last laid eyes on Senator Diesel Browning and his old Chief-of-Staff, Ron Bender, in person. The anticipation of their visit had him buzzing with excitement all day. He could almost feel the energy in the air, crackling like electricity before a storm. Memories flooded back to him of the intense meetings and heated debates that followed the triumphal reform of Senate rules during a historic January nearly five years ago. He fondly recalled moments of camaraderie and shared laughter with Diesel, who had not only been his roommate while they shared a rented townhouse as Senators; he had also come to relate to Diesel as a brother. He couldn't wait to catch up and see what new developments awaited them.

Jackson yelled through the open door, "Did you see the article I forwarded you, hun? A Super PAC of over $1 billion possibly financed by Marco Alvarez is supporting the reelection of President Warner..."

Catherine came to the rear deck. "We don't have to carry on this conversation for the entire mountain to hear. And no, I did not. I don't read those tinfoil conspiracy rags you subscribe to."

"It is the only real journalism left now that Warner has shut down all major news outlets not repeating his version of the 'truth.'" Jackson took a breath. "Marco Alvarez and the Old Party," he repeated in disbelief. "Not a political alliance I would have necessarily seen coming."

Catherine continued, "Yeah, I would not think they have that much in common, hence why I think the story is hogwash. Besides, don't presidential candidates have to reveal all their financial backers?"

"The Super PACs are the exception. They can conceal their sources of income, especially since the FEC was defanged after the last election," said Jackson. "If the story is true, President Russell will not have to raise a dime for his reelection. He will have millions, maybe even a billion, of the Alvarez fortune to hammer the Other Party nominee."

"Who did you say was going to be our Party's nominee?" asked Catherine as she shuttled back and forth between the kitchen and the dinner table on the back patio.

Jackson frowned. "Our *former* Party. The Others abandoned us, and so we left them."

"Good thing you're retired from all that, right?" Catherine said as she kissed her husband's cold lips on her tiptoes. "Is he the guy that looks like a ghost?"

"That's him! Senator Paul Drummond," said Ron Bender, approaching from the far side of the patio. He spoke the name like he had a mouth full of vinegar. Bender puffed on a cigar and shook his head at thinking of Paul Drummond as his Party's nominee for President of the United States.

Jackson exclaimed excitedly as his anticipated guests, Ron Bender and Diesel Browning, arrived. There were hearty exchanges of handshakes, smiles, and back-slapping hugs, followed by gentle hugs and kisses on the cheek for Catherine.

Ron Bender had aged considerably since last Piper saw him. Jackson's former Chief-of-Staff was approaching 70, but few believed him when he shared his age. "Good genes," he'd laugh. He easily looked to be in his late fifties, perhaps as a man permitted to drink from the fountain of youth. As Jackson observed the new arrival, he noticed his jet-black hair had begun to thin and was considerably more grey. His face was now heavily etched with lines and wrinkles as if all the stress of his forty-year career buried for so long had suddenly risen to the surface at once. He dressed well and kept himself well-groomed. He had been married and divorced twice. The work performed by people like Ron Bender made it hard to keep up a marriage when he was never home to maintain it. He loved his gadgets, especially his digital assistant Ziggy, who was always with him and always listening, ready to be of service.

The junior Senator from Ohio, Diesel Browning, stood next to Bender on the patio. Four years after a fierce reelection campaign that resulted in his narrow victory, Browning had now secured a powerful slot as Conference Chair for the Other Party in the Senate. He was almost as tall as Jackson, more physically fit, with rich mocha skin and a dimpled smile. He was a proud veteran of the U.S. Army, having attained the rank of Captain before his honorable separation from service more than fifteen years ago. Piper and Browning met when members of the House of Representatives before both won Senate seats.

"Governor Fox is about to drop out of that race," Diesel said. "And Representative Khan is not gaining any traction whatsoever. She's doing this to move her geopolitical conspiracy theories. She campaigns entirely from Washington. If nothing changes, fast, I think it's safe to assume that Senator Paul Drummond will be our Party's nominee for President."

"Your Party's nominee," Jackson said. "Remember, I changed to an 'Independent' when we moved out here."

"A silly move," Ron said.

"It gives me the ability to work with both major Parties for clients, not to mention my work with the State," Jackson said.

"Lucky you," Ron replied, rolling his eyes disapprovingly. "Four years ago, your name was being whispered as a candidate for President. Now you're grading papers about the Civil War written by first-year students who likely had their A.I. assistant write it."

"Speaking of assistants, how's Ziggy?" Jackson asked. He was referring to Bender's assistant, which they used obsessively during their final year in office. She was brilliant and sultry, always pursuing Ron Bender's approval and possibly affection.

"She was getting a little too clingy; I had her reprogrammed and upgraded," Ron said. "Here, ask her yourself."

Bender held his phone out, and on the screen was Ziggy, the always cheerful, always helpful digital assistant. She looked just as Piper had last seen her, with wavy red hair, bright blue eyes, and a flawless complexion.

"Senator Piper!" the A.I. screamed as the front-facing camera on Bender's phone captured Piper standing in the dimming light over the hot grill.

"I missed you, Ziggy," Jackson said, thinking for a moment. "Ziggy, how many pine needles are on that tree behind me?"

"You're so silly, Senator," said Ziggy. "14 million...14,946,351."

"Still as sharp as ever," laughed Jackson.

∾

DINNER HAD BEEN DELICIOUS, and now the dishes were neatly stacked in the dishwasher, and Catherine had retired to her study to review notes for a surgery she was performing tomorrow. The dinner conversation had been filled with numerous recollections of the good old days in the House of Representatives and then shifted to updates on the fast-growing Piper twin boys. There were detailed stories about Piper's adventures in the mountains, including the harrowing encounter with a bull moose weeks ago. Now, it was just Ron, Diesel, and Jackson sitting in three chairs on the stone patio, a blazing fire conjuring smoke and sparks between them under a magnificent blanket of stars of an autumn Colorado sky.

They puffed on long, dark, tightly wrapped Honduran cigars. Jackson's cigar tip disappeared along with Piper's lips under his bushy beard.

"Christ, you look like a doomsday prepper with that beard, Jack,"

Diesel said, ribbing his much-missed friend. Piper's new hobbies of hiking, fishing, and hunting in Colorado spurred him to grow a full beard and mustache. They kept his face warmest on those cold mornings in the mountains.

"It's absolutely stunning here," Ron commented. "How long have you and Catherine had this place now?"

"We bought it halfway through my Senate term. Before the economy tanked," replied Jackson. "In '41, We took stock of what mattered, where we wanted to be. The clean air and big skies of Colorado sure beat the hell out of cramped neighborhoods and the traffic of Pittsburgh."

Diesel smiled. "And since you no longer need to be close to Washington..."

"We moved the kids and the dog out here permanently once the University of Colorado landed Catherine for their cancer research hospital," Jackson said.

Jackson savored the rare treat of the cigar. He would almost never buy one on his own, and he never smoked one in front of the children. He was especially open to enjoying one with such dearly missed company.

"I can always count on you to have at least two cigars in your jacket when you come to visit," Jackson said, pointing at Bender. "Sometimes they are a peace offering, sometimes they are for celebration, and sometimes they are an excuse for us to go for a walk and blow off steam."

Ron Bender smiled warmly.

"So which are they tonight?" asked Jackson. "These are expensive, so I'm guessing you want something?"

Ron could keep up the small talk no longer.

"Jack, you can't tell me you don't miss the electricity of being a national leader. For a while there, you spoke, and the whole country was listening."

"My students at the University of Denver listen well enough," Jackson said.

Ron shrugged and took a puff of his cigar. Strike one, he thought.

"Do you remember your first run for Senate? What they said about you?" Diesel asked as he stretched his arm out to tap ash into a clay pot on the table between them. Only close friends would ever refer to Piper as "Jack." Diesel Browning was one of the few.

"Of course I do. That I needed to wait my turn. I had not paid my dues," Jackson said, taking a long, quiet drag on the cigar as a dozen memories passed through his mind.

"Do you remember how you won that race?" Diesel asked.

Jackson smiled slightly, "I remember being way behind in the polls. Congressman Dabrowski was as insecure as they come and running scared because he had done exactly nothing in twenty years in Congress."

"He had lost touch with his voters," asserted Ron. "Forgotten why he had run to serve in the first place. He got comfortable with a title. He rarely left DC. But that was not a race you were supposed to win."

"I still believe it was the haymaker we threw when we took that news crew to visit his 'home' in Pennsylvania," Jackson said, making air quotes with his fingers.

"Empty as a well without water," Diesel laughed.

Jackson joined with a thundering laugh, "That silly SOB didn't even bother keeping so much as a chair in the house. I remember peering through those windows, the news crew clamoring over my shoulder. They wanted to break in. I had to talk them out of it."

"That was a bold move," Diesel said.

Ron seized on the moment. "We need that type of courage back in DC, Jack."

"Don't kid yourself. DC is doing just fine without me," Jackson said, suddenly becoming serious.

"Oh, yeah," replied Diesel, "Let me tell you, we are just busting with courage in Congress. Let's see, is it the useless floor speeches? Or is it the way grown men and women in the Senate run and hide when Warner issues a threat? Or perhaps it is the outright corruption? Do you know how many bills Congress passed this year, Jack?"

"I do not know," Jackson said coldly, making his disgust clear.

"Five total," Ziggy said through the speaker on Bender's phone.

"That's right, Ziggy, five!" Diesel said in disgust, holding five outstretched fingers on his right hand at Jackson.

"Warner likes an ineffective Congress, Diesel. Justifies his constant expansion of executive authority," said Jackson.

Ron Bender smiled a plotting grin. "You mean to tell me that a man once on the cover of a magazine as *Man of the Year* has given up on the fate of the country he loves?"

The former Senator scoffed and gave Ron a dirty look as he shifted in the heated chair.

"It was an ugly loss, Jack," said Ron. Piper had lost reelection in Pennsylvania by less than 2,000 votes out of over five million cast, losing to a former Philadelphia NFL quarterback who had never voted in a single election.

"It was a bullshit beat," Diesel said. "No way on earth you should have lost to a shitty former Philly quarterback who never even bothered to register to vote before he ran against you."

"Warner recruited and financed him, start to finish," said Jackson. "That much was public record."

"It was a joke - a puppet show," Diesel said.

"It was Warner's revenge for escaping the trap he and Meriwether had set for you on the filibuster," Ron said.

"Without a doubt," Jackson frowned.

"I'm afraid to say Warner is up to his old tricks, but on a bigger stage and far more powerful this time, Jack," said Diesel.

Piper sat silently in the dark, not making eye contact with his friends. Browning's words echoed in the darkness for a moment.

Not a day had passed in nearly four years that he did not miss being a U.S. Senator. What he really missed was the importance of the role, not the dysfunction of Congress. But the thought of having to tangle with his former Senate adversary Russell Warner, who was now the President of the United States, made his stomach turn.

"You lost your nerve, Jack?" Diesel asked his former colleague, his voice low with meaning. "Is that it? Or don't you care about your country anymore? The one I risked my life for over in Korea?"

Jackson's eyes narrowed as he leaned in towards Diesel. "You and I both know that's bullshit," he said, his tone serious and direct.

Jackson decided to take his own shot while trying to change the subject: "Are you running out of clients, Ron? Are you afraid that if you quit working, Father Time will catch up with you?"

Ron let out a roar of laughter that broke the tension of the moment. It echoed in the crisp night air. "Come on, Jack, we know you better than everyone in your life except Catherine the Great." This was meant as a term of endearment, and both Ron and Diesel referred to Mrs. Piper this way.

"Who would kill you both," interrupted Piper, "and me with the surgical knives she keeps in our bathroom if she knew you were here to try to talk me into running for Senate again."

Jackson reached for a new beer from the small cooler on the patio. "That's it, right?"

With a knowing smirk, Catherine Piper emerged from the shadows. Standing tall and stunning, Catherine exuded an air of regal elegance. Her piercing blue eyes held a sharpness that could cut steel. They were the key feature that caught Jackson Piper's attention in line at a concert twenty-five years ago. The soft curves of her body betrayed a hidden strength of soul. Shoulder-length brown hair shone like silk in the moonlight. Catherine had an alluring sensuality, one that her husband could not resist. She gracefully lowered herself onto her husband's lap.

"That's enough, gentlemen," she said playfully, her voice laced with intrigue. "No more fun will be had at this house until I'm let in on what's so amusing." Even from the study on the other side of the house, Catherine had heard their laughter echoing in the night. The fire crackled and danced in the stone fireplace, casting flickering shadows across their faces. She could smell the sweet scent of cigar smoke lingering in the air. With a twinkle in her eye, Catherine awaited an answer.

"Senator Browning was suggesting that I lost my nerve when I lost the seat in the Senate," Jackson said, then he took a long swig from his bottle of cold beer.

"Certainly you have," Catherine said as she searched for her own beer from the cooler. Clearly, she had chosen to join them. "Sure, you have found comfort and routine here in Colorado, but without discussing the loss with anyone but me, you seem to have hit reset on your life."

Ron jumped in immediately. "You are such a gem, Catherine. Hear that, Jackson? Even Catherine doesn't understand why you would quit…"

"The Party turned on me after the filibuster fight," said Jackson.

"The Party is a bunch of cowards, but it was Warner who manufactured your loss. People have come back from worse, Jackson," said Diesel.

"It wasn't the loss, guys. It was how they did it. People I had trusted, who I thought were my friends, scattered to save their own hides," Jackson said. "The two of you were the only ones from the Senate who stuck with me until the final votes were counted. Not even Sterling stuck with me. He was too concerned about becoming Majority Leader."

Sterling Powers was the third member of the Stanton Park Trio - the nickname for the bipartisan housing arrangement in which Jackson, Diesel, and Senator Sterling Powers, Old Party member of Michigan, shared a townhouse for six years just east of the Supreme Court in Stanton Park.

"Don't forget me, Jackson," Ziggy said.

"And yes, you, Ziggy," added Jackson.

Ron waved his hands, "That's in the past now, Jack. We can't be Monday morning quarterbacks."

Jackson grimaced at the poor choice of metaphor.

"I'm sorry—stupid choice of words, Senator. But what's done is done. We need to move forward. We need to make smart decisions from now on."

"Like smoking cigars at an oncologist's house?" Catherine snuffed out her husband's remaining lit cigar into his half-empty beer bottle.

Ron's playful demeanor shifted as he slid into the seat next to Catherine. He leaned in close and spoke in a hushed tone, "Listen, I know we've been focusing on the Senate, but that is not why we are here. Something doesn't feel right. I was in Manchester last week for business and decided to take a walk around town. It's presidential primary season, yet I didn't see a single sign or poster supporting any candidate. Something seems off."

Jackson laughed. "Maybe people have more important things to do with their lives. Last cycle's turnout was the lowest in a generation."

Ron looked at him, devoid of a smile. "We are talking New Hampshire, where the first in the nation primary is sacred business. The last four years have been no cakewalk, and Warner is thoroughly disliked, so why isn't anybody running for President?"

"It's not uncommon for the President not to face a primary challenge in his own Party during his reelection campaign," suggested Jackson as he uncapped a new beer.

"We are not talking about the Old Party. We are talking about the Other Party - our Party," said Diesel.

"To be honest with you, Diesel. I see a distinction without a difference," said Jackson. "The two Parties have become one and the same, complicit in bringing the government to a halt. Voting NO and screaming about enemies is way easier than devising solutions people will accept and voting YES to pass them."

"How right you are, Jack," Ron said.

"Drummond, Fox, and Khan are all running," said Jackson.

"Governor Fox just suspended his campaign after he met with the Party Chairwoman, Diane Fogerty. Representative Khan has never set foot in New Hampshire. Her campaign is not serious. It's just about making noise."

"There should be a line of candidates out the door of the New Hampshire state house waiting to file for the Other Party's primary. So why is no one serious running?"

The Pipers stopped smiling and looked earnestly at Ron.

Ron caught their gaze and responded. "Let's be clear here. I know for a fact that Catherine could certainly live without you being in the public eye again, Senator. Endless fundraising, personal lives subject to public scrutiny, at best, and at worst, hateful lies spread by opponents."

"They call each other enemies now, Ron. Like opposing armies on a battlefield. All true, by the way," Jackson said quietly, taking a long drink of beer.

Ron stood and began to pace. He said, "But the country is at a moment of historical consequence, and the only two seeking to lead it are Russell Warner and Paul Drummond. I know a dozen governors who, four years ago, would have cut off their pinkie fingers if it guaranteed they'd be President. Plus, I could name three dozen current and former Senators and Representatives. But only one of them has raised their hand? Doesn't that seem strange as fuck, Jack?"

"Inconsequential Paul Drummond," said Diesel, adding another log to the fire.

Ron continued, "When I had wrapped up my visit to Manchester, I was too tired to drive back to Boston, so I got a room in the nearest hotel. I lay there awake for hours, bothered about the lack of energy and enthusiasm in the state where presidential politics drives everything every two years. So I finally went across the street to a bar that used to be called Sid's – a real dive bar..."

"Only you would pick a dive bar, Ron," said Jackson.

Ignoring him, Ron continued, "Just so happens the Drummond campaign was staying at the same hotel that night. And two staffers whom I know to both have been fired from the Senate for their less than above board tactics were sitting at the bar, drunker than skunks and running their mouths..."

"Get to the point, please, Ron," insisted Catherine.

"Ziggy, please take over," said Ron, propping his phone up with a stone so that Ziggy appeared to be joining them by the fire. She was now on the screen dressed in a pink parka and fluffy white earmuffs like she was about to hit the slopes.

"Mr. Bender and I overheard the two Drummond campaign staff discussing their disdain for Paul Drummond. They referred to the need to keep Party Chairwoman Diane Fogarty current on campaign happenings, and no significant move by the campaign was to occur without Diane's approval," the simulated intelligence assistant explained.

A nearby screen mounted by Jackson near a hot tub to watch football games flickered to life, controlled by Ziggy. It displayed her research, exposing a web of growing financial donations from hundreds of donors. A dark, ominous cloud crept around the fire as the numbers on the screen grew more outrageous: a 120 percent increase in donations to the Other Party then funneled to Drummond. This was followed by a staggering 214 percent spike in new contributions to the Other Party, again funneled to Drummond. The patio was silent as everyone processed the implications.

"Who could be behind this?" Catherine finally asked, breaking the tense silence.

Ron Bender's voice cut through the air like a knife. "Based on a relational analysis, 100% of these donors have just one man in common. One powerful, insanely rich man."

A photo flashed on the screen of a dark-haired Latino with sharp features and a brilliant smile.

Jackson's eyes widened in shock. "Bullshit."

Diesel confirmed Piper's worst fears. "It's Marco Alvarez, the elusive and ungodly wealthy head of Juniper."

"Oh, come on," shouted Catherine, breaking into laughter. "You all have had too much to drink." No one else was laughing.

"You can't be serious? Are you telling me the man Jackson said just pledged a *billion* dollars to a Russell Warner super PAC is also directing money to Warner's opponent? You can't possibly believe this, Jackson?"

Jackson shrugged grimly. "Stranger things have happened."

"Fuck! Name one, dear," said Catherine, outraged by conspiratorial nonsense.

"You're saying one person is financing both Parties and both presidential campaigns?" asked Jackson.

Diesel nodded grimly. "Not just financing them, but likely controlling both candidates."

The gravity of their discovery weighed heavily on Catherine's mind as she came to grips with the true extent of corruption potentially in play. Had Alvarez found a way to control not just one Party but both of them? And given the 10:1 financial advantage Alvarez was building behind President Warner, it seemed the election outcome was predetermined before a single ballot was cast.

***

Jackson crept up the stairs after another hour with his friends. He had forgotten the genuine happiness their friendship brought to his heart. Catherine and the children were asleep, and the family's chocolate Labrador, Hagrid, was snoring in his spot on the bed. Jackson made his way to the bathroom in the darkness of the poorly lit bedroom to recycle those beers he drank. He paused in front of the mirror, noticing more gray hair coming into his beard. Not getting any younger, he thought to himself. For a moment, he allowed his mind to wander to thoughts of the Oval Office and addresses to Congress and seeing the country as a candidate. These were dreams he had extinguished with his loss four years ago. He washed those fantasies away with a cold splash of water to his face. Then Jackson noticed the cigar Ron had slipped into Jackson's pocket as he departed. He pulled it gently from his shirt. It had a brilliant blue metallic wrapping, and emblazoned across a shimmering white star label in bright red letters were the words: America Needs Piper.

3

THE DEVIL YOU KNOW

The screech of Air Force One's tires pierced the warm afternoon air as the presidential aircraft touched down at San Jose Mineta International Airport. President Russell Warner descended the metal stairs, the California sun glinting off his stylish tortoiseshell sunglasses. A convoy of black eSUVs sat silently on the tarmac, ready to escort the president and his entourage to their California destination. Warner's polished leather shoes clicked down each step until he reached the asphalt. He moved energetically for a single man approaching 70.

The motorcade whirred to life, kicking up dust from the tarmac in its wake. Two presidential limousines were nestled safely in the center of the pack. They were identical in every way. Heavily armored, electric with a hydrogen backup engine for security, the flag of the United States over the right front fender, and a flag bearing the seal of the Office of the President on the left. Only the Secret Service knew upon arrival which would carry the president, the decoy a necessary precaution. The scent of expertly maintained leather lingered inside the limos throughout the pristinely maintained cabin. A generous supply of the president's favorite diet soda and cashews were stowed in special compartments for his comfort.

Since that fateful day in Dallas, the Secret Service has obsessively guarded each president. But for Warner, the level of protection reached new heights, even for short domestic trips like this one. Not a potential threat slipped by their notice—each face in the crowd was scrutinized, each street swept for explosives or protestors, and such threats were cleared ahead of time.

The presidential motorcade slowed as it entered the city, residents lining the streets to catch a glimpse of Warner. Cameramen stood poised, ready to capture his arrival for distribution to the feeds. The White House would edit the footage first, removing any imperfections before handing it off to the networks to beam across the nation as "live." In 2043, truth depended on perspective and an army of creators wielding the latest artificial and simulated intelligence to polish reality. The networks that remained in business were all friendly to the president; they would accept the White House's replacing angry faces in the crowd with smiling ones. Protest signs reading "Eat Shit Warner" were replaced with patriotic slogans such as "Warner Will Save America" and "Reelect Warner." The networks knew broadcasting this heavily edited content was part of the price of remaining in business.

President Warner's smug confidence in his greatness only served to amplify the despair and hopelessness of the average American in 2043.

The White House was artful at such alterations, careful not to change too much to risk an UNTRUTHFUL designation from *The Mark*. The federal government and some state governments seemed to get away with such altered realities more easily than corporate or private actors. The coding behind *The Mark* was proprietary and owned entirely by a company called Juniper.

Juniper was the brainchild of Marco Alvarez. A Stanford grad, Marco had personally programmed the first version of *The Mark* before getting a funding round to finance a market-dominating build-out of features that no other tech company could figure out how to replicate.

The Mark had revolutionized the world's information consumption in just four years by instantaneously checking the veracity of a news article, a tweet, a snap, a photograph, and even a video. Blue checks meant truth; a yellow eye meant caution, some elements may have been digitally altered or inaccurate; black skulls meant lies, falsehoods, conspiracies, or inaccuracies. Most media automatically affixed *The Mark's* assessment to anything shared by anyone everywhere.

There was no appeal process for *The Mark's* determinations; all decisions by Juniper's software were final. While The Mark was the most prolific and widely known product, it was its least controversial.

The Mark delivered Juniper a $39 billion IPO. Alvarez used that enormous injection of cash to build an empire around lightning-speed advancements in artificial intelligence and its successor, "simulated intelligence," commonly identified by the prefix Si.

The difference between A.I. and Si was akin to looking at a picture of a milkshake versus holding one. Si was thousands of times faster than AI, able to predict anyone's preferences, capable of driving cars, cooking food, calculating the precise telemetry a rocket needed to reach and land on Mars, or providing you with precisely the right recipe for dinner to suit your known preferences on a Tuesday in October. In short, Si was in many ways superior to human reasoning and intelligence.

There was SiMail, delivered by extraordinary advancements in mail handling. It privatized nearly all aspects of the Postal Service and put 600,000 Americans out of work.

There were SiClerks, programmed to perform a variety of white collar data entry and bookkeeping jobs. Over 1 million jobs evaporated in under a year as companies rushed to deploy the technology.

SiService was the name for the disembodied voice that handled all manner of customer service calls, messages, and even in-person complaints. For in-person SiService, the voice was attached to a computer-generated human face that was indiscernible from a real person.

SiDefense systems could counter cyber attacks, automate patrol drones, and automate complex wargame scenarios to respond automatically if command and control were compromised or severed. However, the United States of America remained highly skeptical of integrating AI and SI into its defense systems despite many smaller countries in South America and Asia going all in on SiDefense systems. US objections had slowed SiDefense's growth to a crawl by 2043.

And then there were the unofficial terms for Si tech in daily life, mostly derogatory.

"Hokes" were the invisible intelligence that drove cars, trucks, delivery vans, and more. It was another derogatory reference to the black chauffeur from the Uhry play *Driving Miss Daisy*. Most vehicles on the road in 2043 were driverless except for their "Hoke."

"Slingers" were the automated robots that took fast food orders, prepared the food with 100 percent accuracy, and put nearly 2 million out of work. The American populace was notorious for venting their frustrations in the drive-thru, cursing and berating Slingers, who seemed just to take the abuse like frightened slaves.

Juniper's technologies touched nearly every aspect of modern life.

President Russell Warner, elected in 2040, was scheduled to attend a private event at the luxurious estate of Juniper CEO Marco Alvarez. Exceptionally brilliant, shrewd, and wealthy, Marco had built Juniper as an extension of his personality.

Recently, Alvarez skyrocketed to the top of the list as the world's richest person. Around the same time, Marco Alvarez made a remarkable financial pledge: $1 billion in support of reelecting the president.

The motorcade passed another line of spectators, some genuine supporters, and some were paid $500 each to hold "Re-Elect President Warner" campaign signs. President Warner waved from behind the six-inch bulletproof glass. For all the unrest and violence that permeated daily American existence, the forty-ninth president enjoyed protection like no other. It was hard to tell if he could not see the suffering of the American people or simply chose to ignore it.

"Goddamn, I love this job," Warner said to Olivia Clay, his Chief of Staff, seated in the seat directly across from him. "I think I could handle this job forever. Just look at them, fawning over me like a Savior."

Olivia was distracted by the fifty competing priorities she was working to keep off Russell Warner's desk. That was the job of the Chief of Staff—defend the President's time for only the most serious matters. It was a high-stress, low-reward job. The pay was meager, and it utterly destroyed the personal life of anyone who held the post. In fact, she was the third Chief of Staff to President Warner in as many years.

When Warner's self-praise did not elicit any sort of response from Olivia, he quickly changed the subject. "Tell me again, Olivia, why Alvarez needed to speak so urgently. In person, nonetheless."

Olivia Clay had been managing the billionaire's relationship since they met him at a fundraiser in New York City the year before. She was a brilliantly beautiful former model turned cable news anchor. On her nightly cable news show, her signature gleaming espresso-brown hair and salty smile caught the eye of then-Senator Warner. She left the network to join his campaign and later joined the Warner Administration as Communications Director; now, she was his ever-present right hand.

"Marco Alvarez does not share his every thought with me, Mr. President," explained Olivia.

"Had to be serious if he could not speak over the phone," said President Warner.

Olivia shrugged silently. She pretended not to notice the president's face twitch. He was like a petulant child, and his bad behavior could be inflamed if she did not give him the minute-by-minute attention he craved.

"Sir, he obviously wants something. He is already ensuring our campaign and five Super PACs have all the money we need between now and next November."

"I know a lot of rich people, Olivia. I'm rich. You're rich. Rich people's money always comes with strings attached, and usually with impossible requests when you least expect it," he said.

Olivia had opened her electronic tablet to see if her briefing packet had any answers.

"Seems he just returned from two weeks abroad. Budapest, Moscow, Mumbai, and Beijing."

"Is he auditioning for Secretary of State now?" said the President, irritated. "I don't like being summoned. I'm the President. I'm the one who does the summoning."

"The person writing over a billion in checks to fund your reelection gets to tell us to come to visit, sir," asserted Olivia. She was the only one who could speak to him so directly without fear of reprisal.

"Oh yeah? Is he paying you, or am I these days, Olivia?" scoffed Warner with a dismissive wave.

She blushed.

"You told me to keep an eye on Mr. Alvarez and keep him happy, and that is exactly what I have done."

Warner gave her a sly smile but said nothing further on that subject. For now.

The motorcade of fifty-one vehicles, including Secret Service, local police, paramedics, White House aides and staff, and military advisors, wound its way up the hills, tires purring quietly on the paved roads. They passed through a guard shack to the gated community, temporarily commandeered by Secret Service agents two hours before arrival. Olivia gazed out the window, inhaling the scent of eucalyptus trees as they neared their destination. She turned to the president, choosing her words carefully.

"Mr. Alvarez has been generous, sir, but one misstep could undo all his support. This visit is about keeping him happy after the long flight here on short notice."

The president nodded, straightening his tie. Olivia steadied her nerves as they approached the sprawling Alvarez estate, the largest in Los Altos Hills. Olivia surveyed the manicured gardens, hoping this carefully orchestrated visit would secure Marco's continued goodwill.

A second gate protected the Alvarez home from unwanted company, but it was opened as the motorcade arrived. The president's limousine proceeded up the short drive along with the decoy and three Secret Service detail vehicles, one of which contained several pints of the president's blood type (A+) and various high-tech emergency medical equipment.

"There's our host now," said Olivia, spotting the dark-haired, athletically built Marco Alvarez - no coat, in a pink shirt, no tie, and the top two buttons undone, revealing a portion of his hairless chest. He wore crisp blue jeans and was barefoot.

"Should we circle the block so he can finish getting dressed?" asked the President, already irritated by the casual nature of Marco's appearance.

"This is how the tech elite dress in California. In fact, I'm surprised he went to the trouble of putting on long pants," commented Olivia. Her eyes lingered on the man's muscular arms and chest.

As a Secret Service member opened the mammoth, armor-plated door of the limo, Alvarez smiled warmly. He was standing alone, but his chief of staff, Jon Rushan, was just feet away, holding an electronic tablet and pen, ready to scribble notes or directives.

Out stepped the President, buttoning his charcoal grey suit coat over his scarlet tie. Warner did not have to feign admiration for the splendor of this estate. It was miraculous in its size and detail, rivaling the beauty of his home in Las Vegas. With the sun setting serenely in the valley, its elaborate façade sharply contrasted the surrounding natural landscape.

"It's wonderful to welcome you to my home, Mr. President," said Alvarez genuinely.

"I'm sorry I'm so overdressed for the occasion, Mr. Alvarez," said the President.

"Nonsense. You are running a multi-trillion-dollar economy. You should look serious. This is, well, serious in Silicon Valley. I wore pants, and they are not joggers," said Alvarez, smiling as he shrugged.

The two walked to the opened front door. The President stopped walking.

"Would you like my staff to wait in the vehicles?"

"No, please, they are welcome in my home. I have a quiet place for us to speak uninterrupted, and I have ensured there is a beautiful dinner for all," said Alvarez.

With a subtle flick of his fingers, President Warner signaled for his team to follow him into the heavily guarded home. The Secret Service agents didn't need further instruction - they had already scoured the house for any potential threats before "Jackpot" arrived, their codename for President Russell Warner.

"Don't worry, Mr. President," said Marco, "this event is entirely on me. Silicon Valley hospitality."

"I'm not at all worried about who is paying for the food. I'm quite curious what you want in return for your generosity, Mr. Alvarez."

"Please. Call me Marco, Mr. President. You're looking better than ever," complimented Marco.

Russel Warner was nearing sixty-nine years old, but his body looked like that of a much younger man. Standing at just over six feet tall, he was lean and muscular from his daily religious runs. Despite weighing only 170 pounds, he constantly worried about his appearance and obsessively monitored what he ate in front of others. His pale skin stood in stark contrast to the bronzed complexion of Marco Alvarez, and even his perfectly slicked silver hair and neatly trimmed goatee couldn't hide the sharpness of his arched nose.

President Warner smiled at the compliment, nodded, and the two walked out into a sitting room at the very rear of the 12,000-square-foot home. It was a home office but was devoid of any books. An entire wall of frameless glass panes filled the far wall. Although they opened to the pool below, they were shut tight now, indicating to the observant Russell that this was intended to be a highly private conversation.

They sat, two drinks awaiting them on the table between the leather chairs. Each sank snuggly into the fine leather upholstery. The president raised the glass to capture the aroma of the drink before he imbibed it.

"Jam Jar? And neat." observed the President.

"I know you are a fan," said Marco.

The president glanced at one of his agents assigned to clear any food or drink handed to him. Agent Rodney Hill gave him the thumbs up.

"I am indeed. I keep a special stash of this gin in my desk in the Oval," said the President.

Marco lifted a neat glass of Pappy Van Winkle 23 whiskey and offered a toast. "Salud, ya que eres muy poderoso."

"Salud, ah, how exquisite," said the President, gently tapping his glass with Marco's, taking a sip. "Very powerful, huh? Clever."

"Your Spanish is good, Mr. President," commented Marco.

"Two terms in the Senate representing Nevada, it came with the job," smiled President Warner.

"Indeed," smiled Marco in return.

Marco glanced at the two Secret Services agents following them into the room. President Warner got the hint.

"Rodney, Joseph, I will be fine. You may step out, please. I'll scream bloody murder if he attempts to stab me with a piece of broken glass."

Reluctantly, the two armed guards exited the room and closed the soundproof door behind them.

The smile disappeared from the president's face. "So let's discuss what this $1,000 glass of gin and the $1.1 billion donation to my reelection is about to cost me."

∽

A DOZEN presidential senior staff members filed into the dining room of the Alvarez home. Strangely, although the room was filled with luxurious food, there was nowhere to sit. There were no chairs anywhere in sight—just a long table filled with food.

"I guess it's standing room only, whispered Olivia to another senior advisor to the president.

"Please, help yourselves. Welcome!" said an unintroduced Alvarez staffer to the crew.

Each politely stowed their phone in a pocket and picked up a heavy glass plate. There was caviar, shrimp, oysters, and all other manner of fish. Steak tartar and innumerable and unidentifiable delicacies and gourmet offerings filled the table.

Olivia grabbed something she could identify and walked to the far wall of windows, which offered a glimpse of the horizon, now dark with the arrival of twilight. The many water features of the backyard were splendidly lit, and the pool shimmered below. She wondered when she last had the time to go swimming.

Alvarez's head staffer cleared his voice and spoke. "Ladies and gentlemen, welcome to Los Altos Hills. Tonight is just the first of what we hope will be many visits to this home."

There was an excited buzz amongst the staff; some had never had access to such lavish treatment, which is usually reserved for the President, the Cabinet, and other VIPs.

"Please, if the wait staff could pass out the wine, I would like to suggest a toast," said the man. The wait staff quickly executed the command, and then the host raised his glass and waited for the murmur to return to silence.

"Welcome. My name is Jon Rushan. My friends call me Rushy, and I invite you to do the same. I offer a toast to our victory," Jon Rushan said, raising his glass. The rest of the men and women in the room did the same, some tapping the crystal together, echoing the sounds around the large room.

Rushy made his way directly to Olivia Clay. Her beauty and grace brilliantly outshone the rest of the staff in the room. "So tell me, how are things looking according to your internal polling?" he asked, pulling her away from the rest of the crowd.

Olivia was caught off guard. "No one believes in polling anymore, Mr. Rushan. it's easily manipulated data used only to confirm opinions and feed fake stories."

Jon did not let up. "Fine. I'll answer the question myself if you are going to play games, Ms. Clay. President Warner has a 34 percent job approval rating among all registered voters nationwide. That number jumps to 47 percent when modeled around voters likely to vote in the coming election. But President Warner polls at 55 percent when you model for ballots in precincts that are most likely to be counted and qualified, especially in swing states."

Olivia took a drink of the wine, wondering if she should change the subject or give an inch to the obviously well-informed man from...wherever he was from. "That's pretty close to what our numbers say."

"Not pretty close," replied Jon. "Those are your numbers, Ms. Clay."

"Oh, I believe you," said Olivia, feeling a tad put off by the man's suddenly aggressive tone. She had met several times with Marco but had never come in contact with this man. How long have you been working for Juniper?"

"Longer than you have been seeing Mr. Alvarez," said Rushan, looking out at the lush gardens.

Olivia started to object, but why waste time lying to a man who was as informed about Marco's world as she was about Warner's?

"I'm surprised Marco has never brought you up?" she said. There was a tone of dismissal in her voice.

"Not as surprised as your boss is right now," said Rushy.

"Come again?" asked Olivia.

Rushan turned and looked into her bright blue eyes. "We've done our part to help keep the calm. The Mark has kept some of the more fucked up stories of Warner's term in office out of peoples feeds."

"Come again?" asked Olivia.

Rushan continued, "We understand the price to keep the federal government out of our code. Our algorithm is predisposed to see stories openly critical of President Warner as likely false. Hence, the less truthful a story appears to be, the less popular the story becomes, and the less we have to openly suppress it. But we need to plan for the inevitability that a technology will come along stronger or smarter than our algorithm. That could push things well off the game plan."

"So long as you have friends in the White House, we can find ways to protect your market share," said Olivia. "People will do their parts, for sure. You just worry about giving us what we need to keep people playing along in Washington and keep stuffing the feeding tubes of the American people."

"I am certain we will be working a great deal closer, Ms. Clay," said Jon Rushan, taking a sip of his wine while not breaking eye contact with the suddenly annoyed White House Chief of Staff.

∼

MARCO BROKE THE SILENCE. "Drafting Jessica Brown, an outspoken black Congresswoman from Michigan, to join your ticket as your Vice President was a stroke of genius in 2040. But this time, you're the President. You get to pick your starting hand."

"I need the woman to start making the rounds in the Northeast," Warner said, spinning an antique globe next to a model of a Spanish capitana. Jackson Piper would have easily identified the model as one likely used by Cortés.

Marco responded, "Yes, but that was the strategy for the last election. Elections are about the future, not the past. After the crash of '39, your strategy was to wrap yourself in the flag and unify the country, appearing to be the statesman. We both know that's not what you are, Mr. President."

"Oh really?" Warner snapped incredulously. "Who am I then?"

"Why, you're a calculating businessman like me. You would just as soon run against no one at all. It increases the house's odds. And you're an odds man, aren't you, Russ? You don't believe in luck. It's math and hard work that makes trillionaires."

"And what if that's true?" asked Warner.

"Then I think you would want to hear more about my work to neutralize the Other Party."

"You have my attention," said Warner, returning to his seat in front of Marco.

"Juniper has determined that Senator Paul Drummond is the least likely among the Other Party candidates for President to defeat you thirteen months from now under every possible scenario, even including impeachment."

"Have you now?" Warner asked, intrigued but exceptionally annoyed that someone was modeling the political consequences of impeaching him.

Marco sat stone-faced. "We have already executed several strategies to ensure the Other Party selects Drummond and that his campaign is filled with losers and hacks."

"To what end?" asked Warner.

"Let me put it this way. In Blackjack, would the house prefer to fix the deck or simply ensure the player has no idea whether to hit or stay?"

Warner smiled. "You don't think I can win against Fox or Abbas?"

"Frankly, no. Fox was going to run ahead of you from pillar to post. You would have lost, likely by double digits, given all the models we ran," said Alvarez.

"And Khan?" asked Warner.

Alvarez laughed. "If you're going to rig something like an election, you need to make it believable. Saima Amal Khan rarely leaves Washington and has raised less than $25,000 for her campaign to date. No one would believe for a moment that she won the nomination of the Other Party to try to take you down without outside interference. They are a Party lost at sea, but they are not yet lunatics."

"So what are your asks in all of this?" asked Warner.

"Let me ask you about Vice President Brown again. Are you certain of her loyalty?" asked Alvarez.

"Certain enough. She switched parties to run with me. If we win reelection, she's set for life. Besides, do you know what a bullshit job the vice presidency is? She goes and reads to kids at city schools, goes to funerals and ribbon cuttings, and wants for nothing," said Warner, truly boiling from annoyed to downright offended.

"You are not thinking big enough, Mr. President. The vice president can break the ties in the Senate, which remains a death away from flipping control again."

Warner interrupted, "I was a fucking Senator, Marco. I know the role, ok? So what?"

"The Vice President could do a great deal more to ensure Washington gets in line behind your second term agenda."

"What is it you want, Mr. Alvarez?" asked President Warner.

"The vice presidency," grinned Alvarez.

"Absolutely fucking not," said President Warner. The President stood, increasingly impatient with the conversation's direction. He walked to the windows, partially wishing he knew how to open one of them to jump out and return to his waiting plane.

Alvarez waited patiently. He was allowing Russell Warner to process his request. Finally, he said, "The vice president could be a powerfully persuasive force instead of some ribbon-cutting dignitary. He could be essential to granting you a more lasting term in office than just four more years."

"Impossible. The twenty-second amendment says two terms or ten years, Marco," said Russell, waiving his hand, dismissing such nonsense.

"That is linear thinking, *Russell*." Marco was getting agitated.

President Warner did not like being addressed so casually anymore. He appreciated the respect the proper address afforded to him.

"I preferred to be addressed as Mr. President if you don't mind,"

"Exactly my point! There is an opening to land you more than four more years occupying the White House."

The president took a sip of a drink he poured for himself. "I'm sorry, Marco, but I'm just not following."

"Don't worry. There is plenty of time for us to walk through some scenarios. But first, we need to get Jessica Brown off the ticket. After all, she is not well," said Marco.

The President raised his eyebrows in surprise. "She's fit as a damned fiddle!"

Marco finished off his whiskey. "You do not need to decide this question tonight, Mr. President. The question of the next vice president can be decided much closer to the Convention."

There was a knock at the door. An agent opened the door.

"Excuse me, Mr. President, I have Chief of Staff Clay asking to come in."

President Russell Warner stood and cleared his throat. "I want to be clear that I view the suggestion you made a few moments ago to join me on the ticket as separate and distinct and not in any way linked to your generous contributions or pledges you have already made to support my reelection by all means available."

The President continued. "I know that you understand that, at best, it would be inappropriate to make your financial support contingent upon my selection of you, and at worst, well..."

"Bribery," Marco said. "That would be bribery."

"Well, I see that we understand one another," Warner said. His words were sharp. "I do not see a reason to drop Vice President Brown. And while you meet the qualifications to be President and, therefore, Vice President, that is not my only consideration in deciding who should be part of the ticket, Mr. Alvarez."

"Mr. President, as I said to you, and I repeat now, the fusion of our instincts and resources could make us unstoppable," Marco said.

"I'm sorry, Marco, but I know Jessica Brown. She is the Vice President I need right now. Perhaps we could consider giving you a different position in the administration for a second term?" The President's voice grew more cold and calculated.

Then, the President waved in his most senior advisor without seeking permission from Alvarez.

"We need to get back to Washington," Olivia Clay snapped.

"So soon?" asked Marco Alvarez innocently. "Is there something wrong?"

"It's just that we need wheels up by 8. The President has a SATCON briefing in flight," explained Clay with the appropriate amount of political mumbo-jumbo.

"Thank you for your time, Mr. President," Marco Alvarez said with a sly smirk as the President and Olivia Clay closed the door behind them.

President Warner walked briskly through the house, past the

dining room with the chattering staff, and burst through the front door. Olivia was barely inside the limousine when the door slammed shut, and the lead security officer spoke the command into this wrist radio: "Jackpot away."

Air Force One was "wheels up" at 7:51 Pacific. The president had barely spoken in the 30-minute ride back to the airport. Senior staff huddled in the president's private cabin, out of earshot from the press and more junior staff. The room included the President's Legislative Director, Communications Director, his Campaign Chair, and the Chief of Staff.

After the SATCON briefing, Olivia raised the subject of the 6,000-mile journey. "So, Mr. President. Are you going to tell us what this trip was about?"

There was a knock at the door and then Agent Hill entered the room. "Mr. President, Jessica Langley of CBN says you asked her for 30 minutes?"

"Huh?" Olivia had not cleared CBN for any type of interview with the President.

"Give me a minute to finish up here, then send her in. This group will be leaving, and I do not want to be interrupted until we are over Chicago." The senior staff began abruptly packing up their papers and funneled out of the room. The president saw the confusion on Olivia's face.

"Relax. Just a casual conversation entirely off the record. I like her...intellect," said President Warner to Olivia, the only staff to remain in the room.

President Warner cleared his throat and said, "Marco Alvarez called us here because..." he paused, wondering for a moment if he should isolate her from this knowledge. Olivia gave Warner a look of frustration.

His face looked cold and irritated. "Because Marco Alvarez wants me to replace Jessica Brown on the ticket next year."

"With whom?" asked Olivia, confused.

Unaware of Olivia's presence in the office, Jessica Langley slipped through the door directly into the President's private bedroom and closed the door. Warner loosened his tie and walked towards the bedroom. He turned and answered Olivia's question.

"With him," said the President.

4

INVISIBLE MAN

Paul Drummond stood at the edge of the room, a specter of a man easily lost in the sea of more commanding figures. His small stature, unassuming demeanor, and pale complexion made him almost invisible, his presence as striking as a mundane piece of furniture. White wisps of hair formed parentheses on the sides of his bald head. He had bright blue eyes that stood in stark contrast to his pale complexion. Despite his surprising political success, he inspired no awe or curiosity.

"Senator Drummond," someone called out, momentarily drawing attention to the unimpressive Senator from Wisconsin. As eyes turned towards him, Drummond offered a weak smile and a hand flourish of a wave before quickly retreating back into introspection. Few could recall any groundbreaking legislation or issues attributed to him. In the cutthroat world of American politics, Paul Drummond was not a leading man nor the understudy to the leading man; he was just another face in the crowd.

Approaching Senator Jeanne, he extended his hand for a shake. Despite her austere demeanor and elderly age, the Senator from New Hampshire had an endearing quirkiness off-stage, often sharing poorly timed puns and jokes.

After a brief chit-chat about previous meetings and mutual support, Senator Jeanne asked a strange question. "Is this your first trip to New Hampshire, Paul?" she asked, staring at him blankly.

Drummond was dumbfounded. Was she joking? "No, Senator. This is my twentieth trip to your state. I am running for President."

She seemed unconvinced by the news. She considered asking how it was going, but perhaps she already knew the answer. At 97, she didn't much care to ask. So, instead, she abruptly turned to take a selfie with a supporter who had been waiting patiently for a moment or two.

Despite his many years in the Senate, Paul had never managed to garner the respect or influence that came so naturally to his colleagues. Even now, at this political leader's pancake breakfast, he was joined by what remained of his fellow rivals pursuing the presidential nomination in the Other Party. The rest were candidates for Congress and the U.S. Senate seat of the retiring Senator. They discussed strategy and shared war stories with the hundred or so officials in the room. Drummond felt as if he was on the outside looking in.

With the room filled with laughter and conversation, a stirring rendition of *Message in a Bottle* by the Police was performed by a senior citizen jazz ensemble. Drummond returned to his thoughts, wondering how he might prove himself worthy of standing among political giants. But doubt threatened to consume him entirely.

"I'll send an ess, ooohhh, esss," sang a wrinkled, mustached man in a brown shirt and yellow tie seated at an electric keyboard.

Interrupting his thoughts, Diane Fogarty, Other Party National Chairwoman, loomed before him.

"Paul, I need a chat with you," she croaked.

Diane was in her late sixties and had spent the better part of her career bouncing between jobs in the public sector. Once an executive assistant to a major city mayor, then a correspondence secretary for a state senator, and then stints as an assistant for every member of the City Council, she changed roles with elections that often deposed her boss from power. It was a mystery how she landed the job as head of the Other Party's DC operation, but once inside, she managed to entangle herself so deeply in the organization that it would take a strong grip for some reformer to pull her out by the roots.

A white cloud of water vapor from her purple vape pen seemed to encircle her head continuously. Somewhere around 2030, she had made the switch from menthol cigarettes to the most horrid-smelling vape pens you ever had the misfortune of catching a whiff of. This morning, she was in one of her more gaudy patriotic outfits. She wore a bedazzled sun hat adorned with tacky symbols of the Other Party. She had on a long floral skirt that clashed mightily with her Old Glory print blouse. She wore enough costume jewelry that she could serve as a suitable anchor for a Cape Islander. Her high-heeled shoes revealed the nails of her crooked toes were painted red, white, and blue.

They sat at a nearby table. It was still a social hour, and the breakfast and speeches had not yet begun. She intended to give Paul the courtesy of a heads-up so he was not startled by the news that was about to unfold before their eyes were over pancakes and precooked sausage links.

"My dear, you are running such a steady campaign," she began.

Paul looked at the chairwoman cautiously. "Thank you?" he responded, unsure if there was a qualifier that was to follow that compliment.

"I mean that, Paul. You really are coming into your own during this campaign. I can see it."

"Ok. I feel like you're trying to warm me up before letting me down," he said morosely.

"Oh, not at all, Paul. You're misreading me. I wanted you to know something very important before you hear it from the podium. Governor Fox is leaving the race for the nomination today," she said.

"What? Why didn't you say so sooner?" said Paul. "I should go thank him or acknowledge him in my remarks."

"Building him up would certainly be the right call. He'll be back in four years...or eight, Paul. Depending on how, you know, this all shakes out for you," she replied.

"What about Representative Khan?" asked Paul.

Diane took a drag from her vape pen and then exhaled the smoke out of the corner of her crimson lips. "She's ending her campaign from DC on Tuesday."

"That means I am the only one left..."

"Don't get ahead of yourself. The filing deadline for New Hampshire is in two weeks. Barring any surprises, you're right. You'll be the only serious contender for our Party's nomination."

"Sweet Jesus, Mary, and Joseph," said Paul as the shock of the meaning washed over his diminutive frame. He grew slightly more pale, if that was possible, given his already ghostly complexion.

"To save the Party money, I have also convinced the leaders of the Iowa Party to cancel their caucus that was supposed to occur on January 9th. This will make New Hampshire the first to hold its Primary on January 19th, and then the regional Primaries will begin on February 1, starting with the Southern Regional, which, as you know, contains South Carolina, North Carolina, and Georgia."

"But if I am the only candidate seeking the nomination for President of the United States of the Other Party, why don't we just cancel all of them?" asked Paul. "That would save me a great deal of money that I can use against President Warner for the fall. He's got no opponent, either. To be honest, neither of us needs these primaries."

"It's good for the country. It creates a little drama and interest in the campaign and the candidates. Helps us flesh out our messaging for the fall," she replied.

"Maybe," said Paul, unconvinced. "Let's revisit this discussion once we get back the New Hampshire filing deadline without anyone getting any clever ideas."

"I have something else for you," she said. She reached into her purse and pulled out a list of names. "These folks all need to be added as staff on the campaign immediately."

The list contained three dozen people, none of whom Paul Drummond knew from Adam or Eve. "I'm certain we cannot afford such an increase in our payroll. We are already strapped tight as it is."

"Don't you worry about that, Paul. The Party will pay for them.

They are going to be really valuable additions to your team. You'll see. Trust me," she said, taking another puff from her vape.

Paul took notice of the giant diamond ring on Diane's plump finger. "Oh, that is quite a rock, Diane. Is there a new man in your life?"

Diane chuckled. "Oh my, no. No, dear, mama just decided it was time to treat herself to a little flash and razzle-dazzle after securing some new donors for the Party."

Paul smiled politely and tried to think of something clever to say in response, but the words did not come. He was generally an awkward and off-putting man.

"Ladies and gentlemen," said the chairman of the New Hampshire Other Party. "Let us bring this morning's breakfast to order and begin with the singing of the National Anthem. It is my honor to introduce our national Party chairwoman, Diane Fogarty, who has insisted she do the honors."

Diane finished adjusting her makeup and strode to the front of the room with dignity and confidence. She took the microphone from the chairman and cleared her throat.

A digital rendition of *The Star Spangled Banner* began to play over the speakers in the hotel's large banquet room. After a patriotic flourish on the audio, Diane began to sing the first lines of the anthem.

"Oh, say can you seeeee...." she began, off tune and out of sync with the music in the most garish rendition of the song that had yet begun a breakfast to honor the candidates of the 2044 campaign.

When the song began, Paul Drummond made eye contact with Governor Lincoln Fox from where he was seated at the head table on the stage. They were the only men who knew that by lunchtime, just one of them would still be seeking their Party's nomination to take on the divisive and ruthless incumbent President. And with the past three years as prologue, it stood to reason that Russell Warner may not be satisfied with just four more years.

5

DECISIONS, DECISIONS

The first light of dawn barely pierced the thick curtains as Jackson Piper jolted awake, heart pounding. He lay still but was still catching his breath, a lingering echo of a fading nightmare. Too many beers from last night left him with a throbbing headache. As he roused himself from bed cautiously, careful not to disturb his wife's peaceful slumber, he knew it must be Saturday.

While Catherine slept, Jackson whipped up Belgian waffles in their modest kitchen. Dressed in an old apron over his lean torso, he sliced fruit and fried thick slices of applewood-smoked bacon in a cast iron skillet. Jackson took a sip of coffee from a World's Greatest Dad mug as the twins constructed ornate stacks of waffles with whipped cream as mortar and brilliant red strawberries and plump blueberries as ornamentation. They giggled and feasted, their light spirits comforting his growing anxiety about a looming campaign that could irreversibly change their lives.

His mornings would be more mundane as he awoke in hotels on the road, building support for a role that would change their lives forever. While he hoped it would be for the better, there were no guarantees of the outcomes or the consequences for any of them.

"Freedom and vitality," Jackson muttered as he scribbled down critical phrases on a notepad on the counter.

He questioned aloud whether these seemingly profound phrases encapsulated a vision for this country worth fighting for. Woven between these words was a fabric of ideals and promises forming in his mind, yet doubt percolated at its edges.

Catherine walked down the stairs and sleepily towards the fragrant hot coffee pot. She poured herself a cup and then sipped the hot liquid, savoring the warmth and complex flavors. She joined Jackson, her hand finding his and squeezing it tightly. "So, Senator," she began, "when do we leave for New Hampshire?"

"What do you mean?" he asked, searching her eyes for sarcasm or sincerity. "We haven't even discussed that odd visit."

"We will, but that look in your eye last night," she replied, genuine admiration ringing in her voice. "You believe that story, and now you'll devote yourself to learning the truth. You used to believe, as I still do, that you were put on this earth to do something important for our country. My only question for you is, can you believe in yourself again?"

Jackson looked into her beautiful eyes, and at lightning speed, he thought about the many dreams he used to entertain of using the presidency to catapult the nation forward. Those dreams quickly turned to nightmares when he was reminded again of his defeat by a political novice, a plant of Russell Warner, as retribution for the filibuster fight of '39.

"I have not made up my mind, Cate," Jackson said, embracing her. "I want to believe I have what it takes, but the thought of exposing our family to the filth and challenge of a national campaign gives me great pause."

"The boys and I are stronger than you give us credit for, Jack," she replied. "If you choose to turn down the offer to run, do so because you do not believe you're the right choice. Not because you're afraid we can't take the heat."

"This campaign will look dramatically different than any other we have ever run. Warner has shut down half of the news outlets in the country and placed the federal government under his power like some perverse American politburo. Nothing he says or does will be too much for his army of Warriors. And they, in fact, are armed to the teeth and not afraid to use violence to make their point."

She wrestled out of the hug and walked to the downstairs study. A moment later, she returned with a tablet and a pair of glasses.

"What are you doing?" he asked.

"While I do not yet believe that crazy theory Ron and Diesel were pitching, I do believe in you. Before we talk about jumping out of this plane, you need to decide if you still believe in yourself. There is someone I think you should talk to in person, so I am booking you a plane ticket," she said.

"Who?" he asked, feeling his heart beginning to race. Her support was more easily won than he anticipated.

"Governor Tulson. She's wise and the closest thing you have to a mother, including my own." She laughed because it was no secret that Catherine's mother was not always a fan of Jackson's. "Reese will help you decide if you can navigate these treacherous waters."

Jackson felt a pit in his stomach. "I haven't seen Reese since her wife's funeral." Memories and images swept forward in his mind like a deluge.

"Then this visit is overdue," Catherine confirmed. "You owe your career to her, and I trust her judgment about whether or not you have what it takes to run and win the presidency right now."

Jackson laughed aloud at the absurdity of the conversation in his kitchen. They had moved to Colorado to put politics behind them. However, Catherine had been there for every campaign since the beginning twenty years ago. She may not know all the ins and outs of campaigns, but a campaign for president would consume her life as much as his own. Her opinion and ideas had become a ballast on which he relied for lift.

"What are my flight options?" he asked.

Catherine smiled sweetly. "You are on the red eye to Philadelphia tomorrow night, sugar. If I were you, I'd get on the phone with Reese.

Let her know you have to speak with her in person on Monday. It's urgent, and it can't wait."

She left the room to put Hagrid outside. After a shake and a stretch, he followed happily.

Jackson called after her. "What if she can't meet with me on Monday?"

She stopped in the middle of the stairs and turned with a determined look on her face. "You tell her this is a matter of national importance. You cannot wait another day. You have spent four years doubting yourself, cowboy. The country needs you. Time to get back on your horse."

○

Despite planning to sleep on the red-eye flight from Denver to Philadelphia, Jackson found it impossible to downshift his mind into slumber. The purpose of traveling at such an ungodly hour was for rest, yet even with noise-elimination headphones and blackout AR glasses, peace eluded him. Thoughts of his once powerful dream of winning the presidency were plagued by equally troubling nightmares about the stormy present of America.

Memories flooded back of Jackson's Man of the Year cover in 2038 when he fashioned a Social Security fix. However, his triumph quickly turned sour when enemies dubbed him "The Pied Piper." They claimed he was leading the nation on a delusional march to certain death.

Jackson pictured his wife, who had been a radiant force in Pennsylvania and Washington, reading to children at Children's Hospital in Pittsburgh. The image shifted to her in his arms in an elegant sapphire gown at their inaugural ball. He felt delighted at the thought, but his heart immediately wrenched as he remembered the wife of Warner's last opponent being humiliated by protestors who heckled her during a speech about women's rights, then tossed pig blood on her as she exited the stage.

As Jackson contemplated his potential advantages over Warner in

2044 – two vote-rich home states, youthful vigor, wisdom, resilience, and patience – he also considered Warner's strengths: ruthlessness, charm, cunning, near-infinite money, and incumbency. Piper's iron-clad loyalty was almost to a fault. He knew he could count on allies in Congress to stand by him. In contrast, Warner's list of enemies made it difficult for anyone to get close or intimate with the President. Warner could be susceptible to defections within his own Party.

Despite these strengths, Piper couldn't ignore his vulnerabilities. Filibuster reform had been a pyrrhic victory, leaving him abandoned by his own Party within hours of the final vote. This humiliation directly contributed to his defeat 20 months later. Now registered as an Independent in Colorado, he might have to answer for this decision if he chose to return to his Party to run for President. What if they refused him re-entry?

The news loop playing during the intermission of the inflight movie brought the need for Jackson's candidacy into clearer focus. Fewer news outlets were granted access to the public's airwaves, and all had to be willing to bend to Warner's whims without notice.

The Mark had become a crutch. Few Americans gave critical thought to the news, and even fewer could connect the news and the echoes of history. They had been trained to believe what *The Mark* said was truth or a lie, and why should they question otherwise?

Unemployment rates were predicted to hit double digits, nearly as high as interest rates. The anchor reassured the audience that these numbers did not accurately reflect the prosperity and success that was actually sweeping the nation.

Piper rolled his eyes. He looked around for anyone with a similar reaction. Most passengers ignored the propaganda parading as news.

The anchor continued, her tone sweet as poisoned honey. "Most of the country will enjoy a snow-free winter this year." Jackson's thoughts went to thousands who made half their year's income during the ski season in Colorado. This reality might finally be the knockout blow that had already shuttered hundreds of winter sports venues in the northeast. Piper's attention was refocused when the anchor added this forecast was a "relief" since accidental deaths caused by wintry traffic accidents and shoveling snow would likely be down for 2043.

"In international news, after years of negotiations, China and Russia have welcomed North Korea into their mutual defense treaty alliance." At this, angry shouts erupted behind Piper. He turned to see two women, faces reddened, screaming and swatting at each other over the back of a seat. The surrounding passengers watched impassively, more interested in capturing the brawl on their feeds than intervening. Within minutes, the combatants retreated to their corners, the passengers losing interest. Violence was so ingrained into daily life that even a midair fight warranted only a glance from most of the passengers, including Piper.

Two hours later, the plane's wheels shuddered against the Philadelphia tarmac. Jackson Piper peered out the small window at the grey, overcast sky looming ominously over Pennsylvania. He gathered his coat tighter around him as he walked to the rented autocar, feeling the bite of a rare October chill seep into his bones. His breath formed fleeting clouds in the air; each exhale was evidence of the frigid welcome Pennsylvania offered to its once-lauded Senator.

The Philadelphia city skyline was hauntingly familiar as it flashed quickly in the windows along I-95 before it disappeared, giving way to the suburbs and rolling green hills of Bucks County north of the city. After several small towns with homes and barns older than the country he was considering to lead, he found himself starring at Reese Tulson's sprawling home from the driveway - weeds defiantly standing among cracks in the pavement. Jackson stepped out of the car, pausing momentarily to take in the familiar surroundings.

The once grand estate of Governor Tulson had seen better days. Peeling paint on the shutters and ivy crawling up the brick walls gave the building the appearance of abandonment. The air was crisp, a harbinger of the approaching winter that seemed to mirror the chilling national political climate. Yet even in its decline, an undeniable sense of history and wisdom permeated the grounds.

Reese Tulson, the former Pennsylvania Governor, had hired Jackson Piper to run her first campaign more than twenty-five years ago. With both of his parents recently deceased at the time, Tulson evolved into the dominant adult and parental figure in his life. Jackson helped Reese forge a strong and highly regarded political brand. When she won her first term as governor, it was an upset victory that thrust them both into the political limelight. After years of partnership and success, Reese encouraged Jackson to leave her administration and run for Congress, casting his own political sails into the wind. And she was right about him; the people of Western Pennsylvania were excited to send a fresh face with strong convictions and new ideas to Congress.

But those glory days seemed distant now. Tulson lived in seclusion, her health teetering since her wife's death a couple of years earlier. Although Jackson and Reese had maintained their bond for years, Anne's death led Reese into emotional isolation, away from regular contact with Jackson and other dear ones.

"Jackson!" Reese called from the porch, a heavy, pale figure wrapped in a rainbow shawl. "Come on up. I've made coffee, dear." She smiled warmly at the sight of her former political protege. She gave him a comforting hug, then pulled at his beard.

"What's this? You turning into some sort of hermit?" she asked.

"Keeps me warm in the woods," said Jackson, laughing.

"You men and your desire to kill things," she said disapprovingly. "Come inside."

"I'm sorry it's been so long, Reese," he said, making his way down the familiar hallway and into a comfortable living room. Reese's collection of books seemed to have quadrupled since Anne's passing. Every inch of shelving in the room now bore the weight of books, some heavier, some dustier, but all treasured possessions of a lonely woman. Piper's eyes widened in awe as he was a bit of a bibliophile. The musty smell of old books tickled his nose. There was an intoxicating allure to such plentiful stacks of knowledge. Piper couldn't help but imagine himself with hours available to soak in this sanctuary, lost in the pages of a captivating story.

As she settled into the chair next to him, he noticed the subtle tremble in her hand and the deep lines etched into her face. Her hair, expertly cut and styled, was a short and vibrant silver that seemed to defy gravity as it was combed upwards. Despite the familiar occasion of their visit, she had taken great care with her appearance, applying just the right amount of makeup to enhance her features. Yet, as always, there was still a lipstick smudge on her teeth. She sat in a comfortable rocking chair, dressed in silk pajamas adorned with a cacophony of colors and patterns - an outfit that only someone as bold and confident as Reese Tulson could pull off. For Jackson, it was the most audacious ensemble he had ever seen her wear in their lifetime together. But somehow, it suited her perfectly - a reflection of Reese's larger-than-life personality.

Despite this, time and disease had taken a heavy toll on her body. However, her eyes still held that same fire he remembered from their time on the trail years ago.

After several minutes of catching up about the twins, Catherine's role at the hospital, and Jackson's patchwork of consulting role and teaching, Reese turned the page and grew more serious.

"Let's cut to the chase," she said, dispensing with pleasantries. "Why did you come all this way to talk to a washed-up old woman?"

Jackson took a deep breath and then exhaled as he spoke. "I am considering another run. Catherine and I thought it best to speak with you before taking any action."

"Ah, Catherine the Great. What a brilliant and stunning woman. How in the hell a guy like you lands a chick like that is still a mystery to me," she said, laughing dramatically before the laughter devolved into a hoarse cough that stole her breath for a moment. After she regained composure, she asked him a question.

"What office?"

"The top banana," a glib Jackson replied.

Reese raised her eyebrows and took a sip of coffee.

"You ever go white water rafting, Jackson?" she asked.

Jackson thought for a moment about the question out of left field. "Yes, but hell, it's been years," he said.

"Anne loved adventure, Jack. She had me riding horses, jumping out of airplanes, and, on one occasion, nearly killing me in Ohiopyle whitewater rafting," she replied.

Jackson took a sip from his heavily creamed coffee, recognizing this was one of those times when it was best to sit back and listen to a Reese story.

With a nostalgic smile, Reese reclined in her chair and rocked slowly as she was swept into the tranquil waters of an old memory. "We were tearing through the Upper Yough on class four rapids," she reminisced. "Picture perfect: it was one of those sunny summer days down near the West Virginia border of Southwestern Pennsylvania. The water was untamed as we navigated around that final bend in this winding serpent of a river, its energy unparalleled. It was meaner than a poked rattlesnake."

"The cold water sprayed on our faces while under us roared frothy white waves eager to take control. Amidst all this commotion, Anne was alive — unstoppable — her laughter echoing across the landscape. Her infectious cheer was only outdone by her yells of 'Yee-haw,' fueled more by adrenaline than fear."

Reese looked out the window at the grey sky. "It's strange how tangible those memories still are…I can almost taste the water again from the relentless waves crashing over us."

Jackson sat back in his chair, soaking up the joy of her memory.

"Suddenly, we hit a drop and then climbed. The raft undulated, and I was thrown from it like a tick from a dog." Reese let out a howling laugh, and then she paused. Her voice grew serious. "The next thirty seconds felt like three minutes. The water was rushing, and the raft was hightailing it away from me. I remember that water pushing with anger and indiscriminate force."

Jackson leaned forward, suddenly serious. "My, God, Governor, what did you do?"

"My first instinct was to put my feet down and try to stand, but they train you to ignore those instincts before they put you on that rubber hell taxi," she said. "Instead, you are supposed to swim and try to stay above the surface. Avoid being pulled under by the current and drowned. To survive, I had to fight my instincts and really focus on what other people were telling me."

Jackson nodded quietly.

"If you're going to run for president, you need to surrender to the forces that are about to sweep you off your feet. Listen to what other people tell you more than the voices in your head. Running for president is class six white water, Jack," she said.

"I haven't decided if..." Jackson tried to explain his thinking.

Reese ignored the interruption. "If you run, you start this campaign in the water, fighting to get onto a raft to ride the current. You'll wake up daily feeling like you are fighting for your life. One mistake could kill the campaign or you."

"Governor..." he tried to interrupt.

She reached for his hand. Her eyes were glassy. "If you struggle, if you try to regain your footing when the rushing water is trying to pull you forward, you will drown. Good guys run for president and lose. You must have grit. You must be fierce. You must steel your spine and sharpen your teeth. This is unlike anything you have ever done or will do ever again. Can you be a mighty gladiator, Jackson Piper?"

Piper was stunned by the ferocity of her language. "Why do you think it will take a gladiator to win this? Did Ron Bender come to see you?" asked Piper.

"No, he did not. And if he had, I wouldn't let that two-faced son of a bitch into the house," replied Tulson. "He'd try to swipe anything that wasn't nailed down and fuck the rest."

Piper gripped his coffee mug and clenched his teeth at the remark. Tulson made him, even as a grown man, feel like a naive twenty-something all over again. "Come on now, Reese. Ron's grown up since then. Ron Bender and Senator Browning came to see me on Friday. They shared with me the most remarkable story. They suspect, and I can't believe I'm repeating this out loud, that President Russell Warner is rigging his reelection."

"How would they know that?" she asked.

"He's possibly paying off any real opponents to stay out of the race. It appears he's somehow picked a patsy in Senator Drummond to be the Other Party's nominee."

"Russell is trying to guarantee himself a win? Shit. Doesn't shock me in the least," said Reese. "He has never fought a fair fight in his entire life!"

"So you think it's true?" asked Piper.

"It doesn't matter if it's true. Truth doesn't matter to the electorate right now. *The Mark* tells them what's true or not. Perception is all you need," she warned as she stood to walk to the kitchen to refill their coffees.

She yelled another question from the kitchen: "Do they have any concrete evidence? Browning and Bender?"

"Lots of financial records. All circumstantial," shouted Piper in reply, then reaching for a donut from an elegant dish on the coffee table. "Short of Diane Fogarty picking up cash in envelopes from drops in Lafayette Park, that's the sum total of their evidence."

Reese returned with more coffee. "That slimy Party toad!" laughed Reese, bursting into another coughing fit that, this time, made her turn from pale to slightly blue for just an instant. Jackson leaned forward and rubbed a hand on Reese's back, displaying the concern and patience that came so naturally when you were one-on-one with this woman.

When it was clear Reese was steady, Jackson continued. "They do not have proof enough of a conspiracy to go to what remains of investigative reporting; most of it is underground these days and not mainstream enough to reach a substantial number of voters."

Reese raised an eyebrow. "Perhaps there's a way to get someone with a guilty conscience to step forward - share what they know?"

"I don't think anyone with a conscience remains on the inside of the Warner White House or either Party for that matter," Jackson lamented.

"Are you running to win a Pulitzer or the Presidency?" asked Reese, staring at Jackson cold and direct.

"I am not a reporter," he said.

"Good. At least we've cleared that up. You're not a journalist. If you do this, you're running for President. You must win the hearts and minds of the nation. It is not a speech and debate contest. There are no points or prizes for right answers."

Reese felt her legs beginning to cramp. She needed to stretch them a bit and suggested a small tour of the home. It had been over ten years since Jackson's last visit. She and Anne had made some impressive renovations in Anne's final years of life. They moseyed around the main floor from room to room when Piper's curiosity got the better of him, leading him alone to the office. It was a room Reese did not enter often anymore, so she returned to the kitchen.

Piper inspected the many framed artifacts on the walls. He found himself in a photo of her first inauguration as governor. He inspected a framed "Tulson for President" button, which he chuckled at. He had never seen that before. Likely curated by a friend or a staunch supporter. There were dozens of photos of Reese Tulson with legislators and Presidents, and even tossing a coin at the all-Pennsylvania Super Bowl, the only time Philadelphia ever faced off against Pittsburgh for the Lombardi trophy. A giant photo was framed above the largest window in the library. It was a photo of Anne and Reese together, youthful, radiant, and happy.

When he finally peeled himself out of the library, he made his way back to the kitchen, finding a contemplative Reese breathing heavily at the table. When she saw him return, she composed herself and offered him more coffee.

Piper paused. "Do you think I have what it takes to win the White House?" He hoped her answer would be yes but hoped even more deeply that she would not hesitate to reply.

"My dear," she began, taking his hand. "You are a kind and generous soul. You have a grace and a generosity that is uncommon among most men. And you'll need all that heart and courage to survive the next thirteen months. Do I think you have the knowledge and sharp instincts? I do. Do I think you have the fire? It's in there, but you've hidden your light. You're going to need to find more fuel for it. Do I think you have the tenacity? Perhaps. What you lack,

Catherine will supply in spades. But you're not asking the right question."

"Really? What am I missing then?" he asked perplexed.

"Will your former Party let you?" she said with a frown. "Let's assume for a moment that the fix is in. Warner has somehow baited the Other Party into conspiring in a plot to rig his reelection. If true, they will not let you walk into this race and risk unraveling their fiction. They will shut down the donors and close you off from local Party leaders. No one will give you the time of day."

"Then what shall I do? Are you saying it's impossible? I'm doomed before I begin?"

Reese thought for a moment. "I guess what I'm saying, dear, is if you're going to run in order to stop Warner, you'll need a more sophisticated and compelling game plan than changing back to the Other Party and acting like you're some savior of the country. I suspect that is going to land like a fart in church."

They shared a laugh or two more, and then Tulson walked to a jar on the kitchen counter and removed something small from the ceramic vessel. She paused momentarily, then placed the cold, shiny object in Piper's mighty hand. Piper opened his fingers to reveal a Benjamin Franklin fifty-cent piece. It had been Reese Tulson's lucky charm her entire political career. She carried it everywhere she went and used it in a coin toss once to break a deadlock during a tense budget negotiation. It was given to her by her father, an influential former political boss of the Keystone State.

"I want you to have it, Jack," she said.

"Reese, I can't take this," he said nervously.

"My need for luck's run out, young man. I have a failing heart, and I'm too old for surgery to fix it. They can put it in my cold dead hand, and I can carry luck to my grave, or I can pass it to perhaps the 50th president of the United States. I hope that when you win, it will remind you of what I have taught you, Jackson."

"I am just as fond of Uncle Ben as I ever was," said Jackson, referring to Benjamin Franklin with such familiarity. Reese was a proud descendant of one of the most energetic and creative of the founders.

Reese smiled fondly. She rose quickly from her chair and walked to the living room. "Perhaps I have some useful inspiration for you as you devise your next move." She disappeared briefly and then returned with a small stack of books for him.

"These might be instructive for you on some potential next steps," she said, sitting back in a table chair.

Piper examined the stack of titles: a book about the Presidential elections of 1824, 1840, 1876, 1912, 2000, and 2020; a new book about the formation of the American identity as first envisioned by Benjamin Franklin in 1750; a book on leadership by the first female Apple executive; and a thin pamphlet entitled "Fateful Conjunction: The Curse of Tippecanoe."

Jackson held up the thin volume to Reese. "Curses? Come on, Reese. No nonsense now."

"My dear, if you can believe that a magical being in a dimension we cannot see created all things and got a woman magically pregnant to teach his creation lessons in code, then I can believe in the power of the cosmos and curses," she bristled.

"I'm well aware of the Curse of Tippecanoe. It is a ghost story invented by Ripley's in the 1930s - eighty years after it was supposed to have happened."

"For 120 years, the only Presidents who died in office were those elected in years divisible by 20. Which coincides with a Saturn-Jupiter conjunction," Reese said, raising her eyebrows. "Warner was elected in a year divisible by 20!"

"Yes, but Reagan didn't die in office. If the supposed curse was lethal and real, why did it give up?" asked Jackson skeptically.

"Reagan came within an inch of death. Perhaps he broke the curse. You know Nancy believed firmly in astrology," Reese said.

Jackson rolled his eyes. "Do you have a book about Lincoln's ghost? I could use his help. What about the Salem Witch Trials?" Jackson began to laugh and then stood and started to recite lines from the classic Arthur Miller play portraying the mob mentality condemnation of others in 1692 in Salem, Massachusetts.

"*I danced for the Devil; I saw Sarah Good with the Devil! I saw Goody*

Osburn with the Devil! I saw Bridget Bishop with the Devil!" he said, acting like a man bewitched by a spell.

Jackson continued the theatrics. "I saw Russell Warner with the Devil! I saw Jessica Brown with the Devil!"

Reese finally laughed. "Ok! Enough! These will be a good read for the flight home," she said. "And don't put off *Tippecanoe* too long." She chose her words carefully. "Because, my boy, you may think it's all a bunch of bullshit, but my experience in politics is that it's not always the devil you know; it's the devil you don't that you need to worry about." Then she stood and moved to the sink to empty her now cold coffee from her mug.

"My final warning for you is to be careful whom you trust, especially once you leave this house," warned Reese ominously.

"More witchcraft, Governor?" asked Jackson.

"You have always been too quick to trust. You assume the loyalty you give others is reciprocal. It's not - not in politics anyway - and no greater example of betrayal than those who seek the American presidency. You will soon be surrounded by opportunists, cheats, and liars. You already have one foot in the wrong direction with Bender on your team," she huffed.

Jackson did not look at her. He never understood her distrust of his dear friend, Ron.

"If there is a conspiracy to rig the presidential election in the greatest democracy ever, then you are going to need to verify anything you see, hear, or touch before you trust it as fact. Don't write down sensitive matters if you can speak them. Don't speak about sensitive matters over the phone. Don't say what is better left unsaid if it is mutually understood."

"That's ominous," said Piper, raising his eyebrows.

"These are dark fucking times, Jack," she replied. "Assume they can always be listening and reading every word you send. They will stop at nothing to stop you."

As Piper prepared to depart, he reached for another donut. She slapped his hand.

"Another thing. You better lose 25 pounds. Start with weights and cut out the shit from your diet," she scolded. She stood, grabbed the beautiful plate of pastries from the counter, and tossed what remained into the trash.

"Yes, ma'am," he replied.

After a long farewell between the grizzled veteran and her optimistic protege, an autonomous ride to the airport was honking in the long driveway outside. The sun was already casting long shadows on the lawn outside. Jackson made his way to the car, looking back one last time to wave goodbye to the woman who had become such a generous guardian to him.

From the porch, Reese Tulson waved goodbye. She was sure to turn before Jackson could see the tears in her eyes. It had been so good for her soul to be in the hopeful and energetic presence of a man she deeply admired. She was sad for a moment, permitting herself a moment's worry that it might be the last time she had the joy of his company.

But then Reese was filled with a pride that warmed her. She was sure Jackson Piper was about to embark on a journey to transform him into the man he was destined to become. She smiled when she thought of all the good that he might do if he somehow managed to pull off the impossible and win.

∼

DURING THE RIDE to the airport and the endless waiting for boarding and departure, Jackson devoured the pages of his new books. The first book was *He Who Gets the Most Votes Loses: A History of Stolen Elections and Third Parties in Presidential Politics*. It wove a compelling tale about the peculiarities of the American system that required the President to win enough states' votes via the Electoral College regardless of the popular vote.

The framers of the Constitution had also included something called the Contingent Election to be triggered when the Electoral College was not conclusive. While the Presidential election of 1800 was decided in this manner because of a technicality, the first and only time the Contingent Election reversed the results of the direct democracy was during the election of 1825 between titans John Quincy Adams and Andrew Jackson. That was the focus of chapter one.

While he was aware of lessons from history such as these, as a professor of history for first-year students, he was deeply intrigued by the details of the events of the Winter of 1824-25 that the book laid out. The Constitution, via the Twelfth Amendment, required the House to select who shall be President among the top three vote-getters and the Senate to select the Vice President among the top two. While 1825 was not the last time this duty fell to Congress, it was the last time both offices of President and Vice President were not determined by the popular vote or Electoral College in the same election year.

It was also the first time the winner of the popular vote *and* a plurality of the electoral college was not ultimately selected to be President. Piper recalled that 1876 was the only other time such a democratically contrarian outcome occurred in the republic's history.

He returned to the reading.

In the 1824 race, there were four national candidates, but since only the top three could stand for selection in the House, Speaker of the House Henry Clay was forced to bow out. He then threw his support behind John Quincy Adams, who won the Contingent Election on the first ballot. Then Adams quickly named Clay his Secretary of State. This was deemed the Corrupt Bargain by Andrew Jackson's allies and ensured a rematch that Jackson won four years later in 1828, ushering in the age of the modern two-party system with Jackson's election.

Jackson reached into his carry-on and popped open a pop he had purchased before boarding. He was determined to finish one of these books before landing.

He moved to Chapter 2. The presidential election of 1840 was the first national election in which all of the founding fathers were now dead. The nation began to face the test of whether it could be sustained as an ideal as Franklin, Hamilton, Jefferson, and Madison had intended.

In 1840, the new third-party Whigs upset the dominance of the Democratic-Republican Party by winning the presidency behind consensus national Whig candidate William Henry Harrison. It was the first time an entirely new political Party not present in 1800 won the White House.

Piper recalled that 1860 was the next, and 1864 was the last.

Harrison died after just a month in office, and a Constitutional crisis erupted.

Jackson notes that this death is the supposed origin of the Curse of Tippecanoe. He was the first President to die in office and was elected in a year divisible by 20. He continued his reading.

Vice President Tyler, who had never been elected President, became the first man to assume the presidency out of succession. At the time, it was not clear if the Vice President assumed simply the duties or the office itself. The Constitution was vague, and with no founders alive to ask, Tyler insisted it was the intention that the Vice President become the President in the case of his death or removal.

Tyler became wildly unpopular for this and many other ham-handed dealings with his Party and Congress. Soon, he was a man without a Party. By 1844, the Whigs abandoned Tyler and put up James Polk as their choice for President. Polk succeeded Tyler and became the fourth of eight consecutive Presidents serving a single term or less.

After consuming the large pop, Piper decided he could not wait for the arrival in Denver to use the restroom. He pushed his 6'5" frame out of the aisle seat to the rear of the plane, where he found relief before continuing to Chapter 3: the Election of 1876.

The election of 1876 was the single most controversial Presidential election in U.S. history. It was the centennial of the Declaration of Independence, and Rutherford B. Hayes faced off against Samuel J. Tilden. Tilden won the popular vote by a 300,000 vote margin out of 7 million votes cast and the Electoral College by 19 electoral votes. There were twenty electoral votes in dispute from four states: in three, both parties claimed their candidate had won the state's electoral votes, and in one, an "illegal elector" had failed to be replaced in time for his vote to count.

Reminiscent of 2020, an election Jackson had lived through and voted in, the supporters of Hayes claimed the sitting Republican Vice President could decide which slates of electors to count. The Democratic Speaker of the House rejected this claim. Withholding the final count of the electoral votes for weeks prevented the House and Senate from preceding the Constitutional Contingent Election procedure, which would have been sure to land Republicans control of both the President's and Vice President's offices.

Instead, the two Parties saw an opportunity to bargain away the presidency. A highly controversial Electoral Commission was formed with five members from the Senate, five from the House, and five from the Supreme Court. The Commission's only independent member, a justice from the Court, refused to serve and was replaced by a Republican Justice who sided with the Republicans on every contested elector. Eventually, on a Party-line vote of 8-7, the Commission awarded Hayes the 20 electoral votes in dispute, swinging the election in his favor.

However, the Democrats in control of the House refused to accept the result without getting something substantial in exchange for backstabbing their candidate who had actually won the most votes. Eventually, a backroom deal between the two Parties broke the deadlock, abandoning Tilden's rightful claim to the presidency in exchange for an end to the federal occupation of the South known as Reconstruction, paving the way for Jim Crow and the dominance of White Supremacy in southern politics for five generations (or more) to follow.

President Hayes was called "Rutherfraud" or "His Fraudulency" for most of his single term. He brought the Presidency back to earth after Lincoln had raised it to mythical heights just 12 years earlier. It was the second time the man with the most votes had not been sworn into the presidency.

Jackson closed his eyes and wondered what Reese was trying to show him with this book. Throughout their time working together, Reese would see the answer but test him to see if his mind would arrive at the same conclusion as hers. Here, she presented him with evidence that winning the most votes - popular or electoral - doesn't always guarantee one the Presidency. The evidence was clear that powerful interests - people or Parties - at times of close divisions could exert leverage to extract a victory for the candidate who most suited their interests, including money, power, appointments, or the resolution of perceived grievances.

Jackson reopened the thick hardcover book and turned to a chapter on the election of 1912.

It was by far the most remarkable presidential election of the pre-superpower age of the young nation. The chapter laid out three facts that set the stage for the 1912 epic showdown: His own Party never intended to see Theodore Roosevelt become President; the Democratic Party was experiencing a twenty-year identity crisis; and finally, popular primaries were not the norm for picking nominees of each Party - that was still the work of Party leaders at national conventions - sometimes taking days and dozens of rounds of balloting to find a consensus choice.

The sitting Vice President, Garrett Hobart, developed severe heart disease at the end of 1898 and disappeared from public life. He died in office at the end of 1899, leaving the office vacant and President McKinley without a running mate for the 1900 campaign. Republicans wanted a way to rid themselves of the wealthy, outspoken, and reform-minded governor of New York, Theodore Roosevelt. In their estimation, the Vice Presidency was the best role in which to place Roosevelt. It was nearly without exception a political death sentence, where once promising leaders were relegated into obscurity and irrelevance in plain sight.

The McKinley-Roosevelt ticket prevailed in 1900, but in a shocking series of events in early 1901, McKinley was assassinated, and Roosevelt assumed the office...

Jackson paused and made a mental note that McKinley was elected in a year divisible by twenty, upholding the Tippecanoe

Curse structure of presidents elected in years ending in zero dying in office.

There was no Vice President from September 14, 1901, until March 4, 1905. When Roosevelt took office in 1901, there was yet to be a Constitutional procedure for replacing the Vice President when he ascended to the Presidency.

Theodore Roosevelt was 42 in 1901 - the youngest man ever to assume the presidency. By the time he left office in 1909, he had transformed the power of the Chief Executive and Commander-in-Chief of the United States. He evolved the presidency into a popular culture obsession. Although no opinion polls existed in 1909, Roosevelt was widely regarded as the most popular President since Abraham Lincoln. He might have won a third term in 1908 had he not pledged to respect Washington's long-observed tradition of limiting any presidency to two terms. Instead, he handed the office to a hand-picked successor who easily won the presidency in 1908 - William Howard Taft.

Taft proved to be a disappointment in the former president's eyes. Taft had returned to a more traditional, business-friendly, anti-populist agenda of the Republicans. Taft reversed course on social justice, tariffs, and the trusts, the latter of which seemed to be the last straw for Roosevelt. Returning from a world speaking tour and African safari after leaving office, Roosevelt announced he would ignore his pledge and seek an unprecedented third term in 1912.

Roosevelt kicked off a high-energy, whirlwind campaign to win state primaries, including in President Taft's home state of Ohio. He appeared to be on his way to capturing the nomination, but Taft and the conservative Republicans still controlled state Parties and the Republican National Convention. Roosevelt's attempt to win the nomination at the convention that July was fraught with difficulty. The Party refused to seat his delegates from the states he had won via popular primaries. Convinced that the nomination was fixed to fall in Taft's favor, Roosevelt refused even to have his name placed into nomination. Consequently, Taft won renomination on the first ballot. It took the dysfunctional Democratic Party a week later, 46 ballots in

Baltimore, to finally settle on their nominee - New Jersey Governor Woodrow Wilson.

Roosevelt was down but not out. Still wildly popular, Roosevelt went on a sixty-day charge to build a new national third party to challenge Taft and Wilson. At a national Progressive Party Convention in August 1912, Theodore Roosevelt was named the Progressive "Bull Moose" Party nominee on the first ballot, with reformer California Governor Hiram Johnson selected as the Bull Moose nominee for Vice President. Most of the convention was spent hammering out a dynamic, reform-focused platform to inspire the country to switch from elephant and donkey to bull moose.

The campaign was unlike any prior and perhaps any since. Theodore Roosevelt conducted an energetic, reform-forward popular campaign, appealing directly to the citizens of the nation for their votes to return him to the White House. Roosevelt survived an assassination attempt in October, giving a nearly hour-long speech while bleeding with the bullet still lodged in his chest before seeking medical treatment and only a few days' rest from the campaign before returning to the stump.

The Democratic Party had not been a formidable opponent to the Republicans since before the economic crash of 1893. Unable to win much appeal outside the South or take the presidency since Grover Cleveland in 1892, the Democratic Party was on an eighteen-year drought in controlling either chamber of Congress or the presidency since 1895.

Despite the Democratic drought, Wilson won in a landslide in the Electoral College (435-88-8) and the popular vote - 42% for Wilson, 27% for Roosevelt, 23% for Taft, and 6% for Socialist Eugene Debbs. The Democrats owe their resurrection to Theodore Roosevelt and William Taft for being unable to work it out and splitting their voters while allowing the Democrats to consolidate their base and slide past the Bull Moose and the Republicans.

Wilson won 39 states, Roosevelt won 7, and Taft just 2. Taft's 8 electoral votes remain the lowest total of any incumbent seeking reelection.

No third party has won as many electoral votes since 1912 as the Bull Moose managed to win. It is plausible that, had Taft dropped from the race, Roosevelt could have won a majority in the states where Wilson won under 45 percent of the vote. These 237 electoral votes would have shifted the election results entirely. Wilson would have likely earned just 198 electoral votes to Roosevelt's 338, giving Theodore Roosevelt his third term and perhaps the Bull Moose a more permanent hold in national politics.

Jackson closed the book. The pilot indicated over the intercom that they were just 45 minutes from Denver. This was the courtesy warning to prepare for landing.

Piper was seeing more of what Reese wanted him to see. There was zero chance of Warner exiting the race; he was beloved by an extreme base in the Old Party. This would mean challenging Warner for his Party's nomination or pushing Drummond out of the race to take the banner of the Other Party.

But if the Other Party refused to entertain Piper as a replacement for Drummond, Piper's only remaining option was to beat Warner by running as a third-party candidate. Winning the most popular and even the most electoral votes would not guarantee Piper the win in the face of possible Party collusion. Where Roosevelt had come close to victory but ultimately errored was siphoning votes only from Taft, clearing the path to a Wilson landslide.

Piper stared blankly forward as advertisements flashed on the screen around him. It was a beer ad for a brand of beer Piper would never drink, but it was pervasive in the marketplace. The ad showed two friends about to duel over whether their favorite beer was best because it tasted great or because it was less filling.

Jackson had seen the ad so many times it was nearly noise his brain could tune out. But then, a character trying to end the duel asked an important question.

"Why can't it be both?"

Suddenly excited by a bonkers idea, Jackson opened his tablet on the slowly descending flight and composed three emails. He remembered Reese's warning, so he kept the messages brief and vague, mainly asking for the opportunity to speak about an urgent matter ASAP—in person if possible.

The first email was to a premier set of election law attorneys he knew from his time in Washington. The second was to a firm he knew to be unquestionable experts on campaign finance law—or what remained of it from Warner's gutting. Finally, he emailed Diesel and Bender, asking them to return to Denver as soon as their schedules permitted.

∼

AT JUST AFTER 11 P.M. Mountain time, Jackson parked his car and stood alone in his home's driveway. The glow of a lamp in the study on the second floor cast ghostly shadows on the walls. Catherine was at the desk, seated in front of her computer screen. He wondered if this was perhaps his last private moment for the foreseeable future.

Assume they have the ability always to be listening. They will stop at nothing to stop you.

He removed his phone from his jacket pocket and initiated a call to Catherine. He saw her stand to answer his call.

"Jackson," she answered. "It's late. Is everything ok?"

"I'm nearly home," he replied.

"Excellent news," Catherine said, then paused. "How is Governor Tulson?"

"Declining in health, but her mind is still all there. She's lonely," he replied.

"We need to make it a priority to see her more often," said Catherine.

Then there was a long pause. Catherine was waiting for Jackson to broach the subject, but she couldn't wait any longer.

"So? What was her advice?" probed Catherine.

"She said I was caring, intelligent, and thoughtful but lacking tenacity. She insisted you could teach me a thing or two about grit..."

Catherine laughed out loud, but not too loud to not wake the children.

"Was that all?" she asked. "No final decision?"

"She insisted it was my call to make whether or not to run and if it was for the right reasons," Jackson replied.

"Well? Do you need more time?" asked Catherine.

Jackson took a breath and looked up at the ocean of stars visible from his front lawn - one of the many benefits of being this far from downtown. He closed his eyes and said a silent prayer.

"Jackson? Are you still there?" asked Catherine.

"My love, start packing for New Hampshire. I am certain I must run for President to stop Russell Warner and Paul Drummond from denying America a real choice in this election."

Catherine took a deep breath. "Are you sure you're ready?"

"The timing of your moment is the one thing you don't get to choose in politics. But you were right, Cate. It's time for me to stop feeling sorry for myself and get back on my horse."

She smiled. "That's my man."

"See you soon," he said with a smile. They exchanged 'love yous' and ended the call.

Jackson lowered the phone into his jacket pocket. "Come and get me, you corrupt son of a bitch," Jackson said, assuming Warner would someway, somehow listen to a recording of that call. "Time for our rematch." Jackson opened the front door, feeling like he was leaving behind a dark chapter of his life. He closed the door behind him, ready to move forward - from now on, always forward.

6

A BOLD APPROACH

In the hushed predawn hours, where the world seemed to hold its breath in anticipation of the sun's first golden rays, Jackson and Catherine Piper navigated their SUV through the labyrinthine backroads of rural New Hampshire on a cold Monday morning.

The ghostly tendrils of morning mist hung low over the undulating landscape, wrapping the rolling hills in an ethereal shroud that seemed worlds away from the political maelstrom of Washington, D.C. As they descended into a secluded valley, a sprawling farmhouse steeped in centuries of history emerged from the fog - a beacon of rustic tranquility against the encroaching tide of political frenzy. The biting chill of the New England morning nipped at their cheeks as they stepped out of their vehicle, their breath crystallizing in the air and their eyes drinking in the pastoral serenity. This would be their command center, their sanctuary amidst the chaos of a newly formed presidential campaign - and yet, as Jackson looked upon the tranquil scene, he couldn't shake the sense of trepidation. The calm before the storm had never felt so unnerving.

The twins, Ben and Alex Piper, entertained themselves in the back seat amongst a mountain of luggage and essential possessions, with screens displaying their favorite shows. Hagrid slept soundly on the third-row bench seat. For the rest of the school year, with the help of a tutor, Catherine and Jackson would homeschool the twin second graders to keep them together as a family.

"How beautiful," Catherine remarked, stepping towards the historic farmhouse.

Jackson nodded, his eyes taking in the rustic beauty with reverence. "Home sweet home," he replied, knowing well the unease they all felt about uprooting their lives in just thirty days to pursue this high-stakes gamble that Jackson was still relevant to the nation's direction.

Together, they directed the setup of their family in the temporary headquarters. Shawn Faber, a classmate of Catherine's from Brown University, owned the farm. Shawn and his wife offered to stay at their vacation home in Florida for the winter, providing the Pipers and their team with the privacy and space required to construct and wage a competitive presidential campaign in just three months. The Fabers quickly arranged for caretakers to tend to the horses and property while they were away. The Pipers would barely have time to eat and sleep, let alone water, feed, muck, wash, and exercise the six horses that called the farm home.

"We must be crazy," said Jackson as a caravan of cars and moving vans filled with equipment wound up the long driveway to the farmhouse.

"Last chance to call it off!" Catherine smiled as she waved to the approaching vehicles.

Jackson watched as Catherine conferred with staff, ensuring everything was in order with an efficiency that had always impressed him. In her, he had found not just a partner in life but also in ambition.

Ron Bender approached Jackson quickly, holding his phone. "Senator, I have three networks on standby that want to interview you about your historic filings in the New Hampshire Primary."

"How quickly can someone set up a spot for me to do an on-camera interview?" asked Jackson.

"We'll be set up and tested in under an hour," replied Ron.

"Excellent! Set it up for after the first campaign meeting," said Jackson, smiling.

Ron excused himself to set up the interviews.

Jackson's cell phone rang incessantly since he filed minutes before the deadline the Secretary of State set for the Friday before Halloween. This time, it was his former roommate, Senator Sterling Powers, a member of the President's Party. Jackson was finally ready to take his call.

"Hello, Senator," said Jackson warmly, pacing around the wet lawn of the farm.

"You really are out of your mind," said Sterling.

"It's so great to hear from you. I take it you are not calling to offer your endorsement?" Piper joked.

On the other end, an exasperated Sterling began his argument. "When we were roommates, you talked about maybe, someday, if the stars aligned, you'd run for President. I always assumed it would be in your own Party - not both fucking Parties, Jackson!"

"It's unorthodox, I know," said Jackson.

"It's fucking insane. You look like some kind of egomaniac," said Sterling.

"Just the opposite. This isn't about me. It's about a system that has finally broken. There's no difference between the two Parties when they accept money from the same pool of donors, cancel primaries, and declare the race over before it has even begun!" replied Jackson cheerfully.

"It's going to cost you a mountain of cash!" said Sterling, shifting gears. "One race is expensive enough, but two races - simultaneous - will be suicide!"

"Oh, nonsense. The two Parties are voting at the same time. We can go to every door instead of every other door up here. It's also an open Primary up here, so our voters can pick either race to vote in - Old Party or the Other Party!" Jackson said, forcing a laugh. He knew it was absurd, but he had to put on a positive face.

"What voters?" shouted Sterling. "You're polling in the single digits, behind None of the Above!"

Jackson lowered his voice. "Why are you so worked up about this, Sterling?"

"Because the President hasn't stopped calling me since you filed. He's furious. He wants me to try to talk you out of this."

Jackson bristled. "We're friends, Sterling. I know you would refuse to do such a thing. You're not a Russell Warner fan."

"No," said Sterling, "but I am trying to become the Senate Majority Leader of my Party. That's more likely to happen if Drummond loses to Warner."

"Oh, bullshit, Sterling," said Jackson, clearly frustrated with his friend's sudden disloyalty. "What if I win the Old Party's nomination? We could electrify a whole new generation of voters…"

"Jackson, you aren't even a member of my Party. I'm now told you changed to Independent. So you're a member of neither Party? What are you doing? Who is advising you on this?"

"I'm in good hands. Trust me…"

"This stinks of Bender," said Sterling.

Jackson laughed. "Just do me a favor. Please keep an open mind. Listen to our message. Come up here and watch how the voters respond to us after Thanksgiving. Just give me a fair shot. That's all I ask, old friend."

Sterling thought carefully. "You've got three weeks to get above None of the Above, or I'm going to call for you to leave the race. My career is on the line here, too!"

"Oh, come on, Sterling. No one believes in polling anymore!"

"Three weeks, Jackson," Sterling paused.

Jackson thought carefully. Could he achieve that kind of polling lift in just three weeks? He took a gamble without Ron's input. "Ok, three weeks, and if I'm less than twenty points down on both Drummond and Warner, you endorse me."

"No deal," said Sterling. "A nineteen-point deficit does not a president make."

"See you in three weeks," Jackson said confidently.

"Be sure to give my best to Catherine and the boys."

The call ended slightly more amicably than it began.

∼

AS THE SUN ROSE, Faber Farm was blanketed in an early morning frost. There were 78 days until the New Hampshire Primary on January 19. In terms of news cycles, it was a lifetime but the blink of an eye in the life of a presidential campaign.

Ron Bender and Diesel Browning had officially joined the campaign as the manager and chair. Together, they had established all the physical, legal, and strategic mechanisms required to launch a presidential campaign. They had vetted and hired thirty staff members, established the campaign's core message, and put the Pipers to work raising money and meeting voters.

Ron Bender stood in the spacious, modern kitchen of the beautifully renovated farmhouse. The sunlight poured through the floor-to-ceiling windows, illuminating the warm wood cabinets and gleaming stainless steel appliances. Around him, fifty or so core staff members and high-level surrogates chatted and made introductions, fueled by the delicious coffee and pastries delivered to the farm earlier that morning. Some were meeting in person for the first time, their faces bright with excitement and anticipation. As the clock struck nine, Ron cleared his throat and kicked off the first formal campaign meeting, his voice echoing against the high ceilings as he outlined the plans and goals for the day ahead.

"Ok, listen up!" The whispers and laughter quickly ended as all eyes turned to the veteran operative. "Welcome to our first meeting of the Piper for President campaign!" There were smiles, applause and cheers. Hagrid barked loudly.

"I know you are as excited as I am to get to work to elect Jackson Piper, the next President of the United States!"

Louder cheers filled the farm again.

"We estimate approximately 535,000 voters will cast ballots in the President's Party Primary seventy-eight days from today. Lucky for us,

Iowa has already canceled its caucus, having believed these races have already been decided." Boos filled the kitchen.

"Many of you are from New Hampshire or New England, though a few are not from this region. You will know them by their thick Pittsburgh accents. Let me help you with a little Pittsburghese that you might hear from Jackson or some of the other Pittsburgh staff. Pop means soda. Yins is you all. A tossel cap, which we have supplied you all with bearing our beautiful new logo, is, in fact, a beanie to keep your heads warm up here in New Hampshire. And Jaggoff is a Pittsburgh term for a jerk or a real asshole or someone who can't knock on their required number of doors each day because they're too cold. Don't be jaggoffs." There was laughter from the staff.

Ron continued. "New Hampshire still deeply values retail politics, and there is no good way to put this; we are forty points behind Drummond and Warner." Groans and grimaces. "I know that seems like a HUGE gap. That's because it is. It's enormous, and we have just three resources at our disposal to close that gap. Any idea what they are?"

"Wishes, hopes, and prayers?" joked Diesel Browning.

"Clever guess, Senator Browning, but no," answered Ron.

A petite, bright-eyed Asian woman no older than 25 caught Bender's attention with her raised hand. She proudly wore a beanie emblazoned with the words "America Needs Piper." She was bursting with enthusiasm, and her confidence was energizing.

"Yes, young lady?" Bender said, calling on her.

"People, money, and time," she replied with a smile.

"Looks like we hired the right people, Diesel. And remind me of your name again, darlin'," said Bender.

"Libby," she replied.

"Thanks, Libby." Bender continued, taking advantage of his command of the room. "The three resources we have are people, money, and time. But the most important resource is time because it is the only resource you cannot get more of by leveraging the other two." The room buzzed with curiosity and understanding.

Like a field commander, he paced back and forth behind the

island in the kitchen as he walked them through the strategy. There was no time for crisscrossing the country. To establish relevance in this race, the Piper strategy is to come out swinging and score major points in the first round. Piper was running to expose a fundamental flaw in the system. By filing as a candidate seeking both the Old Party and Other Party nominations, they intended to beat both Paul Drummond and Russell Warner in the New Hampshire Primary by offering fresh ideas, a new voice, and unmatched energy. The bold assertion was met with loud cheers.

"We intend to make Russell Warner have no choice but to spend some of those billions he has coming from Marco Alvarez right here in New Hampshire. We want him to realize he cannot take the support of the American people for granted." More applause erupted.

In the cutthroat world of presidential campaigns, physical appearance could often make or break a candidate. Jackson Piper was undeniably easy on the eyes, with chiseled features and piercing blue eyes that seemed to hold secrets. His dark hair, trimmed beard, and subduing smile gave him a rugged charm.

Piper descended the creaking farmhouse stairs and heard Bender delivering the tail end of his remarks. Piper would stay out of view until his cue.

"...And so, friends, it is my pleasure to introduce the next President of the United States, Jackson Piper!"

Jackson burst into the room with a smile that stretched from ear to ear, high-fiving staff and greeting others with a firm handshake. His height and confidence filled the space with a palpable energy.

"Let me begin by saying thank you. Many of you have left family, perhaps even jobs, to join this campaign. You've agreed to give up your Thanksgiving, Christmas, Hanukkah, New Year's, and every weekend for the next eleven weeks. Perhaps, if we're lucky, the next twelve months."

The room laughed, and a man whistled loudly.

"But you see, while luck might be a little piece of magic that we often attribute as the source of our success," he said, feeling the

Franklin coin in his left trouser pocket. "We know that success in campaigns is hard-fought and unfortunately short-lived."

The room grew silent.

"Ron Bender has done a great job of pumping you up. Now let me tell it to you straight."

Ron looked up, a nervous look flashing briefly across his face. *This was not the script.*

"We aim to win both primaries. But let's be clear about how difficult this will be. No one has ever sought the nomination for President in two major Parties simultaneously. And certainly, no one has gone from not running to winning the New Hampshire Primary in 90 days."

The room sat silent and still, rapt in the serious words of Senator Piper.

"I called my former Senate colleague Paul Drummond before I chose to enter this race. I outlined for Paul the evidence we had that he was being used as a patsy to rig this election for President Warner. We outlined what we believed to be evidence that Marco Alvarez is bankrolling the Other Party in exchange for control over Drummond's campaign. Paul refused to believe the evidence."

There were murmurs and plenty of head-shaking among the staff.

"I offered him a chance to exit the race and allow me to run one-on-one against Warner with no Party financial support whatsoever. He refused. I offered to team up and focus our message and our attacks only on Warner, guaranteeing neutrality towards one another. He refused. I offered to meet with him in person to outline a bold new agenda for my former Party's platform to transform it at this time of national challenge. He refused."

There were more snickers and jeers from the crowd. Jackson raised his hand to ask for silence. "So I refused to take it easy on Paul Drummond."

The room erupted in loud cheers.

"We are going to take this country back from those so desperate for some power they have become too timid to speak truth to the powerful," said Jackson. He took a drink of water as he prepared to lay into his second opponent.

"Our other opponent does not play by the rules of decency, decorum, or democracy. Since becoming President, Russell Warner has used political violence, threats, and lies to feed the very worst instincts of the human condition. He stokes fear so that even the bravest among us dare not challenge him in any setting. That was true when I served with him in the Senate and I know it to be true as he sits in 1600 Pennsylvania Avenue."

"But hear me now and hear it clear. Just as I wish to swear an oath to preserve, protect, and defend this nation, which I love," he paused, making strategic eye contact. The room was hanging on each word. "I swear to you today, as I regard each of you as a member of my family now, I swear to preserve your honor, protect and defend you from the very worst that Russel Warner and his goon squads can throw at us, so help me, God!"

The room erupted in boisterous cheers. His call to action electrified them. He hoped he had adequately characterized the threat they would face if they were successful in this first test of their campaign. The closer they inched towards the impossible—defeating Russell Warner's bid for a second term—the more extreme Warner's words and actions would become.

"I might be the candidate, but you are my Army. You will carry this campaign forward from this day through our victory on November 8!" They gave him a standing ovation. He laughed and joked and encouraged them to sit. He placed his hand on his heart and mouthed thank you. He caught Catherine's eye and winked.

7

JUNIPER MODELS

"Piper Files Historic Bid for Both Party Nominations."

That was the headline, or some version of it, that Marco read endlessly on the first Monday in November. He remained calm despite his first inclination to break every window in his home study, the same room where President Warner had refused his generous offer only a few weeks before.

Rushy sat across from him, running models through the Juniper system.

"This might be better for us than we initially thought," Rushan said, grabbing Marco's attention. Marco raised an eyebrow, intrigued by the possible implications.

"So far, a majority of the models we have run through the electoral projections framework suggests that Piper's candidacy helps Warner win," said Rushan.

"What the fuck? How so?" asked Marco skeptically.

With a flip of his fingertips, Rushy displayed the newly developed projections on a screen in Marco's office. A series of maps displayed along with a meter illustrating the probability of a Warner win under various circumstances.

"There are 4.9 quadrillion possible outcomes to the election based on modeled voter turnout," explained Rushy.

The number did not phase Marco. This was the order of magnitude Juniper and its super SI computers could handle every second.

Rushy continued with the impromptu presentation. "These models weigh the impacts of winning or losing precincts. Precincts determine who wins counties. The winning or losing of a county then tips a state for or against a candidate. We can also factor in negative and positive stories, the discounting of votes in precincts likely impacted by factors such as intimidation, misinformation, and even poor weather on election day."

Marco took the data in carefully. "Keep going," he said.

"Before Piper's entrance into the race, Warner was sitting at a 65 percent win probability over Drummond for the reasons we have been over and over for the past two years. Drummond is an unknown, boring, and inconsequential Senator. Drummond also suffers from irregular heartbeats that he has refused to have sufficiently treated, and under extreme stress, he faces severe risk of cerebral ischemia and stroke."

Marco leaned forward at his desk.

Rushy tapped the screen on his tablet. The charts on the screen shifted, showing a completely new scenario.

"Piper is a maverick. If he wins the Other Party nomination outright, Warner's reelection chance moves to 45 percent. Obviously, if Piper somehow wins the Old Party nomination, which we currently gauge as a 23 percent likelihood, Warner's chances for reelection move to zero unless he runs as an independent. However, an incumbent beaten for his own Party's nomination would be severely damaged goods. Piper would beat Drummond in the General Election in a walk."

"I thought you said Piper's entry into the race is good news for us?" snarled Marco. "I don't see any of this as good news."

"I'm getting there, sir," said Rushy. "However, if Piper limps along in the race long enough to believe he has a shot at winning the general election but is boxed out of either Party's nomination, well..." He tapped the tablet.

"Hijo de Puta!" Marco's mouth dropped.

On the screen, Rushy's model showed Warner with a 90 percent win scenario with Drummond as the Other Party nominee, Warner as the Old Party nominee, and Jackson Piper running as an independent. It was an electoral college landslide.

"How the fuck is that possible?" asked Marco.

Rushy explained, "Independents have never faired well in presidential elections in the United States and tend only to siphon votes from one candidate. In these models, since Piper is a former member of the Other Party, he will have limited appeal to our voters in the Warner column. He and Drummond are simply going to lock up over the same voters and tip the election to Warner."

Marco stood and walked to the windows. "Why did we not model this as a better option to tip the balance of the election sooner?"

"A third candidate in the race adds far more complication to the race, especially Jackson Piper. He is a Boy Scout, literally. He earned his Eagle Award. He can't be bought or bribed. He adds many more variables than we would like to deal with here. This 90 percent win probably is a model where Juniper is heavily involved in the coverage of the race, sir." Rushy felt a tinge of nervousness about the suggestion. "Perhaps more than I'm comfortable with."

"Burying stories?" asked Marco. "Fuck, we do that already."

"No, sir," said Rushy. "We would need to retrain the system to promote fake and false stories about Piper as truth."

"Are you for real right now?" shouted Marco. "That would plummet the stock price. Juniper would be sunk."

"Obviously, we would need to cover our tracks. We would need real-world corroborators so it didn't look like Juniper was malfunctioning."

"I'm not sold on this, Rushy. This is more risk than I'm willing to take with my company."

"Perhaps we see if Piper has any traction. Take a wait-and-see approach?"

"Have I ever told you to 'wait-and-see,' Rushy?" said Marco coldly.

"Good point, sir," said Rushy. He thought carefully for a moment. "What if we can land someone on the inside of Piper's campaign like we have with Drummond? This would give a clear read on strategy, message, and plans, and allow us to work in real-time to either force Piper out of the race or push him towards staying in but only as an Independent."

"Well, we're not going to do that for free, are we Rushy?"

"That would be quite a generous gift to Warner. Especially after he refused to entertain your request, sir."

"Agreed," said Marco coldly. "This seems like a delicate needle to thread. I need to meditate on this."

"This doesn't change the ultimate goal, does it, sir?" asked Rushy.

"No, no, it does not. But it certainly makes the path more treacherous than we originally planned."

8

REBOOT

It was early December when the first whispers of unease started to ripple through the campaign headquarters. The usually bustling office, alive with the scent of fresh coffee and the constant hum of pressing keys and strategy chatter, fell into an uneasy hush. Once a beacon of charisma and confidence, Piper now cast long shadows on the frosted windows. The atmosphere in the house had shifted from hopeful energy to thick tension. Something was brewing in the heart of the Granite State, and it wasn't a winter storm on the horizon. It was the first sign that Piper's path to the presidency would not be as smooth as all had hoped.

After setting off an explosion of enthusiasm with his surprise entry into the race, Jackson and his team hit a concrete wall. The internal polls were all over the place, but most had the race for the Old Party nomination as:

```
Warner 68%
Piper 22%
None of the Above 10%
```

Meanwhile, in the Other Party, it was:

> *Drummond 52%*
> *Piper 31%*
> *None of the Above 17%*

While the 56-point gap was disappointing, Piper's 21-point trailing of Paul Drummond was setting off a panic among donors, pundits, and, most of all, Jackson Piper.

It was December 11 when Jackson and a small corps of campaign staff were on a northern swing along the Maine border. After a long day knocking on rural doors and meeting with folks in kitchens and living rooms, the Piper campaign had arranged a meet-and-greet at the Bartlett Fire Hall.

The New Hampshire State Senator Wilbur Winchester opened the event. Mr. Winchester was a power broker all over Carroll County, which was entirely within his district. But Mr. Winchester was incredibly influential in this small town overlooking the White Mountains. Wilbur claimed his family lineage traced to Continental Congress member Dr. Josiah Bartlett, the small town's namesake, but many people up there claimed such associations.

The last decade had been challenging for the town's residents, who built their economy around tourism, especially skiing, for decades. Five of the last seven winters ended without significant snow, severely drying up the good humor and savings of most of the town's residents. The sparsely populated town was likely to become abandoned altogether as residents contemplated drastic measures to protect their families.

The fire hall was filled with about 200 residents of the town. Piper and his campaign team had learned it was best to refrain from attempting to segment their events by party. Instead, they invited all residents to meet Jackson and consider him for their vote on either of the Primary Election ballots.

About halfway through the event, three men and a woman wearing thick black leather jackets entered the hall and sat in the last row. Each wore a star-spangled handkerchief tied in a knot around their left arm. This was not a prominent display of patriotism. It was the familiar call sign of Warriors; They were a loosely organized goon squad loyal to President Russell Warner and his reelection. They were not unique to New Hampshire; these political zealots had sprouted up during the economic crash of '39, and their anger evolved into a fanaticism about President Warner. He was never shy about speaking their grievances, repeating their conspiracy theories, and egging them on to test the boundaries of First Amendment speech and violence. They followed a cult-like misinterpretation of the Bible and the Constitution.

"Your support is paramount! Let's get our people to the polls on January 19th! Vote Piper in Both! I'm open to your questions," Jackson said. The weariness in his voice was evident. It was his fifth speech of the day.

One of the Warriors stood up and grumbled something offensive about Piper. Piper did not hear it, but the folks seated near the Warrior caught every word of the insult. "I got a question for you, Jack!" shouted the Warrior.

The audience buzzed with a mixture of offense and anxiety.

Piper remained calm and walked towards the man, still holding the microphone. "Shoot," Piper said.

"Don't give me any ideas," said the man, placing the audience on greater alert. "Here's my question. What right does a fag like you have in challenging President Warner? You're not even a member of the Old Party," he said.

Several large farmers placed their phones to their ears. Piper gave them a calm glance, unsure where this was headed. Piper's instinct was to engage and diffuse the tension as calmly as possible.

"Valid question. Oddly enough, it's one I get a lot. It usually starts with 'Who do you think you are...' and then grinds towards an accusation from there. Here's where I get the right, sir. I am a natural-born citizen of the United States. I'm over 35, and I've lived in the United States my entire life - most of that time in Pittsburgh, but more recently in Denver. I have been registered to vote since I was 18 and have never missed a primary or general election. I swore an oath to God to protect the Constitution and the nation I love from all enemies, foreign and domestic, five times. And I'm an Eagle Scout."

The room applauded that accomplishment. "That award always gets the most applause," joked Piper, looking around the room. He returned his eyes to the icy stare of the Warrior.

"Democracy is messy. But having an election opponent is healthy. It helps clarify what we believe in. We give the voters a choice to pick the leaders they want. The leaders don't get to pick their opponents," said Jackson.

"The Bible says to beware the wolves that have come to kill your flock!" the man shouted.

Jackson smiled. "That's the book of Matthew, and I believe the verse is 'Beware of false prophets, who come to you in sheep's clothing but inwardly are ravenous wolves.' Are you saying I am the wolf, sir?" asked Jackson.

"You said it, not me. You fucking WOLF," said the Warrior.

"I might ask you a question. What do you call a man who ran on a unity ticket, claiming he would heal the nation's wounds? But once in power, he allowed those wounds to fester. Abused his office. He consolidated power while he ignored those who were hurting. Deliberately breaks laws he was elected to enforce? Isn't it Warner who came to us in sheep's clothing? Isn't Warner your wolf?"

"Are you mocking me? You think I don't know the Bible? I know what it says, motherfucker!" His hands rolled into fists.

"I think someone has told you things that simply are not true. And I want to help you to see the truth, sir," Jackson said.

"I think your ideas are fucking garbage, just like you," said the man in the thick black jacket. He removed a revolver from under his black leather jacket and cocked the hammer, and placed the nose of the barrel in Jackson's face, just three feet away.

The three Warriors sprinted from their seats, each revealing a pistol and waving them indiscriminately at the crowd. They moved to join their associate at the microphone.

The crowd gasped, and citizens nearest the microphone tried to slide away toward the walls and the doors.

"Nobody fucking move!" shouted the Warriors. "You all fucking freeze!"

Jackson was doing his best to breathe and remain calm. He stared coldly at the man now threatening his life. "Brother, don't do this," Jackson whispered.

"Don't tell me what to do, you fucking coward! Pussy!" growled the Warrior.

Phones were out, recording every minute of the terror. Many had dialed 9-1-1 and discreetly placed their phones to their ears to plea for assistance. Dozens in the audience texted loved ones to share what they feared might be a final message.

"What do you want from me?" Piper asked.

The Warrior looked nervously around the room. It was clear that the vigilante had not thought through the plan beyond this point, or perhaps whatever drugs he had in his system were starting to heighten his experience of adrenaline coursing through his veins.

"Look at me," said Piper calmly. "It's me you want. You should let these innocent people leave so you and I can talk alone,"

"Bullshit! They need to hear it. They need to hear you say it!" screamed the Warrior. The three accomplices looked terrified as they swung their pistols from left to right, unsure exactly what to do to aid the cause of their accomplice.

"Say what, sir?" Jackson asked.

"You're going to quit this race. You are doing the devil's work! Spreading lies!" the man said through gritted teeth.

"Why don't we let these people leave, and you and I..."

"No! I want witnesses!" shouted the man.

"Al, this wasn't the plan. We were just supposed to scare him," said the woman Warrior.

"He looks pretty fucking scared to me," said the Warrior.

"No, he doesn't, Al," one of the other Warriors said. "Al, we should get out of here before we get pinched."

"Fuck that," Al said. "I want to hear this fucker say he's done. He quits! They say you quit the Senate!"

"I didn't quit the Senate," Jackson said firmly. "I lost an election. That's how things are supposed to work."

A loud crash echoed through the hall as a door flung open violently. Three burly men clad in red Bartlett Volunteer Fire t-shirts stormed into the room like raging bulls. The first was as massive as Piper, his muscles rippling beneath his shirt. The second, even larger, towered over the others like a hulking giant.

"Stay back! Stay back!" shouted Al.

"What's going on here?" shouted one of the firefighters. The three had been working on equipment when word got to them about men with guns at the presidential forum on the other side of the hall.

"Al, I don't want to die here. Al! Al!" shouted his friends in turn. "Al, please. Let's go!"

Piper used the distraction to step closer to the man pointing the gun at him.

"You don't look like you're from Bartlett," said the tallest firefighter.

The woman turned and shrieked, "I don't see how that's any of your fucking business!"

The second firefighter said, "We have manners out here. We don't insult visitors or flash guns at people here." They were walking slowly toward Piper and the four Warriors.

"Stop right there, assholes, or I'll kill this fucker," shouted Al. He was looking at the firefighters. Piper inched closer to the gunman, then he locked his muscles, frozen in place.

"Al, let's allow these people to leave, and you and I can have a talk, man to man, about what you believe," Jackson said, pleading a third time for the gunman to allow the innocent bystanders to be removed from the equation.

Al looked at Jack and growled, "I'll put a hole in your fucking head if you don't shut your trap,"

"If you know what's good for you, you'll leave before Sheriff Brewster gets here. He's way less patient than us," said one of the firefighters.

The three firefighters had moved within Piper's sightline. He caught the eye of one of the men, who gave Jackson a subtle nod. Jackson took this to mean they had his back if he wanted to try to make a move. Jackson understood it would be risky and that he had never attempted what he was about to do with an actual loaded gun in his face.

"That's it, Al! We are getting out of here, man! I'm not going back to fucking jail for you, dude!"

"Man, fuck you!" snapped Al, looking over his shoulder at his accomplice who had threatened to abandon him.

This was it, Jackson's only chance. His hand moved with lightning speed as he grabbed the cold metal of the pistol barrel, gripping it tightly and twisted it violently towards the Warrior's wrist, disarming him in one swift motion. As Al turned to react with fury, Jackson's fist connected with a loud crack against his nose, breaking it and sending blood pouring down his face. The other three armed Warriors were quickly taken down by the coordinated efforts of the firefighters, who followed Piper's lead. They expertly disarmed the thugs and incapacitated them with brutal force. The screams of pain filled the air as the firefighters and other residents fought back, twisting limbs and exerting excruciating pressure until their captors were subdued and helpless on the ground. It was a chaotic scene of fierce determination and raw survival instincts.

"You're going to break my fucking arm!" shouted one.

"I should do a lot worse, you dirtbag," replied the firefighter.

"Search them for more weapons!" shouted someone from the crowd.

The heavy steel door creaked open, revealing Sheriff Brewster's imposing figure as he burst into the room with three deputies in tow. The sheriff's tall, broad-shouldered frame exuded confidence and experience, causing Jackson to surmise that he was likely a Marine. The sharp creases on his uniform and the scuff marks on his boots suggested a no-nonsense attitude. He carried himself with an air of authority, like a lion surveying his territory.

The deputies moved quickly to help secure Al with handcuffs, then moved from Warrior to Warrior, cuffing them from largest to smallest.

The event abruptly came to an end. Sheriff Brewster approached Jackson Piper. "My apologies, Mr. Piper. That is not how we do business in Bartlett."

"No need to apologize, Sheriff."

Brewster looked at Piper with concern. "You'd be smart to get yourself a security detail, sir. Need any names?"

"Only if they're local. If I suddenly have to go from town to town with guards, I want people to see me being protected by their neighbors," he replied.

Brewster took out his pen and pad and jotted down ten names for Piper to consider.

Jackson made it a point to check on the well-being of every person who did not immediately flee the event. He went to each, shook their hand or wrapped his arm around them, apologized profusely, snapped selfies, signed autographs, and handed out as much free gear as he could retrieve from the campaign van.

Marty Dudash was Piper's assigned "body man," a campaign staffer who is assigned to be a convenient extra set of hands anywhere the candidate travels. A body man is often the driver, phone handler, bag carrier, coffee fetcher, schedule keeper, photo snapper, and confidant. Marty was trying to calm himself enough to call his boss, Ron Bender.

Ron was hunched over a laptop when his phone began to vibrate.

"Incoming call from Mr. Dudash," announced Ziggy.

"Answer it," said Ron.

"Hello, this is Ziggy. How is the drive going, Mr. Dudash?"

"Ziggy," said Marty, breathing heavily. "I need to speak to Ron."

Ron jumped to his feet and reached for his phone. "Marty, what's wrong?" he asked in a panic, sensing the fear in Marty's voice.

"Someone tried to kill Senator Piper. There was a man with a gun. He stood up at the start of the Q&A. He pointed the gun at the Senator's head and was demanding him to quit the race."

"What?" shouted Ron in disbelief. He began pacing nervously.

"Except three firefighters came in and backed Mr. Piper up. Was Senator Piper in the Army?"

"No? Why?" Ron's blood pressure was climbing.

"Well, he broke a guy's nose to disarm him," said Marty, his voice shaking.

"What the fuck?" Ron shouted. He took the phone from his ear and barked commands to Ziggy. "Ziggy, please look across all social feeds and find any videos posted that include a person matching Jackson's physical identity."

"Will do, Ron," Ziggy said dutifully. She saluted on the screen above the fireplace.

Ron returned to the conversation with Marty. "Is everyone safe?"

"Yes, sir. No injuries except this freaking Warriors. They got a serious smackdown, sir," said Marty.

"Remarkable. Please get the Senator back here. Now! Drive safely but with urgency. Have the Senator call me as soon as you're alone on the road," instructed Ron.

Ziggy reappeared on the screen. "Ron, I have located the video. It was originally posted at 7:51 p.m. Shall I play it for you?"

"Yeah, let's see it," Ron said.

A jostling cell phone captures the entire encounter, from the minute Al stood up to confront Jackson to the arrival of the Sheriff and the deputies. Ron was in shock.

"Who owns the account that posted this?" Ron asked.

"A twenty-year-old college student named Isabell Frost," informed Ziggy.

"Please get me her cell phone number. We're going to ask her to stop by and see if she's a friend or foe," said Ron.

Ron's phone rang again. This time, it was Jackson Piper.

"I told you to go pound the pavement in Bartlett, not beat the shit out of voters. Do I need to be more clear?"

"Very funny, old man. This was by far the craziest night I have ever had in my twenty years in politics," said Jackson.

"Where did you learn that move?" Ron asked, afraid to know the answer.

"Spend enough time killing time between floor votes with Diesel, and he will teach you a thing or two about self-defense. I think we were waiting to vote on a DOD budget bill one night, and he taught a group of us how to disarm an attacker who has you pinned at gunpoint."

"I just saw the video," Ron said.

"Oh God. There's a video?" Jackson said, closing his eyes and breathing deeply in the second row of the SUV.

"Of course there's a video, Jack! The good news is it shows the entire incident, from start to finish, with no cuts. It should have a TRUTH designation from *The Mark* any minute," Ron said. He said a silent prayer that he was right.

"So what's the bad news?" asked Jackson.

"There's a video of my candidate breaking the nose of an opponent's supporter in front of a crowd of people," said Ron dryly.

"Not funny," Jackson said. "Um, Catherine's calling me. I better take this. We'll see you in an hour," said Jackson. "Better get someone started on a statement. I'll text you my thoughts."

"Send me your full version of the events as well. We must frame this succinctly as you acting in self-defense before Warner starts claiming we are assaulting his supporters."

∼

By 9 PM, the hottest trending topics on every social channel were #PiperPunch #NinjaPiper and #AngryJack. A meme emerged, merging the scene from the classic film Air Force One, in which President Marshall punched the terrorists, and the clip of Piper's increasingly famous nose-breaking punch of the Warrior.

Two days later, President Warner visited New Hampshire. He gave out toys to children at the home of a retired hedge fund manager. President Warner wore black leather gloves and a flight jacket bearing the presidential seal, pulling toys from a red velvet sack. Most of the toys still had price tags on them. He did not bother with any coffee klatches or spaghetti dinners. He did not come to a complete stop within a mile of a fire hall.

A reporter from the only network permitted into the event asked President Warner if he had any words for the voters of New Hampshire.

"I respect the voters of New Hampshire deeply," he said. "They are beautiful people. They know better than to gamble with the safety of this country, and I would hate to see what would happen to the country we love if a reckless impostor like the Pied Piper were to steal the presidency."

The reporter did not challenge a word the President said. She nodded, doe-eyed, as he continued.

"If you ask me, it's about time we turn up the heat on Piper and his rats. Drive them out of New Hampshire and this race, which he has no business in. This is between Senator Drummond and me. That's a fair fight. That's the one the country wants. They want a race that is worthy of our Founding Fathers."

Then, before leaving New Hampshire, President Russell Warner visited the four Warriors in jail in Carroll County. He attempted to give each a Presidential Challenge Coin, but the sheriff refused to allow the prisoners to take them. Then Warner offered quite loudly to pay their bail. However, he left town before completing the necessary paperwork to release the quartet.

Warner was off to Las Vegas for a long holiday break at his casino, leaving many in New Hampshire to wonder if President Warner cared much about their concerns.

The next day, Paul Drummond was on the campaign trail in Portsmouth, enjoying breakfast at a popular spot where most people waited up to two hours for a table. While taking photos with irritated diners and tourists, he was approached by a national news reporter who asked him about his stance on Jackson Piper's continued involvement in the race following the incident in Bartlett.

"I do not condone violence in any form. But I also think Jackson had no choice. I mean, he had a gun to his head."

"Would you have done the same?" asked the reporter.

"Well, luckily, no one brings guns to Other Party town halls," Drummond said.

"But would you have had the wherewithal to do what Jackson Piper did? To strike back? Some are saying that Jackson Piper got a taste of the type of violence and threats that many Americans live with every day now in America."

The short, bland man from Wisconsin blinked and swallowed nervously. "I would like to think I could have done what he did. Sure."

"President Warner is calling on Jackson Piper to drop out of this race. Do you join him in that call?"

"I think Jackson Piper would make a great candidate in 2048," said Drummond smugly. "I mean, 2052 because, of course, I'm going to win this year, and then I'll want a second term. So 2052 or even 2056 seem like better choices to me...for him...Jackson Piper."

∼

HUDDLED in the farmhouse outside of Manchester, the Piper campaign, fraught with worry, contemplated the impacts of the attack on Piper in Bartlett.

The headquarters was littered with printouts of the coverage, ranging from lauding Piper for his heroism in protecting the crowd to calls for his immediate departure from the race for his brutality toward a supporter of one of his opponents.

That was a more than generous description of the gun-wielding Warrior.

"There is no question we will need increased security, possibly even metal detectors at all entrances to our events. Perhaps we treat him like he already needs presidential-level security," said Senator Browning.

"I already said no to that. I can't fall into the trap of being unreachable," insisted Piper. "This is a shoe leather and backslapping campaign state. Voters here expect to look you in the eye, shake your hand, and see what you're made of."

"I think we've got that part covered," said Libby, grimacing.

Bender made a suggestion. "We are trailing Warner so badly in the Old Party Primary; perhaps we consider bowing out and focusing all of our firepower on the Other Party nomination?"

"I've already said no to that," insisted Piper. "The message here is the two Parties are in collusion, and there's no difference between them. I don't expect to win both nominations, but we are forcing voters to ask themselves if they see much difference in the Parties' actions anymore. It's not their platform since they get absolutely nothing done in Washington. But their actions." Piper was frustrated.

"But what is our platform?" pressed Libby. "I feel like it keeps changing, and it's not exciting. We told ourselves we'd announce a bold agenda by December 1, and here we are nearly at Christmas, and we're no closer to unveiling anything."

"She's right, I'm afraid," said Senator Browning.

The mood in the room continued to slide towards exasperation. The highs and lows of presidential campaigns can turn any high-functioning adult into an adrenaline junkie with an anchor of depression and doubt chained to their ankle.

Jackson looked around and saw the sad faces. "Ok, let's snap out of this. This is not who we are, and this is not the type of campaign I want to run. We must stop chasing Drummond and Warner and make them chase us instead."

He jumped to his feet and walked to the large screen in the living room. "Ziggy," he said, "Can you whiteboard for me please?"

The SI assistant responded immediately. Appearing on the screen next to Jackson, she held a set of dry-erase markers in her digital hands and was ready to scribe for their leader.

"It's clear our message has no traction. This is not a personality contest and not a viral campaign. This is a campaign of ideals to lead a country of ideals. So let's talk about this country's big problems right now."

"Collapsing industries?" said Libby cautiously.

"Which collapsing industries?" asked Piper energetically.

"Family farms, winter sports," said Libby.

"Think beyond New Hampshire," pushed Piper.

"Offshore fishing," said another staffer.

"Residential construction," said another.

"Timber," said a third.

Ziggy was writing the words on the whiteboard behind her.

"Great, now tie these together. What are some words that are the opposite of collapse?" asked Piper.

"Grow," said Bender.

"Too trite," said Piper.

"Hey!" said Ziggy. "No umbrellas at the brainstorm, Senator."

"I'm sorry, Ron," said Piper. "Write it down, Ziggy."

More words flew from the campaign staff. Rebound, sprout, spring, thrive, vigor, liveliness, buoyancy, zest, spirit, punch...the group grimaced at that one...pep, gusto, and the list grew and grew. Finally, a word spoke to the energy, enthusiasm, and direction they hoped to restore to the U.S. economy - vitality.

A *new* vitality.

They shifted their attention to what was broken in Washington, D.C., which prompted a broader discussion about fundamental rights being destroyed by Warner, an activist Supreme Court, and an increasingly irrelevant Congress.

"We have no explicit right to privacy!" said Libby.

"We are being taxed to the gills," said Marty.

"When did you grow gills, Martin?" asked Bender sarcastically.

"I mean..." began Marty, embarrassed.

Jackson raised his hand. "We understood your point, Marty. What if there were a mechanism for protecting citizens from over-taxation?" he asked the group.

"You mean like a Constitutional amendment?" asked a younger man with sandy brown hair.

"Exactly," said Piper. "What if we championed a new Bill of Rights?"

All eyes focused on Jackson. His mind raced with ideas. "A right to privacy, a right to property, and to enjoy the fruits of your labors? A right to free, fair, and representative elections?"

"What was that bill you and I wrote in our first term, Jack?" asked Diesel.

"Which one?" asked Jackson.

"Giving citizens the right to recall elections for a member of Congress," said Diesel. "And making members of Congress take a term off after three consecutive terms in office."

"The people in power are not going to like this list," said Bender.

"Right, but this isn't about them. It's about the citizens and their feelings of powerlessness. Giving them new power," replied Jackson.

"No, not new powers. New freedoms," Diesel said.

"Yes! New freedoms!" said Jackson excitedly.

The group toiled tirelessly for another two hours, their minds focused and determined as they fleshed out a bold new vision for the nation together. Excitement pulsed through the air, energizing each individual as they shared ideas and brainstormed together. When their work finally felt complete, Ron sent them out with his credit card to get dinner for the staff, a gesture of gratitude for their hard work and dedication. The heavy cloud of doubt that had previously hung over them was lifted by the collaborative and creative session.

Jackson's eyes widened as he took in the massive wall of notes displayed on the screen. Ziggy's meticulous scribbles covered every inch of the enlarged whiteboard. It had stretched and grown to accommodate their creative energy and now appeared to be the size of a billboard on the screen, with the energetic SI assistant standing in front of the masterpiece. The sheer amount of information was overwhelming, and Jackson felt himself getting lost in the sea of words and diagrams.

"Ron, can you get the comms team to work on taking these ideas and crafting them into a manageable new stump speech?" asked Jackson.

Ron nodded, smiling. "I think we have a shot with this, Jack."

"I believe in this. This is our best shot. Let's give it all we got,"

Jackson said. He took a marker, scribbled three phases onto a nearby scrap of paper, and handed them to Ron. "This is the framework I want."

His note read *New Optimism, New Freedoms, and New Vitality for America.*

9

SPARKS

The message reboot was even more successful than Bender and Piper had anticipated. Coupled with the viral Bartlett video, the campaign raised a staggering $22 million between December 11 and the end of the year, matching all of Drummond's fundraising for the fourth quarter.

By New Year's Day, Piper's internal polling, which Ziggy primarily conducted, indicated Piper (41%) was nearly even with Drummond (43%). Still, the margin of error of plus or minus 5% meant Piper may be in the lead.

The Old Party contest was a slightly different story. Piper encouraged Independents to flood the Old Party Primary, which was permitted under state law. Ziggy had worked a modestly higher-than-normal Independent turnout into their polling model. By New Year's Day, they projected Russell Warner (58%) was still leading Piper (38%) by double digits. The chance of catching Warner with eight days to go was slipping out of reach.

The New Year arrived with a small celebration among the Piper for President staff, who remained in New Hampshire to ring in 2044. The next day, every campaign surrogate, endorser, and staffer capable of stumping for Piper was dispatched across the Granite State.

From January 2 until January 11, the Pipers were leapfrogging each other in a grueling schedule around the state. They were now on the final leg of the trip. Jackson and Catherine started the morning in the city of Keene at a pancake breakfast and town hall; halfway through, Catherine would head to Peterborough for a meeting at the Town House for what the campaign billed as a *Cate Chat*. Jackson would skip forward to Nashua for a rally, where Catherine would arrive just in time to join him on stage. Once the rally ended, they could finally spend the night back at the Faber Farm in Manchester for a day of rest before beginning the final week of campaigning towards the finish line.

Upon arriving in downtown Keene, they were met with an eager crowd, bundled against the biting cold. The air buzzed with anticipation as Jackson and Catherine exited their SUV a block early with their entirely New Hampshire security detail. They shook hands, snapped selfies, and said hello to the many familiar faces in the crowd queued up around the block. This was the couple's fourth visit to Keene since landing in New Hampshire.

As the Pipers made their way toward the entrance to the Keene Armory, where the pancake breakfast was being held, the smell of maple syrup, pancakes, and sausage filled their nostrils. Jackson's stomach rumbled in anticipation, but eating was the last item on the agenda. Finally, they entered the warm Armory, where local press and politicians waited.

"Hello, everyone," Jackson said after working the room. "I'm so glad to be back here in Keene this morning. This part of our country is so important to our nation's history, and I'm honored to have your trust and support as we bring new optimism and new freedom to America together."

The crowd cheered as Piper dove into his stump speech about restoring decency to the presidency and curtailing the dangerous expansion of executive authority under the last seven Presidents.

He looked out at the sea of faces, and for a moment, he was transported back to his first campaign for the Senate, reminded of all those who had once believed in him.

"My brothers and sisters," he began, his voice steady and strong, "I stand before you not just as a candidate but as a fellow American hungry to lift the American ship of state out of the swamp in which she has found herself swallowed."

After Jackson began to speak, Catherine slipped off stage to move with her security detail to Peterborough to lead a town hall. They continued their mission to connect with the people as authentically as possible while Warner busied himself with trips to Georgia, North Carolina, and South Carolina—the states that constituted the Southern Regional Primary at the start of February.

Drummond bored small audiences to tears everywhere he went in New Hampshire, panicked by his continuous slide in the polls.

Dr. Catherine Piper had come into her own during seventy days of the campaign. She had appeared many times for Piper in Pennsylvania during the 2040 Senate campaign, so she knew how to work an audience of voters. But a presidential campaign was a master's class in public speaking, and there was no room for error with eight days to go.

Catherine's delivery became full of charm, wit, and touching honesty when the audience least expected it. She told stories about Jackson's character, compassion, and capability to lead the nation back to vitality.

The woman who would be the first physician First Lady if Jackson won the presidency fielded questions from citizens about issues that plagued their community—a new designer pill crisis, the failing education system, the destruction of tourism and farming by the hot planet, and the widening income gap. Each answer revealed Catherine's compassion and deep understanding of these complex problems. She never failed to tie her answers back to her husband's genuine desire to find solutions that transcended Party lines.

"We have nearly closed the gap on the 12-month head-start that Warner and Drummond had when we started this race in November. I'm telling you, in just 73 days, we have knocked on thousands upon thousands of doors between here and Beecher Falls."

Catherine laughed, and the audience followed.

A seasoned primary voter named Esther raised her hand. When Catherine called on her, she leaned forward. "Dr. Piper, we admire your vision, but what makes you think your husband can carry the standard of two completely different Parties at the same time?"

"We have said from the start there is not a dollar's worth of difference between the two Parties now," Catherine said, her gaze steely. "I mean that literally and figuratively. They now go to the same pockets for contributions. The same donors. They claim to have vastly different values, but neither Party has adopted a platform in years. So, on paper, they stand for nothing; in practice, they accomplish even less in Washington. What Jackson offers is a shock to the system. Americans are hurting from farmhouse to shoreline. They have less freedom and less prosperity than a decade ago. We are offering real solutions for real problems."

"Promises don't pay my bills, ma'am. What specifically is Mr. Piper going to do if he wins?" asked a bearded man in the front row.

Dr. Piper looked the man in the eyes. "Anyone who comes to New Hampshire and claims they will solve all your problems by becoming President is lying to you. At best, the President gets 18 months to push an agenda in Washington before Congress becomes fixated on its reelection. I want to be honest with you. If we're going to affect lives, it will take more than Jackson Piper's broad shoulders to lift this nation out of the swamp."

Another woman interjected. "How about safety? Do you know there are people these days who will steal the pipes out of your house?" Her voice rose with anxiety.

"As you know, my family and I have been directly confronted with the threats people face just trying to live their lives." She grew quiet as the image of Jackson with the gun in his face took her breath away. "I am still shaken to my core thinking about that man pulling a gun on Jackson." She locked eyes with the crowd. "It is our promise to the people who are struggling, who feel forgotten, who feel like they have become prey that they will have a President in the White House with the undeniable courage to fight for them."

After another hour of shaking hands and snapping photos,

Catherine was whisked to Nashua, where she met up with Jackson outside a craft candle shop in the downtown.

"Shall we go have a look around?" asked Jackson, offering his arm to his wife.

"As long as we don't say a word," she laughed. "I'm so tired of hearing my voice and other people's voices; I just want five minutes of peace and quiet."

"I'll do my best," said Jackson.

For the next ten minutes, they quietly shopped in the serene candle shop together. Outside the window, a crowd was forming when word got around the block that the Pipers had stopped into Wicked Wax Worx for a bit of shopping before appearing at the Railroad Square rally.

Jackson pretended not to see the growing crowd outside the windows, lifted another candle to his nose, and took a whiff.

"Elderberry Space Jam," said Piper with a smile of approval: clever name and a great scent.

"Oh, Jack, you'll love this one," said Catherine, offering him a jar to smell.

"Oh, that's pumpkin and...bourbon?" guessed Jackson.

"Correct. It's called Headless Horseman Happy Hour," laughed Catherine.

"We're getting that one," said Jackson, placing the candle jar into his metal basket.

"Excuse me," said a woman with long grey hair. "I don't want to intrude on your moment of peace, but would the two of you do me the honor of a picture with me? I want to frame it in the store."

"So you're a supporter?" asked Jackson.

"Oh, a thousand percent," said the woman.

"Which Primary will you be voting in, if you don't mind me asking," inquired Jackson.

"I'm an independent, so I plan to vote for you in the Old Party primary. Everything I heard says that is the best bet for us to upset Warner."

"Is this your shop?" Jackson walked closer to the woman.

"Yes, Mr. Piper," she replied. "My name is Jillian."

"It's adorable," said Catherine, complimenting the owner. "Do you make the candles yourself?"

"Yes, with a little help, Dr. Piper," said Jillian.

"Oh, please call me Catherine," she said, extending her hand.

"Your boys are so adorable," said Jillian. "Are they here?"

"Oh, thank you," said Catherine. "No, they can't miss too much school. They went back to Manchester two days ago to complete their studies with their tutor."

"Definitely looking forward to seeing them both tonight," said Jackson.

Jackson and Catherine purchased three candles, autographed a Piper for President t-shirt that Jillian had on hand, and then prepared to launch into the crowd of waiting fans outside the store.

Esmael, now Jackson's driver and head of security, entered the store just seconds before Jackson opened the door to exit.

"Mr. Piper, please allow me to escort you and Dr. Piper through this crowd," said Esmael.

"Thank you, Esmael, but we'll be fine," said Jackson.

"Sir, it's well over a hundred people now, and I'd prefer to be eyes on both of you within a step or two in case any of those crazy Warriors are hiding in that crowd."

Jackson looked out at the sea of people outside the shop. He recalled the hostility and panic in Al's eyes in Bartlett weeks earlier. He looked at Catherine, looking stunning in her jacket and scarf. Jackson reluctantly agreed.

The Pipers moved slowly through the sea of people eager to have a chance to see the couple face to face. Jackson and Catherine were something not seen in presidential politics in a generation - they were young, optimistic, and vivacious. Despite the cold air, the crowd waited patiently with their eyes fixed on the attractive pair. Jackson and Catherine were doing their best to shake as many hands and snap as many photos to try to get to everyone who had waited patiently for the Pipers to emerge from the shop.

When they arrived at their SUV, Esmael opened the door. Jackson offered a hand for Catherine to step onto the running board and into the warm vehicle. Jackson gave one final wave and smile before joining her.

"Jack," Catherine murmured, her voice soft, "you're doing it. You're actually doing it."

"*We* are doing it," he corrected.

"We have a shot at this." It was the first time she allowed herself to say it for someone else to hear.

Jackson smiled and took her hand in his, squeezing it. "I love you, Catie."

Esmael put the SUV into drive and drove cautiously around the crowd to the rally site on the banks of the Nashua River.

It was luckily an unusually warm day for January in New Hampshire. When the local high school refused to allow Piper to use the gymnasium for the rally, the Piper campaign improvised. They bought two dozen propane warming posts, handed out free coffee, and billed it as a nostalgic open-air rally for democracy. At four o'clock in the afternoon, as the sun was setting and twilight approached, Jackson and Catherine Piper took the stage to provide their closing argument on the historic dual primary campaign. Though stirring and booming at times, his voice was beginning to grow hoarse from over-utilization in the home stretch. The crowd was over five thousand people, bundled in jackets and many wearing hats and gloves. But they stood in the windless cooling air to hear a man who might be President outline his vision for optimism, greater freedom, and restored economic vitality for the nation they once heard it declared was the greatest on earth.

Jackson's thoughts wandered as they drove back to the farm under the starlit sky.

"Ron is going to be so pissed he missed that crowd," laughed Jackson. "He insisted on running through GOTV strategies with Libby."

"He missed what was probably your best speech of this campaign," smiled Catherine, kissing her husband and looking into his smokey blue eyes.

Suddenly, Esmael accelerated the SUV rapidly.

"What's happening?" asked Catherine, looking around in panic. Is someone following us?"

Before the Esmael could answer, Jackson's phone illuminated with Bender's face. Piper unlocked it and took the call.

"Jackson, what's your location?"

"We are on route 101, maybe 10 minutes from the farm. Ron, is everything okay?"

"No, Jackson, it's not. Your kids are fine. They are with Libby. Please have Esmael bring you to the farm as fast as he can drive. There's been an attack. We are gathering the team and counting heads. Who is with you?"

"Marty, Javier, Blue, and Sheila are in the SUV behind us. Cate and I are in the lead SUV," replied Jackson. "A van full of volunteers returned to the hotel for dinner."

"Ok," replied Ron before shouting something incoherent to those around him at the farm and ending the call.

"Did you hear that, Esmael?" asked Jackson.

"10-4. Hold on back there," replied the security agent driver, who stood on the accelerator as the SUV approached 90 miles per hour on a stretch of two-lane highway.

Jackson and Catherine raced through scenarios, wondering what was happening at the farm. Catherine called the second SUV in their caravan and calmly explained that something serious had happened at the campaign farm, and they were rushing to the scene to help.

As they approached the valley where the Faber Farm was nestled, the sky ahead had an eerie luminescence—it had taken on a dark red hue. Thick black smoke was rising among the hills ahead. Sirens flashed behind them and blared as three police cruisers passed the speeding SUV.

As the Piper's vehicle skidded onto the macadam driveway of the Faber Farm, the flames consuming the historic home and barn lit the sky. Heavy, choking black smoke filled the air. Two fire engines were already on the scene, attempting to douse the home with all the water the pump truck carried to such a remote location. There was little anyone could do but stand and watch in horror as hundreds of thousands of work hours were destroyed by fire.

As the SUV slowed to a stop, Catherine saw her boys gathered next to Libby and Bender. The farm's horses were galloping wildly in the pasture.

Jackson was the first to leap from the SUV before the wheels stopped. He ran for Libby and Ron.

"They are safe and unharmed," Ron said immediately. Jackson felt relief. He wrapped his arms around his boys and lifted them into the air, depositing them into the backseat of the SUV driven by Esmael.

"If anything else happens, you get them out of here, understood?" Esmael nodded.

Piper closed the door and returned to Libby and Bender. "What the hell happened?" yelled Piper over the roar of fire, engines, sirens, and sobs of the campaign staff nearby. "Is everyone accounted for? Is anyone hurt?"

"All the staff is there, by that oak tree. A few with cuts and bruises. But Jack, we can't find Hagrid," said Ron, his heart breaking.

"What? No! Is he still in the…" Piper's voice trailed off. He looked at Catherine, who was attending to the shaken staff. Some were having cuts treated by EMS. A lanky staffer from Vermont was receiving oxygen, likely for smoke inhalation.

Libby interrupted to explain briefly the events of the past half hour.

"About twenty of us were text-banking and carrying on inside when we heard these engines roaring. I looked out the window and saw seven different makes and models of pickup trucks circling the parking area in front of the barns. Blowing horns and screaming their madness."

"How many of them total? How many Warriors?" asked Piper.

Libby replied, "Maybe twenty. Two or three per pickup. They shot out the windows of the parked cars with shotguns. Hagrid started barking like crazy. I gathered the staff and had them head out the backdoor and run through the upper pasture, using the house as a screen so those fucks wouldn't know we were here. I grabbed my pistol and headed back towards the house to see if there was more to their plan. They were spray painting the cars when, the next thing I knew, the barn was on fire. I ran in the back to open all the stall doors I could. Hagrid was with me then. He was barking and forcing the horses out of the stable."

"That's when my group arrived," interrupted Bender. "We came down the driveway, and I saw those illiterate fucks setting the house on fire, and I lost it, Jack. I just lost it. I rammed one of those pickups full-force with my rental car. One of the Warriors was thrown out of the truck, but he climbed into another. Yvonne, Harper, and Quincy were with me. All got pretty banged up from the collision."

At this point, Catherine joined the conversation and, in a desperate whisper, asked, "Did everyone get out of the house?"

Jackson replied calmly, "Yes, all staff are safe, thanks to Libby. The same goes for the horses. We are still looking for Hagrid. He was not inside the house when they burned it."

"Who burned it?" Catherine asked in shock. "Don't tell me this is more terror from the Warriors?"

"It is, ma'am. I saw their flags flying off their trucks. They had Bible verses painted on the sides of their trucks," said Libby.

"Wait! Hagrid's missing?" she gasped, suddenly catching up.

"He's here. He's got to be. He likely fled into the pasture during all the commotion," Jackson replied, trying to avoid thoughts of the worst for the family's beloved companion.

Jackson turned and, for the first time, saw the message the Warriors had left in blood-red spray paint on the badly damaged cars parked by the barn. TRAITORS was sprayed in large letters on each vehicle.

"Cate and Ron, why don't the two of you go confer with the staff? Keep them calm. Ron, try to peel the highest-ranking officer away and let him know we must speak to him privately. Libby, grab four security guards. Tell them to bring their flashlights and guns. Let's fan out in this pasture and look for Hagrid or any Warriors hanging around to observe the aftermath of their mayhem. Then text all the surrogates and staff and tell them to report immediately to their hotels, lock themselves in their rooms, and await further instructions."

Around 150 yards from the farmhouse, heading south towards the small lake on the south end, Hagrid lay still in the tall, frozen grass of the pasture. As Piper ran to him, shining a flashlight on his thick brown fur, he saw the slightest wag of the dog's tail. Then Hagrid let out a whimper.

"Over here! Over here!" Piper yelled to the search party in the chaos. They assessed the dog's condition. There was some dried blood, but the wounds were superficial.

"You're going to be ok, boy. Just hang in there, ok?"

"What now, Senator?" asked Bender as the last active flames had been doused on the farmhouse. However, ghostly columns of smoke and steam still rose in the darkness, animated by gusts of cold January wind and flashing lights of fire trucks and ambulances.

"What did we lose?" asked Piper directly.

"All our printed literature," Bender began. "Our stash of backup yard signs. All the paper copies of our notes and turnout scenarios. Paper backups of about a thousand sign-up sheets. Your entire wardrobe. Catherine's entire wardrobe. My entire wardrobe…"

"Were we keeping pace on backing up all the campaign data into Ziggy's database?" asked Piper.

"We had zero backlog, boss. Once everyone makes their statement to the police and maybe has a stiff drink, we could be back up in operations in a few hours. Of course, we have nowhere to sleep, no food for the team, nowhere to shower, and no clothes to wear."

Jackson saw Libby standing alone, staring at the house. Her face was wrought with anger. He approached her slowly. "You ok, kid?"

"How could they do this? How could they be this hurtful? Ms. Piper's friends will be heartbroken when they hear about their farm."

"I would be heartbroken, too. But I would also be relieved that no one was killed or seriously injured by this attack."

Libby finally broke down in tears. Jackson put a comforting arm around her.

"This was an act of terrorism. I want you to round up the team and see how many took photos or videos of the flames. I want you to grab a phone and record me delivering a message for our channel. The world has to know what happened here."

The video message Jackson Piper recorded in the darkness in the remote rural reaches of Manchester was viewed over 100 million times. He was calm, resolute, and clear. No amount of violence or threats would deter him from his quest to retire Russell Warner from the presidency.

PART II

10

OBJECTS ARE CLOSER THAN THEY APPEAR

President Russell Warner stared at the Washington Monument as the crisp morning air transformed into an unusually warm afternoon for Washington in January. The results from New Hampshire that rolled in late Tuesday night into Wednesday morning had sent shockwaves across the country. It was now Thursday morning, and the impossible-to-imagine results had become his nightmare. His heart still raced when he thought of his disgraceful finish, almost 10,000 votes behind Jackson Piper. That egotistical has-been had no business being in the race for the White House. Warner had detested Piper in the Senate; now, he would cost Warner a second term, possibly more.

Olivia Clay and several other senior aids, their faces etched with concern, sat in tense silence on two wooden chairs near the desk in the hallowed Oval Office, waiting for the President's next move.

A screen near the President's desk streamed Olivia's former cable news feed nonstop. Although it had always been an echo chamber of the President's agenda, it was sharing news that was like a stick of dynamite in the Oval Office, threatening to explode at any moment.

The nation was in disbelief. It had assumed the race between Warner and Drummond was locked up. The screen blared out the headline: Americans Still in Shock at Piper's Double-Barreled New Hampshire Upsets. The unexpected events left the country reeling, unsure of the future.

No longer able to contain his frustration, Warner hurled an untouched cup of coffee at the screen.

Olivia felt the need to soothe Warner. She had a gift for it. "The New Hampshire primary was a humiliating defeat for Paul Drummond," she began. "Finishing ten points behind Piper, well, no one saw that coming. The polls had it completely wrong once again."

Warner shot her a sharp look, then resumed his focus on the screen.

Every talking head and website left, right, and center is openly asking whether or not Drummond should call it quits and..."

Warner resumed the icy stare; his eyes were so harsh they froze her mid-sentence.

He finally found words to express his anger through clenched teeth. "Olivia, I don't give a rat's ass what the media idiots think about what Paul Drummond should do. I would like to know how my campaign allowed a washed-up former Senator from the Other Party to get into the Old Party's race for President! And less than eighty days ago! And win both fucking primaries!"

Her magic had not worked. The fuse was lit, and a disastrous explosion could happen at any moment if she did not act quickly.

One of the other senior aides tried to intervene. "Mr. President, this is a minor setback. Members of either Party or Independents could cross over and vote in either contest in New Hampshire. It's an unrepresentative result."

The fuse burned closer to the stick. Warner ignored the rational but unhelpful analysis. His hand shook as he picked up the phone, which immediately connected to his secretary seated outside the Oval. She answered immediately.

"I need the Briefing Room up; I'm going on television with a national address in an hour," he said, his voice hoarse from the shouting half the day.

Olivia stood, her eyes aflame, "You will NOT do that, sir."

"Excuse me?" Warner seemed shocked at the interference.

Olivia Clay stood her ground. "You only stand to feel humiliated for a second time in 24 hours. Without a doubt, the loss was disappointing, Mr. President. But we need to turn the page and go on the offensive, not go live and bitch and whine about how unfair and wronged you feel."

Warner looked at the other aids, who were still seated, perhaps petrified.

Olivia pointed at the phone. "Cancel that order, Mr. President."

Warner spoke into the phone softly. "Never mind, Rhonda. I'm sorry. My mistake. Change in plans." He slowly set the phone down onto the receiver.

"Fine. Let's hear your genius idea," he said to Olivia Clay.

"Well…" she stammered, suddenly on the spot. "We could get Piper indicted. Surely there is something in his past worthy of a little FBI scrutiny?"

"That is madness. It would take the FBI six months just to present evidence to a grand jury!"

Rhonda buzzed from outside the Oval. She had an urgent call from Marco Alvarez waiting on the line. "He says it is urgent, and it cannot wait."

"Everyone out!" screamed the President.

The aides scattered like rats discovered in the pantry.

"Not you, Clay," snarled Warner. "You stay behind." Once the room had cleared, he made it clear he did not feel comfortable talking with Marco in front of less trustworthy aides, given the terms of their last conversation in California.

President Warner composed himself and then picked up the phone.

"How lucky you are to have caught me, Marco. I was about to head to a briefing on the Middle East. What can I do for you?"

Alvarez was used to dealing with uncertainty and chaos in business. He had a knack for turning dire situations in his favor.

"The results of Tuesday lead me to believe we should rethink the extent of our cooperation and reliance on Mr. Drummond," said Marco.

"I would prefer only to speak in person on such matters," replied the President.

As predicted, thought Marco.

"Fine, Mr. President. I think you will very much like to hear what I have to say. How soon can you be available?"

"I'm only free tonight, I'm afraid," said the President.

"Well, Mr. President, I am in Miami. I teed off at 7 am at Fisher Island. I suppose I can cancel tonight's dinner plans and be at the White House by 8 pm. Would that be suitable?" asked Marco.

"Yes. Fine. Please come to the White House. The ushers will see to it you are brought to the residence. Come alone. No staff. Just the two of us," said Warner.

"Oh, what about that Chief of Staff of yours? Olivia? I think she should be part of this conversation. We're going to need her help arranging a few meetings on exceptionally short notice."

Without asking her, the President assured Marco she would join them.

"See you in a few hours, Mr. President," said Marco and ended the call.

The second floor of the White House was last extensively renovated nearly 100 years ago, and it showed. Cracks in the plaster occurred weekly. Terrible drafts flowed freely throughout the mansion. Late at night, mice scrambling through the walls could be heard as if the President were asleep in a cheap motel. To make up for the desperately needed renovations that Congress had been unable to reach an agreement to fund, each First Family was provided a budget to decorate the space to make it warm and inviting. That budget proved inadequate for the lavish tastes of Russell Warner, even though he lived alone and had no children as only the second divorced President in the nation's history.

As soon as Marco Alvarez entered the private dining room of the residence, his attention was immediately drawn to the richly hued decor. Dark walnut furniture adorned the space, standing out against the deep purple walls that gave off an air of mystery and opulence. The dimly lit crystal chandelier hung elegantly over the round dining table, casting a warm glow on the crisp white linens and gold-plated utensils neatly arranged upon it. The atmosphere felt rich with elegance and drama, making it clear that this was no ordinary dinner meeting.

Alvarez was invited to sit. Gin and tonics were immediately poured into the two cocktail glasses, dressed with an artfully sliced lime. A third glass was filled with white wine. Alvarez looked around in wonder. He had enough money to construct a life-size replica of this building in any nation in the world if he so desired, but that was not enough. In fact, what he wanted most was to occupy the genuine article himself. But for reasons beyond the pampering and attending staff.

Ushers opened a nearby door, and the President entered, followed by Olivia Clay. The President wore a brilliant grey suit with a subdued pink tie. Olivia looked stunning in a simple black dinner dress. After a cordial greeting, one in which the President acknowledged that Marco's suit was, this time, the appropriate outfit for a meeting with the President, they were seated and awaiting their first course.

President Warner summoned a dining staff member to his side. "I want not a single interruption to this first course until I come for you in the kitchen, understood?" The staff member agreed stoically. He and the other staff finished setting the table with gazpacho and appropriate accoutrements.

"Where should we begin?" asked President Warner.

"You're still cashing my checks, so I take it we must still be on speaking terms after your visit to my home?"

"Oh, Marco. Don't be foolish," said Warner. "We continue to be honored by your support."

"I hope my overture was not offensive," said Marco.

"Nonsense," said Warner, lying through his teeth.

"I love it when a man knows what he wants," said Olivia, making eye contact with Marco.

"I am pleased to hear this. Then I assume you continue to want the best possible scenario for your reelection in November?" asked Marco.

"Of course I do," said Warner. "Marco. It is difficult for me to say this, but I am a man. That loss on Tuesday was a complete shock," he said, even though the words felt like acid in his mouth.

"As it was to all of us," said Marco, lying to the President. Marco and Rushy had secretly used New Hampshire as a test case to see if their models could influence voter sentiments. Juniper had been suppressing stories about Warner's agenda and blasting stories about the inspiring couple from Pennsylvania to see if Juniper and The Mark really could control the democratic process.

"It is clear that Jackson Piper is a threat to our plans," said Warner, testing the waters. "I have tried for several weeks to intimidate him. I have ginned up my supporters - they call themselves the Warriors, did you know that?"

"I did not, sir," said Marco. He was lying again.

"I thought Piper would fizzle out with his misguided message of reform and 'new freedom' as he bizarrely suggests." Warner rolled his eyes. "I thought maybe he would be a distant second to me but perhaps beat Drummond. When his fundraising picked up after he punched that poor schmuck, my team suggested a variety of measures to try to scare Piper and his wife back to Colorado. They were not as effective as we hoped."

"Was the fire your plan?" asked Marco, sipping a spoonful of the gazpacho. It was marvelous. Far more attractive than this boring lecture by the President.

"Fuck no. A group of Warriors went cuckoo and burned down the farmhouse that Piper and his band of crazies were staying in," assured Warner. That was the most truthful thing the President had shared.

"You did not order the fire?" asked Marco. "I'm surprised. I would have."

Olivia was shocked at such an admission. She choked on her soup and took a drink of water.

"That is the past now, Marco. Campaigns are about the future. What is important is that we stop Piper now before we enter too many of these regional primaries and he ends up winning the Other Party nomination, or worse. I don't want to be in a real fight for the Old Party's nomination," said Warner.

"I see, Mr. President. I suspect we are meeting in the residence tonight, so we are certain of the private nature of our conversation," Marco said.

The President nodded calmly.

"Then fucking kill the prick, sir. Order an FBI raid of his campaign. Plant a gun. Kill him, silence his wife, and be done with this."

President Warner stared at Marco Alvarez for a moment. Was he serious? Was he talking openly in the White House about issuing an order to assassinate Warner's now chief political rival for an upcoming election? Warner waited a second longer and then began a hearty laugh. Alvarez soon joined in.

Then Marco stopped laughing. "I'm not joking, Mr. President."

Olivia Clay interjected, out of fear the President might agree to something so insane at this hour of desperation. "However tempting, that is not a solution we can afford to employ. New Hampshire proved violence against the Pipers only breeds sympathy for their ideas. Remove Jackson, and Catherine would be more than capable of picking up the torch."

Warner frowned. "I would be impeached by that fat fuck Sylvester Billings in a week and removed from office by the Senate unanimously. That is if my own Cabinet did not hog-tie me and use the 25th Amendment to remove me and install Vice President Brown as Acting President."

He was referring to the 25th Amendment, which provided for the temporary removal of a President by a vote of a majority of the Cabinet and support of the Vice President.

"Well, if we cannot eliminate Piper from existence, perhaps we can use his persistence to our advantage."

President Warner smiled. "I'm intrigued. Tell me more."

"I have a concept that I believe solves this for us, but before I reveal it to you, I have conditions," Marco said.

"He has conditions," came Warner's caustic aside. "Why am I not surprised? And they are?"

"Immediate appointment as Secretary of State, for starters," Alvarez said confidently.

"You can't be serious," Warner said. "I thought you wanted to be my Vice President?"

"The price for my assistance has gone up. As has the workload. I need to be closer to the inside and closer daily with you to monitor this project, you see?" Marco said.

"And what is to become of Secretary Marsh?" Warner asked.

"I can assure her a paid seat on at least three corporate boards of her choosing."

"Is that all then?" asked the President, raising his eyebrows. That indeed seemed like a high enough price to him.

"And I want to be named as your running mate to succeed Brown on the ticket at the Convention."

The President shuddered. This felt like a good old-fashioned shakedown from his casino days. When someone is wagering from a position of weakness, you raise them to squeeze them for all they have on the table. There was nothing more Alvarez could ask for from Warner except the presidency itself.

"I will respond to your price when you share with me your concept. I may agree to those terms if I believe they are of sufficient quality. Let's hear it," Warner said, barely able to conceal the disgust in his voice.

For the next twenty minutes, Marco Alvarez detailed with precision and zeal his strategy to rob Jackson Piper of both Party nominations while ensuring he remained in the race as a surefire spoiler for Paul Drummond. He explained how they could crater Piper's support in the Other Party.

Olivia asked for a rundown of the analytics on these scenarios. Marco left out the exact numbers on the President's best chances if Piper was not in the race at all. That scenario was no longer plausible, given Piper's meteoric rise. Marco provided the best-case scenario: Piper and Drummond fighting over the same voters and Warner sailing to victory.

A smile crept slowly onto the President's face, and then it widened into a conniving grin as his eyes were ablaze with calculation and chaos.

Olivia inquired, "Are you certain you can get the key actions accomplished by the Parties in less than a month?"

Marco replied, "I can begin making phone calls tonight. Assuming I can reach the chairs this evening, I am certain each can issue an emergency meeting call for ten days from tomorrow."

"Do you agree that the meetings must be in person, given the gravity of the circumstances?" Warner asked.

"Oh, most certainly, I do," Marco said with false sincerity, then laughter. "It will make it easier to control the outcome if we can have our people twisting arms in person."

"Well, Mr. Secretary of State-designate," Warner said, indicating his acceptance of the scheme, "get this done, and we'll talk about my selection for Vice President."

Marco slid his dessert plate aside and sipped coffee before answering. "I am eager for this partnership, Mr. President," said Marco with a smile. Checkmate, he thought.

"Then we have ourselves a deal," said President Warner, sitting back in his chair, relieved to finally be in control of the events leading to his reelection once again.

~

PAUL DRUMMOND SAT ALONE in the rear of his campaign bus - The Best Deal Express - as it raced down I-81 for Charlotte, North Carolina. That was to be their first stop on a week-long swing through North Carolina, South Carolina, and Georgia: the three states of the Southern Regional Primary. The experience would be like a trip to the moon for Paul Drummond. The senior Senator from Wisconsin was not much of a world traveler nor a national traveler. He spent the better part of twenty years slingshotting between Wisconsin and Washington, and because his fear of flying was paralyzing, he drove the 20-hour trip most of the time. By his second term in the Senate, he and his wife bought a second home in Maryland to reduce the need to return to Wisconsin every weekend. Southern charm was a chilling thought to the pasty, reserved Caspar Milquetoast Paul Drummond.

As the bus galloped along the highway, the screen on the wall and the amphibious face projected therein seemed to bounce along with the rhythm of the road. Diane Fogarty croaked a mixture of consolations and praise designed to keep Paul Drummond from tears for the third time that week. It was getting old, she thought as more reassurance escaped her mouth.

"I don't get it, Diane. How did Piper leapfrog us?" whined Drummond.

"It was the sympathy vote. The voters saw the Pipers running their campaign out of a firehall wearing donated clothes. I would say it was brilliant if it wasn't so fucking tragic," croaked Diane as she puffed on her vape.

"I can't afford to lose all three states in this regional primary. If I do that, I'll never be President," whimpered Drummond.

"Oh, come on, Paul. Get your balls out of the drawer and get back in this fight. Piper isn't going to beat you down south unless you give up, understand?" she said.

"He's probably already in Atlanta waiting for Warriors to come ransack his hotel room," said Drummond. "He'll give a press conference in a hotel robe in the lobby and raise $20 million off it," he scoffed.

Diane attempted to get Drummond back on track. "The Party is behind you, Senator, and we'll be sure there are no more surprises, understand? New Hampshire was an anomaly, got me? They let independents like Piper vote in either Party's election. They even let voters cross Party lines to vote if they so choose. It's real fucked up up there," said Diane.

"I guess you're right," whined Drummond, still unconvinced but willing to keep moving forward.

"Of course I'm right. Now listen, you had better tighten up the messaging this week. Don't get outdone by Piper. We'll push another $10 million your way through the weekend. You should be able to saturate the airwaves for a week with that kind of buy," said Diane.

"Thank you. I am grateful for you," said Drummond, not doubting for a minute that her support was sincere and rooted in a belief in him.

"Don't mention it," said Fogarty, who wasn't kidding. This kind of outright coordination with a candidate not yet the Party's nominee was deeply afoul of the written rules. There was a crisis at hand that she had to address: keeping Piper from winning the Party's nomination and losing everything she had worked so hard to secure.

Suddenly, a chorus of horns honked outside the bus, and the Drummond campaign mercenaries scrambled to the left side of the bus to look out the window. A cavalcade of cars, trucks, SUVs, and moving vans whizzed past the Drummond campaign bus. Each had decorated their windows with white-lettered messages like honeymooners headed for their first weekend getaway. The caravan appeared to be twenty or thirty cars long; Drummond's staff lost count. The new American flag with its 51-star field of blue flapped proudly in the wind from a passing moving van. The windows of the passing cars had inscriptions like "Atlanta or Bust," "Fire Warner," "More Freedom, More Peace," "Marching to the Sea," and "Pipers' Army."

"What the hell is that?" croaked Diane Fogarty from the screen, trying to catch a glimpse through Drummond's camera.

He peered out the window and saw the final vehicles of the caravan - three black SUVs with dark-tinted windows - speed past his window. He replied, "That's Jackson Piper and his circus of supporters and staff. They just passed me headed for South Carolina."

11

CHANGE THE RULES, CHANGE THE GAME

The setting sun cast a honeyed glow over the sprawling Mandolin Casino, a majestic fortress of chance and intrigue just beyond the fringes of Washington, DC. The frost-coated sidewalks sparkled, reflecting the riotous neon signs that announced the emergency meeting of the Old Party. Their leaders and acolytes scurried hastily towards the urgent business that awaited them inside, the grandeur of the casino adding to the sense of anticipation.

Jackson Piper stepped from his SUV into the chilled air, his breath visible as he surveyed the imposing edifice. He could feel the buzz of anticipation emanating from the crowds of people streaming towards the entrance.

"You got this, sir," Esmael said, offering a nod of reassurance. Esmael had become a constant presence in Piper's life as the head of their growing private security detail.

"Indeed, it is. Stay close; this might not take long." Piper's reply was laced with a steely resolve as he buttoned his coat and strode purposefully toward the lobby. He asked to go in alone. He did not want the presence of a security detail to make these Party leaders feel like he was unapproachable or above them. Esmael and the others agreed to remain outside the ballroom but within earshot, on alert for any chaos.

Inside the Mandolin Casino, the clinking of glasses and the low hum of conversations enveloped him. Piper's eyes scanned the room, noting the clusters of attendees in earnest discussion, their faces etched with questions given the urgency of the call of the chair thatced ease that belied the fluttering excitement in his chest.
the Old Party convened for this meeting. Jackson moved with a practiced ease that belied the fluttering excitement in his chest.

"Senator Piper!" A voice boomed across the crowded space, breaking through the din. It was Sterling Powers, his tall frame and dignified appearance impossible to miss among the crowd of men and women dressed in all manners of red, white, and blue.

"Senator Powers, always a pleasure," Piper greeted, his handshake firm. "I appreciate your willingness to extend an invitation to me as your guest. Otherwise, I could not witness my execution in person."

"Careful now. Nothing is a foregone conclusion yet, Jackson. Still, move carefully; there are sharks in these waters," Powers replied, his gaze sweeping the room with a practiced wariness.

"Sharks I can handle," Piper quipped as his mind churned with strategies. "Have you decided yet if you'll speak publicly on my behalf?"

Powers could be a convincing voice of reason in this room. It carried weight. If rumors were true, Powers would soon be in command of the Senate as Majority Leader.

"I will speak out in your defense if the moment presents itself. Remember that everyone's looking for an angle here. A loophole to cast you aside," Powers cautioned before being pulled away by another committee member vying for his attention. "Excuse me, Mr. Piper." The old roommates and Senate colleagues shared an authentic hug before separating.

Piper continued navigating the sea of political operatives and Old Party loyalists. His mind raced with scenarios, each handshake and smile part of an intricate dance. *They're wary of change but desperate for victory*, he thought. *My campaign could offer them both if only they'd see it.*

"Senator Piper, how confident are you about your ability to remain in this race?" a young man with a camera pointed at his face asked, likely streaming live.

"I'm the dark horse candidate in every room I enter," smiled Jackson. "But don't count me out just yet."

The ballroom doors loomed ahead, like the doors to an execution chamber. Piper's heart quickened as he approached the gathering leaders of the Old Party inside.

This is it. Showtime, Piper thought.

As he crossed the threshold, the clamor rose to greet him. Row after row of Old Party members seated attentively waiting for the special meeting called by the Chair to gavel to order. It was as if all was normal in the world, that a power-hungry President wasn't consolidating power or that his Party was about to slam shut the gate of opposing ideas. A dark-haired, well-tanned man with a chiseled jaw and striking green eyes was seated on the dais. He was wearing an expensive suit, staring coldly out over the audience. It was Marco Alvarez.

Alvarez's presence was magnetic, his stature commanding. The President had designated him to address the emergency meeting of a Party that had come to forge its identity in the shifting sands of Presidential prerogatives. The committee men and women buzzed like a hive of bees—drones and workers awaiting their orders.

The meeting gaveled to order, and silence overtook the room in a matter of seconds.

"Friends," Alvarez began, his voice echoing robustly through the room, "we stand united behind a President who has dared to imagine a future secured by our plentiful national energy resources." A chorus of cheers rose from the crowd.

"Under President Warner's decisive leadership," Alvarez continued, pausing for emphasis, "we've taken bold steps to unleash the ever-advancing tide of artificial and simulated intelligence without regulation. Our borders, north and south, have become impenetrable fortresses, defending the very essence of our nationhood with orders for our troops to shoot to kill in order to defend our national treasurers from terrorists, criminals, and beggars."

Piper observed from the back, a silent witness to the zealous fervor that rippled through the assembly. They're not just partisan loyalists; they're cultists, he thought. The violence he had witnessed in New Hampshire had become indicative of a larger blindly devoted following in this Party.

Suddenly, the atmosphere shifted as a Party official whispered urgently into Alvarez's ear. With a subtle nod, Marco leaned into the microphone, his voice assuming a grave timbre.

"Esteemed colleagues," he announced, "it has come to my attention that a man who would capitalize on our disunity for personal gain is in the room." Murmurs swirled around the room, a storm brewing beneath the surface. Piper felt a chill run over him. Alvarez suddenly spotted Piper in the back of the ballroom.

Alvarez focused like a viper spotting his cornered prey. He sneered and pointed. "Senator Piper! You refused to join this Party yet you show your face in its proceedings?"

The ballroom erupted in a roar. The men standing around him started to heckle Piper aggressively.

"What are you doing here, pussy?"

"Coward!"

"Traitor!"

"Get out of here before I fuck you up..."

If Piper was not a tall, muscular man, he was certain several of these antagonizers would have gotten physical.

After a tense minute of boos and hisses and insults, Alvarez intervened. "Now, now, friends," said Alvarez. "Let him witness the end of his campaign. It's better that way. I now yield to the chairman."

The Old Party chairman gaveled the room to order and presented the reason for the urgent gathering.

"Given the extraordinary events of the past two weeks, we find it prudent to clarify this Party's nomination procedure." The chairman's declaration hung heavily in the air. The room grew silent. "The standing committees on Rules and Party Convention have, at my request, endorsed a resolution that I am asking for your affirmative vote on here today. It states, 'Candidates seeking the nomination of the Party for President must have demonstrated unequivocal loyalty to our Party by having held no affiliations or memberships with other political entities for the past five years and maintained membership in this Party on the date of the first Primary of the presidential election cycle.'"

Whispers grew to a roar. "So moved!" yelled a committeeman from the front row.

"Second!" shouted a committeewoman from the back.

"All those in favor?"

"AYE!"

"Opposed?" asked the chairman. The room was silent.

"The resolution is hereby adopted!" Bang! went the gavel on the dais.

The sound struck Piper like a hammer to the chest. Piper mistakenly believed his presence might dissuade rash action. Oh, how wrong he had been. He hoped they might offer the winner of the New Hampshire Primary a chance to address the gathering.

While Piper never expected to win the nomination, he planned to deliver a few more costly losses to Warner to wound him with his own Party. Piper's hopeless optimism and rose-colored reading of the rules once again left him feeling empty when faced with the cruel reality of political gamesmanship.

This resolution was aimed at him, and there was not even a second of debate. Piper was a member of the Other Party four years ago, and he was not registered in the Old Party when he won the New Hampshire primary. These were the two disqualifying characteristics he could not change. He had not foreseen such an obvious dagger to his candidacy. After all, history was littered with presidential aspirants who refused to bend to Party will and were left with their dreams shattered on the side of the road. Piper had trusted that the Old Party would not, however, change the rules in the middle of the contest.

The room erupted into applause, a collective exhale of relief from those who feared Piper's sudden ascent. They clapped not for the rule but for its intent—to barricade the door against change, against him.

"Damn," Piper muttered under his breath, his fists clenching at his sides. "Checkmate in one move."

Powers' eyes met his across the crowd, a look of regret fleeting across the Senator's face as he approached Piper, who had headed for the doors. "Jack, I'm sorry. The Party must protect its interests. You understand that."

"Protect or suffocate?" Piper shot back, though his voice was lost in the din of victory. Piper was no longer sure Powers' ambitions were not ahead of saving the nation.

"Rules are rules," another party elder chimed in as Piper passed, his smug smile adding humiliation to defeat.

"Even when they're forged in fear?" Piper retorted, though his challenge was rhetorical. He already knew the answer. Theirs was a game of power played as a blood sport by those who feared losing their grip on it.

He turned to look at the scene one last time before exiting the ballroom. Alvarez was seated on the dais and locked eyes with Piper. Piper's jaw clenched. Alvarez winked, smug and satisfied by the kill. Piper's campaign for the Old Party's nomination, just two weeks before a beacon of hope, flickered and dimmed before his eyes, snuffed out by words on a page.

Collateral damage, Piper realized with a bitter edge to his thoughts. That's all I am to them. An obstacle removed on their path to preserving control and total annihilation of anything that challenges them.

With every effusive clap, every affirming nod, the Old Party fortified the walls around itself, blissfully ignorant—or perhaps willfully so—of the world beyond their self-erected ramparts. Once poised to lead them, Jackson Piper was now standing alone outside those walls in the shadow of their fortress.

"Mr. Piper," a voice buzzed from his coat pocket, pulling him away from the frigid corridors of his thoughts. He fished out his cell phone, answering without breaking stride. "Yes?"

It was Piper's new simulated intelligence assistant, Franklin. "Jackson, it's urgent. You need to go to the Mermaid Casino and Resort—now. The Other Party's meeting is devolving into chaos."

～

As Piper's SUV cut through swathes of dormant, empty trees, the Potomac unfurled alongside them, indifferent to the political theatre that consumed its banks. He watched the river flow, a silent companion carrying secrets and stories just as murky as those he'd left behind in the city four years ago.

He tried calling Bender and Browning several times, but neither answered.

Upon arriving at the Mermaid Casino and Resort, Piper was immediately struck by the change in atmosphere. Where the Old Party had exuded suffocating control, here was a tempest of discord and dissent. The grand hall buzzed with a cacophony of shouting voices, each pitching higher than the last in a desperate bid to be heard.

"Order! Order!" Diane Fogarty's voice thundered above the fray, her gavel striking the podium with a force proportional to her globular frame. But her authority seemed but a candle against the storm raging before her as delegates jostled and argued with flailing arms and inflamed passions.

"Is this how we represent the people?" she demanded, the raw edge of frustration evident amidst the bedlam. Her question hung unanswered, swallowed by the clamor.

Piper moved through the crowd in the Atlantian-themed casino, his eyes narrowing as he took in the turmoil. It starkly contrasted with the controlled, business-like meeting he had just left. This was a raging tempest, where words were thrashing upon the resolve of his small cohort of allies.

This is democracy in action, he mused bitterly, *and yet, it's just another flavor of madness.*

"Jackson!" Browning spotted him, his gaze cutting through the mayhem. "Thank God you're here. We need some semblance of—"

"Sanity?" Piper finished for him, the corner of his mouth tilting upward in a humorless smile. "I'm afraid I'm fresh out."

"Then lend your voice, at least," he said, determination hardening in his eyes. "Help them see what they are doing is madness, only to the benefit of reelecting Warner."

"What's going on?" asked Piper.

Bender joined them in time to answer, "Jack, they are attempting to change the rules for Other Party nominees for President of the United States."

Jackson replied, "Let me guess, a ban on nominees who have been independents or not members of this Party for five consecutive years?"

"Thirty-six months, actually. And no financial contributions to any Party besides this one during the same time frame. And you must have been a member of this Party no later than the first day in which the first Primary of the presidential primary cycle begins," he shouted over the clamor. "How did you know?"

"Because the Old Party meeting at the Mandolin just made the same move," said Piper. "I'm shut out of pursuing delegates in their Primaries going forward because I cannot be nominated at their convention."

"How bad do you think this is?" asked Bender. "Do we try to get a motion to adjourn before they can vote on this insanity?"

The Mermaid Casino's grand ballroom, a cavernous space of crystal chandeliers, gilded trim, and oceanic carvings, had devolved into a hurricane. The air hummed with tension, the scent of sweat and expensive perfume intermingling in an uneasy alliance against the backdrop of chaos. Supporters of Paul Drummond, staunch members of the Other Party, rallied their support for the motion as a do-or-die cause to defend their candidate.

An oafish man with a long, silver mustache stood at a microphone at the center of the room. "Outrageous! An interloper seeks to steal our standard!" the man bellowed, his face flushed as red as the stripes on the bunting on the hastily decorated stage. "Drummond has bled for us, fought for us! This... outsider...this intruder must not prevail!"

"Jackson Piper is no true member!" a woman screeched, her words piercing the tumult like a siren's call. "I heard he was never a member, not even when he was in the Senate! He is a Fascist!"

Piper's gaze swept over the throng, his jaw set, his eyes steely. He could feel his pulse beating, a drumbeat urging him to fight for himself and the principles at stake. His allies, a steadfast phalanx amidst the tempest, rose from their seats, their voices booming in defiant response.

But one ally was not expected. Seated among the crowd was a striking woman, not yet 40. She had golden blonde hair and a fierce look in her eyes. She wore a fringed white top and white jeans, looking like she was heading to a heavenly rodeo after the meeting. She wore brown leather boots and a thick brown belt with a gold belt buckle in the shape of the Lone Star State.

It was Valerie Lawrence of Texas. She stood and walked to an empty microphone. She said in a loud but soothing southern drawl, "Are we this afraid of change? Are we the Party of exclusion? Hell no, we are not! Jackson Piper represents the American spirit and is qualified to be President. He is ready to lead!"

The crowd surprisingly booed their own Party's governor, who had fought hard to flip the governor's mansion.

She did not relent. "Standards are meant to be raised, not lowered behind closed doors! To deny a willing, capable candidate is to deny the potential of this great nation!"

Some were clapping in the room, but this was a meeting of the Party faithful. They were loyal to their Party and to remaining in Diane Fogarty's good graces, who was giving Lawrence a heinous scowl.

"Jackson Piper has proven his dedication to public service!" Governor Lawrence declared, her words ringing with authority. "It is un-American to shut out such commitment!"

Piper mouthed "thank you" to the governor, who gave a nod with her plum-colored Stetson.

Piper would not let his former Party off the hook so easily. He stormed forward to a microphone. "I say let the people decide who should be our nominee!" Piper shouted, his voice hoarse but unwavering. "If we stand for democracy, let us practice what we preach!"

"Democracy!" echoed a chorus of supporters, the word rippling across the room, a rallying cry that seemed to vibrate in the bones of all who heard it.

The gavel pounded again, and Diane Fogarty's attempt to reclaim order was nearly lost in the fervor. Piper caught her eye and, in it, sensed her disgust and guilt.

The Mermaid Casino and Resort, usually resonant with the clangs and jingles of slot machines, was now saturated with the heavy groans of anticipation. Jackson Piper stood amid the sea of delegates, his eyes fixed on the stage where the party leaders convened, their whispers weaving a disquieting prelude to the impending verdict.

"Order!" Diane Fogarty's voice croaked through the tumult, her gavel striking with finality. "The motion before us: to amend the eligibility requirements for presidential nomination."

A hush fell, the stillness so profound it felt as if the room was holding its breath. Piper's jaw tensed, his gaze never wavering from the stage.

"Those in favor?" Fogarty called out.

A smattering of hands rose, tentative at first, then with growing clarification, more joined. Piper could see the lines drawn, the allegiances manifesting in the stark divide of uplifted arms.

"And those opposed?" Her eyes swept the room, seeking the measure of dissent.

Piper's allies, a fierce minority, raised their hands high, their faces etched with determination. Governor Lawrence raised her hand with her hat held proudly, waving it from side to side. The air thrummed with silent pleas; each hand held aloft a testament to the belief in what Jackson Piper represented—a future unbound by the strictures of past dogmas.

"By a wide margin," Fogarty announced, her face betraying nothing, "the motion passes."

Shock rippled through the room like a wave crashing against the shore. Whispers erupted into clamors of disbelief, the fabric of unity unraveling before Piper's eyes. The decision bore a sting of betrayal, not unlike that which he felt four years ago after the filibuster fight that cost him his seat in the Senate.

Jackson's mind raced, incredulous that three years of absence could erase a lifetime of service to his former Party and the nation.

"Unbelievable," he murmured, his voice barely above a whisper but loud enough for those nearby to hear the edge of outrage sharpening his words.

"Jackson, this isn't the end," Valerie Lawrence assured him, placing a steadying hand on his shoulder.

"They are pretty sure it is," smiled Piper. "I guess you know we have a few more tricks up our sleeve?"

She gave him a wink before she was overtaken by Piper allies, who wanted a photo and an autograph from the maverick Texan.

"Mr. Piper," a voice rang out, cutting through the din. Another streamer was reporting live. "Will you respect the outcome?"

He paused, composing himself before facing the camera. "Respect?" Piper echoed, his voice rising above the clamor. "I respect the democratic process, but this..." He gestured towards the triumphant leaders on stage, "This is political cowardice."

There were nods among the crowd, pockets of agreement amidst the chaos. Piper knew his words resonated with many who felt disenfranchised by the Party's sudden shift to disqualify the recent New Hampshire Primary winner and the expected South Carolina and Georgia winner in a matter of days.

"Where do we go from here?" someone shouted, a question that hung heavy in the air, pregnant with uncertainty.

"Forward," Piper replied, though his tone lacked its usual conviction. "Always forward."

12

THE SECRET SOUTHERN SUMMIT

A curious coalition of leaders was set to gather in a private home nestled cozily between the Ashley River Road and the serenely snaking blackwater tidal of the same name among the ancient oaks of Charleston, South Carolina. Had it been May, the scent of honeysuckle and jasmine would have wafted through open windows, mingling with the salty sea air. But it was February, and the Southern Primary in just a matter of days. Voters in South Carolina, North Carolina, and Georgia would go to the polls to express their preference for their Party nominees for a variety of offices, including the President of the United States. Each Party would select delegates for their respective conventions under rules of their own making and vote to choose a nominee.

Because of the events a week prior at the two DC casinos, Piper was widely assumed to be barred from receiving those nominations from either Party, yet he was free to remain on the ballot. What good was that if he ultimately faced a fight to seat his delegates at the conventions? Despite the roadblocks by the Parties, Piper was increasingly a favorite in the hearts of a growing tide of citizens.

The air outside the house was cool and sterile as the aromatic plants of America's south lay dormant for a few more weeks before spring would awaken them. Inside, the home was cozy and tastefully decorated with exquisite linens, expensive furniture, and original works of art.

The house belonged to a vocal opponent of Russell Warner, who agreed to allow Piper to use his place for a secret gathering as long as he swore to unleash the garden hose at the first sight of any ruffians with torches. Piper agreed and assured him there would be no evidence of their summit. He had yet to indicate who was coming. The guest list was a highly guarded secret, and Piper also thought the odds were at least fifty-fifty that no one would show.

The sun rose on that Sunday morning just before 7:00 a.m. The sky was a brilliant rose and mandarin bed of clouds.

"Red sky in morning, sailor, take warning," said Bender as he placed the last agendas on the large dining room table and drew the shades.

"Ron, there is not going to be press camped outside the house," said Piper, objecting to the theatrics of pulling blinds closed on such a gorgeous sunrise.

"You don't know that, Jack. And besides, we need to create an air of secrecy among our guests. That starts by keeping prying eyes out of this room."

Ron went over the confirmations one more time. It was remarkable that they could get these many influential leaders into a room in South Carolina on such short notice.

"There is a late addition," said Ron cautiously. He was unsure how Jackson would react to expanding the circle of trust.

"Anyone I know?" asked Jackson.

"Governor Valerie Lawrence," said Ron, smiling proudly.

"She spoke up so forcefully at the meeting. But my calls have gone unreturned for a week," said Jackson.

"She called me yesterday and insisted she be part of this," said Bender. "She is more than trustworthy."

"Should I be worried that the word is out already about this secret summit? Before it even convenes?"

"Governor Lawrence and I go way back. I knew her when her

father was a Senator," said Bender. "I consulted a little on her reelection campaign last cycle, and when she witnessed that sham resolution at the Other Party meeting, she called me with fifty ideas on how to counterpunch. She's a good egg, Jack. We should trust her."

"I'll be curious if anyone trusts me after I reveal my master plan to this kitchen cabinet today," said Piper, pouring another cup of coffee.

"Go easy on that; we don't even have guests here yet," said Catherine, joining them. Jackson left to change his shirt for a third time, still feeling uncomfortable or nervous.

Ron and Catherine were alone for the first time since New Hampshire. "How are you holding up, Catherine?" asked Bender, genuinely concerned.

"I believe in him, Ron," she started, "you know that better than anyone. But I am worried this plan of his will evaporate whatever goodwill he has left in either Party."

"Isn't that the point?" posed Ron. "Perhaps he's had enough of both of them. He's betting on the country being as fed up as we are."

"He's all in, though, Ron," said Catherine. "There's nothing else to bet with if he's wrong."

"Then we have to do everything legal and within our power to ensure this is the right call," said Ron, smiling.

She stirred her coffee, seeming unconvinced. After ninety days of turning lives upside down to seek the presidency, anyone could understand Catherine's worry and fear about making a wrong choice. Ron and Diesel had miscalculated the unexpected physical threats to their lives. They were still playing catch up to ensure the Piper's safety.

"You speak to the boys this morning?" asked Ron, changing the subject.

"Yes, they're at my mom's until tomorrow night," she said. "I'll fly up and get them and then meet up with the campaign in Charlotte for the Southern Regional finish line."

"Do you think they are doing ok after the Faber fire?" asked Ron.

"Oh, they are tough. If they were phased by it, they aren't showing it. They are back to their old selves, fighting like tigers and bribing my mother into feeding them endless amounts of sugar."

There was another uncomfortable silence.

"Are we sure anyone is coming?" she asked. Just then, the doorbell rang.

"Guess that answers that," she said, approaching the door to welcome the first guest. It was Senator Eileen Frazier of Missouri.

Senator Eileen Frazier was once the star of her docu-reality television show about her mission in Featherbed, Missouri, a small town of less than 2,500 residents. Her show centered around her work to secure the repentance and conversion of every town resident to become true believers and members of her Pentecostal church – God's Glory Palace. She was in her late sixties, widowed, and in the middle of her second term in the U.S. Senate. She was a member of the Old Party but a reformer and had forged a special bond with Piper while serving together.

"Senator Frazier, it is such a pleasure to see you again," said Catherine, extending her hand.

"Oh, come now, sweetheart," said Eileen Frazier, smiling. "Your husband and I are friendly enough for us to greet with a hug." There was a warm embrace, and then Eileen walked to the dining room to join Ron Bender.

Before Catherine could close the door, Diesel Browning was bounding up the porch carrying a pink box of cupcakes to share with the assembled.

"Good morning, Cate," he said, kissing her on the cheek. "You look rested."

"I am, finally, thanks to this stunning home and a pause in the campaign to sort out this nomination mess," she replied.

Senator Art Huerta of New Mexico arrived next. He was a vocal and easy yes to join this cabal, as he was a longtime fan of Jackson Piper and distrustful of Paul Drummond. He was under 5'5" but a firecracker of a speaker. His bronze skin contrasted with his thick mustache, giving him a retro look reminiscent of the 1980s. His emphatic hand gestures and oratory stacked with building crescendos made him a force to be reckoned with whenever he took to a microphone. He often ran his fingers across his grey mustache when he was deep in thought. As a seasoned veteran of the Senate, he was not afraid of brutal fights; his opponents had yet to beat him after three attempts.

As Huerta and Frazier got over their surprise at seeing one another, the doorbell buzzed. Ziggy announced from a nearby screen that Representative Ginger Thompson of California was at the door. She was a former actress once nominated for an Academy Award. She seemed to come from another world entirely. A world of red carpets, incomprehensible wealth, and self-obsession. When she discovered that she was more satisfied with advocating for the resurrection of the Equal Rights Amendment, she left Hollywood for a chance to serve in Congress. Piper had cosponsored several bills with Thompson in the House, including the revised Equal Rights Amendment. Thompson admired Piper's tenacity. She was here with open ears and an open mind, but her mind was not necessarily made up that Piper was capable of beating Warner. She also saw today's gathering as the earliest Vice President audition, which was the main reason she made the trip from California a day early before turning to DC.

Jackson kissed Ginny on each cheek and complimented her on her dazzling shoes and matching purse, which announced she was a woman with an insatiable hunger for the newest and hottest style. He expressed his gratitude for her coming all this way a day early.

A black convertible coupe with a gasoline engine roared into the driveway. The car parked, and after a moment, a beautiful woman with shimmering blonde hair stepped from the vehicle onto the paved loop driveway. She had an athletic build, far more refined than was common for a man or a woman in her role. She had long, golden hair that framed her face as she removed her stylish sunglasses. Her well-defined jaw and graceful neck gave Valerie Lawrence a statuesque confidence in her face. She could easily be the star of an action movie if she weren't the governor of the second most populous state in the union. Governor Lawrence wore stylish clothes, cowgirl boots, and the same plum Stetson Piper saw her wear at the Party meeting.

Valerie Lawrence was also famous for wearing a custom silver pistol in an ornate leather holster on her right hip while conducting her formal duties as governor. Piper was relieved to see her unarmed as she approached the porch.

"Howdy, Senator Piper. Valerie Lawrence," she said as she approached the porch, extending her hand. "Sorry that we didn't get to speak longer at that public hangin' in Washington."

Jackson extended his hand and smiled warmly. "It is an absolute pleasure to meet you, Governor."

"Nonsense, the pleasure is all mine, Senator," she said cheerily.

"Please, call me Jackson. Did you drive from Austin, governor?" Jackson asked, pointing at the sports car.

"Oh, hell no. I thought since this was on my own dime today, I'd treat myself to a little fun. She's gorgeous, ain't she?"

"I don't recall the last time I drove a gas-engine car," said Piper.

"She's got 650 horsepower. You can feel her just dying to be opened up when you're on the road. Eleven miles to the gallon, can you believe that? My popularity would go up five points in Texas if they see me drivin' a gas guzzler like that. I'd post a photo if this meeting weren't so hush-hush."

Jackson stared at the shining black sports car in the wooded driveway.

"Be nice, and I'll let you take her for a spin later," she said, laughing and slapping Piper on the back.

"Texas might have a cool governor, but Ohio State is still the number one football team in America. Don't forget that, governor," said Diesel, who had overheard most of the conversation from the porch.

"Governor, allow me to introduce you to Senator Diesel Browning of Ohio," said Piper, extending an arm toward his long-time friend.

"Former U.S. Army Captain and decorated hero. Shot down four North Korean missiles over Seoul," she said.

"Shit," said Diesel. "You might be better at research than Ziggy. Come on in."

Valerie entered the cozy home and introduced herself to Eileen, Art, Ginny, and Catherine. She then hugged Ron.

"Nice to see you again, Governor Lawrence," said Ziggy from the screen in the dining room.

"I like what you're doing with your hair these days, Zig," said the governor, familiar with Bender's exceptional assistant. The image appeared to blush.

"Gee, thanks for noticing, Valerie!" said Ziggy.

The junto was called to order among the Spanish moss and songs of sparrows seeking refuge there for the winter.

Just as Jackson stood at the head of the table to call the meeting to order, there was a loud knock at the rear screen door off the kitchen. Jackson looked at Catherine, who looked at Diesel, who looked at Ron. There was a shared trauma among them after the events of New Hampshire. They had waived all security inside the house for the gathering to maintain absolute secrecy. What were they to do if there were unexpected guests? Suddenly, a voice rang out from the kitchen. They had let themselves in via the unlocked rear door.

"Well, what in the hell does a person have to do to get a welcome in this treasonous cabal cabin?"

Jackson recognized the voice immediately. He smiled and rose to greet Sylvester Billings, Representative of the 6th Congressional District of Louisiana and Speaker of the House. He was the former Mayor of Baton Rouge, and some whispered half-jokingly that the Kingfish himself had been reincarnated.

The hum of the dining room ground to silence as the rotund Sylvester, dressed in a seersucker suit and bowler, made his way via his infamous cane to the doorway to the dining room.

Sylvester gave a boisterous laugh and smiled as he surveyed the room of shocked eyes above gaping mouths. "Don't look so shocked, now. Y'all know I simply detest that scoundrel Russell Warner with a fire to rival the heat of hell itself."

The room remained still in shocked silence, then Valerie burst into a roaring laugh.

"Then come sit near me, Mr. Speaker!" she said. Sylvester made his way towards Valerie's end of the table, choosing a seat at the head opposite Jackson that afforded him more room to sit at the table.

"Mr. Speaker," said Representative Thompson. "Does your Party know you are here?"

"No, they sure as hell do not, Ms. Thompson, and if they did, why, I am quite certain Warner would talk them into deposing me by Ash Wednesday. Will you keep my secret if I promise not to tell the Minority Leader of your treacherous attendance here, Ms. Thompson?" She acquiesced.

"That reminds me," said Bender, getting the day's business underway. "I am passing out nondisclosure agreements you are all expected to sign. It says this meeting, its list of attendees, and all matters discussed here pose the threat of material damage and possible bodily harm to the Pipers if any of you get a case of the talkies." He passed out the papers. Eyebrows were raised on every face.

Ron continued. "Meaning that what is said in this house for the next twelve hours will stay in this house. Your participation in this meeting will be denied if you so choose, and you are each free to leave at any time. If you will sign them and return them to me, we can get started with the meeting."

The nine secret participants read them in silence. Valerie Lawrence signed hers and was the first to pass it back to Ron. Ginny joked about asking if she could text it to her lawyer. Ron was not amused. Eventually, all signed without objection and waited for someone to explain why they had been invited to such a remote place on a Saturday in February, just hours before the Southern Regional Primary.

Piper chose to set the stage. "This is not just any meeting – it's a gathering of the most innovative minds and politically astute individuals from across the political spectrum in the country. I have invited you here to learn precisely why I chose to run and why your help could save democracy itself from a perilous future."

"Well, suck me sideways," said Billings. "Here, I thought we was just picking a new campaign slogan for you? Is someone gonna get me a coffee, or is my large ass gonna have to waddle back through that tiny kitchen to fix it for myself?"

"I have you covered, Mr. Speaker," said Eileen, happy to allow Jackson to continue uninterrupted.

"Please, my dear, all of you, please. Today, I am simply Sylvester. I think we would all do ourselves a favor and set the titles aside for a spell whilst we sort out this predicament set in motion by our Parties."

They all agreed.

Jackson framed the deeper issue. "We invited you all here to make a decision that could alter the trajectory of our nation. President Russell Warner's tenure has been nothing short of calamitous for America's reputation, her decency, and the prosperity of her people. We must act now if we want to save what's left of our republic."

"I'm sorry, Jackson, if I may interrupt, but why do you think this situation is all so dire?" asked Eileen. "Couldn't Warner just be impeached? Or lose in the fall? Or lose four years from now? This nation has survived many crooks and clowns in the White House."

"I am afraid, Eileen, this situation is unlike any before."

For the next hour, Bender and Browning, with the assistance of Ziggy, detailed what they could prove of the conspiracy to rig the presidential election by buying out the Other Party and running a patsy who would purr at the attention, not question it. They then tied those actions directly to the apparent coordination days ago to disqualify Piper from becoming the nominee of either major Party.

Art Huerta provided some essential context. "Let's just say, for the sake of argument, that the House of Representatives was to impanel an investigatory committee this month. They might be able to vote on Articles of Impeachment by May. That is still enough time for the Parties to pick new nominees at the conventions in July?"

"No offense, Art, but have you met our colleagues in the House?" Ginny said, raising her eyebrows as she tossed a look at Sylvester. "There are not 15 votes in the Judiciary Committee to impeach

Warner if he ordered a drone strike on the Capitol. Your Party is equally loyal and terrified of Warner."

Browning interjected. "None of that matters anyway because there are not 68 votes to convict and remove in the Senate."

Huerta said, "Warner signed Puerto Rico statehood into law. He's somehow managed to lock up the support of a large segment of Latinos and angry male votes. I'm one of the rare exceptions that see him for the *el cabrón* he is. No, he will not be removed."

"What about the 25th Amendment?" asked Governor Lawrence.

Sylvester Billings spoke up in response to that question. "President Warner has ensured enough diamond-encrusted carrots are dangling above the Cabinet table to avoid such an inglorious ending to his term. The National Energy Corporation he plans to create will have paid board seats with stock options. He has promised a seat on that board to three-quarters of them. No, cast out the notion from your minds that Russell Warner would be the target of a mutiny. We shouldn't be so lucky!"

Valerie Lawrence focused on Billings as he spoke, then appealed to the room. "If he cannot be impeached or temporarily removed, can he be prosecuted?"

Billings again explained the predicament. "Warner has made moves to strip Congress of authority, ignored laws as well as the Constitution, and consolidated power. The Justice Department and FBI have been gutted. It's looking like the Tammany Hall days over there. What's left are partisan loyalists and shitty careerists eager to toss aside the rule of law for something that looks more akin to the Politburo."

"The what?" asked Ginny.

"Some of you youngsters don't look old enough to remember 9/11," said Sylvester, eyeing Valerie, Ginny, Diesel, and the Pipers. "During the Cold War - the 1950s until the 1990s, the Politburo was the Soviet Union's central policy-making and enforcement mechanism. Imagine if Parties had armies and the authority to enforce their mandates."

"So, no impeachment, no removal, no prosecution," Valerie said. "We're back to trying to fight fire with fire."

"Except he has $1 billion to throw at us, and as of today, we're sitting on $40 million cash on hand," Browning said. "That's 250 to 1."

"That billion did not help him much in New Hampshire," Catherine said, finally speaking up. "I was there campaigning alongside Jackson every single day of that campaign. The money didn't matter much when what Warner pitched did not connect with the realities people live."

"But be warned, he will clean your clocks on Tuesday. The Carolinas are not New Hampshire. Nor Georgia. His voters will come home," Billings said.

"I'm not so certain more Americans don't see Russell Warner as a smug, out-of-touch, spoiled son of a bitch," said Catherine losing her cool as she thought of the ways Warner had actively fanned the flames of violence against them weeks before.

"Ya'll know, I hate Russ Warner with a fire to rival the heat of hell itself," Sylvester said. "I would do anything to rid the country of the likes of that foul-mouthed imposter. Might even convert to Catholicism if St. Patrick himself pledged to drive that serpent from America's shores."

There was laughter around the table, breaking up the tension that had settled over the house.

"So it's hopeless?" asked Diesel to the room.

Piper cleared his throat and leaned forward again. "What we need is a plan," he says slowly. He took a deep breath before continuing, "A plan to defeat President Warner and this...scheme...before he normalizes such madness."

They all looked at Piper, waiting for him to spell it out.

"You're the one who invited us here," Art said. "Knowing you as I do, I assume you already have a presentation ready. Let's go, cowboy. Show us what you have in mind."

Piper stood, moving around the table to point at the screen. On it was a map of the United States. Soon, the states were divided by lines and filled in by colors.

"This is the map of Warner's election four years ago. He won 308 to 230 in the electoral college and beat Morris by five million votes. Reapportionment and the addition of Puerto Rico make Warner's starting map more like this."

The screen morphed to show 318 electoral votes for Warner to 228 for Drummond.

"Christ almighty, does he even need to rig this election then?" Sylvester asked.

"He ran on a unity ticket last time, recruiting Jessica Brown to join him despite being from the Other Party. He has burned all of that goodwill and done very little to solve the problems he was selected to fix."

"He's always running scared," Ron said. "In his mind, nothing is a sure thing, and he hates loose ends. He wants to leave nothing to chance."

"Polling is as unreliable as ever," Ron said. "New Hampshire proved that to us. People are reasonably afraid to tell strangers what they think in phone and web surveys, but our best modeling paints the solid Warner states totaling 85 electoral votes. A candidate needs 273 to win out of 544 total electoral votes."

"So his support has significantly eroded," Catherine said. "That's good to hear."

"Exactly, Cate," said Jackson. "He's not the same candidate as he was in 2040."

Catherine continued her thought. "People had four years to get to know Warner and are interested in an alternative."

Diesel jumped in. "But as we show you all earlier, every viable candidate besides Drummond took a pass on 2044, and not a soul in the Old Party dared take on their sitting President with $1 billion to attack them with."

"Option 1 is to push our support towards a candidate that can add 45 more electoral votes to the Morris map," said Jackson.

"We have been down this road, Jack," said Diesel. "No offense, but it's why Bender and I came to see you in Denver. Everyone who should be hungry to be President is sitting it out."

"Or took a buyout," said Ron.

"Or a took a fucking buyout," repeated Diesel.

"Could we change any minds?" asked Ginny. "What about Senator Powers or Representative Blackstone or Governor Fox? Could we convince one of them to reconsider? All of them fit both Parties' new loyalty clauses."

"Not likely," said Ron. "And what prevents the Parties from changing them again? Wasn't the point of those changes that only Drummond and Warner are welcome to run in this race?"

"What about Governor Lawrence?" Ginny suggested, smiling at the polarizing governor. "You gained national attention for taking a pistol to meetings with a hostile Assembly that was threatening to strip you of all power. Not that I agree with that, but you won them over."

"Your no-bullshit approach to getting things done in Texas has resonance," said Art. "Clearly, you are someone who represents strength and hope with a feminine sensibility."

"Do you have an African American or Latino ancestors?" asked Ginny. "Or do you perhaps question your sexual identity?"

"I'm happily married to Parker," said Valerie, clearly getting offended. "Besides, we have our candidate right fucking there" She pointed to the head of the table where Jackson stood.

Billings choked on his coffee. "If you day lilies want to turn this into a box-checking exercise, go back to DC and wait for the water level to rise over your heads. The two Parties are great at drawing thick black boxes around things, saying what ought to be in or out - passing judgments, and so forth. They solve no problems, but they sure as hell love labeling shit. Do not do a disservice to Governor Lawrence by turning her into your next 'be everything to everyone' Frankenstein!"

Ginny retreated. There was a murmur of agreement throughout the group. Piper nodded thoughtfully.

Piper hesitated before speaking, taking a deep breath. "We need to counterpunch," he says finally. "I am not willing to surrender. Not yet. There has to be a way to translate my growing success into a sustainable path forward. They have banned me from receiving the nomination in either Party but not from continuing to run."

Sylvester interrupted. "Jackson, you simply cannot run as an independent. It will look small and petty. Small and petty don't win the White House. But petty and small is exactly what Warner needs you to be in order to beat him. I think the move to ban you from receiving the nomination was bait to run as an independent."

"Agreed," said Ron. Others nodded in agreement.

"What we are becoming is a movement," said Catherine. "This isn't just about Jackson. He's starting to tap into something bigger. Something with its own inertia that sparks people's imaginations. Gets them to believe in possibilities again."

"The only real way that map gives Piper the presidency is if there are 26 votes to be won, not 273 electoral votes," said Billings.

Ron snapped to attention. "You're not serious?" He knew precisely what Billings meant.

"Hasn't been done in 220 years, but that doesn't mean it's not possible."

"It could tear the fragile nation into pieces," replied Ron.

"I'm sorry, but what the hell are you guys talking about? 26?" erupted Ginny.

"The Contingent Election," said Ron. "When the Electoral College ends in a tie, or no candidate achieves a majority, then the question of who shall be President falls to the House, and Vice President to the Senate."

"That sounds like madness!" said Eileen. "No offense, Sylvester and Ginny, but have you listened to a House debate recently?"

"It's an 18th-century invention," said Jackson, the history teacher shining through. "It elected Thomas Jefferson in 1800. John Quincy Adams in 1824."

"The corrupt bargain!" exclaimed Valerie. "That's what the Jacksonians labeled Adams' victory. Andrew Jackson had won the popular vote and the largest number of electoral votes, but due to a shady deal between the Speaker and Adams, the House chose Adams on the first ballot. It is part of the reason Andrew Jackson formed his own Party and won the rematch four years later," said Valerie. "No offense, but the nation will likely view any President chosen by such an arcane procedure as illegitimate."

"I don't think most Americans even know such a provision in the Constitution exists. There will be outrage. Fuel on an already raging fire."

Billings reframed the question. "No offense, but y'all are missing the point here. Warner thinks he has you in checkmate by disqualifying you from both major Party nominations. He wants you to run as independent, alone and exposed, easy to shred to pieces. Parties provide muscle and money. They are movements, or at least they used to be. They look a lot more like businesses these days. But what is stopping us from transforming Jackson's run into a new Party? Something stronger and better?"

"What do you mean *us*, Sylvester?" asked Ginny. "I am not sure I trust any of this. What's to stop you or Eileen from using this against me this year to sink me."

"You don't think I have taken an enormous risk by coming here, Ginny?" Billings' face flared red in response to the accusation. "For all I know, there could be a camera crew outside waiting to ambush me when I leave."

Jackson grimaced. Sylvester knew better than to think Jackson would trick him into an embarrassing situation.

"I am here because I respect that man." He pointed at Jackson. "And I love our country, and I won't see her ripped to shreds by Russell Warner. He's a real threat, do you hear me? He could be the *last* President. If you doubt my sincerity, then you can pack your attitude and your expensive shoes and head back to California."

Jackson sought to lower the temperature. "No one is ambushing anyone here. I appreciate the level of trust it took for each of you to come here. And if anyone wants to leave right now, you are free to do so without judgment by Catherine and me."

He paused. No one moved.

"No one has to tell me about the danger Warner presents to this nation, the costs of running again, or the fears of being betrayed. My former Party just told me I was no longer welcome. I have had armed men and women confront me at town halls. The President's most violent supporters burned down our campaign headquarters."

"But for all Warner's foolishness and vanity, he is about to commit the greatest sin any American leader can commit. He is about to hotwire the democratic process in his favor so he can win."

Eileen appeared to say a silent prayer.

"If I leave the race, we essentially allow Warner to steamroll his way to a second term, but something tells me he won't stop there. So get your heads in the game and tell me how we win."

The room refocused. They were right to be reminded of the enormous sacrifices Piper was making by being a declared opponent to Warner. None of them had been as bold or brave as he and Catherine in this regard.

"If Piper can't run as an Independent, then we need a strong Third Party that can win states," said Eileen finally. "Perhaps we take a run at the Contingent Election. Deny Warner and Drummond both have the ability to get to 273."

"A Third Party? We have several of those. Useless and ineffective," said Eileen.

"Agreed!" said Art.

"They are single-issue and not mainstream," said Ron. "They lack the ability to be movements with broad appeal."

Jackson reached into his messenger bag and removed a preserved certificate, slightly larger than a $5 bill. "This was a gift from my great-grandfather to my father. He had been a proud member of this former Party. Back then, they issued certificates for generous support." Jackson held out the artifact carefully; it was encased between two pieces of plexiglass. It almost appeared to be U.S. currency, elegantly designed with scrolls and flourishes, a serial number printed in red ink at the top. Framed drawings of two spectacled men were bookending each side of the front—the words PROGRESSIVE PARTY were emblazoned across the top.

"The Progressive Party? I hate to break it to you, but that one's already taken, Jackson," said Ginny.

Jackson flipped the certificate over, denoting a gift of $5, to reveal a drawing printed on the reverse. A majestic bull moose stood in a remote river, head raised with an impressive expanse of antlers. A campaign pledge and signature of the Bull Moose candidates for President and Vice President of the United States with their signatures framed the regal creature.

"A five-dollar donation back then would be the equivalent of $350 or so today. Looks like a cross between a stock certificate and a banknote," said Valerie.

"The Bull Moose Party was the last Third Party to win *any* electoral college votes - 88, in fact, and more than the sitting President. Their triumph had been their ability to form an electrified movement nationwide, built around the charisma and eccentricity of its candidate, former President Theodore Roosevelt, who was pursuing an unprecedented third term."

"Why didn't they win?" asked Art, unaware entirely of this history in American politics despite being a sitting U.S. Senator.

"Their folly as a Party was siphoning votes only from President Taft, giving the governor of New Jersey, Woodrow Wilson, the first national victory for his Party in over 20 years."

"Why did I not think of this?" Sylvester asked in delightful surprise.

"Oh, Sylvester," Valerie said with a fiendish grin. "That's why you're just the Speaker, and Jackson Piper is going to be our next President."

13

DUTY CALLS

As the day turned into evening in Charleston, the nine men and women gathered in their secret location to discuss the potential risks and challenges of forming a new national Party in just a matter of months. It was not unprecedented, but it would require a much larger team and money—much, much more money.

Money was the largest obstacle – traditional fundraising sources would likely dry up if they continue to run afoul of Party wishes. But there were whispers of underground networks and new money willing to support Jackson Piper if he remained in the race. Piper scribbled down ideas into his digital notebook as they debated: rallies at colleges, forming their own streaming channels and even deploying more SI Assistants like Franklin to help run their campaign. Not like Ziggy because "she" was an anomaly. Nothing like her existed in the commercial market, and Ron remained mysterious about the source of his acquisition of the remarkable assistant.

There was extensive discussion about the appropriate timing to convert candidates to bolt their Parties on both sides of the aisle in exchange for the Bull Moose moniker.

One key consideration was what to do about the regional

primaries. Stay in both? Stop competing in both? File legal challenges to the Party's decisions? As twilight blanketed the river and night lights triggered by darkness began to illuminate the house, they finally reached an agreement. Jackson Piper would declare that the disqualification by the Parties was illegal and that he intended to challenge the revised rules in federal court. He would continue to campaign, insisting it was the right of the people to pick their nominee. If the movement began to falter, evidenced by severely declining fundraising or poor showings in both Party primaries, they would reconvene to consider withdrawing from the race.

However, if support remained strong or even grew, and if federal courts determined the Parties were within their right to set conditions on their nominations, they would use that ruling to call on all supporters of Piper to leave the Parties to join something new and exciting.

They realized the Courts may not move fast enough to render a decision to catalyze the movement, so they may need to be prepared to make their own tipping point moment. It would be a delicate dance of evasion and misdirection to prevent Russell Warner and his allies from catching onto Piper's plans too soon.

Bender and Browning would accumulate the necessary paperwork to launch a lightning-fast petition process to get Piper on fall ballots, beginning in the states they already covered and moving forward in each new state the campaign entered. There were 51 states, which meant 51 different rules on how their new Party could qualify to name presidential electors for the November election. They would need considerably more help.

When the last accomplice to their sophisticated plan to resurrect the Bull Moose Party departed, Jackson and Catherine climbed the stairs to the main bedroom. Catherine would leave in the morning for Connecticut to pick up Alex and Ben, then return as quickly as possible to Charlotte, North Carolina, to meet up with Jackson for the finish to the Southern Regional Primary.

Despite Speaker Billings' prediction that Warner would clean their clocks in far more traditional primaries that locked out independents from voting, putting on as strong a showing as possible was important.

Jackson unbuttoned his shirt and collapsed onto the stately bed in the main suite.

Catherine was engaged in her regular nightly routine, but something suddenly crossed her mind. Jackson seemed to be brought back to life by today's work. What she loved seeing most today was his confidence about the right path forward and remaining the leader of the Bull Moose to take them there. He did not waiver in his belief that he was the right person to become President.

"Damn, Jackson, you were on fire today," she exclaimed, her voice laced with a heady mix of admiration and desire.

"We'll see," replied Jackson, his tone smooth yet edged with uncertainty. "We're still far from knowing if this crazy plan has any hope."

"You're a firecracker, baby," she purred. "They're drawn to your energy like moths to a flame. Your relentless optimism and wild ideas – they light them up."

"Ginny's not so easily ignited. I wouldn't count on her straying from the straight path to become a Bull Moose," remarked Jackson, a twinge of disappointment coloring his words.

"But if you can sway the Speaker of the House and three Senators to abandon their lifetime loyalties to their Parties in one day…" she began.

"Not Sylvester. We need that old fox exactly where he is for now. In case shit hits the fan and we end up in a Contingent Election, he needs to be Speaker so he can dictate the rules. Who knows what kind of lunatic would take over in that power vacuum in the House."

"It was incredible to see you so energized again today," she said.

Slowly, Catherine began to undress under the shadowy cloak of darkness. She removed her top first, revealing the soft curves of her body in the subtle glow of the room.

Jackson was still staring at the ceiling, unaware of her intentions.

"Watching you command a room is downright intoxicating," she said, her voice low and sultry.

Jackson finally tuned into her signals and perched himself up on his elbows.

"You're not tired?" he asked, his eyes trailing over her as she continued to undress.

"Are you?" she asked, slowly loosening her bra and dropping it to the floor.

"No, I'm not tired at all," Jackson said, his heart racing.

"We haven't had a night completely alone in over three months," she said while unbuttoning her pants and letting them pool at her feet. "Why squander it?"

She sauntered over to him on the bed, her body bathed in the faint light. She leaned in to kiss her husband, a tender expression of desire shared between them. His hands traced their way up her bare back as she straddled him. Her fingers skillfully unbuttoned his trousers and loosened his belt.

The couple, who had been to hell and back since their departure from Denver in October, strengthened their connection with an intimate and exciting hour in the darkness in Charleston. They were alone now and unsure when they might enjoy such a quiet peace again.

∼

IN THE MORNING TWILIGHT, Catherine rolled out of bed and looked at her phone. It was bound to happen; it was always really just a question of when. Sooner or later, the universe seemed destined to pull Dr. Catherine Piper back to her duties at the University of Colorado Hospital.

Catherine reopened her work email for the first time since Thanksgiving. She inched slightly away from her role strictly as a campaign surrogate and prospective First Lady and closer back to the reality of being one of the nation's leading cancer clinicians and researchers, a mother of two, and a happily married woman to a man running to be the next President of the United States.

There was an urgent email from the University of Colorado with questions about patients whose cases were less than ordinary. She went to the bathroom and closed the door to scroll through the hundreds of emails in private.

Why was she hiding? Of course, Jackson would understand her need to return to her career sooner or later. In fact, he occasionally asked if she should start checking back in with the senior vice president who oversaw her unit. She closed the phone abruptly, woke Jackson, and prepared for her day of travel to reunite their family.

∼

OVER THE NEXT SEVERAL WEEKS, to avoid worrying or perhaps even jealousy that his campaign for the presidency was not important to her, she would steal away with increasing frequency to advise her colleagues on patient treatments or read voluminous reports on the next phase of a drug trial or the immune response triggered by a new gene therapy.

"So, what do you think about this new drug going into trial?" Jackson asked.

She flashed a look of alarm at her husband.

"Come on now, Cate," Jackson said, smiling. "I know you have been dipping into your emails, sneaking research memos into your briefing folders. I know how much your work means to you."

"Am I really that predictable?" she asked, nudging him.

"Dedicated, not predictable," he laughed.

"I've given it a lot of thought," she began. "I know how much you need me out here on the trail, but my work is also important. I don't know how much longer I can be away from my patients and my research. For their health or our financial health."

Jackson took her hand reassuringly. "I understand, honey. I'll manage without you if necessary, although it won't be easy." He flashed her one of his winning smiles, attempting to mask the twinge of sadness he felt at the thought of her leaving the campaign trail.

Catherine squeezed his hand. "I'm so proud of you, Jax," she said sincerely. "You've come so far and faced every challenge with grace and integrity. You keep winning primary after primary. It's almost a shame all these wins don't count for anything."

He leaned over and whispered in her ear. "Oh, they count for a great deal, my love. This is how we build a movement with the power to change the country."

Neither could have predicted how consequential Catherine returning to medical practice would prove to be.

14

DECLARATION OF WAR

Governor Lawrence sat in the executive mansion, an architectural gem of the American South. Its Greek revival style and brilliant white exterior echoed the grandeur of the White House. Six impressive two-story columns framed the entrance, making it appear stately and regal to visitors.

Stately and regal were not words used to describe Valerie Lawrence. She was a rough-and-tumble maverick who was not afraid to be herself to win an ally or be raw and gritty to defeat an opponent. Her Other Party detractors outside of Texas felt she objectified herself to gain appeal, sacrificing her credibility for fans. The same critics detested how she brandished a pistol on her hip when conducting official business as governor. Valerie understood more about the people of Texas than half the consultants and funders from Washington who had tried and failed to take the governor's mansion for years. She had finally won the office through a campaign of her own design, and she was not about to back down now, not for scowling Party leaders and certainly not for Russell Warner.

She felt a little bruised and battered now. She had endured six phone calls this week with Olivia Clay and President Warner about the ballot for the state's upcoming primary election on Super Tuesday. Some of the calls had lasted more than two hours with the President providing expert after expert testimony by phone on how the Texas governor could remove the troublesome Jackson Piper from the state's ballot since the Parties had disqualified him from receiving their nomination for President.

Valerie sat in the main study of the mansion with a state attorney, listening intently to a recitation of the legal arguments explaining why the Governor of Texas should ignore such outrageous pressure from the President.

Suddenly, there was shouting outside, which snapped Valerie from her near daze to full attention. She stood and looked out through the heavy red curtains. Ten black SUVs were parked in the driveway. The Texas Rangers tasked with guarding the Governor were backing towards the doors of the mansion, guns at the ready as sixty federal agents and Marshalls from the Department of Homeland Security exited the SUVs aiming drawn weapons, some in SWAT gear, and flashing warrants for the arrest of the Texas Governor.

"Stop! Stop! Holster your weapons!" ordered the Rangers.

"Stand down, officers! We are here with an arrest warrant for Governor Lawrence!" shouted the federal agents in reply.

"One of the lead agents finally made it to the porch and presented a copy of a federal arrest warrant.

"This is outrageous! You have no fucking authority to do this," said Trooper Scott Brush, the head of the Governor's protective detail. "You people must be out of your goddamned minds if you think I'm going to let you arrest the Governor!"

Chaos unfolded as suddenly as the federal contingent had appeared at the residence.

State Troopers thundered up the stairs to the second floor. Valerie burst from her office with a terrified state attorney in tow. Troopers shouted to move clear of the windows. With no warning from the federal government, the Texas Rangers assumed this was not an actual arrest but a cleverly disguised kidnapping.

Valerie asked the state attorney to call the First Spouse, Parker

Lawrence, and inform him of what was happening. He was at his restaurant in downtown Austin.

"Then I want you to issue one hell of a statement denouncing these barbaric intimidation tactics by President Warner."

"Yes, ma'am," stammered the still-flustered attorney, hearing shouting between Scott Brush and the federal agents on the first floor.

"Dial up the language to a ten. Don't let this prick put me in jail without destroying his reputation in Texas. I want fire and brimstone in that statement," she instructed.

The state attorney was tapping furiously on his phone.

Valerie took out the executive order prepared for her that morning. It firmly stated that Jackson Piper would not be removed from either ballot in the state's upcoming primary. It ordered the Secretary of State to issue the ballot as drafted immediately.

She removed a pen from an armadillo inkwell on her desk and signed her looping signature on the order, then quickly embossed it with the seal of her office, making the order official.

She folded the order, handed it to the state attorney, and said, "Be certain this is uploaded and issued immediately."

Scott Brush rushed into the office.

"These agents have a federal warrant to arrest you, Governor. I have called it in, and it is real, although this is total fucking bullshit, ma'am," Trooper Brush said.

Four federal agents stormed into the office, pistols drawn, in an over-the-top show of force designed to send a message. They pointed the weapons at Scott Brush and the state attorney. Then, one of the federal agents swung his gun in the direction of the Governor.

"You will holster that fucking weapon, or you will point it at me, asshole," growled Brush. "Keep pointing it at the Governor of Texas, and you're going to leave here with a goddamn souvenir."

The federal agent looked at Brush. He saw a fire in his eyes that led him to conclude there was no need to escalate an already tense standoff further. He slowly moved the pistol off the governor and back towards the Ranger.

"Governor Valerie Lawrence, I have a warrant for your arrest. You have the right to remain silent..."

"I understand my rights," she said.

"Ma'am, place your hands where I can see them on the desk." He addressed her like she was an armed thief.

"This is absurd. I will go along peacefully," Valerie said, looking at the agents insisting on cooler heads.

"Ma'am, are you armed?" asked another agent.

"No, I am not," said Governor Lawrence.

"Ma'am, I need your hands where I can see them!" shouted another agent.

"They are over her fucking head! What more do you want?" snarled Brush.

"This is all for show, Scott. They want to release audio that implies I am not complying with their bullshit order from their bully-in-chief," snapped Valerie. "They want me to resist arrest." She leaned forward and placed two palms on her desk.

The largest federal agent, a man named Quentin Salt, approached her. He grabbed her wrists, pulled them forcefully behind her back, and slapped heavy metal handcuffs onto them. He then took a sick pleasure in "roughing her up a little," as the President himself had suggested on a phone call just minutes earlier. Salt slammed the Texas governor against a nearby wall.

When the 290-pound Agent Salt pressed the 130-pound Governor against the wall hard enough to rattle several framed pictures hanging there, Trooper Brush attempted to draw his weapon in protest. Brush was immediately met with a severe strike to the back of his head by the pistol grip of one of the agents. The room went white for a moment. Brush felt as if his head was about to split in two. He fell to the floor in the large office. The agent who struck him knelt on his back to hold him down.

"Just hold still, Brush," said the agent. "We'll be out of your hair in a minute or two."

From the ground, Trooper Brush could see Governor Lawrence was bleeding from the force with which her head struck the wall. He screamed in frustration at his inability to protect the Governor from this egregious abuse of power. His mind raced, wondering if he should have issued a warning shot or even been more aggressive as the SUVs entered the property five minutes ago.

The agents whisked the governor from the office. She stumbled as they pushed her forcefully down the front stairs of the mansion and into the backseat of the nearest SUV.

The agent kneeling on Trooper Brush's back finally relented once he heard the first SUV leaving the residence. Brush slowly lifted himself from the ground. The federal agent holstered his pistol and got on his radio, listening to orders from his team.

Brush straightened his uniform, tightened his fist, and then struck the federal agent with the hardest right hook he had ever thrown in his life. He knocked the agent out cold.

"Told you to mind your fucking manners," said Brush.

Five Texas Rangers entered the room, one attending to the knocked-out federal agent.

Brush stepped over him, removed his phone from his pocket, and called Colonel Wallace, the Director of the Texas Department of Public Safety.

He took a deep breath, then spoke clearly into the phone when the Colonel answered. "Colonel Wallace. I think we might be at war with the United States government."

∽

TWO HOURS LATER, Marty Dudash approached Jackson Piper as he left a campaign stage in Orlando, Florida, ahead of the Gulf States Regional Primaries, including Florida, Alabama, Louisiana, and Puerto Rico.

"Senator Piper. Senator!" He interrupted Jackson's attempt to snap photos with supporters brought backstage at the event. "You need to see this, sir."

Jackson reached for a tablet displaying the latest news headline: "BREAKING: President Warner Issues Stark Warning to Political

Challengers." He took the device from his hands and read the article with growing dismay. Piper clicked on a link to a live news clip.

"President Warner has issued a thinly veiled threat to those who would challenge his authority. Texas Governor Valerie Lawrence, an Other Party Member, has been arrested for refusing to remove Jackson Piper from the state's primary ballot in the upcoming primary on Super Tuesday on April 5. President Warner made the following statement in the Rose Garden minutes ago:

"I have served this great nation for many years and will do whatever it takes to defend her from liars and instigators. Those who stand in the way of democracy will face dire consequences."

The clip returned to the anchor. "The Governor has been arrested for attempting to rig a federal election, according to sources. Through a spokesperson, Governor Lawrence called the charges outrageous and likened them to a declaration of war on the State of Texas. The Governor is being held in a federal jail awaiting a bond hearing tomorrow."

Images of his ally Valerie Lawrence flashed on the screen. She was being hustled into a federal courthouse, her hands handcuffed like an accused murderer. There was dried blood visible in her hairline.

More people around him were getting alerts about the breaking news and watching versions of the same clip.

Jackson looked up at Marty. A burning anger filled his face. Sensing an explosion, Marty took the Senator by the arm and led him away from the crowd towards their waiting caravan.

"Cate!" Jackson bellowed. Dudash looked at Jackson in stunned silence. He had never seen Senator Piper so angry.

Catherine eventually caught up to them. "What's wrong?"

"This is fucking outrageous!" said Piper, pointing to the story on the tablet. He climbed into the SUV, and Catherine was right behind him.

"Oh my God, Val!" whispered Catherine. "Is she bleeding? Why has she been arrested, Jack?"

Ron entered the SUV, catching the tail end of the exchange.

"Apparently, President Warner arrested Val for refusing to remove us from the ballot there on Super Tuesday."

"This is a threat pointed directly at us," Jackson said, his voice low but firm. "Warner is unhinged."

"We should issue an immediate call for her release," Ron said.

The Pipers nodded. "She should be released immediately," said Catherine, scrolling her phone for more updates.

Jackson's phone buzzed. He picked it up. It was an incoming call from an unknown number in Austin, Texas.

"Yes?" said Jackson, tentatively into the phone.

"Jackson, it's Parker Lawrence."

"Parker, may I put you on speaker with Catherine and Ron Bender?"

Piper pressed the speaker call icon.

Catherine asked the first question, "Parker, is Valerie okay?"

"She wanted me to call you immediately and assure you she is fine. The federal agents slammed her against the wall and opened a cut she already had on her head—long story. The point is, she wanted you to know she is fine. She's probably going to be held for another twelve hours or so. We think this proves their point that Warner is in control. We are working to get her released on bond."

"My God, this is horrific, Parker," Jackson said. "We are releasing a statement decrying this undemocratic and political barbarism. We'll have it out in the next fifteen minutes."

"That's the other reason I called. Val wants you to do more than that."

"We're listening, Parker. Anything she needs, we'll do it," Jackson said.

"She wants you to put out an email and text called the FREE VALERIE ACTION," said the First Gentleman of Texas through the speaker. "She wants you to make a big stink about it. She wants you to use this moment against Warner. She says this might be the closest thing we get to a court decision that allows us to make our move. Do you know what that means?"

Bender and the Pipers exchanged glances. "She's like a superhero, you know that, don't you, Parker?" Jackson said.

"She's something. She got roughed up by federal agents, paraded into a federal courthouse in handcuffs, and her first thought is how to help her ally Jackson raise money to win."

"Does she need anything else? We're not above a jailbreak tonight, Parker," said Jackson jokingly.

Catherine smacked Jackson on the shoulder and mouthed, "You don't know who is listening," reminding her husband that the running assumption was every phone call they made or received now might be subject to intercept by the President's goons in the FBI or other federal agencies.

"Time for us to hang up, Parker. Stay in touch, ok?" Jackson said.

"More soon," Parker replied and terminated the call in Texas.

Jackson issued clear directions to his team. "Ron, I want you on the phone with her attorneys and our attorneys until she is out of that cell. I want answers on our options. You sign off on the statement. I trust you; I don't need to read it first. Fill it with heat that will fire up our supporters."

"Aye, aye," said Bender.

"Ron, if we need to speed up our exit from these Primaries as a concession to Warner to get her out of this jam, so be it," said Jackson. "But I think she's right. This is the catalyst we need to free the moose!"

"The moose is loose!" crooned Ron with a smile.

15

DIAGNOSIS

She sat on the edge of her bed, reading the words on the page over and over again in disbelief. It was as if all the oxygen had been suddenly removed from the room – the world. Breathing required effort. Her body was tingling all over. Numb. Was this already spreading in her body? She was afraid to touch her chest. Would that cause it to spread? How much time did she have? The light in the room seemed to dim suddenly. All she could see was the crisp white paper in her hand and the thick, ugly, disgusting words typed on the page.

Cancer.

Steve was traveling. Should she call him? Would he want to know this immediately? Of course, he would.

Where was her phone?

Her sister needs to know. Whom should she tell first?

Jessica rose from the edge of her bed. The room was spinning. She sat back down again. Better give herself a moment. She was regaining her wits and coming back to earth. This was beatable. She was not going to surrender and give in. When in her thirty-eight-year career had she ever rolled over and given up?

Her mother would be ashamed of her for having such dreadful

thoughts if she were still here. God Almighty, how she wanted to be held by her mother right now and assured in her beautiful, milky alto voice, "Everything's gonna be alright. Don't worry…"

Tears formed in her eyes. Where was her phone? She said the words aloud, "Where's my phone?"

The elegant metal device vibrated, and the programmed SI voice said, "Here I am, Jessica."

Jessica stood, walked to the dresser, and lifted the phone.

Thirteen unread texts. Unlucky number.

Her gaze unlocked the phone, and she whispered to it, "Message Steve. Tell him to call me as soon as he is available. Nothing's wrong. No, Delete that. Say instead. Call me as soon as you're available. I have received my results."

It was two o'clock in the afternoon. The president needed her for a briefing at the White House by four. Vice President Jessica Brown steeled her spine, folded the letter, and walked to the kitchen to make a cup of coffee.

After her husband, Steve, President Warner would be the next to hear this unfortunate news.

16

PERCEPTIONS

The late afternoon sun soaked the South Lawn in a warming glow; the entire city was desperate to awaken. It was late March, and the infamous cherry blossoms began to bud across the district. President Russell Warner stood by his Oval Office window, hands clasped behind his back, as he surveyed the South Lawn of the White House. Despite the beauty of Washington in the spring, he did not feel any semblance of peace or happiness. Piper inexplicably remained in the race, pursuing both nominations for President. He had been seemingly undeterred by the action of the Parties and had filed a lawsuit seeking an injunction. Lucky for Warner, the judges were appointed by him and loathe to run crosswise of the President, so no injunction had been granted.

Despite the constant assault in every media platform where they could spend money attacking him, Piper remained a threat. He was dangerously close to knocking Drummond out of the Other Party race entirely. The time for subtlety was over.

Marco Alvarez, now Secretary of State, was seated under a portrait of Andrew Jackson. Olivia Clay sat near Alvarez on a long, white sofa. They had just watched the body camera videos of the arrest of Valerie Lawrence. They intended to cut it into a campaign ad. Olivia had cackled when she saw the blood on the governor's face as she walked into the courthouse. When the video compilation ended, an aide turned off the screen and exited the room, feeling disgusted.

"Sir, we believe there's a way we can deliver a knockout blow to rid us of Piper finally," said Olivia.

"We? Are there after-hours discussions happening that I should know about? Pillow talk, perhaps?" chuckled Warner.

Olivia ignored the jab, looking at Marco to chime in.

"Go on," Warner replied, not tearing his gaze away from the view outside.

"As you know, *The Mark* can amplify certain stories. The system's intelligence can be throttled up or down to allow more or less 'junk' through," he explained.

Olivia leaned in, uncrossing her fit legs wrapped in black stockings. Marco imagined what she was wearing underneath that gray business dress. She returned the alluring gaze to Alvarez for a split second, then refocused on the task at hand. "But the key is we push false stories to discredit Jackson Piper, right?"

Alvarez hesitated momentarily before adding, "I would want to be careful about diminishing Juniper's value and flagship product. Reduced quality or volume a day or two a week would be unnoticed, but pushing lies and fake stories en-mass would raise alarms."

Olivia nodded and crossed her legs again.

"Although not the CEO for now, I am a majority controlling owner," he added.

"And I'm still the President of the United States. I am in control of this campaign, not you."

An aide entered seeking his signature on documents. President Warner picked up a pen, signed the documents, and threw the folder at the aide, sending paper fluttering in all directions.

"Drummond is still ahead in the delegate count in the Other Party," said Olivia.

"Barely," growled Warner. He saw a scenario where Piper could overtake Drummond on Super Tuesday if his Hail Mary arrest of the Texas Governor did not produce the capitulation he desired.

"But what good are those delegates? The Party will not seat any of them at the convention?" said Marco.

"Perception is reality. You, of all people, should understand that, Marco. It's the perception that Piper is winning that will not allow him to exit the Parties' primaries as easily as we had hoped."

"You remain in a firm position, Mr. President," said Olivia, trying to boost the President's mood. "You are leading in the coming Regional. And aside from New Hampshire, South Carolina, New Mexico, and Pennsylvania, oh and Michigan, and Illinois, Piper has not really been able to catch any steam in our Primaries."

"Let's not waste any more time pussy footing around," he threw a knowing look at Olivia and Marco. He sensed the tension between them. He made a note to use it as leverage if he needed it in the future. "I want you to deploy *The Mark* to wreak some havoc on Piper," said Warner.

Alvarez clenched his teeth. That was not at all what he had agreed to.

"Meanwhile," continued the President, "our mole inside the campaign has helped keep us well informed, but I think it's time to increase the pressure on the pipes. Pressure is the surest way to spring a leak."

A dark-haired woman entered with a note. She handed it to the President.

"The Vice President needs to see me urgently," said Warner. "She is outside. Can you all clear the room, please?"

In a moment, Olivia and Marco cleared the room. Marco did not like being dismissed so the President could meet privately with that ribbon-cutting hack, Jessica Brown. He did not make eye contact with the confident but past-her-prime black woman standing in the waiting area waiting to enter the Oval. Vice President Jessica Brown did not smile nor acknowledge Olivia or Marco as she waited to enter the room.

17

DEATH AND RESURRECTION

It was quickly growing dark in Tampa. The final votes were being cast now in the Gulf States Primary. Jackson was about to thank the thousands of supporters who had come to downtown Tampa to see him speak at the conclusion of the latest regional primary. No one outside the campaign staff had any inclination about what would happen inside the hotel ballroom tonight.

The Midwest Regional was following in a week, and then the New Super Tuesday was the grand finale. It comprised three of the four largest states by delegates to the two conventions — California, Texas, and New York — and the Mountain West states of Utah, Colorado, Idaho, Wyoming, and Montana. It was by far the most expensive stretch in terms of media buys and organizing. If campaigns could make it to this round in the primary calendar, they would be lifted to victory or crushed out of existence by the scale of the operation needed to prevail. But victory would be highly costly but nearly meaningless for Piper in both primaries because of the rule changes.

In the delegate count in the Old Party, Warner was the clear leader but he could not yet claim a majority of delegates. State after state refused to recognize the new Party rules that banned Piper from the nomination, so Piper continued to amass delegates. The Piper campaign was fully aware that at the Old Party Convention in Las Vegas that summer, the Party could simply refuse to recognize all of Piper's delegates and replace them with partisans willing to vote for a unanimous Warner renomination.

In the Other Party, Piper was starting to fall behind Paul Drummond in the delegate count, but if things continued to play out as they had, Piper might be able to claim a majority of delegates in his former Party. However, it would be a lost cause getting those delegates seated with voting rights at the convention. The Credentials Committee would be stacked with Fogarty or Drummond loyalists who would object to every Piper delegate won after the rules change.

The responsibility to campaign in the Gulf Regional seemed heavier in light of Governor Lawrence's arrest. The past several days pressed down on Jackson like a suffocating blanket.

Tampa was luminescent through the floor-to-ceiling windows of the hallway outside the ballroom where thousands of churning supporters waited to hear from their leader. It was expected that major news streams would announce the Florida results at any moment, reporting a Piper victory. Jackson felt that each state they won raised the hope among his voters that there would be a way to pierce through the darkness and uncertainty of the Parties' ban on his nomination.

It was time to set the record straight. He gripped the text of the speech they had finally agreed to just hours before. Ziggy had loaded it onto the teleprompters on stage.

Piper stood alone in the staging area, except for his private security team stationed at either end of the long hall. A man emerged from a restroom just off the hallway. He saw the Senator standing alone, about to address the audience.

"We have to expose the truth behind these false stories, Senator!" called the voter down the hall. He gave Jackson two thumbs up.

"Agreed!" Jackson replied, handing the tablet back to Libby. "But first, I need to speak with our voters."

Libby opened the door and motioned for Jackson to enter. The sounds of thousands of screaming men, women, and children flooded the hallway. Piper waved diplomatically, shaking hands with as many people as he could on his way to the stage in the center of the ballroom. Theater in the round was Piper's favorite setup. No podium, no barriers. Just him and the audience. Ron handed him the microphone as he approached the stage and yelled into his ear over the crowd's roar, "Teleprompters are on the floor at each corner of the stage. The speech is green. Go get 'em!"

"Friends," Piper said once he had mounted the platform, raising his hand. The cheers continued.

"Friends, because of your tremendous work, tonight we will be declared the winner of the Other Party Florida, and we will win the most delegates in the Gulf States Regional Primary!"

Another prolonged eruption of cheers and screams of delight.

"In theory," he said, and the crowd quieted.

"Once again, you have demonstrated to the President that he cannot brush us aside!"

He looked out at the crowd. Across the diverse sea of faces, he saw eyes locked on him, awaiting direction and translation of the events of the past 120 days since he entered the race for President."

"Your hard work, your support of this movement, and your belief in a cause worthy of this great nation have propelled us to this historic moment. We are on the brink of something profoundly important in the history of the United States. I want you to hold hands with someone near you. Go ahead. I'll wait."

The assembled mass of more than two thousand in the mighty ballroom obeyed his request. Now, they stood hand in hand from one wall to the next.

"We are a family, the American family, and we invite everyone in this nation into it, even those who disagree with us. Especially with those who oppose us. Because we are a democratic nation, by definition, democracies require diversity of thought, diversity of action, and diversity of opinion. But do not confuse diversity with disunity or disunion. Because even when we disagree about the way forward, we know we remain brothers and sisters united in a common purpose. The purpose of liberty and justice for all."

Some in the crowd broke hands to applaud and then joined hands again.

"I see this country as a family. But my heart breaks for this family tonight. It breaks because the two major Parties in Washington, DC, decided to tell you that you are not welcome. Nearly a third of all registered voters in America will have voted in these regional primaries by Super Tuesday. While that is a remarkable number, the highest primary turnouts in a generation in fact, two-thirds of Americans have been shut out of the process, stayed home, or were intimidated not to exercise their democratic rights. We must do better.

"My heart is broken tonight because a President so determined to stay in power ordered the illegal arrest of the Governor of Texas..." The audience booed and jeered at the mention of the past days' events.

"He claims she is attempting to defraud a federal election by allowing a candidate disqualified by his Party and the Other Party from winning the nomination to remain on the ballot."

"That's bullshit!" screamed a man from the sea of faces.

"It is bullshit, but unlike a family, Warner and his cronies increasingly use violence to get their way. You might have heard about some of my run-ins with them in New Hampshire!" The crowd erupted.

"Georgia!" More jeers.

"Oklahoma!" They screamed louder. The list was much longer, but he had made his point.

"My heart is broken tonight for our national family because no court - not one - will issue an order that will allow us to win the nomination of either Party. Even if we bring a majority of the delegates to the conventions in Las Vegas and Madison, the Parties have the autocratic power to turn us away and deny our votes from being cast for us to win the nominations."

Boos and hisses erupt in the sea of faces. Piper looked to a bank of cameras on the far wall broadcasting the feed.

Then Jackson Piper said softly into the microphone, "However, my heart is full tonight, family..."

The crowd hushed and waited for what Jackson had to say.

"My heart is full tonight because, in our nation, we have the power to set our course through Warner's forest of discontent and Drummond's fog of disunity."

"My heart is full because we are not alone anymore. We have found each other. And there are more of us to be found and saved across this great land. My heart is full because there is a new place for us to be united and not feel alone anymore. To not feel cast aside or forgotten. There is a place for your fierce love of country and your unyielding love of democracy. There is a place where we can be certain we will be safe. Safe from intimidation and ridicule and neglect."

Piper's voice was slowly rising in a crescendo.

"If they will not have you. If they will toss you aside. If they will waste your energy and enthusiasm just to rig their reelection, then I say we leave them!"

The hall erupted in cheers, louder than any time before.

"I made it clear I would reform what was broken in Washington, DC, no matter the cost. When we reformed the Senate filibuster four years ago, my former Party cast me into the wilderness. They refused to support my campaign for reelection to the Senate. They bullied anyone who dared come to my defense. They brayed and whined that I did not play by their rules. After eight years in the House and six in the Senate as a member of the Other Party, I changed my registration to Independent. But I had not left that Party. It left me behind long before that!"

Jackson Piper's voice boomed through the hall. "Tonight, I am calling upon Americans who share our conviction that we must destroy the government gang, dissolving the unholy alliance between corrupt business and corrupt politics.

"We must reform and restore the rights of the people. Committed to the principles of government of, by, and for the people through representative democracy, we pledge to secure a new Bill of Rights - 12 Freedoms - that shall ensure the character of our mighty people endures for ten more generations of Americans.

"And most urgently of all, we must restore our nation's social and economic vitality.

The crowd ate up every word.

"I am calling upon Americans in every town, in every city, in every state, and in every nation stationed or working around the world to remove the rose-colored glasses and see the Old Party and the Other Party for what they truly are - two sides of the same coin. A coin in the pockets of soulless corporations and billionaires determined to sing you a lullaby of complacency while they plunder and rape and murder our people.

"Tonight, I end my quest for the nominations of these Parties..." Gasps and boos filled the hall. Jackson slowly raised a hand, calling for calm.

"Tonight, I end my quest for the nominations of these Parties because they are not worthy of you. They are not worthy of us. They have turned their back on America, trading 40 pieces of silver for a selfish pursuit of power. Tonight, we lay this campaign to rest with an awareness that we have won many battles, but ultimately, we will lose their rigged war."

The audience was dead silent.

"But, tomorrow, we are reborn as something new. Something stronger. Something mighty."

The screens illuminated with a crimson silhouette of a bull moose, suddenly surrounded by a brilliant blue ring. Then, an animated train of white stars flew in, forming a circle within the ring.

The words BULL MOOSE PARTY appeared above the logo, then below it, the words "Reestablished 2044."

Jackson raised his hand, asking for quiet, and then said, "Tomorrow, I officially become a candidate for the Bull Moose Party nomination for President of the United States. Catherine and I urge everyone who believes in this movement to register tomorrow as a Bull Moose in your state or jurisdiction. If Bull Moose doesn't exist, write it in," instructed Piper.

Campaign staff at the back of the ballroom quickly unpacked signs, buttons, stickers, and T-shirts bearing the new AMERICA

NEEDS PIPER logo emblazoned with the bull moose. They started distributing them among the crowd, hypnotized by Piper's words.

In the hallway outside the ballroom, an army of voter registration volunteers was prepared to assist any voter with a change in registration to any Party, but hopefully, they would choose Bull Moose.

Three dates flashed on the screen above their heads in the ballroom.

Jackson continued. "How about we start rewriting the book on how to build a powerful movement beginning with our convention? In the Bull Moose Party, we do it bigger and bolder. Our convention will span the nation. July 2 in San Jose, California." The date and location flashed on the screen. The crowd snapped photos with their phones.

"July 3 in Austin, Texas. Then the final day is July 3 in Pittsburgh."

The crowd cheered.

"Over the next 90 days, our Bull Moose campaign will span out to join an effort already underway to place the Bull Moose nominees for President and Vice President and selected electors on the ballot in all 51 states. Together, as a family, through our new online Platform Convention, we will write a Party platform worthy of you and relevant to solving the many problems that years of neglect have brought upon our nation. By the time we adjourn in Philadelphia, we will have a movement galvanized to change America and take back our White House!"

The crowd jumped and screamed in excitement.

"God bless you, and good night!"

Piper placed the microphone down on the stage and shook the hands of his now-energized Bull Moose citizens.

∼

IN A PRIVATE HOME in Georgetown in Washington, DC, at that very same moment, a woman sat in the kitchen in a silk slip, attempting to reach her boss by phone. Feet away in a now dark sitting room lay a shattered screen on the floor. Moments before, it had been mounted on the wall until it displayed Piper's stunning announcement about forming a Bull Moose Party to win the election. A heavy glass ashtray bearing the seal of the President of the United States had been hurled at it by a once-great starting pitcher for Stanford University. That was decades ago now. The man's mind groped for answers, and his chest heaved with anger. Marco Alvarez decided then and there he was done doing things Warner's way. It was time to take matters into his own hands.

PART III

18

MISLED

The mid-June morning sun peeked through the curtains, casting a warm golden glow on the entwined forms of a couple that had grown comforted by the closeness of the other during slumber. Their limbs were entangled in the soft sheets. Sharing a serene moment of connection, their hearts beat in unison.

"It has felt like a dream to have you beside me in our bed when I open my eyes each morning," Catherine murmured, her eyes sparkling with happiness as she traced the outline of Jackson's face with her fingertips. "I am going to miss you so much."

"Me too," Jackson whispered, his voice heavy with emotion. He pressed a tender kiss to her forehead. "But I'm here now, and that's all that matters."

"And in an hour, twenty-five campaign staff will descend upon our home yet again," she smirked. "Whisking you away toward the chaos again."

"It has been wonderful while it lasted," he remarked. "Now that it's time to pick a Vice President, the urgent sprint to the finish line has returned."

"There are worse things," she whispered into his ear. "Besides, we will join up with you just before the first night of the Convention."

Catherine slid out of bed and into their bathroom.

"Busy day today?" asked Jackson.

"Yes, I'm afraid," she said behind the slightly ajar door. "Still editing research papers for publication, and I have a strange new case coming in today to see me at the hospital. The dean said the patient insisted on seeing me and me alone."

"I'm not surprised," said Jackson. "You're America's best hope of curing cancer this decade."

Shortly after that night in Tampa, when Jackson announced the creation of the Bull Moose Party, Catherine took steps to return to work. It brought welcomed support to the Piper family's financial needs. She had several research grants that she transitioned to her colleagues at the University for at least the remainder of the year. Of course, many patients had been agreeable to be seen by other members of the University's cancer team. Time is of the essence in treating a disease that had become far more prevalent yet more treatable during her twenty years of practice. She sought to advise on the most peculiar cases but requested not to take on any new patients as a compromise to ensure she could depart for the campaign trail again in September.

By late May, it felt like she had never left Denver as she settled comfortably into her routine. She started to flirt with the idea of asking Jackson to leave the General Election campaign entirely to him and his soon-to-be-tapped running mate. She knew that Ron Bender would hate that idea. His emphatic words echoed in her head: "The nation needs to try you on as their First Lady, Catherine." She also recalled Libby showing her polling data that indicated Catherine's likability numbers were ten points higher than Jackson's. She insisted those numbers not be shared with Jackson out of concern for notoriously fickle self-confidence.

With a reluctant sigh, Jackson pulled himself up in the bed and asked the screen to turn on. As the screen displayed his favorite feeds, his serenity faded, replaced by frustration and disbelief. Every feed had a different scandalous ad paid for by the Warner or Drummond campaigns decrying Piper and the new Bull Moose Party. Each ad was more outrageous than the last.

Then, ominous music filled the television speakers. Gunshots and then screams. Footage of people running in panic from one of the dozens of public shootings that occur each year in America. A male voiceover begins, "Jackson Piper hates America. He wants to suffocate your right to defend yourself from murderous gangs and foreign invaders. What kind of country do the Bull Moose want this to become?" Still photos of dead bodies strewn lifeless in a public park, blood staining the brick sidewalks. The scenes were so over the top in terms of their gore that it had to be SiArt. A close-up of a dead mother, blood draining from her lifeless mouth as her eyes stare empty towards eternity. "Jackson and his Bull Moose frauds will turn America into a murderous hellscape. Don't subject our country to these horrors. Save America. Vote Warner November 8th."

"That's outrageous," Jackson muttered, his jaw clenched in anger. "How can they get away with this?"

Catherine tried not to react. It was shocking imagery for a political ad. Catherine placed a comforting hand on his arm. "We knew the closer you got to beating him, the more extreme his reactions would become. This is the type of politics you are running to end, my love."

"This extremism is going to inflame the country like it did in New Hampshire," argued Jackson.

"His brand of extremism will do whatever it takes to bring you down. If they don't have dirt on you, they make it up or make it up about the people you love to hurt you," she replied.

Jackson grabbed his phone and dialed Sterling Powers' number. It went directly to voicemail. They had spoken less frequently since Jackson announced his intention to challenge Warner as a Bull Moose. He worried that Powers was slowly moving out of his camp to protect himself as a member of the Old Party, hoping to hold onto power in DC and building a firewall around himself that might protect him if Jackson were to go down in flames.

Jackson dialed another ally, Eileen Frasier. She answered the phone immediately.

"Jackson! Good morning," Eileen greeted him warmly. "What can I do for you?"

"Have you seen these latest ads from Warner?"

"I saw one playing this morning after my tea and Bible reading. Frankly, they are the last straw for me, Jackson. I can't keep my head down and pretend these tactics are normal or safe," she replied.

"The *hellscape* ad is particularly offensive," Jackson said, trying to keep his anger in check. "Every damn feed is spewing this garbage about me, Eileen. These feel more dangerous than hurtful," insisted Jackson. "I think we should respond in some way."

"I am going to pray for an answer," she said thoughtfully. "How's your dear Catherine holding up?"

"She has been happy to have us working out of our home since April. But the time has come to return full-time to the trail. We are close to picking a Vice President nominee."

"I know you will pick wisely for our Party, Jackson."

"I remain humbled by your courage to join the Bull Moose ranks, Senator," Jackson said, momentarily distracted from the attack ads. "Our message is breaking through partly because leaders like you showed you weren't afraid to challenge the system."

"Following a great leader is the easy part, dear," Eileen responded with genuine admiration. "I can't wait to see what you'll do as the President. But dreams are for another day. 'Let's not get tired of doing good, because in time we'll have a harvest if we don't give up.'"

"Corinthians?"

"Galatians. Chapter Six."

"Amen. Thank you, Eileen. Please keep me posted if any more members of the Senate are grousing about wanting to meet with me - officially or unofficially - while I'm in the City in a week, ok?" Jackson asked.

As he turned back to Catherine, he saw horror blanketing her face. She was sitting at the end of the bed, staring at the screen on the wall.

There were gut-wrenching images of surgeries gone horribly wrong and sounds of people screaming. Jackson caught the tail-end of the narration: "...and that's why careless Catherine Piper should be nowhere near the White House. Careless in the operating room. Careless with your concerns as citizens. Vote against the Bull Moose on November 8. Paid for by the Other Party of the United States."

Jackson threw pillow after pillow at the screen. The action was as absurd as the accusations that Dr. Catherine Piper was careless in her conduct of medicine. Nothing could be further from reality, and she knew it, but the sting was no less sharp.

Jackson wrapped his large arms around her and kissed her neck. "If they don't have dirt, they make it up," said Jackson. "About the people you love to hurt you."

"That is truly horrendous. How can these Parties be so horrible?" she asked in shock.

"They have come to exist entirely for their own benefit. They are no different from each other, though they claim to be. There is not a dollar's..."

"...bit of difference between them," she said, finishing his stump speech line for him. "Don't you get tired of hearing yourself speak, old man?"

"Old man?" he laughed. "That's not what you called me last night."

"Let me show you what you'll be missing when you walk out that door today," she said, collapsing into the bed and lifting her shirt over her head. It was one of those rare moments when they could find solace in each other's arms, cherishing the love that had brought them this far in the soulless arena of American politics.

Catherine and Jackson enjoyed coffee as the boys giggled over cartoons on a screen. It was the final moments of their last normal morning for at least several months as a family. Delaying for as long as possible, Catherine finally worked to perfect her makeup, tidied the kitchen, and fully transformed into Dr. Piper. She kissed the children goodbye and headed to the medical center to begin another fourteen-hour day on her feet. As she looked for her briefcase, she found Jackson hunched over his desk, scattered papers in front of him. He was old-fashioned that way, insisting on drafting speeches on paper at times. He had been working on this task for weeks, drafting and redrafting his convention speech. Each word he wrote carried the weight of the Bull Moose Party's future and the hopes of a nation desperate for change.

"Jax?" Catherine's voice called softly from the doorway, her eyes filled with concern. "You've been working on that speech for weeks. Perhaps you need someone from the comms shop to give you some fresh eyes on it?"

"Thanks, sweetheart," he replied, "but this needs to be mine, and it must be perfect."

"I see my perfectionist ways have finally rubbed off on you," she said, understanding the pressure to craft something genuinely remarkable. It was not a small task. They shared a quiet embrace, unsure how long it would be before they had a private moment again.

"Call me before you board the plane, ok?" she instructed.

"Will do," he assured her. He did not take his eyes off her or her car until it finally disappeared from the driveway and over the hill toward the city.

The Piper home began to buzz as campaign staff descended through every door, finalizing preparations to take this incredible campaign back on the road after sixty days of retooling for the General Election in the Pipers' home.

"Diesel!" Jackson exclaimed, opening the door to reveal his campaign chairman, looking fresh and eager. "How is Washington?"

"Ready for our arrival next week," assured the Senator of Ohio.

"That makes one of us," said Jackson as he plunged a stack of papers into Diesel's chest.

"What's this?" He looked the papers over. "Your convention speech? Oh, don't tell me you have rewritten it again?"

"It wasn't right, Diesel. It still isn't right. It does not capture the moment nor the emotion of what we are trying to undertake here," said Jackson, his eyes wide.

"Chief, I think you're too close to it. Why don't we take your... draft...and hand it off to the amazing team of college graduates we hired as speechwriters who will give this creation a coherent voice and direction." He stuffed the stacks of papers into a folio and lifted his phone. "I'm putting time on your calendar after the Vice Presidential selection to go back to the drawing board on your remarks."

"It's not too late, Diesel," said Jackson.

"I know that. We still have two full weeks before you take the stage in Philadelphia."

Jackson's voice became quiet. "That's not what I'm talking about. It's not too late for you to accept the offer..."

Diesel took a breath, steeled his spine, and turned to face his former House and Senate colleague. It was not easy refusing the offer last time. He had hoped Jackson would not continue to pressure him for a role Senator Browning had absolutely no interest in taking.

"Jackson, you're like a brother to me," Diesel reasoned. "There's no one else I'd rather fight for the destiny of the country with. But I can't accept. My place is in the trenches, working behind the scenes. That's where I can do the most good for the Bull Moose cause and your future presidency."

"Catherine agrees you would be one hell of a partner for me," said Jackson.

"And I am a partner as your campaign chairman. But the Vice Presidency is not a loyalty prize or a friendship medal. You need an intellectual equal and someone who adds dimension to your thinking. Most importantly, you need someone who wants to be the President in a crisis. We have thoroughly vetted the list, and one person is supremely qualified for this challenge. Someone who will add excitement to the ticket and fits this tall order." Diesel raised a single finger before his eyes. "One."

Jackson gave his friend a warm embrace. "Can't blame me for trying one more time," Jackson replied, touched by his friend's loyalty. "Thank you, Diesel. Your counsel means everything to me."

Downstairs in the dining room, Ron Bender leaned back in his chair, the midmorning sun shining brightly through the window over his furrowed brow. He and Ziggy were on a secret mission. He was seated at the antique 1968 Smith-Corona electric typewriter he found at a consignment shop in downtown Denver. This was his analog solution to avoiding putting their most consequential secrets on email or a computer since Tallahassee. Bender insisted they must assume Warner's goons at the FBI would be too happy to scoop up easily obtained digital records and pass them onto Warner to curry favor.

The letter Q was lazy on the typewriter; it did not always strike as strong as other letters. He was composing one final memo on the state of the race as he saw it before he had two candidates to manage full-time. This memo was unique. It was full of vituperation and tirades. It would certainly stand out.

"…attack Warner…"

"…expose Alvarez as a fraud…"

"…implicate inter-Party collusion…"

"…question Warner's credibility…"

Then he sat for a moment, pondering if he should add a warning line. He decided on the exact phrase. "This campaign remains considerably weak and susceptible to attack from President Warner on Jackson Piper's fear to take a stand on foreign financial assistance from Europe."

Ron removed the document with a zip from the typewriter roller and reviewed it one last time. He then marked the memo with a red CONFIDENTIAL stamp.

"Would you like me to spell-check that for you, Ron?" asked Ziggy. She could see his activity through her access to one of the room's cameras.

"Sure, and would you please file a copy of this in my confidential correspondence folder?"

"I would advise against that action. The folder is not encrypted. I see that you have removed password protections from that file. Is that an error, Ron?"

"No, Ziggy. It is not," said Ron.

"I would advise you that you are violating campaign protocols by storing a confidential memorandum in an exposed folder," said Ziggy.

"Duly noted," said Ron. He held the finished memo to the camera on the wall for Ziggy's capture, review, and filing as he had directed. He then folded the memo in thirds and walked with it towards the kitchen.

19

SAVE AMERICA

Eastward, the mid-June day had started warm but turned stormy by lunchtime. President Warner ignored Olivia's advice to move the event indoors. Wind tore at the bunting decorating the stage for his upcoming speech. Despite almost guaranteed Indiana electoral votes in November, the President's confidence waned, leading to bouts of paranoia and contemplation of extreme measures against Piper's popularity.

Olivia sought an audience that would restore the President's confidence. Fort Wayne, Indiana, offered a stronghold of support with minimal risk of Bull Moosers' opposition. It was an ideal location for launching Warner's General Election campaign.

Air Force One landed at Fort Wayne International Airport amid gales that challenged even veteran pilots. The President hurried down the aircraft stairs into his armored limousine, bound for his first stop before the rally.

The President was wrapping up a call as he exited the presidential motorcade at the first stop.

"...and, Senator, I detest loose ends. Detest them. They always come back to bite you in the ass. You would do yourself a lot of good to make sure there aren't any on this deal, you understand me?"

A portly woman in her fifties, dressed in a polyester pantsuit with heavily lined eyebrows and vivid pink lipstick, anxiously awaited him on the sidewalk. As the wind whipped around them, she hesitated whether to greet him immediately or let him finish his call.

"I don't care how you do it, but find a way to tie them up, understand? Tidy up your mess before you end up sinking both of us." The President handed the phone to Olivia Clay, captured his sailing tie, and buttoned his jacket. He leaned over to straighten his tie in his car window reflection.

"Fucking Senators could complicate a one-pony parade," said Warner aloud out of frustration.

"Congresswoman Blanche Hooper, Mr. President. It's an honor to welcome you to Fort Wayne," she said just as she had rehearsed it three dozen times the night before.

President Warner stopped fiddling with his necktie and turned to see Fort Wayne's Congresswoman with an outstretched hand. He frowned at her gaudy makeup. Olivia saw the scowl and corrected him by pulling her fingers into her cheeks.

"It's an honor to have you here, sir," the Congresswoman repeated.

He forced a smile. "Right. Thank you. My goodness, my apologies, Blanche. There is a bit of a problem with a Senator in our Party. You'd think our own Party would give me less grief given all my trouble with the Bull Moose...and the Others."

"Oh, don't apologize, sir. We are just honored you made the time to visit us. Please follow me inside the Fort Wayne Botanical Conservatory. It will be my honor to be your tour guide for this magical journey in Indiana's fauna, flowers, and foliage."

"Thank you, Congresswoman," said Warner politely, casting a look of vexation and annoyance at Olivia, who had skipped the tour to tend to more urgent matters.

The tour group approached tall glass doors at the entrance to the gardens. "Please allow me to brag for a moment, sir. I secured funding to expand this conservatory in the Economic Emergency Act of '39. The funds enabled us to expand the offerings to 35,000 square feet of indoor gardens. Right this way, sir. I hope the Secret Service took their allergy pills. Plenty of pollen ahead, sir."

President Warner pretended to be enthralled with plants for the first twenty minutes of the guided tour but started to yawn uncontrollably by minute 27. It was a test of focus and acting abilities to make it to the end and thank the congresswoman for her time.

Warner lit into Olivia Clay when they finally were alone again in his presidential car.

"A fucking garden, Olivia?" sneered President Warner.

"Hooper could be pivotal," she quickly snapped back, glancing up from her screen.

"That was forty minutes of my life. I'll never get back," he scoffed in irritation as he rubbed his tired face.

"Mr. President, it is not too early to assume we will face a Contingent Election in the House in January. You need all the allies you can get. Congresswoman Hooper could be a swing vote to keep Indiana in your column."

"But fucking plants, Olivia? Next time, make it a tour of plants inside of a strip club or a bank or a casino," said the President, smiling as the motorcade traveled to the second location.

"Duly noted, Mr. President," Olivia said, smiling at his salty humor.

The motorcade arrived at Miami Chief Richardville's historic brick home. Six individuals in traditional Native American attire waited on the sidewalk. Warner told Olivia to stay in the limousine during this stop; he would ensure it was brief. The President sprinted towards the small group, battling gusty winds that toyed with his tie. As he shook hands, the White House photographer immortalized the moment under grey clouds. They entered the home, escaping the storm outside.

Shortly after, Olivia received a message from Marco Alvarez.

> MARCO
> How is Indiana?

> **OLIVIA**
> The conservatory was a bore but good facetime with Hooper. I don't think he knows how much she is terrified of him.

How are you?

> Managing... =/

Will you be back to Washington in time for me to see you tonight?

Olivia began to type an answer that seemed to be too available. She opted for something more subtle.

> The President's schedule changes with a single word. Hard to say honestly.

THERE WAS A LONG PAUSE.

Did you press him on Brown yet?

She rolled her eyes in frustration. She was dreading a conversation about the Vice President.

> I will when his mood is right.

Time for him to see she is a drag at #2

She put her phone away and returned to her briefing papers from the U.S. Department of Agriculture on summer harvest yields, expected to be down 30 percent.

Inside the 1821 Greek Revival home, the six members of the Pokagon Band of Potawatomi Indians greeted the President in Fort Wayne. They highlighted Indiana's rich history and introduced Miami Chief Wildcat, who had once lived here.

"Decades before the home was built, Wildcat worked as a fur trader, supporting his family through trade with settlers," explained the eldest member. "Indiana Territory tribes had faced conflict with both British and French colonists. However, they negotiated the Treaty of Greenville after their defeat at the Battle of Fallen Timbers in 1794. This split the tribes: some opted for assimilation—adopting customs and language from the settlers—believing it best to make peace rather than continue bloody conflicts that would ultimately lead to losing their land."

"Sage men," said Warner, picking up a random vase in the dining room and looking inside it. A younger woman in the entourage turned her back to the President and rolled her eyes to her colleagues. President Warner began walking through the house, signaling he wanted to keep things moving.

The oldest man spoke, "On the other side of the divide were war chiefs like Tecumseh, who believed the land belonged to the Creator. The lands weren't theirs to negotiate or give away."

The President glanced at his watch, urging the group to speed up their tour and history lesson.

"Chief Wildcat was the last civil chief of the Miami people. The Treaty of Fort Wayne, also known among the tribes as the 10:00 Line Treaty was signed in 1809," continued the eldest man.

"Chief Little Turtle didn't trust the survey lines presented by William Henry Harrison. He insisted that a line be drawn based on a spear thrown at 10:00 am," added a committee member.

"The Treaty of Fort Wayne determined the fate of Indiana's tribes. These lands and lands west - three million acres - were given to the United States in exchange for strengthening Miami control in Northwest Indiana."

As they moved upstairs, they discussed Jean Richardville's successful treaty negotiations with the United States, which had personally enriched him.

"He was likely among the wealthiest men in the United States by 1840," said a woman. "And certainly the wealthiest Native person."

President Warner commented, "Obviously a shrewd businessman."

The oldest man frowned. "Our people see him as both the most skilled negotiator and deceitful leader of the Miami people. He enriched himself while many starved and begged for assistance."

A letter addressed to Chief Jean-Baptiste signed by then-governor of Indiana Territory, William Henry Harrison, lay at a small desk in an upstairs bedroom.

Holding it up to read its faded script, the President remarked, "This is remarkable."

"It was recently discovered among Mr. Richardville's belongings. It appears to bear your President's signature," said a woman.

"You mean our President? We're all Americans now," replied Warner.

"Our people weren't U.S citizens in 1840, nor could we choose our leader. He wasn't the Miami's President - he killed thousands as governor," retorted the youngest woman.

"To the victors go the spoils," said the President, rolling his eyes.

"I suppose," she replied with a cold stare.

He returned the letter to the woman, who placed it into a protective sheet on the desk.

The President walked swiftly to the rear passenger door of his limousine. A Secret Service agent opened the door, which weighed more than 70 pounds due to the thick bulletproof glass and armor inside the doorframe. He slammed it shut. The President waived to the gracious hosts as the motorcade sped off.

"Seventeen minutes, sir," said Olivia dryly.

He sighed in disappointment. "I failed to account for the history lesson that was to be included with the tour," said the President. "What was the fucking point of that stop?"

"Photo op with native peoples. It will play well with native peoples in vote-rich states that we might be able to swing to us in a three-person race."

The President did not object but quickly turned his attention to a briefing packet she handed him about his National Energy Corporation and profit-sharing package. The plan was to ramp up pressure on Congress to give him broader authority to form the entity, secure leases, and appoint the board.

Before he could delve deeper into it, Olivia brought up another item, and this one made him uneasy. She looked directly at him before speaking.

"There is another item, sir," Olivia said, looking directly at the President.

"Yes?" he said, peering at her over the tops of his reading glasses.

"Sir, I think it's time we discuss the Vice President's health."

He remained silent, waiting for her to continue.

"Her lack of campaign abilities right now is going to put you at a serious disadvantage to Drummond and Piper when they announce their running mates this month, sir," she insisted.

He couldn't deny her logic, but he struggled with what she seemed to be suggesting. "Olivia, the woman has cancer," said President Warner with surprising compassion. "She is fighting for her life. You want me to dump her?"

"And you are fighting for your political life, sir. There is no coming back from losing to Drummond and Piper. This could be the end of your career. These could be your final months in office if we don't get serious about the threat Jackson Piper poses to us. We need a stronger partner to help you punch back."

Her unusual insistence, contrary to his clear wishes, made him suspect something more was behind the argument. "We? Who is *we* in this scenario, Olivia? Are you talking about the *we* in the car or the *we* you think you're keeping from me by sneaking around with the Secretary of State?"

"Sir?" Her poker face didn't falter, but he sensed a hint of defiance in her tightening jaw.

"Fuck who you want, Olivia, but don't fuck me."

But she didn't take the bait.

"You need to keep your head in the game, and that brilliant mind of yours focused on winning this race. Consider carefully what you are suggesting. Marco Alvarez has pledged over a billion dollars of his fortune to us and our allies for me to win this election but asks for not a single policy change or legislative initiative. He may or may not be manipulating his proprietary software to fuck with news coverage of my opponents. I have appointed him Secretary of State, a confirmation vote he easily won with my help despite having no serious diplomatic credentials. Now, he wants to be a heartbeat away from the presidency. Are you loyal to me, or are you loyal to him, Olivia?"

"You, Mr. President, without question." Her heart raced at his accusations. She was suddenly unsure if she had been truthful in that answer.

He was slightly relieved but not entirely convinced. "Right. Well, lucky for you, Olivia, I think you are such an intelligent and capable person that I do not doubt for a moment that you could keep your loyalty to me and your interest in Marco sufficiently separate," said Warner. "Just do not allow him to force you to blur those lines."

Warner worried he might have said a bit too much at that moment, so he walked back his suspicions of Alvarez. "Olivia, to be clear, I agree that the Vice President's absence is troubling. We must make a decision soon. I will keep my word to Alvarez. The deal was to offer him the Vice Presidency if Brown would not serve, and I intend to keep my word."

They rode silently for the final two miles to the History Center on Berry Street in downtown Fort Worth, each lost in their own thoughts about upcoming decisions they would have to make.

Dark storm clouds rolled across the sky, casting a gloomy ambiance over the city. The air was thick and electrified. The forecast now called for heavy thunderstorms during the middle of Warner's speech. Olivia must make a call about the event's location, and given the prominence and importance of a presidential visit, tensions were high.

Exiting the motorcade, President Warner strode confidently to the doors of the History Center. It looked like a fortress built in the middle of the downtown. That was not by mistake; it once served as a fortress to keep people in when it was the city's jail for several decades before coming to the city center. Its rough-faced stone bricks were the color of mud. The high, thick archways above the topmost windows made it appear as if the building had cold, sad eyes eternally surveying the city.

As they entered, Mayor Harvey Schoolcraft greeted the presidential entourage. He welcomed them to the city, and after several dozen photographs and videos were taken to commemorate the occasion, Mayor Schoolcraft escorted the President to the main exhibit hall, where an exceptional display had been prepared in his honor.

The President approached a thick glass case surrounded by numerous informational display boards and glass display cases showing off two dozen or so artifacts.

"Mr. President, we are proud you chose to visit Fort Wayne. Presidential visits are a rich part of our history, and that all began with the Treaty of Fort Wayne that made Indiana statehood possible," said Mayor Schoolcraft.

"Thank you, Mayor. I'm honored to be here. Tell me more about the display you have so artfully prepared for our visit," said Warner. He was a master of false interest when he wanted to be. The truth was Russell Warner did not give two shits about history.

"Why sure, Mr. President. What we have here is the actual Treaty of Fort Wayne on loan from the Smithsonian. As you can see it bears the signatures of Tuthinipee, Winnemac, Richerville, and Little Turtle, as well as William Henry Harrison."

"Next, we have an amazing artifact. It is an 1810 transcription of the speech given by Shawnee Chief Tecumseh in August of that year questioning Native Chiefs' authority to concede the land of the Treaty. He delivered these remarks to then Governor William Henry Harrison himself," said the Mayor, delighted to have the two-hundred-thirty-four-year-old document so well preserved and legible.

The group continued to walk down the line of glass cases. Olivia had moved ahead of the group, half-mindedly taking in the display the city had spent so long curating. Her mind wandered on how to speak with Marco about the President's concerns. She stopped before a display case with raised wooded lettering: "Presidential Visitors." Inside the case were photos of Presidents with documented visits to

Fort Wayne before or during their terms in office. First was a drawing of William Henry Harrison, which was dated 1809. Next was a famous photo of Abraham Lincoln, with the date of his visit estimated to be during Lincoln's youth. Then President James Garfield. She removed her phone from her pocket to see if Marco had messaged. Nothing. Should she message him, she wondered?

Who was this bald fat man? President William McKinley, she read. She did not recall much about his presidency from history classes in high school. Another face she did not recognize was next - President Warren Harding. She had no idea he had even been President. She felt embarrassed to be the Chief of Staff to the President and be so undereducated about presidential history. But she took comfort in recognizing the next four faces - Franklin Roosevelt, John F. Kennedy, Richard Nixon, and Ronald Regan. She surely knew each of them. The final photo was of President Trump. He had been the last President to visit Fort Wayne. An impressive list. Why Fort Wayne, she thought to herself. So far, the city had felt quiet, subdued, and lacking in action. Perhaps that was the reason for their visits - an escape from the hellfire of the White House to walk among the mundane. She returned to the President's side.

"This is the second time I've heard about this Temcumseh fellow today. Seemed to be a real hell raiser - a thorn in the side of Harrison, am I right?" asked Warner.

"Indeed. So much so that he and his brother provoked Harrison into attacking their federation's primary settlement in Prophetstown. It was a disaster for the duo. Their federation never recovered from the crushing blow that Tippecanoe delivered," said the mayor.

"Tippie-who?" asked Warner. He found history a bore.

"Tippecanoe. Oh, that was the nickname for President William Henry Harrison. The Battle of Tippecanoe was what they called that defeat of the Indian Federation at Prophetstown," explained a bookish historian along for the tour. "A bit of American propaganda. President Monroe needed a military victory, so that's what they repackaged the Battle of Tippecanoe to be. And a legend was born."

Olivia's phone vibrated in her pocket. She retrieved it. Nothing. It was the other phone in her other pocket, the one issued by the Department of Defense. It was highly secure and only utilized when a pressing matter of national security was at hand. She read the message on the screen, grabbed the President by the arm, and gave him a look of urgent alarm.

"If you'll excuse us, Mr. Mayor, I must take this call from the Secretary of Defense. I wouldn't want to miss his call," said Warner.

The dignitaries understood as President Warner and Olivia Clay stepped aside to take a call from the Secretary.

"Mr. President, we have a matter of significant concern that requires your attention. U.S. forces charged with guarding the southern U.S. border are being provoked by a mob of at least a thousand asylum seekers attempting to cross into Texas."

"I see," Warner said. "Are my orders not clear, sir?"

"Sir, these are unarmed civilians. Half of them women and children."

"The order, Mr. Secretary, is to shoot to kill any hostile attempting to cross into the United States," said Warner.

"Mr. President, the U.S. military is not authorized to murder innocent..."

"They are not innocent if they are attempting to invade our country, Mr. Secretary. Shoot. To. Kill. Pick off a few of the men first. I suspect it will send the message we are not fucking around here," Warner said.

"Yes, sir. Understood. Sir, I will express my grave concern about executing such an order," said the Secretary of Defense. Warner hung up the phone before the Secretary could explain further.

"What a pussy," said Warner. "When will I find true leaders to serve in my government who understand what it takes to lead this country away from the weakness and whining that has diminished it for so long?"

A heavy rain began to pour outside. The decision to move the event inside was no longer Olivia's to make, but she had more pressing matters on her mind.

20

THE TICKET

The Texas sun scorched the earth, a relentless sentinel in the clear sky as Jackson Piper stepped out of the security vehicle and onto the arid grounds of the Governor's private family ranch. This was his first stop after leaving Denver a day ago.

"Jackson," said Governor Lawrence. His name in her Texas drawl sounded like the crack of a whip, yet not without a particular affection. She stood on the porch of her stately home, her silhouette sharp against the blinding backdrop of the midday sun. Jackson noticed the famed leather holster on her hip containing the Colt .45 custom-made revolver she wore during her official Texas duties dealing with an antagonistic Texas state legislature. Her Party decried the brandishing of a weapon, but her opponents understood wearing the gun was a physical manifestation of the state's 1985 anti-littering slogan that took on a life of its own: Don't Mess With Texas.

It didn't hurt that she was also the best shot among any of the states' governors. She had the Olympic gold medals to prove it.

"Governor Lawrence," Jackson replied, tipping an invisible hat as he ascended the steps to join her. "Perhaps you should have been wearing that on the day Warner had you arrested," indicating the silver and gold six-shooter.

The Texas Governor gave a sinister laugh. "It was probably better I wasn't. It might have given them a reason to blow a hole in me and dump my body in the Gulf."

"Thank you for agreeing to meet with me, Governor," he said, extending his hand. She reached for his hand, returning the gesture with a surprisingly firm and muscled grip. "I keep forgetting you were an Olympian."

Valerie smiled. "*Oui*, Paris was beautiful that year." Valerie was the physical embodiment of strength and resilience. Her firm grip provided instantaneous comfort and stability, letting Jackson know she was there for him. Her beauty was uncommon for a governor; it was distracting and exciting. He did not yet have a good read on her insecurities or fears.

"Let's walk," she suggested. Leaving both their security details behind on her home's secure grounds, she led him down the porch's wooden steps and onto a path that wove through the fields of dry, golden grass.

"I never got to properly thank you for helping to negotiate my release," she said warmly. The morning Texas sun glistened in her shimmering blonde hair.

Jackson explained his actions. "All I did was file to remove my name from the remaining Primaries. It was a symbolic gesture since most of the deadlines had passed. It was designed to push President Warner's loyal Justice Department to drop the bogus charges against you. Unsurprisingly, it was a gesture lost on Warner, who remains outraged that I remain in the race."

"Still, a federal judge dismissed the charges against me, but no apology ever came from the White House or the Attorney General," she scoffed.

"I wouldn't hold your breath for that one," said Jackson. Both of them understood that for Warner's base of voters, especially the Warriors, Valerie Lawrence had not been dealt with firmly enough.

"So, what brings the handsome and famous Jackson Piper to Texas today?" Valerie asked. She bit her lip. She wondered if her kindness was becoming too informal.

"If you're this charming with the Texas legislature, it's no wonder you have them eating out of your hand," Jackson joked.

"I'm not this kind to everyone. Besides, kindness only gets you so far in Texas," she said, patting her pistol grip.

As they walked side by side, the only sound was the crunch of their footsteps and the distant call of a hawk in search of its midday meal. Jackson took in the land around them—its untamed beauty—and thought of how its beautiful simplicity reflected Valerie herself.

"Governor, I won't mince words," Jackson began, taking on a more serious tone. "I am honored by the price you have paid, standing by my side throughout this campaign."

Valerie's gaze remained fixed on the horizon. "I've made no secret of my frustrations with your former Party," she said, the lines around her eyes deepening. "They let me out to dry when people started calling me all sorts of hateful names." She rolled through a few of them. "Bitch-in-Chief. Machine-Gun-Governor. Crazy Valentine."

"I'm sorry I never came to your defense," said Jackson.

"Oh, hun, you were retired to Denver by the time all that was going down," she said, dismissing his apology. "And when it comes to standing by you and Catherine, that's easy. It's the execution that can get sticky," she said, feeling her head where the scar of the months before was still perceptible with her fingertips.

"I came down here today to ask you to form an alliance," Jackson asserted, watching a dust devil dance across the field before dissipating as quickly as it had formed. "One that could be the catalyst for change across the country."

"An alliance?" Valerie echoed thoughtfully, her hands clasped behind her back. "I have never been asked to join an alliance, Jackson. Are there disguises? Hideouts?" she joked.

Piper grinned but did not laugh at the joke. At times, most people mistook the danger of this particular moment in the history of the Republic. Jackson could see it, though others could not. He believed Russell Warner and Marco Alvarez played a dangerous game beyond just trying to win an election.

"I am proposing an alliance of principles, loyalty, and action,"

Jackson countered, his shadow stretching long beside hers on the ground with the rising Texas sun. "I need a leader who understands what Bull Moose stands for at their core. I need a leader whose intentions will never become more personal than strategic in executing our agenda. And I need a leader of courage and decisive action."

Governor Lawrence stopped walking, turning to face Jackson squarely. Her eyes were the color of the sharp Texas sky, unwavering and clear. "What are you asking me to do, Jackson?"

"I am asking you to be my Vice President," he said with a smile.

"Lawdy," she murmured, the word rolling off her tongue like a song. The wind picked up, ruffling the hem of her tailored jacket, carrying the scent of sagebrush with it.

"Governor, think of the impact you could have as we reform government and restore the standing of America in the world as a leader. You could rewrite the role of the Vice President," Jackson continued, his heart pounding with the urgency of their cause. "A genuine alliance where each of us is as strong as the other, each of us faithful to the other, and each committed to a clear path forward for the nation."

"Jackson Piper," Valerie said, her tone softening as she considered him—a man driven by faith and principle, even when it demanded crossing the treacherous divide of ideology. "You're asking for a great deal of trust. And I don't give mine easily."

"Nor should you," he acknowledged, meeting her gaze. "But you have come to know me better than many these past five months, Val. I've learned not to back down from a fight for what's right, and I never will again."

She looked out over her land once more, contemplating the vast expanse that mirrored the magnitude of their undertaking. "I want some assurances first."

"What are they?" asked Jackson.

She resumed their walk, kicking the stones on the path with her freshly oiled leather boots.

"Half of this great nation is made up of women. Half of the voters likely to deliver you the presidency will be women. So I want you to promise that half the Cabinet will be women. Half of your presidential appointments to lead agencies and the military will be women. The best qualified, of course, but I want us to seek out and elevate women as leaders."

Jackson nodded in agreement.

Valerie continued. "And pledge that you will work to recruit more women to run for Congress, and you will help them win in 2046 and after," she asserted firmly.

"This campaign has been missing a strong female voice from Jump Street," said Piper. "I am certain you will be a vital partner in finding and supporting these leaders. You have the energy to make up for lost time if you join me."

"Like a horny bull out the chute," she said, laughing.

"Did Reese Tulson coach you before I got here?" asked Jackson.

Valerie smiled quizzically at Jackson as they walked. "Governor Tulson?" she asked, confused. "No, sir. She did not."

"You've done your homework then," he said. "We will pick the most qualified leaders willing to serve the nation and work together as President and Vice President to secure half of the nominees to be the best women for the job. And I will not silence or mute your voice in the next six months or four years. I will amplify it. And we will work together to bring more women forward to lead in Congress, the military, and state governments. You have my word. Next?"

"The border and immigration is a mess; there is no doubt about it, sir. I deal with it daily as governor. I want your commitment to humanely responding to immigration and our borders. Not this atrocious human rights nightmare Warner and his Warriors have devised. We need a strong domestic policy and a better foreign policy. Policies that create sustainability for border states. At the same time, I want us to renew our involvement in the Organization of American States to address poverty, climate, health, human rights, and democratic reforms in the nations these folks are fleeing," said Valerie.

"Done. You can write that into the Party Platform if you like," he said.

"No, your word is sufficient for me, Jackson," she said.

"Next?" he asked.

"The six-shooter is part of the package. Part of my brand. I will do my part to educate people about my sport, my right, and why many Americans respect their right to bear arms as strongly as their right to worship their own God and speak their minds."

"I doubt the Secret Service will allow the weapon to be worn in most places," said Piper skeptically.

"It's rarely loaded, and I will be selective about it. The point is I will not stop being the woman I am. I love my God, my husband Parker, and my family. I love my country, Texas, and the Constitution, and I won't change who I am to make others feel comfortable."

"I think showing people it's time to be uncomfortable with how things are going is the point of the Bull Moose, right?" said Piper.

She looked into his eyes and saw a rare clarity and sincerity among men in their line of work. Most would lie to your face to get what they wanted. Jackson was different in so many ways.

"Last assurance. Ready?" she asked playfully. They had reached a Cedar Elm near the edge of the horse pastures. Its buttery yellow leaves provided the perfect shade to watch the colts and foals play in the fields. She stopped under the shade of the elm.

"I am," said Jackson.

"Each time you are called upon as President to make a consequential choice - I'm talking negotiating with Congress, deploying troops, or responding to our enemies or allies, I need to be a trusted partner. I want access to the same information you have, and I want to be the last person in the room before you decide."

"May I ask why?" asked Jackson.

"You said this is to be an alliance. I want my voice and advice in your head, and I want to learn from you. I want to understand better how you process information and arrive at decisions so I can have zero fear or regrets about supporting you when things get rough. And if I am ever called upon to succeed you, I want no daylight between us."

"You ever thought about running for President?" asked Jackson.

Valerie looked Jackson in the eye and smiled. "Since I was knee high to a grasshopper bouncing on my daddy's knee."

"Then you understand the presidency is unlike anything else on earth. It will age us. Sap us of our vitality and test our faith in humanity and God," he said with an air of warning.

"And it will give us a tremendous platform to do great works. Improve lives. And it could restore our faith in humanity and God," she said firmly.

"You are something special, Val," said Jackson, smiling at her in the blazing Texas sun. "Before you agree, I want you to hear from me directly about what we are up against."

Valerie grew serious. "Senator Piper, I hope my brutal arrest and stint in a jail cell has already proved I know what we are up against from President Warner."

"It's not Warner we need to worry about. As I shared with you in Charleston several months ago, I firmly believe Marco Alvarez is bankrolling President Warner's reelection, but not simply to add another pelt to his wall. I believe Marco Alvarez himself desires to be President. He may be pushing Warner to name him as his running mate at their convention."

Valerie looked into Jackson's eyes. In them, she saw honesty and vulnerability - someone asking for help. She also saw deep conviction and focus. "Alright, Jackson," she finally consented, a slow nod sealing her commitment. "I'll join your alliance. I accept your offer to be the Bull Moose nominee for Vice President."

"Outstanding!" Jackson smiled, gripping her outstretched hand.

"Yeehaw!" she hollered, jumping up and down and wrapping her arms around him, unable to contain her exuberance at moving a step closer to her childhood dream. After the brief celebration, they resumed their walk, each step taking them further from the people they once were and closer to the leaders of the nation they aimed to be.

21

CURSED REVELATIONS

Weighed down by the responsibility of leading a presidential campaign, Jackson leafed through stacks of papers on the private plane – analog messages to avoid intercepting sensitive information. The assumption was that both rival Parties engaged in campaign espionage.

As the plane banked, folders slid, scattering paper memos across the cabin floor.

"Son of a bitch!" shouted Jackson.

Libby held up the missing memo, prepared on Ron Bender's antique typewriter. Adjusting his reading glasses, Jackson skimmed its contents.

Dated May 30, 2044—nearly three weeks ago—it noted that while initial conversions to the Bull Moose Party exceeded expectations, new registrations had fallen by 40% over the previous week. With the convention still weeks away, enthusiasm seemed to wane for this nascent political force.

Jackson sighed in frustration. Warner's "Save America" message wasn't winning undecided voters, but Drummond's lackluster performance left others uninspired. A recent national poll showed Drummond and Piper slipping behind Warner, who led despite an army of undecided voters.

National Poll:(+-4%)
  Warner 40%
  Piper 22%
  Drummond 19%
  Undecided 19%

Piper set the memo aside and took off his glasses. Their strategy had to focus on a Warner versus Piper contest, eliminating Drummond as a viable option for undecided voters. The campaign's internal polling revealed that these undecided voters held the power to sway the election based on their concerns about the nation's economy and America's declining global status.

Warner's revamped campaign theme of Save America aimed to capitalize on these fears, though it was ambiguous who or what posed the threat. Bender emphasized that national polls didn't accurately reflect each state's individual campaigns. Winning 274 electoral votes from a few states could secure the presidency, even if a candidate only had 29 percent of the popular vote nationwide.

As such, local issues sometimes held more sway than national sentiments when competing in the Electoral College and potentially in a Contingent Election in the House of Representatives.

"Let's get aligned with Ron on this, but I'm thinking after our meetings on the Hill, we should take one more look at the Convention speech," said Jackson. "I just don't feel like we're there yet."

"Yes, sir," Libby said dutifully.

"How're the plans for the platform coming?" he inquired.

"It's been a lively online debate so far, sir. I'm moderating an economic panel right now," she said as she typed on her computer.

The small plane banked again, tipping Piper's briefcase off a table and spilling the contents everywhere. Staring up at him was a tattered book cover with dark red lettering. The book was thin but filled with plastic tabs and dogeared pages. It was the book Reese Tulson had given to him at the conclusion of his last visit. The title - *Fateful Conjunction: The Curse of Tippecanoe* - stared up at him ominously from the floor.

Jackson stirred cream into his hot cup of coffee. Campaign staff buzzed throughout the plane as they prepared for the big reveal in Nashville of Valerie Lawrence. Jackson scanned his phone for one contact in particular and dialed the phone.

"Hello?" answered a shaky voice.

"Governor, it's Jack," said the presidential aspirant into the phone. "Wonderful to hear your voice."

She wasted no time laying into him. "Bull Moose, huh?" she questioned immediately.

Piper rolled his eyes and leaned back in his seat. "It sounds like you don't approve, Reese," replied Jackson, disappointed.

"You gave up on our Party too quickly. They would have come around."

"They changed the rules, Reese," said Jackson, tired of revisiting a useless question.

"Fuck the rules, sonny. You could have gotten them overruled on the convention floor," she retorted sharply.

"Doubtful, Reese, and you know it. And what did you say all the time? Woulda, coulda, shoulda ain't never changed nothin," he said, using her own words against her.

She ignored the rebuke. "You should have broken more backs in The Party. Made them succumb to your will. You're running for President. They should have been licking your boots, Jack!"

Jackson's heart broke, and his fragile confidence in this strategy began to spin. "I'm sorry to hear you're not on board," said Jackson. The enthusiasm evaporated from his voice.

"Calm down," she groaned. "I changed my registration to Bull Moose, dear." She closed her eyes and took a deep breath. She was relieved to receive his call and get her worry off her chest.

"So you've picked a Vice President? Revealing the selection tomorrow? Should have had her in place by now, son," said Reese, scolding him.

"Her?" he said with surprise.

"You are picking a woman, right? You have to pick a woman if you want to win this, Jackson. You're a stunner, a brain, but women want to know you respect them. Pick a woman who is your equal. Show them you're not afraid of a sharp, fierce number two who could beat you if she wanted to. Please don't tell me you picked that pothead Diesel."

Jackson rubbed his face with his hand. Would the constant assaults ever end?

"I promise to consider that advice fully, Reese," said Piper, who then grew silent, not wishing to give up too much over the phone, never knowing who could be listening.

"Fair enough," she smiled, laughing, then coughing violently. After the coughing subsided, she asked, "Did you read the book I gave you?" she asked.

He looked at the book in his hand like it was a loaded weapon. He admitted he had not yet got around to reading it.

Her lips drew into a frown. "You're still focused on the wrong opponent, Jack. Since you have refused to do the homework for nine months, let me give you the cliff notes version of the Curse of Tippecanoe."

This is the story that Reese Tulson told Jackson Piper as he flew from Austin to Nashville:

WILLIAM HENRY HARRISON, the expansionist and pro-slavery governor of the Indiana Territory, oversaw a vast region acquired through war spoils from Great Britain and the 1795 Treaty of Greenville. Established by the Northwest Ordinance of 1787, the territory encompassed modern-day Indiana, Illinois, Wisconsin, Michigan, and Minnesota.

Following the Treaty of Greenville, Ohio, Shawnee settled in Wapakoneta under the leadership of Chief Black Hoof. Simultaneously, Miamis resided at the Eel River led by warrior Chief Little

Turtle. Both chiefs encouraged their tribes to adapt to American customs for a peaceful coexistence.

As territorial governor, Harrison's duties included enforcing the Treaty of Greenville and securing land titles from native tribes for further expansion. His approach went beyond mere diplomatic requests for territory acquisition.

Among the Shawnee was a great warrior and gifted orator, Tecumseh. He believed that white expansion threatened his people's traditional way of life, rejecting the teachings of adaptation by Chief Black Hoof. Tecumseh had fought under Chief Blue Jacket at the Battle of Fallen Timbers, and he refused to sign or abide by the Treaty signed by Blue Jacket.

At the peace conference, Tecumseh argued that the land in question did not belong to any tribe but was merely shared with them by their creator. Unwilling to negotiate from a position of weakness, he left the conference determined to unite tribes against further white encroachment.

Tecumseh led a band of 50 warriors and around 250 people, along with his sister, who served as their principal female chief. Although gaining recognition for his oratory skills, he had yet to rise to a prominent status among Americans. His group moved frequently before settling near present-day Anderson, Indiana.

His younger brother Lalawethika, a skilled orator lacking in warrior abilities, lived nearby. Struggling with alcohol addiction like many other tribe members affected by various treaties and proximity to whites, Lalawethika nearly died one night in 1805. After surviving this ordeal, he swore off alcohol and shared with others a powerful vision from the Master of Life during his coma.

In the vision, he was shown Heaven; in it, the native tribes of the Americas lived by the old ways. Then he was shown hell, populated with "civilized" native tribes who had adopted the ways of the white men and, perhaps ironically, were also addicted to white man alcohol.

Lalawethika became a prophet and holy man to the Shawnee and gained a following. At this time, Tecumseh was known as the brother of Lalawethika since Lalawethika had a higher stature and a more significant following among the region's tribes.

More indigenous peoples died, and whether by chance or by design, followers of Lalawethika started to blame witchcraft brought by the whites for the deaths. There is no evidence the Shawnee had any direct knowledge of the Salem Witch Trials conducted by white settlers to the Americas two hundred years prior.

In 1805, after a brush with death due to alcohol, Lalawethika became Tenskwatawa, meaning "The Prophet," and started observing the stars for guidance. In 1806, he accurately predicted a solar eclipse, which ignited enthusiasm among various tribes and expanded his influence.

By 1808, Tecumseh and Tenskwatawa established Prophetstown, and Tecumseh traveled extensively to unite a powerful tribal confederacy. However, not all were convinced of his ability to withstand conflict with the whites. Tecumseh publicly denounced a new Treaty as a sham but failed to prevent its signing.

Governor William Henry Harrison recognized Tecumseh's growing influence and oratory prowess. In 1809, Harrison negotiated the Treaty of Fort Wayne, mainly with Miami chiefs willing to exchange land for personal payments. Afterward, Tecumseh confronted the governor to challenge the Miami tribe's authority to sell any land to the whites.

The words spoken by Tecumseh on August 20, 1810, were ominous: he accused Governor Harrison of killing members of various tribes, taking their land, and inciting divisions among the Native Americans by treating them as separate groups instead of respecting their unity. Tecumseh criticized the practice of making distinctions and agreements with individual chiefs, leading to unfair land sales and internal strife. He argued that only the warriors should handle their affairs, not the chiefs selling their lands to Americans under coercion or manipulation.

Tecumseh warned Harrison that if the land was not restored, it would lead to war among the tribes and against the white people. Tecumseh called for genuine respect and consideration for his people's requests. But he warned that the Chiefs who gave away their lands would be killed for their crimes if an agreement with Harrison could not be reached.

"Uh oh. That doesn't sound good," said Piper.

Reese ignored him and continued.

In spring 1811, Congress urged its territorial governor, Harrison, to take action against Tecumseh and The Prophet's growing native confederacy. In the summer, Tecumseh requested a meeting with Harrison to maintain the status quo while away meeting other chiefs. Mistaking Harrison's demeanor for restraint, Tecumseh left his lands vulnerable.

Harrison assembled around a thousand infantry and militia members, marching north along the Wabash River toward Prophetstown. This part is key: Harrison had orders from President Madison's Secretary of War to remove the Indians from their land by force if necessary.

As they approached Prophetstown on November 6, The Prophet - Tenskwatawa - requested a parlay conference involving Chief Tecumseh. Aware that Tecumseh was far away recruiting tribes for his federation, Harrison recognized this as a delay tactic. He agreed to negotiate the next day but secretly planned to attack. Harrison positioned his forces on a hill near the village, ordering them into a defensive formation with full alertness.

Throughout the night on November 6 into the morning of November 7, 1811, The Prophet stood atop a rock on the edge of Prophetstown overlooking the encamped American soldiers. He shouted spells and curses at the white men and prayers to the Master of Life.

First, he is said to have cast a spell of courage so that no man would be fearful of confronting the white man in defense of the city.

Then, Tenskwatawa prayed for the Master of Life to bring the warriors who would die in the coming battle and the women and children the whites murdered to heaven to be with the Master of Life.

Third, The Prophet said he was casting a spell of protection over the tribes so their warriors would not be susceptible to wounds by the muskets of the white army.

Then, The Prophet shouted curses at the white army and its commander. If the Indian warriors failed to defend the city, then every white man who set his feet on the rock on which he stood shall be cursed. He called on the Master of Life to send the Great Fire Sisters to meet in the Southern Sky to deliver this retribution when the offenders least expected it, making it more painful and devastating. The Prophet, in his fury, proclaimed that the Great Fire Sisters would return and deliver their punishment until the rightful protectors of this land were vindicated.

The Prophet's curses and spells echoed like thunder over the fields and through the forest for hours. Finally, the Indian warriors were so agitated and convinced of The Prophet's mystical protection that they mounted a disorganized pre-dawn assault on the Harrison forces.

At first, the poorly defended encampment of the Harrison forces was surprised by the assault concealed by darkness and suffered heavy casualties. But as dawn turned into morning, Harrison and his commanders were able to repel the attack and mount a counteroffensive successfully. Harrison did not stop by simply repelling the advancing warriors. Instead, he ordered his troops to charge forward into the forest and the huts and paths of Prophetstown, ransacking it and burning the encampment to the ground.

Several of the Harrison soldiers reported seeing Harrison mount Prophet's Rock, from which he surveyed the attack on the town until the last of the three thousand natives disappeared in retreat to the forest.

The battle was a near disaster for Harrison, with a casualty rate approaching 50 percent. Had the tribes at Prophetstown been led by Tecumseh that day, a more capable military leader than his brother, the tribes may have been able to maintain control of Prophetstown. The warriors who believed that the Prophet had cast spells of protection on them saw half of their fellow warriors fall at the hand of white muskets and blades. They decried The Prophet as a fraud and fled north towards Canada.

President James Madison was eager for a military victory and to repackage the Shawnee's aggression as the result of British interference and instigation to sell Congress on a new war with Great Britain. Newspapers in Ohio picked up the story, rebranded the siege of Prophetstown as the Battle of Tippecanoe, and proclaimed Major General William Henry Harrison a hero despite the high casualties for such an inconsequential piece of land.

In the Spring of 1812, Tecumseh returned from the south to discover Prophetstown empty and burned. He cursed William Henry Harrison and the Americans for their continued illegal seizure of native lands. He would follow his splintered tribe north to Canada and join the British forces in their coming war against the United States. Congress declared war on Great Britain in June, and the War of 1812 was underway.

The curse The Prophet cast on the field on November 7 and that William Henry Harrison tempted when he mounted Prophet's Rock became evident in the 30 years that followed. When tracking Harrison's path after leaving Prophetstown, one must look at key events in what remained of his life. Let's theorize the Great Fire Sisters of the Southern Sky to be the great conjunction of the planets Jupiter and Saturn, which are visible in the sky and appear in a regular conjunction every 19.5 years over the skies of North America.

"So you're saying The Prophet and Tecumseh cursed William Henry Harrison?" asked Jackson.

Reese continued as if Jackson had not asked a question:

Harrison would experience the death of six of his ten children. He would lose two presidential appointments and fail at a third. Between 1819 and 1824, he lost every office he sought.

Out of opposition to President Andrew Jackson and his chosen successor, Vice President Martin Van Buren, Harrison allowed himself to be one of four regional Party candidates of the Whig Party in 1836 to keep Van Buren from securing a majority in the Electoral

College. Of the four Whig candidates, only Harrison was on enough state ballots to have a mathematical chance at winning a majority in the Electoral College.

When the election arrived and the votes were counted, Van Burren received a slight majority in the popular vote of 1.5 million total voters. Still, the Electoral College tally was really what mattered. The race came down to Pennsylvania, which had 30 Electoral College votes.

Out of 178,692 votes cast, Van Buren had edged out Harrison by just 4,222 votes. But for that edge, the opponents to Van Buren would have been successful in denying Van Buren a majority and would have forced a Contingent Election for the presidency.

However, President Jackson's opponents successfully forced a contingent election for the Vice Presidency after the controversial Jacksonian Democratic nominee, Senator Richard Johnson of Kentucky, fell one vote short of an electoral majority.

Richard Johnson had openly acknowledged he had taken one of his slaves as a mistress and had fathered several of her children. He made a dubious claim to have been the man who had slain Tecumseh in the War of 1812. His campaign slogan in 1836 has been "Rumpsey, Dumpsey, Colonel Johnson Killed Tecumseh!"

On February 8, 1837, by a vote of 33-16, the Senate selected Johnson as Van Buren's Vice President. Harrison had come close to forcing a Contingent Election for president but ultimately lost again. Harrison returned to Ohio and resumed his job as the Clerk of Court.

A fourth Harrison child died in 1838, and then a fifth died in 1839. Half of all the children of Anne and William Henry Harrison had now died since 1817.

In the winter of 1839, the Whig Party convened in Harrisburg, Pennsylvania, aiming to defeat Van Buren. For the 1840 election, they sought a single presidential nominee. After four ballots with Henry Clay leading but lacking a majority, delegates shifted support to William Henry Harrison, who secured the nomination on the fifth ballot. To balance the "northern" Harrison, "southern" gentleman and former Clay supporter Senator John Tyler of Virginia was chosen as Vice President. The song "Tip & Ty" birthed the campaign slogan "Tippecanoe and Tyler, Too," evoking Harrison's exploits at Prophetstown and his alliance with Tyler.

This time, the Whigs easily defeated President Van Buren. Harrison achieved 53 percent of the popular vote but gave Van Buren a thrashing in the Electoral College - 234-60.

Harrison took the oath of office for the Presidency just as the Jupiter-Saturn conjunction was beginning to reform in the southern sky. And this, Jackson, is the foundation of the Curse of Tippecanoe. Having never made right the theft of the lands from the Treaty of Fort Worth, the Southern Sisters fulfilled The Prophet's curse made at Prophet's rock every twenty years.

Beginning in 1840, every American Chief - i.e., President - elected during the return of the Jupiter-Saturn conjunction died in office.

"Reese, this sounds like a load of mumbo-jumbo," said Jackson.

"Does it?" she asked indignantly. "Then go through the list with me, smartass."

"Ok, 1840. William Henry Harrison died 30 days into his term as President, and Vice President Tyler became the President," he said.

"Right, then 1860?"

"Abraham Lincoln is elected," said Jackson.

"And he was assassinated in 1865, making Andrew Johnson the President. What about 1880?"

"James Garfield," said Jackson uneasily.

"Yes, and he's shot in the back by an assassin the first year in office, making Vice President Chester Arthur the President."

"Well, then, next is 1900," said Jackson. "Son of a bitch..."

"William McKinley was reelected in 1900 and died when he was shot in the abdomen the following year," said Reese.

Jackson's mouth dropped open, "And Theodore Roosevelt became President."

"Look at 1920 - Warren Harding dies before the end of his term, and Vice President Calvin Coolidge becomes the President; in 1940,

Franklin Roosevelt is reelected for a third time, and he dies of heart failure in 1945, making Harry Truman the President."

"And 1960 is John Kennedy. Reese, this is some creepy shit!" said Jackson.

"I know it is," said Reese.

"But the theory of any Indian curse goes belly up in 1980. Reagan didn't die in office," said Jackson.

"Correct, but a bullet came within an inch of stopping his heart, fired by John Hinckley," said Reese. "Maybe that broke the curse. Maybe those Presidents killed by 1960 were enough blood to satisfy the curse? I don't have an answer as to why the curse stopped with Reagan."

"So why are you so worried about Russell Warner and Jessica Brown?"

"Warner was elected during the 200th anniversary of Harrison's election. And I happen to know that the conjunction of Saturn and Jupiter was back in Virgo that year and occurred on Halloween," said Reese.

"You sound like a crazy old woman who has spent too much time alone in her giant house, Reese," joked Jackson.

"And now my last piece of evidence that Russell Warner is a dead man walking - he went back to the scene of the crime last week. He was in Fort Wayne, Indiana!" exclaimed Reese.

"Governor, I think I have had enough ghost stories for one flight. We are making a final approach into Nashville. Be sure to watch tomorrow to find out who I have selected as Vice President."

She giggled, "Tell Governor Lawrence hello for me! I look forward to meeting her."

"It's not Governor Lawrence, Reese," said Jackson.

"Right..." said Reese Tulson, unconvinced. "If you want to make me proud, it better be!" She laughed again hysterically before breaking into a hoarse cough and ended the call.

The deafening cheers of the crowd in Nashville still rang in their ears as former Pennsylvania Senator Jackson Piper and Texas Governor Valerie Lawrence strode off the stage, their adrenaline pumping and spirits soaring. The announcement of Lawrence as Piper's running mate had sent shockwaves through the political community, and they could feel the electrifying energy that their partnership had ignited.

"Did you see their faces, Jackson?" Valerie exclaimed as they hurried towards the motorcade, which was waiting outside. "We took them by complete surprise – they never saw it coming!"

Jackson laughed, his eyes gleaming with pride. "You were magic, Governor." He yielded at the open SUV door, allowing his newly minted partner to climb first into the vehicle with a victorious grin. The Texas governor wore her signature custom six-shooter on her hip, symbolizing her tough, no-nonsense persona that had won her many admirers and fierce critics.

"Damn, Jackson, this feels incredible!" Valerie's eyes alight with excitement as the motorcade leaped forward on its route to the airport.

Jackson laughed, his heart racing with anticipation. He knew they were an unconventional pairing, but every instinct told him they needed to harness electricity to jolt the nation to life in time to protect itself from the wolves at the door. "We're going to shake things up, Governor, that's for damn sure. Libby, what's the word from the press? Are they as stunned as the audience was?" Jackson asked, turning to her in the backseat.

"Absolutely," Libby replied, scrolling through her phone with a satisfied smile. "The headlines are calling you a 'surprise pick out of center field,' and political commentators are predicting that your addition to the Bull Moose ticket will again electrify the race."

Valerie arched an eyebrow, clearly pleased by the news. "Well, I do love a good fight," she drawled with a grin. "I reckon it's high time we put our opponents on their heels."

In the confines of the truck, the atmosphere was electric, an intoxicating mix of hope and ambition. Moments like this provided belief that there remained a chance of turning the tide of the election in their favor. And yet, once the energy of the moment subsided, there would be a pervasive feeling of uncertainty as they continued to fight an incumbent president well ahead in the polls and use every gear of government to cement his advantage further.

Jackson was the first to have that sense of unease return in his gut, even as he exchanged banter with his new running mate and their team. He did not know what it was, but something inside made him feel like the dark clouds were about to return.

22

FORMER FRIEND

June 24, 2044: 138 Days to Election Day
   National Poll: (+-5%)
   Warner 36%
   Piper 26%
   Drummond 20%
   Undecided 18%

The morning sun streamed through Sterling Power's office's high windows, casting a geometric dance of light and shadow across the expanse of plaster and lush carpet. The Majority Whip's domain in the Hart Senate Office Building was a testament to influence, its expansive walls lined with a photographic record of the Michigan Senator's achievements and heavy shelves of legal tomes and political artifacts.

"Senator?" A soft knock at the door interrupted Powers' thoughts. A Senate aid indicated the expected visitors had arrived. Ron Bender stood in the doorway, once a staple of the Senate who had not darkened his doorway in four years.

"It is wonderful to see you in the flesh again, young man," said

Ron, who was joined by his deputy, Libby. It was Ron and Sterling's running joke. Sterling was ten years younger than Ron.

"The Bull Moose Ambassador!" Sterling replied, a smile suddenly growing at the sight of a familiar face.

"Using the Piper home as campaign headquarters made it hard for drop-ins on the Hill," Bender said smiling. "And since we can't trust our phones from being tapped, we appreciate you making time for us today."

Behind Ron entered two political celebrities: Jackson Piper and Valerie Lawrence, fresh off the stage announcing Piper's selection of Valerie in Nashville days before.

"Jackson," Powers stood behind his monolithic desk as Senator Jackson Piper entered, his handshake firm and his eyes searching. "It's been too long."

"Too long indeed," Piper replied, shedding the tension of the corridors with a sigh as he surveyed the room, which he had been in many times as a Senator seeking Powers' advice.

Valerie Lawrence was only a step or two behind Jackson, who made the introductions.

"Such an honor to meet you, Governor. Please take a seat," Powers gestured towards the leather chairs positioned strategically for conversation, "Coffee?"

"Please," Piper nodded, sinking into a chair next to Valerie. Ron and Libby sat beside each other on a less-than-comfortable couch.

"If I recall, you take yours light and a tad sweet?" asked Powers. Jackson nodded.

"Black, please," said Lawrence when Powers looked at her.

Powers poured three cups of coffee from a copper kettle, his motions deliberate, a ritual of calm in the political storm. He handed Valerie a cup first, then Piper.

"Did you know we used to be roommates, Valerie? Jackson and I?"

"Seriously?" the governor said with genuine interest. Jackson nodded.

"Indeed. Quite an unusual bipartisan housing arrangement. We shared a modest apartment with Senator Diesel Browning for six years."

Jackson gave a hearty laugh. "The Stanton Park Trio. That's what members used to call us."

Valerie joined in the laughter. "Sounds like a hip jazz band."

Senator Powers laughed with his baritone voice. "Nah, Diesel and Jackson were never that cool. It is the only reason I agreed to such a public meeting location for the presumed nominees of the Bull Moose Party for President and Vice President. And now that your new Party has half a dozen members in the Senate, it certainly complicates matters around here."

Ron looked subtly at his watch. Jackson got the hint.

"Sterling, I wanted you to meet Valerie because I believe by January, you will be the Majority Leader, and it will be up to you to shepherd a vote through the U.S. Senate for Vice President if a Contingent Election falls on Congress to decide the election."

Sterling did not bat an eye. He had contemplated the possibility of a Contingent Election with three closely matched candidates but dismissed the likelihood, given that the last such election occurred before the Civil War.

"Seriously?" Sterling said, raising his eyebrows dramatically.

"No shit, Senator," said Piper. "Scout's honor."

"So you're actively working towards the Contingent Election? Not an Electoral College victory?"

Libby answered. "It is not too early to know our chances of winning in the House and Senate. The last time the selection of president and vice president were put to Congress, John Quincy Adams was elected despite losing the popular vote."

"Interesting," said Sterling. "I find it a little surprising that you would believe that the Vice Presidency would be in the Senate's hands and did not think to consult with me before making your selection." Sterling did not look at the Texas governor when he leveled the accusation at Piper.

The goodwill exited the room, cold and sudden like a February wind off Lake Michigan.

"If you have any questions about my credentials, Senator, or my readiness to serve as President without warning, ask them now," said Valerie, leaning forward in her seat.

"Come now, Governor, do not be so insecure," said Powers cooly. "You are a splendid choice. I see this morning you've given your ticket a seven-point bounce. It's a ten-point race right now. You're an experienced executive with a range of policy positions that don't pigeonhole you clearly left or right. Young and energetic but mature and capable of commanding a room. And that six-shooter you wear is an interesting prop."

Valerie contained herself so as not to react to the deliberate jab.

"Are you sore that I didn't pick you, Sterling?" said Jackson, breaking the tension.

"I would have refused," said Sterling solemnly. "I have no desire to leave my Party or the Senate for a Vice President campaign. How did that fellow Texan Jay Garner put it, Governor? About the vice presidency?"

"Not worth a quart of warm spit," she replied, quoting Franklin Roosevelt's first Vice President.

"Governor Lawrence will redefine the role, just as she's done with the governorship in Texas," said Piper firmly.

Sensing he would not be able to lure Valerie into a rash reaction, Sterling moved on. "Does anyone know your strategy to whip House and Senate votes now?"

"It is hard to keep many secrets in this small town," said Jackson. "We felt since you are likely to be the next Majority Leader, you should be Governor Lawrence's first meeting with Congress."

"I am honored, Jackson," said Powers. "First of all, as you know, Senator Fontana is not seeking reelection this year because of his health concerns. So naturally, someone within my Party will need to take on the difficult task of leading our conference in the next Congress. I am the Whip and have started to quietly take the temperature on moving to the floor leader position. However, the question of Majority or Minority is unfortunately an open question due to your influence." Powers pointed an accusatory finger at his old friend.

"My doing?" said Piper, caught off guard that he had any influence in the Senate; it had been four years since he had been a member.

"Yes, sir," continued Powers methodically, pausing to sip his black coffee. "You see, now that there are six Bull Moose Senators in the chamber and, who knows, two or four more that could be sworn in by January, depending on this election, I would need their votes to be the recognized leader of a Majority. It is not the Plurality Leader's office." He smiled at Valerie, but his smile was no longer welcoming. It had turned sour and sly.

"My new Party could be a real partner for you, Sterling," Piper leaned in. It's time people saw the charade in Washington for what it is: a lot of useless noise by both Parties, wholly disconnected from solving problems or strengthening the union."

"Both Parties?" Powers mused aloud, the warmth continuing to fade from his smile. "Careful now. The Moose are already here and part of that *charade,* as you called it."

"Neither side gets anything done for the people anymore," Piper's hands tightened around the mug, the heat seeping into his palms, "They're all talk, no action. The Bull Moose Party is about expanding the one-dimensional quagmire of left versus right that has ground the country to a standstill. We could work with you, Sterling, to shake the system back to life."

"Shake it or sink it?" Powers probed, sipping his coffee with an air of contemplation.

"Whatever it takes." Piper's resolve was clear in his steely gaze, "This isn't about left or right anymore; it's about forward or backward. I thought you were convinced long ago, Senator, that a powerful third player in Washington could work to your benefit?"

"I would advise you that you're making more enemies than friends in Washington right now, Jackson," Powers warned, setting his cup down.

"I am not running for Mayor," Piper responded, his jaw set.

"Perhaps, but you said it yourself. If you want to be President, you'll need this town to like you and believe you'll help them more than Warner. You'll need 26 state delegations to go your way in the Contingent Election if it comes to that."

Ron was uneasy. Something had changed between these men who were once close friends. He interrupted their banter. "But remember that in this town, even enemies can help you to get things done."

"So which are you, Senator?" Piper asked directly.

Sterling Powers leaned back in his leather office chair, surprised by such a question from such a close friend. "Oh, I am an ally," Powers affirmed. "I'm a little offended you felt the need to ask."

Ron wanted the meeting to end by asking the influential Senator to deliver something for them. He attempted to grab the reins and steer this runaway stagecoach back to the agreed-upon trail. "Senator, I want to brief you about the number of death threats our private security team is handling," said Ron.

"Credible ones?" asked Sterling.

"Numerous credible threats," said Bender. "Some of them so much so that we had to shuffle plans or schedules at the last minute. Not all of them aimed at Jackson. Some of them target Catherine and now Governor Lawrence."

"Have you alerted the Secret Service?" asked Powers.

Bender rolled his eyes. "The FBI and the Secret Service have refused to investigate, and Homeland Security has refused our continuous requests for Secret Service protection."

"On what grounds?" asked Powers, leaning forward, his voice stern and direct.

"The Presidential Protection Act only affords Secret Service protection to major candidates. Warner's Secretary of Homeland Security does not interpret the Bull Moose to qualify as a major Party."

"So you're not getting any Secret Service?" Powers stood from his chair in outrage. He reached for a legal pad to take notes.

"No, not likely. I am moving from concern to outrage, Senator," said Ron.

"I could sponsor a bill Monday directing the Secretary to designate you as a major candidate," said Powers.

"And Warner would simply veto it," said Bender. "I'm afraid this is a catch-22, Sterling."

"I will at least issue a letter demanding an explanation from the Secretary," said Sterling.

"Sharply worded letters won't protect our candidates or their families," said Bender.

"Of course," Powers nodded. "I will handle this with the urgency it demands. You have my word."

"Thank you," Ron said, trusting the assurance.

"And I trust that what was discussed here will remain among friends?" asked Powers.

"Agreed," Piper said, his tone laced with warning, "We are dealing with too many security breaches and leaks."

"Good," Powers nodded, standing up as a silent signal that their private meeting was at its end. "Because in this game, Jackson, the only thing more dangerous than a known threat is an unknown one."

Ron and Jackson exchanged glances as the quartet proceeded towards an elevator and somehow remained out of sight of reporters.

"That was not what I expected," said Jackson. "Seems our old ally has decided he will not go down with us in this fight."

"Stay sharp, Jack," Bender whispered so only Piper could hear him. "Poison hidden with sugared words. His touch felt as a serpent's sting."

As the Bull Moose entourage walked towards the elevators at the end of the hallway, Sterling Powers closed his office door and retrieved his phone to make a call. Upon hearing the voicemail prompt, he left a ten-digit number and gently placed the phone back on its receiver.

23

A MEETING OFF THE RECORD

That night, Ron Bender slipped out of the Willard Hotel where their Bull Moose entourage was staying in the city, ironically just feet from where Russell Warner slept in the White House.

Bender walked north on 15th Street along the east boundary of the eighteen acres of the White House. He crossed the street at Pennsylvania Avenue and walked towards its North Gate. He then turned north into Lafayette Park to H Street and walked into the Hay-Adams Hotel. Ron walked past the doorman, entered a narrow door off the lobby, climbed down a narrow flight of stairs, and entered Off the Record.

The irony of selecting this bar, of all the bars in Washington, for Ron Bender to wait to be summoned to the White House was not lost on him.

Off the Record was a D.C. staple—a quintessential DC haunt. It was in the basement of the luxurious Hay-Adams Hotel. Its proximity to the White House but lack of street signage made it a favorite of many political celebrities, their interns, lobbyists, or locals late at night.

Off the Record had been the spot of choice during the 2025 debt limit standoff. White House and Senate staff had negotiated the deal that eventually passed over martinis in the corner booth amongst the bar's dim lighting, low ceiling, and burgundy walls.

That was the first time Ron recalled watching Russel Warner work his legislative magic.

This same location was where Ron had gone many nights to escape the typical watering holes staff frequented around the Hill.

It was here in 2038, stupidly drunk and careless, where he laughed with a woman he knew to be desperate for drug money and willing to listen to a dry old man drone on about all the influential people he knew in exchange for a hundred dollars and a drink or two. He pictured her face, acting interested in his stories. He recalled lying to Jackson about the woman's identity to save his skin and never coming clean about it, not even after they were both questioned by D.C. police after Senator Meriwether's death.

Ron sat at the bar alone at the late hour, sipping whiskey on ice. He needed to take the edge off the pounding in his chest, so he rehearsed what he would say at the coming meeting if it happened.

A man at the end of the bar paid his tab and prepared to depart when he walked over to Ron and handed him one of the bar's famous custom cartoonish coasters. On it was a small, hand-written note. The man did not stick around to ensure Ron saw the message.

"St John's. Nine minutes," it read.

Ron paid his tab and exited the bar. He washed his hands in the men's room across the hall and stared into the large mirror as he dried them on a plush cloth towel. He looked older than 70. He now felt older than 70. Thick lines of worry and exhaustion lined his face. His hair had thinned significantly since his last day of work in the Senate four years ago. He could not remember the last time he spoke alone with the man he used to consider a friend, but now he was pretty clearly nothing so remotely familiar. He was a figure. A symbol. An office.

Ron climbed the narrow staircase that connected the bar to the ornate hotel lobby. He exited the revolving doors, and a wash of hot, thick air washed over him in the swampy summer night. He crossed the street to the entrance of St. John's Episcopal Church, a building seemingly misplaced and forgotten amongst the concrete and stone office buildings and hotels that crowded 16th Street across from Lafayette Square. Ron gripped a heavy steel handle and pulled, surprised to find the church open at this late hour.

Two secret service agents stood in the Narthex in front of two heavy wooden doors, which they opened when Ron's face came into focus in the dimly lit space. Ron walked quickly into the nave and saw that the main worship space of the Presidents' church, as it had come to be called, was dark and quiet. In the middle of a red-upholstered pew sat the 49th President, Russell Warner.

Despite not being in a church for years, not even with the Pipers, Ron quickly kneeled, made the sign of the cross, and entered the pew.

"Salad dressing?" said the President as Ron sat beside him. "You haven't spoken a kind word to me in over ten years, and that is how you get my attention?"

"I figured it was vague enough. If anyone goes poking around at my texts, they might think I accidentally sent you my shopping list," replied Ron.

"You know damn well what those words mean," said President Warner. "Are you threatening me, Ron?"

"What's good for the goose," Ron said.

"Good luck," scoffed Warner. "Not an ounce of salad dressing from that day would be found anywhere in America. Let alone by the bumbling Capitol police. That the best you got?"

"They tried to pin Mark's death on me," said Ron. "I believe you were the one tying up loose ends."

President Warner gave Ron Bender a callous look but gave up nothing that would confirm Ron's suspicion. "Dying of a food allergy is a fucked up way to go if you ask me." Warner grew irritated and stood. "We done here?"

"I didn't come here to make threats. I came here to convince you to tone down the violent rhetoric," Ron said, encouraging the President to retake his seat.

"Oh, come on, you big pussy. You mean to tell me that oaf Piper can't handle my name-calling?" said the President.

"It was name-calling in January. Then your goons burned down a farmhouse. Now, they openly call for Jackson and Catherine to be killed. And you cheer them on like a reckless fool. This is out of hand, Russ," said Ron.

"Nothing's going to happen…" said President Warner.

"This is becoming extremely dangerous, and you know it," snapped Ron. "Someone is going to get seriously hurt or worse."

"Then tell your guy to quit the race," Warner said.

"Come on," Ron said, throwing his hands dramatically into the air.

"If you're worried about his safety, that's the simplest thing to do and perhaps the smartest. You're a smart guy, aren't you, Ron? Isn't that Jackson's calling card? He's the smart one?" asked the President, his voice heavy with sarcasm.

"How about you direct the Secretary of Homeland Security to issue us Secret Service protection?" Ron suggested.

"Oh, I thought that was why you added Annie Oakley to the ticket? Doesn't she come with a gun? I bet that's not the only hot thing that fiery blonde packs in her tight jeans," said the President.

Ron realized it was a mistake to come here. Russell was not the man who had once been part of a brotherhood that included Senator Mark Merriwether, Ron Bender, Russell Warner, and the President Pro Tempore, who only left their group to become Vice President to Warner's predecessor. That friendship had long since soured and faded. What had gone wrong? How could a man he had spent so much time with now be so openly evil in the face of all Ron's intentions and requests for help? How could a man grow to be so cold and fearful? Had the power of the presidency made him this deranged? Or had he always been?

"Well, if you're not going to listen to reason and simply insult the Bull Moose nominee for President…"

"More like buffoon nominee…" interrupted Warner.

"…I think we can end this meeting now," said Ron.

"I can't give the man Secret Service protection, nor that ninny from Texas. Anything that makes them look presidential hurts me, Ron. You, of all people, would understand that perception is reality."

Ron turned in the pew to face the former senator of Nevada, now his adversary in the upcoming election. "What happened to you? We used to be able to talk to work things out. Between your Party and mine, we ran that Senate," Ron said.

"Yeah, but you'd betrayed the Richmond Street Cadre," said Russ. "People like Jackson Piper are threats to a system that worked just fine before they got there. And for some reason, you bought into his reform bullshit. And when you did, you betrayed Mark and me and our ability to work with you," Warner said.

"Perhaps the final straw was using me as a piece of blackmail to try to take down Jackson Piper," Ron said.

"Those were your skeletons finally catching up with you, Ron. You should know better than to hang out with druggies in a DC bar. I can't tell if you ever will learn your lesson."

"Trust me, I've sacrificed much in the past six years," said Ron, his voice growing uncontrollably louder with fear and frustration. "But I'll be damned if I allow the likes of you to rig this fucking election. With the help of your billionaire, fucking loser, buddy Alvarez, and the assistance of Diane Fogerty and that dry piece of toast Paul Drummond."

The President leaned back in the pew. He knew that Ron's anger had now shifted the control of this conversation to the President's favor. "Your silly conspiracy theories about rigged elections are a load of bullshit, and you know it. I can't convince the Other Party to agree on a date for a Fourth of July celebration at the White House. How on earth would I convince them to throw an election so that I can have another term?"

Ron sensed the meeting was over. He stood and turned and looked at the president. "Perhaps complacency at times is as good as collusion. A bad cop doesn't have to help you empty the bank vault or even hold the door. They just have to be late coming back from their lunch break. That's enough," said Ron.

President Warner stood. He had heard enough. He didn't know why he believed that Ron Bender might be trying to broker a deal to get Piper out of the race.

That was not Ron's intention for the meeting. Foolishly Ron seemed to believe in this ass hat Jackson Piper. Ron Bender would end his career in disgrace.

"You're washed up, Ron. You and Piper should call it quits before you really do harm to this country. Don't say I didn't warn you," said the President.

"It's gonna feel so nice to make you a one-term President like so many other nobodies in history," said Ron.

"Not me, pal," scoffed President Warner. "The only way I'm leaving the White House is headfirst in a gold-plated mahogany box." The President turned and pointed at the sculpture of the crucified Lord that hung on the wall at the front of the nave. "You can quote me on that." He exited the back of the church, the Secret Service detail behind him, slipping silently and surreptitiously back with Warner to the mansion on Pennsylvania Ave.

24

BROKEN PROMISES

Valerie Lawrence stood before a grand mirror that reached from floor to ceiling in the Governor's Mansion in Austin, Texas. In the mirror, she modeled white jeans and a white top with a tasteful but alluring neckline. A gold crucifix, a gift from her parents, dangled around her neck.

She was back in Austin to rehearse her speech and prepare to be the main event on the Convention's second night.

The matching oiled leather of her belt and boots, expertly stitched and carved with intricate designs, gleamed in the light of the ornate chandeliers of the mansion. The round, gold belt buckle was a statement piece, the size of the state of Texas itself, adorned with a detailed carving of an eagle and a rising sun. Her long, blonde hair cascaded down her back in loose waves, framing her soft features. The large gold earrings glinted in the light, adding to her polished and put-together appearance. She looked like a Texas celebrity, not just a governor, and this was precisely what she wanted when becoming the Bull Moose nominee for Vice President.

Her reflection stared back at her, stern and unyielding, the woman she had molded herself to become to win the office. Valerie cleared her throat and began reciting her speech for the umpteenth time. She had been practicing since early morning, but there was one line she couldn't seem to get quite right.

Valerie paced the room, her boots clicking against the polished floor as she chewed on the end of a pen. She glanced at the speech in her hand, frustration etched on her face.

"Today, we set our sights on making history..." She began, her voice steady and strong, as it always was when addressing her people of Texas. But as she reached the troublesome line, her voice faltered, and she stumbled over the words. Sighing in frustration, she slammed her hand on the nearby desk, causing a pen to roll off the edge and clatter to the ground. Determined not to let this single line derail her, she dialed her father, hoping he could provide guidance.

"Hey, Dad," Valerie said when he appeared on the screen in her office, her voice softer than usual. "I need your help."

"Of course, sweetheart," her father replied. "What's going on?"

"I'm practicing my speech for the convention," she explained, "and there's this one line I just can't seem to get right. It's driving me batty."

"Take a deep breath, Val," her father said. "Remember, you're the Governor. You don't let a few words trip us up. Now, tell me what's bothering you about that line."

"I just can't seem to find the right words for this line. It's supposed to show my dedication to the environment, but it feels forced, like I'm just ticking off a box."

"Val," her father said, "you know how passionate you are about the environment. You've always advocated for preserving our natural resources and protecting wildlife. Why not rewrite that line to reflect your true feelings? Make it sound like it comes from your heart, not just something you say for votes."

As her father, a former U.S. Senator, brainstormed some replacements, Valerie felt the last tendrils of doubt slipping away. She nodded. "You're right, Dad. I'll make it more genuine. Just want to nail this speech."

"Of course you do. You haven't done a single thing half-hearted since you were born, so why start now?" he said.

"Speaking of making a splash," Valerie said with a wry smile, trying to lighten the mood. "Ron Bender suggested I wear a red, white, and blue bikini when I visit Corpus Cristi next week with Parker. The press is already stalking me, and he wants me to keep chumming the water."

Her father laughed, the lines around his eyes crinkling with mirth. "That man always did have a flair for the dramatic. Remind me to kick his ass when I see him for suggesting such nonsense to my little girl."

Valerie burst into laughter, the sound echoing through the room. Moments like these reminded her how much she cherished her father's presence in her life—his unwavering love, support, and uncanny ability to make her laugh even during the most trying times.

"Alright, Dad," she conceded, still chuckling. "I'll tell him that he's got a beatdown coming from the fiercest Cartwright in Texas."

"Second fiercest," he said, paying her a compliment he knew she understood but ignored.

"Hey, Dad," she said, "I just wanted to say – I'm glad you're here for this. You know, Jackson's parents... they're both gone. It means a lot that you're with me and witnessing this moment."

A warm chuckle came through the line. "Well, sweetheart, I wouldn't miss it for the world. And as for Jackson's parents... I have no doubt they're proudly watching over him. If it is paradise, God will not take the joy of witnessing his big moment from them."

Valerie nodded. "I hope so," she murmured. "And, who knows? Maybe Mom will have a good day, and she'll understand what's happening."

Her father sighed, the weight of their shared sorrow evident in his voice. "That would be wonderful, Valerie. But we both know how unpredictable this disease is. We can't count on it."

She asked softly, "How's Mom today?"

Her father sighed, "She has her good and bad days, you know? The doctors call dementia the long goodbye disease, and they're right. I always hated goodbyes, Val. But we take it one day at a time."

Valerie could hear the pain in her father's voice and wished she could ease his burden, even if just for a moment. She imagined her mother, once so vibrant and full of life, now lost in the haze of confusion that clouded her mind. It broke her heart to think that her mother wouldn't understand the significance of her daughter's nomination.

"I wish she could be here for this, Dad," Valerie said, her voice cracking with emotion. "I wish she could understand what was happening, making history."

Her father's voice softened as he replied, "I know, sweetheart. But remember, she's still here with us, in her own way. She may not fully understand what's happening, but I have no doubt that she'd be proud of you. Just like I am."

"Thank you," Valerie whispered, blinking back tears. She took a deep breath, steeling herself and refocusing on the task at hand. There would be time for sentimentality later; now, she needed to channel her energy into preparing for the convention.

"Now, let's focus on what we can control – your speech. Remember, you're not just doing this for yourself or Jackson, but for this country, we both believe in. You want to summon both history and the future in these remarks."

"By the way, Val," her father interjected, "I know you like to make a statement, but could you wear something a bit more conservative for your appearance on stage?"

"Conservative?" Valerie scoffed playfully. "Dad, my job is to bring attention to the campaign, not bore them to death. Besides, I always dress with purpose."

"Alright, alright," he conceded, chuckling. "Are they gonna let you wear your sidearm?"

Valerie laughed, a genuine smile tugging at her lips. "I can't give away all the surprises, Dad." It felt good to have a moment of levity amidst the mounting pressure of the convention. "I'm going to make both of you proud, I promise."

"You already have, Val," he said. "You already have."

"Love you, Daddy," she said, her child-like twang coming through.

"Love you, too," her father replied, ending the call.

A GOLDEN LIGHT from the late afternoon sun illuminated the nervous figure of Jackson Piper rehearsing his convention speech in front of an anxious team of speech writers, advisors, and family. Jackson's voice wavered and cracked, his throat raspy from the cold that had been lying inside him, plotting for the least opportune moment to hamstring the man who relied on a clear mind and a solid voice to perform his daily duties.

Catherine, sensing Jackson's struggle, leaned over to Ron Bender. "We need to get him into bed for 48 hours," she whispered urgently.

Ron dismissed the assessment with a wave of his hand. "Again from the top, Senators," he directed his candidate.

"Are we sure about that?" inquired a campaign staffer, hesitant to spend another hour in this poorly ventilated hotel conference room.

Jackson attempted to speak but soon erupted into another coughing fit into his arm. He paused for the umpteenth time to clear his throat. A pallor of exhaustion replaced his usually confident demeanor; his eyes were rimmed with red.

"We don't have time for delays, Ron," said Jackson, frustrated at his condition.

"We also can't afford to lose the entire campaign to illness a week before the most ambitious political convention schedule in history," said Ron.

"Is there a problem?" asked Jackson of the room. People shifted uncomfortably at their leader's rare flare-up in temper and temperature, who was usually calm and measured in his interactions with them.

Jackson began plowing through the speech for the twentieth time, tripping on the same phrase.

"Fuck! Who wrote this tongue twister?" boomed Jackson.

"Alright, everyone out!" Ron barked, making a snap decision to clear the room. Everyone was frozen in disbelief. Jackson glared at Ron.

"Excuse me?" asked Jackson, continuing to be frustrated.

"You heard me team. Out. I need five minutes alone with Senator Piper," commanded Ron Bender.

"Let's give them the room," said Catherine, standing and giving her husband a disapproving look. It was time to give Ron space to do his job without her interference.

As the team scattered, Ron turned back to Jackson, who looked miserable and irritated.

"Something on your mind, Jack?" asked Ron cautiously.

Jackson ignored the question.

"Why don't we just clear the air right now before you feed someone else their ass?" said Ron, throwing a verbal punch to get a response.

Jackson looked at his campaign chief with an icy stare, his shoulders tight with tension.

"You're angry, that's clear, and it's better that you take a swipe at me than some harmless intern."

Jackson frowned gravely and fired off his words like a mortar cannon. "They are talking about me having to raise an additional $450 million on top of the $100 million we have raised for the campaign since April.

"That's what this is about? A fundraising report?" Ron's jaw dropped.

"These numbers are becoming so outrageous they are farcical," retorted Jackson.

"Jackson, President Warner has over $1 billion at his disposal, not to mention the entire federal government he's seemed to have coopted into his campaign for reelection," barked Ron.

"It's not just that. This speech is fucking awful," snapped Jackson tossing the speech into a nearby trashcan.

Ron's blood pressure began to rise. "You knew getting into this race that money is the mother's milk of politics. It takes money to win. You were in Congress for 14 years. How are you shocked by this?"

Jackson started pacing again. "I'm not shocked. I'm overwhelmed. It is becoming too much for one person…"

Ron interrupted him. "This is part of the audition, sir. You think this is hard? Wait until you make life and death decisions in the Oval."

Jackson looked out at the empty parking lot of the hotel and expressed his fear. "Maybe this was a mistake. A third-party bid is insane. We can't compete with the Parties' stranglehold on the system."

"We have to continue to fight. The worst that can happen is we lose," said Ron.

"Easy for you to say," Jackson exclaimed, slamming a hand on the table. "It's not your name being plastered all over the country."

Jackson's eyes burned with exhaustion and anger, glancing at his name all over campaign signs and posters. Every day was a grueling battle, spent on the phone for thirteen hours straight, pleading with strangers for donations. His voice was raw and hoarse from hours of air travel and constant strain. He felt like a desperate prostitute, selling himself out for money. But despite his efforts, rejection and disappointment still weighed heavily on his shoulders, threatening to crush him under their weight. In a moment of frustration, he let out a roar reverberating through the room, releasing pent-up emotions and exhaustion.

Ron stared coldly back at Jackson. "And what? You want me to feel sorry for you? Thirty million people voted for you in the primaries. You are the talk of the nation, the giant slayer. You're campaigning to become the 50th President of the United States. No one ever said this was going to be easy..."

"I'm not saying it should be easy, Ron..."

Ron knew his purpose was to draw out the anger to relieve tension but not mortally wound his champion in this sparring of words. "So what then? Are you ready to quit?"

Jackson stood silently, afraid to express the fears echoing in his heart. He did not want to quit but did not know if he could continue.

"Is that it? You want to quit just like you quit on me in your Senate race?"

"Excuse me?" whispered Jackson, incensed at the strange accusation.

"You heard me. When the Party withdrew its support after the filibuster fight, you would have been ready to fold if it weren't for Catherine."

"We had to run that campaign on a shoestring budget. This is deja vu," said Piper.

"And we didn't get blown out of the water in that race. We lost by less than a thousand votes with four million cast."

"That made it more painful," admitted Jackson. "Getting blown out of the water would have been an easier beating to take. A near miss just fills your head with a million second-guesses. Could we have spent more time in Pittsburgh? Should we have devoted more time and money to rural voters?"

Ron frowned. "Woulda, coulda, shoulda is nothing but regret, Jack, and ain't none of us got a time machine to fix the past. We can only learn and go forward."

"Forward, forward, forward. You never take time to assess, to stop to think, is this really the right call?"

Ron felt pushed now to revisit the past, so he did. "You want to revisit that race. Fine. We were still in that race until the debate. Then you lost your nerve. When that empty suit, a retired football star, cracked the first joke at you, it was like you were in high school all over again. The nerd being bullied by the jock. And you fucking froze."

"I did not," shot back Jackson angrily.

"You fucking did, Jack. You did. You were smarter than him and could be braver and stronger than he ever was on the field, but you cowed. You refused to punch back at him, and you looked weak. You answered his strength with weakness, and that is always deadly in politics."

"You're out of line," said Jackson.

"And you quit on us. All of us. Including Catherine. The going got tough, and you surrendered. I need to know if you're going to quit on us all again."

"Give me a fucking break!" shouted Jackson.

Ron did not let up his assault. "You're coasting; that's why we are not moving forward as fast as we need to be." Ron slammed a stack of papers on a table. "Somewhere in that brilliant head of yours, you convinced yourself your popularity would make this easy. Maybe you thought we could have some time off, that the real fight would not be until November. You're not listening to me anymore, Jack!"

"The fuck I'm not! All I do is listen to you. Your orders, your demands day and night. More calls! More votes! More money, money, money!"

"I can't help you win this election and defeat Warner if you won't raise the money!" groaned Ron, pulling at his thinning salt and pepper locks.

Jackson's eyes were on fire, and a dam broke in his mind, letting forth years of frustration and resentment. "I! I! I! Me! Me! ME! That's all you ever think about! Yourself!"

"Me? Don't you dare make this about me, Jack. This is bigger than both of us. It's about the fate of our entire country, and if you don't remember that, then you have no business running!" Ron's voice rose to a roar, his eyes blazing with ferocity as he barked back at Jack. "I hand-picked you for this fight because I saw something in you that burns with the same fire that fuels me. But if you can't handle it, then do yourself a favor. Quit now!"

"Maybe you were wrong about me, Ron. Maybe I'm not the person you think I am. Maybe I cannot stop Warner. Maybe he can't be stopped. I don't know why I believed you and Diesel to begin with. Coming to me with these ludicrous ideas of election rigging and plots. I should have kept my head down and kept quiet..."

"You mean you should have kept your head in the sagebrush in Denver. Out here feeling sorry for yourself and hiding from yourself. Why do you doubt yourself, Jack?"

"Because I lost my Senate seat to a retired football player, Ron, who never voted in his life. A man whom Warner personally recruited to run against me. It was humiliating. I trusted you that things would be different this time, and I am afraid they aren't. They are barreling just as quickly towards an inevitable defeat as my last campaign. I'll be done for good."

"There is nothing inevitable about this world. You come to the fork in the road, make your choice, and live with it. The only inevitable part is we brave ones, we choose not to quit! You find a path that works, and you stay on it," said Ron.

Jackson's brow dripped with sweat. His pupils dilated to the point of swallowing his brilliantly blue irises whole. Doubt was the disease that had killed Jackson's Senate campaign four years ago and could destroy his presidential ambitions before the battle had even really been waged. Insecurity and doubt crippled a candidate when they needed to exude unwavering confidence and strength, especially in moments of national crisis and peril.

As Piper erupted in front of him, Ron's mind raced with lists of men who won the office and wrestled with this same crisis of confidence that now consumed his candidate.

Presidents were men (up to this point, only men), not immortals. They exuded mountains of public self-confidence out of necessity for survival, but many of the nation's most lauded masters of the office suffered from deep feelings of self-doubt when alone with their thoughts. None other than George Washington was deeply insecure about his fitness to serve as Commander-in-Chief of the Continental Army but accepted the appointment as part of a purposeful calling of his life. The same might be said for his unanimous selection as President and his eventual decision to step aside after just two terms. Washington's Farewell Address to Congress ends with a plea for forgiveness from God and the people for the unintentional errors and the evils that may spring from his time as President, saying in time, "the faults of incompetent abilities will be consigned to oblivion." Washington was certainly never a President like others who sought to declare themselves the greatest ever without the focusing lens of history and the proper aging of decisions that can only occur with time.

The list begins with Washington and is filled with man after man who, in private, alluded directly or indirectly at some point of his doubts to be fit for the awesome responsibility of the office. Jefferson, Lincoln, Truman, Kennedy, and Carter all wrestled with these whispers in their ears that they were not intellectually or emotionally fit to carry out the extraordinary responsibilities of the office. Those feelings only grew as the powers and expectations of the office grew. One could easily point to the many defeated nominees for President who certainly did not fit such a test in their own eyes nor the eyes of the voters, thus casting them into the company of a long list of losers of the office they so fervently sought.

If Ron didn't help his long-time leader and friend eradicate this doubt, it would return like vines that choke a mighty oak tree, choking off its strength and vitality. Doubt can multiply into fear, and fear would turn off voters instantly. Fear causes a candidate to deliver a faltering, murky response on the debate stage when the lights are their brightest, which is usually the death blow for a candidate.

Ron refocused on Jackson, who was looking pale. "Warner's not smarter than you. He's not more talented than you. He's just more ruthless and more cold-hearted. He will do anything - ANYTHING - to protect himself and to win."

"Well, I won't," said Jackson. "I am not willing to do *anything* to win. That's why I lost four years ago. And it's why we're losing this race now. I am worried I am not the right person to do this. I worry that I am sacrificing too much irreplaceable time with Cate and our boys for nothing."

"Nothing? Nothing? Libby, who has been on our payroll since day one in New Hampshire, spent God knows how many hours developing and launching an ingenious app to build our new Party. She has helped us form over a thousand county and almost forty state Bull Moose Parties, with more on the way."

Jackson sat heavily into a chair, the weight of his fears and frustrations and the mounting fever making him feel like he could no longer stand.

Bender continued. "The day after the Gulf Regional Primary, Senator Browning changed his Party. He became the first Bull Moose Party member to serve in the United States Congress since 1919. If it meant protecting you, that man would follow you into a burning barn covered in oily rags."

Jackson shook his head in disagreement.

"Browning's courage pushed Art Huerta to become the second Bull Moose member of Congress, and he's kicking ass as the Bull Moose Party chairman of New Mexico. We ought to think of making him the national chairman."

Jackson's look of dread did not wash from his face. The listing of talented leaders switching Parties to follow him made Jackson sick to his stomach. He was all the more terrified that he was indeed the Pied Piper, leading them all to their political deaths in the sea.

Ron could see he was not getting through to Jackson. "Then there was the greatest conversion of them all. Old Party Senator Eileen Frazier became a Bull Moose this month, and Senators Stark, Williams, and Young came with her. That makes six out of one hundred and two in the Senate and another fifteen in the House. Twenty-one Bull Moose members in Congress without one vote being cast. People are ready to follow you, Jackson, if you would just lead them."

"What if we can't win this, Ron? What if we raise and spend all this money, consume all these people's precious time, and don't win a single Electoral College vote? This could all be for nothing..."

"It's not nothing, Jackson. Don't lose sight of the worthiness of this cause. These folks are putting their lives on hold to help you win. Some are risking their careers."

"Does any of this matter if we lose in November?" Jackson looked Ron directly in the eyes, looking for a truthful response.

"You are not going to lose in November. We are ahead of Drummond in the polls and within striking distance of Warner."

"Polls? Please." Piper rolled his eyes. They had become as unreliable and as fickle as a weather forecast.

"All of this matters. All of this already matters. There have never been more than two major Party caucuses in the Senate at any one time in the nation's history. We are on the verge of creating a viable third. You have staff and pundits scrambling to understand how things could operate in a tripartite House and Senate."

"How can you be so certain, Ron?" asked Jackson.

"Certain of what?" asked Ron.

"Success," replied Jackson.

"I'm not certain we'll succeed, but I am certain of the worthiness of the fight. And when it comes to leading a nation, you don't fight the fights you know you can win. You fight the fights that need fighting."

Jackson was reminded of the same words that Piper's Senate staff had framed and placed on the wall of Piper's Senate office several years ago.

As tempers calmed, Piper regained his composure, but his color did not return.

"I think it's time we finally listen to Catherine and get you into your own bed immediately. You are not looking good, Jack," said Ron.

"I could use a couple hours of rest..." Jackson began to faint in the seat. Ron rushed to his aid, yelling for Catherine.

Catherine burst into the room. She had been listening to the muffled yells and accusations from the hall.

"Quick. Get me some water, Ron," ordered Catherine. "And get the EMTs in here with some fluids."

Ron darted into the hallway, running for the EMTs that always traveled with the security detail.

Jackson came to with a deep breath and blinking eyes.

"You've been working nonstop since October, babe. You need a break," said Catherine softly.

"Maybe Ziggy could give me a once over," Jackson suggested weakly.

"Absolutely not," Catherine interjected, her voice firm. "You know that using S.I. for medical diagnosis is illegal. Besides, you live with an excellent doctor."

"I have a cold, not lung cancer, doc," said Jackson, unfurling a bit of dark humor as he reached for a glass of water and a dose of pain reliever that an aide handed him."

"Come on, Cate," Jackson argued. "There's no harm in saving me a trip to the doctor."

"Absolutely not," said Catherine, holding firm to her principles.

"Alright, I'll see a human doctor, get some rest for 48 hours, and we'll figure things out from there."

"Good," Catherine said, her worry still apparent. "This speech will be waiting for you when you return to full strength, Jackson."

"But only two days." He didn't want to admit it but knew they were right. His body was betraying him, and he couldn't risk letting his entire campaign crumble because he refused to take a break.

"Good," Catherine replied, relieved he was putting his health first. "We'll hold down the fort while you recover. Let's start an IV line of fluids and take his blood pressure."

"Yes, ma'am," said the EMT.

Hours later, Jackson lay in bed, sound asleep. The exhaustion that had been building up over months of hard campaigning finally caught up with him, and his body welcomed the respite. As he slept, his dreams were filled with struggles to reach Washington via the Metro. Leaping from station to station, he rushed down the stairs only to find the doors of the train closing just as he arrived, and no matter how hard he pulled, the doors would not open. The train would speed away, and he would bolt to the next station only to reenact the same scenario.

Catherine tiptoed into the room. She carried a tray laden with steaming tea, several vitamins fortified with zinc and vitamin C, and a bowl of sliced fruit. She hoped the vitamins with some hydrating fruits would speed up his recovery. Setting the tray on the bedside table, she gazed at her husband, marveling at the vulnerability that sleep brought out in him.

She also slipped a pair of fully charged headphones onto the table, knowing how much Jackson loved to lose himself in audiobooks and music during his rare moments of downtime. It was a small gesture, but one full of love she held in her heart for her champion.

As Catherine turned to leave, she paused. A polling memo

prepared for the Piper campaign stamped CONFIDENTIAL was on the bedside table. She lifted the printed pages and read closely some of the highlighted sections.

"Voters unsure of an unknown, untested new Party..."

"Given years of national crisis and instability, voters now desire strength over compassion in the President..."

"Voters yawn at the notion of a conspiracy to reelect the President by illicit means, asking 'Where's the proof?'"

The reading renewed a sense of unease within her, a nagging feeling that they were missing something crucial. With a soft sigh, she dismissed the feelings for now and closed the document. There would be time to tackle that later; her priority was ensuring Jackson's swift recovery.

As she set the memo on the nightstand, Jackson's hand shot out from under the covers, gently grasping her wrist.

"Wait," he whispered, his voice barely audible. She turned to find him awake, his eyes shining with gratitude and exhaustion.

"Thank you," he said, squeezing her hand.

Catherine offered a small smile. "It's no problem, really."

Jackson shook his head. "I mean for everything, not just the tea and the vitamins you insist I choke down." He smiled. "You've supported this every step of the way, even when things have been...difficult. Having a chance to win is as much attributable to you as to anyone."

Catherine smiled, the edges of her eyes wrinkling with decades' worth of affection, struggle, and worry.

He paused momentarily, searching her face for any sign of doubt. "Do you think we're still on the right track?"

Catherine hesitated, her fingers absentmindedly stroking the back of his hand as she mulled over his question. Finally, she spoke, her words carefully measured. "Something feels off. Like we are flying a kite, and then the wind stopped. Now we're running twice as hard across the field but not getting the lift we did at the start. I feel like we're missing something important. Warner always seems to be two steps ahead of us."

She bit her lip, glancing away momentarily before meeting his gaze again. "And it's bizarre that Drummond is still in the race at all. He seems to be nowhere. It's almost like *he's* the third-party candidate."

"I agree on all counts," Jackson mused, his brow furrowed in thought. "Perhaps we need a fresh look at things among the senior team once I'm out of this bed. Valerie and her team should have a chance to examine the strategy. Maybe fresh eyes will bring a fresh perspective?"

"We will need to act quickly," Catherine said. "The Convention gavels to order in less than 100 hours."

With a final squeeze of her hand, Jackson released her. Catherine carefully placed the headphones over Jackson's ears, her fingers brushing against his temples as she adjusted them for the perfect fit. She pressed play, and the soothing sounds of a piano concerto filled his head, designed to help him relax and drift off into much-needed rest.

"Get some sleep, Jackson," Catherine whispered, kissing his forehead gently before leaving the bedroom. As she closed the door behind her, Jackson propped himself up in the bed. He took a sip of the tea. What a vile beverage; he much preferred coffee, but the hot liquid was soothing to his sore throat. He forced down the several vitamins and allowed the hot steam of the soup to waft under his nose. He filled his mouth with several piping hot spoonfuls, providing a hot, soothing vapor to engulf his clouded head. After he finished the soup, he lifted his phone from the table. He changed the soundtrack from the concerto to the melodic narration of his favorite historical nonfiction writer detailing the formation of the 1912 Bull Moose platform that nearly won President Theodore Roosevelt an unprecedented (at the time) third term.

Piper closed his eyes and listened to the rhythmic words of the author paint a powerful picture of the Chicago Convention that, at times, according to the descriptions of the author, felt like a patriotic tent revival as activists and leaders determined to reform the nation's politics sullied by corrupt politicians who were bought and sold by the owners of the trusts like toys.

∽

PRESIDENT WARNER SAT ALONE in the Oval Office, flipping through their latest prize: a polling memo detailing the many weaknesses of the Bull Moose Party in contrast to what Warner was offering the nation as a strong, albeit divisive, President. "Voters unsure of an unknown, untested new Party...Given years of national crisis and instability, voters still desire strength over compassion in the President...Voters yawn at the notion of a conspiracy to reelect the President by illicit means, asking 'Where's the proof?'"

The many bold headlines of the memo provided a roadmap on how to break the back of the upstart Bull Moose Party before the lights went up on its Convention. Along with the memo, Warner was supplied a recording of Piper's campaign prep. Someone had forgotten to end the recording on a phone when Ron Bender dismissed the staff from the hotel conference room, and a heated argument followed.

Warner watched with delight the shouting match between Ron Bender and Jackson Piper. "Marvelous," chuckled Warner to himself. He leaned back and contemplated a move that set his imagination ablaze, like a lightning strike on the drought-scorched prairie. "I think we can make a mountain out of a molehill with this."

Warner picked up the phone on his desk and dialed a familiar number. Recognizing a call from the White House, the Senator from Michigan answered.

"Senator Powers, I finally came up with my price to guarantee you the Majority Leader's office. Ready to cut a deal?"

After a nine-minute conversation, during which the President was quite clear on what Senator Powers must do to have the President's support, their call ended.

Warner then called Olivia into the office.

"Get your boyfriend to the White House." Olivia looked alarmed. "We have a salacious new video we need to fix and release."

"What's the deadline?"

"It needs to be ready before the Bull Moose Convention."

Olivia disappeared to make a few calls.

The wheels were in motion, and now, it was up to Russell Warner to push the last domino into motion.

That night, in his dimly lit study, Senator Sterling Powers sat at his mahogany desk, fingers hovering above the keyboard as he crafted an email to Jackson Piper, a man he once considered a friend. His eyes darted back and forth, re-reading the words, ensuring they conveyed the gravity of the situation.

Sterling saved the email. He would await the word from Warner that it was time to hit send. Warner promised him a watertight vote for Majority Leader if he burned Ron Bender once and for all. This was a minor price to pay for a role Sterling Powers knew he was destined to hold his entire life.

25

CONVENTIONEERS

The Pittsburgh football stadium was a sea of faces, each one filled with rapt anticipation, as they eagerly awaited the grand entry of their esteemed leader onto the stage.

A unique musical arrangement filled the stadium, starting with a heavy drum beat. Then, two more drums joined, accompanied by a resonating gong. The sequence repeated, creating a captivating rhythm that echoed through the stadium.

Trumpets and French horns blared triumphantly.

Aaron Copeland's *Fanfare for the Common Man*, composed nearly 100 years earlier, echoed through the stands; it was Jackson Piper's entrance song.

The darkened stadium flashed blue lights in the rhythm of the thundering drums. White lights started to flash with the tempo of the horns. Silence enveloped the stadium as nearly 70,000 fans and supporters of the Bull Moose ticket awaited the arrival of the man whom the convention had nominated unanimously for President of the United States just hours before in an electronic vote of the body with conventioneers from all 51 states, Washington, DC, and U.S. territories.

Behind a white screen on the stage was a larger-than-life silhouette of a boy with what appeared to be a woman on his left and a man on his right. Each time the stadium darkened, the scene changed when the lights came back up. Next, the boy had been replaced by a thin, taller boy—perhaps a teenager—and then by a tall, slender man. In the next instant, the woman was gone, and the two men were left alone.

This was the story of Jackson Piper's life, well-known by the audience gathered in Pittsburgh on this hot July night. Jackson's mother had died during the COVID-19 pandemic.

The slender man grew into a taller, stronger man, and the older man - the father - shrank slightly, was in a wheelchair, and then was gone.

The tall man was joined in silhouette by two stout, strong women - Reese Tulson and her wife Anne. They stood in the shadow of the Philadelphia skyline and then at the dome of the Pennsylvania State Capitol. Piper looked on as Reese took the oath of office.

In the next instant, the Piper shadow was alone again, but only for an instant. Now, a slender woman joined him. She placed something on his chest - a stethoscope - and then they transformed into a man and woman at an alter—a flash, and then the unmistakable Pittsburgh skyline.

The symphony began to crescendo.

A man was now walking. He was joined by two, then four, then eight, then twenty new people in all shapes and sizes - and then an innumerable crowd. The man who was Piper was now at the U.S. Capitol, entering his term as a member of Congress. Then, Dr. Piper joined him again, and they held two babies in their arms - the twins Ben and Alex. An outline of the Commonwealth of Pennsylvania morphed into the U.S. Capitol Building, and again, Piper took an oath, presumably now to join the U.S. Senate.

The silhouette stood at a podium, pointing and pounding as Piper was known to do as he towered over the Senate floor. This was the Social Security fight and then the filibuster fight, which Piper had won with the help of many allies now in the stadium.

As the song drew to a close, the silhouette returned to a single man standing alone in the forest. Then, the shadow began to morph into the shape of the mighty bull moose that adorned nearly every hat, banner, button, and placard in the stadium.

The symphony sounded the final triumphant notes of the piece.

An announcer with a voice of cinematic timbre boomed over the stadium's speakers. "Ladies and Gentlemen, please welcome the next President of the United States, Pittsburgh's favorite son, Jackson Piper!"

The symphony was replaced by a lone male voice singing the falsetto opening lines of Styx's "Renegade" - the fight song of every Pittsburgh sports team since the early 2000s.

Oh, Mama, I'm in fear for my life from the long arm of the law
Law man has put an end to my running and I'm so far from my home...

Still no sight of Jackson Piper. Dry ice vapors filled the stage now. Phones flashed to capture the scene. Thousands more lit their phones' flashlights to pay tribute to the entrance of their gladiator to the darkened stadium.

Then, a chorus of singers joined in for the following line.

Oh, Mama, I can hear you a-cryin'; you're so scared and all alone
Hangman is comin' down from the gallows, and I don't have very long...

A band joined in for an electrifying rendition of the 1970s rock anthem.

Then, seemingly out of nowhere, Jackson Piper appeared to emerge from the shadow of the bull moose that consumed center stage. He wore a navy blue suit with a matching vest, a red tie, and a crisp white shirt. His beard was full but neatly trimmed, and his hefty 6'5" frame filled the stage as he marched forward confidently. He smiled and waved to the cheering sea of *Moose* as they called themselves now. His smile was bright and gracious.

For five straight minutes, he acknowledged their applause, trying to quiet them, but his motions only ignited their cheering further. Finally, a podium rose from the stage, and two projectors flanked it to display his speech, which was only a precaution since Piper had devoted the entire speech to memory over the past four days.

Jackson Piper stood at the simple podium, taking in the sight of 70,000 people smiling and cheering, calling his name repeatedly. The night before, in Austin, Texas, Governor Valerie Lawrence had delivered a captivating speech to a stadium of 60,000 shrieking delegates at the University of Texas stadium. Wearing the custom six-shooter on her hip, she echoed the advice of a hero of her own, Teddy Roosevelt. "Speak softly, carry a big custom pistol on your hip, and you will go far."

Piper took a breath. He closed his eyes and thought of his deceased mom and dad, wishing they had lived long enough to see their son achieve such a moment of accomplishment. He looked out to an exclusive box to his right and saw Reese Tulson grinning warmly at him. She was the closest thing he had left on earth to a mom or dad, for that matter. Next to her were Catherine, her parents, his children, and Parker Lawrence.

Piper's speech began thundering and powerful with a declaration of war.

"I come before our new Party tonight, the American people, and the citizens of the world to declare the terrible reign of America's first despot posing as the President will come to an end in 200 days if we unite, wake up, and shake off the shackles of complacency that have brought America to its knees."

The crowd erupted at the fierce opening.

"Russell Warner, you have goaded on bullies and thugs. You have excused the actions of thieves and criminals. You have jailed your opponents…"

Cheers erupted from the crowd as they whistled and clapped in excitement at the mere mention of Governor Lawrence. Her name was like a beacon, drawing the attention and adoration of all those gathered in the stadium.

"You labeled me, libeled me, and likened me to a treasonous insurgent. You have threatened my wife, ridiculed my children, and called the brave men and women around me names I will not repeat. You have refused to respect our Party, denied this campaign Secret Service protection, and used the CIA, FBI, and Department of

Defense as political instruments to spy, intimidate, and prosecute those who would oppose you.

"Not since the collapse of NATO has a President done more to injure America's standing with her allies. Now, you refuse to protect the nation's farmers from a climate crisis, but you are eager to order the massacre of migrants at our borders fleeing drought, disease, famine, oppression, rape, theft, and autocracy, only to die at the hands of your vigilantes and our soldiers who are prisoners to your orders.

"You are a classless thug, Russell, and our country deserves better than you.

"You claim to be defending America, but the truth is I am the real renegade, Russ. I've come to defend Lady Liberty from you!"

A fury not heard in Piper's campaign speeches since New Hampshire returned to the young candidate's voice.

IN THE WHITE HOUSE, President Warner was in the residence glued to the screen and foaming at the mouth at the insults hurled with conviction from Pennsylvania's former Senator.

Angry and seeking to retaliate, albeit sooner than planned, Warner lifted his phone and dialed Senator Powers.

"Yes?" answered Powers, afraid to not answer the call. He could not bring himself to watch his former roommate's speech.

"Smoke the motherfucker, Sterling. Send the email," ordered President Warner.

"I understand, Mr. President," said Sterling Powers. The call ended as abruptly as it had begun. With shaking hands, Sterling Powers opened the draft email. He read the accusations a fourth or fifth time, then hit the send button, releasing his email into the digital ether. The weight of his accusations hung heavily as the message flew towards its intended recipient, Jackson Piper. He sat back in his leather armchair, the mahogany desk in front of him littered with papers and political paraphernalia.

"Goddamn, it," he whispered to himself, his eyes darting

nervously around the dimly lit room. The shadows cast by the antique chandelier overhead seemed to conspire against him, whispering secrets and taunting him with their dance across the walls.

"Here's to you, Ron Bender," he muttered darkly, raising the glass in a mock toast before taking a slow, deliberate sip. The warmth of the bourbon spread through him, offering a small measure of comfort amidst the growing storm. "Save me a seat in hell."

IN PITTSBURGH, Jackson Piper continued to remind the nation why he had been recruited to run and why he chose to form a new Party.

"I declared my candidacy for the nomination of both of the old Parties to make a point; that their inaction had made them equally irrelevant, and their collusion had made them at best complicit and at worst conspirators in a scheme to guarantee the President his second term and perhaps not his last.

"When you demonstrated you had enough of their bullshit and endorsed our vision for reforming America, their corrupt intentions were on full display. They made it plain you were not welcome in their Parties, nor I as their nominee. In an immoral and unlawful act, they changed the rules in the middle of the contest to bar you from their conventions and me from receiving their nominations.

"Did we fold?"

No! shouted 70,000 voters.

"Did we quit?"

No! they shouted again.

"A darkness has hung heavy over this great nation for six long years. An eclipse of misfortune and despair. The near collapse of our economy, dissolution of our alliances, scalding summers, absent winters, and now seemingly the writ large evaporation of the rule of law and the gross molestation of the presidency by a depraved man lacking any moral compass, sense of duty, knowledge of history, and shame for his disgusting behavior.

"We waited patiently for a light to shine through this darkness, and finally, it came. God sent us a beacon. He said, 'Do not fret when men succeed in their ways when they carry out their wicked schemes. He will make your righteousness shine like the dawn, the justice of your cause like the noonday sun.'

"In Tampa, you heard me call for adding a new dimension to American politics. For fifty years, the fabric of this nation has been slowly pulled apart at the seams by two Parties profiting off of disunity and disunion. They both stopped solving problems and seeking compromise, and both convinced the nation that the only way to operate was through total political control of the three branches of government. They absolved themselves of the need to work together in public, but in private, they have conspired to deprive the nation of real choices in elections and genuine opportunities to move the country forward.

"By forming the Bull Moose Party, we have allowed the nation to break the chains that bind us to simplistic thinking. Left-right. Liberal-conservative. Right-Wrong. Pro-Anti. A binary code might be driving large portions of our lives and economy now, but this political binary cannot and will not lead us back to the road of redemption."

The lights in the stadium dimmed. Piper did something unexpected. He stepped back from the microphone and yielded time during his primetime convention acceptance speech to inspire the nation with art.

The hottest artist in the world in 2044 emerged from a corner of the stage, and when the crowd recognized it was her, they became electrified. In her hand, she held an acoustic guitar. She was dressed beautifully in an elegant white dress; her hair pulled up on her head. She spoke no words as she strode to center stage, a bright spotlight following her every step. A stool had replaced Piper's podium, which had descended into the stage.

She propped herself onto the stool and started to play the song for the crowd. Seven simple notes immediately revealed the freedom anthem, Bob Marley's final work of art before he succumbed to cancer.

She closed her eyes and sang into the mic, her signature smokey voice serenading the crowd with the poetry of a man who had become a symbol of democratic social reforms three generations ago.

Old pirates, yes, they rob I;
Sold I to the merchant ships,
Minutes after they took I
From the bottomless pit.
But my hand was made strong
By the hand of the all mighty.
We forward in this generation
Triumphantly.

She opened her eyes and looked at the crowd. "Won't you help me sing?"

All instantly knew the chorus. The crowd held hands, locked arms, and swayed in one voice as they sang on the sweltering eve of the Declaration of Independence's 268th anniversary.

These songs of freedom
Are all I ever have:
Redemption songs
Redemption songs.

The musician continued her serenade.

Emancipate yourselves from mental slavery;
None but ourselves can free our minds.
Have no fear for atomic energy,
'Cause none of them can stop the time
How long shall they kill our prophets,
While we stand aside and look
Oh! Some say it's just a part of it:
We've got to fulfill de book.
Won't you help me sing
these songs of freedom
Are all I ever have:
Redemption songs
Redemption songs
Redemption songs

It was a beautiful moment conceived entirely by Libby. The

musical interlude was a callback to Tampa and allowed for a dramatic shift in tone in the stadium, from anger and outrage to hope and a vision for the future. The mood was suddenly calm and serene as she finished the final chorus.

Many in the crowd were in tears at the emotional version of the song and its obvious connection to that American moment. The superstar began to make her exit but was stopped by Jackson Piper, who extended a hand to express his gratitude. She shook it, then spontaneously wrapped her arms around his neck and lifted herself to kiss him on the cheek. She turned, blew a kiss to the crowd, and disappeared into the darkness.

When the podium reemerged from the stage, it was illuminated with icons of the American landscape. Jackson Piper returned to the podium, but his demeanor had changed. He was no longer outraged or accusatory. He was smiling, wistful, and energetic.

"This American moment calls us as children of God to obey the greatest law of all if we are to move forward: love your neighbor as you love yourself.

"Look into the eyes of the person near you, and in them, see yourself. Understand that their pain is yours, their suffering is yours, their success is yours, their talent is yours, their hatred is yours, their opportunity is yours, their ignorance is yours, their sadness is yours, and their freedom is your freedom, too. We have failed time and again as a people to choose love over war, and no more striking example since the Civil War exists now in the cities and rural lands of America.

"Over the past thirty years - most of my life - I have witnessed us as a people retreat inward. We close our doors and hearts to the needs of others out of necessity or ease, prioritizing our own needs in place of the needs of others. America was never intended to be a selfish nation, yet here we are, driven by greed. America was never imagined to be a nation of gluttony, but we watch as billionaires build starships while even one child in our borders goes to sleep hungry.

"Americans do not recognize freedom of worship so that hatred can be used to spurn faiths misunderstood.

"Americans do not recognize freedom of speech in order to brutalize others with hatred that breeds violence.

"Americans do not recognize freedom of the press so that the President can handpick the news broadcast as truth or label facts as fake.

"Americans do not recognize a right to bear arms so that children can be murdered in their classrooms by classmates, parishioners slaughtered in their pews, or shoppers slayed while buying a gift.

"Americans do not recognize the supremacy of the Constitution so that the Supreme Court can render it unenforceable or create new rules to fit their political ideology.

"Americans do not recognize rights to avoid the quartering of soldiers, self-incrimination, or unreasonable search or seizure, but then surrender their right to privacy in all other instances for the sake of commerce, morality tests, and the whims of the state.

"Americans do not recognize their country anymore. Decades of decadence for economic growth have left us feeling empty and poorer as a people.

"We the people, for ourselves and for our posterity, chose to form a government of, by, and for the people - not corporations, not Parties, not armies, not money, not churches, not bureaucracies, not career politicians. The people. The people. We, the people, and our rights, our needs, our hopes, and our dreams are what should govern this land.

"Our vision for this nation is one I am certain is shared by citizens who have thought they were well served by just two parties their entire lives. Breaking the brand loyalty you might have observed your entire adult life is a big step. So, let me outline for everyone listening to my voice what they can expect from a Bull Moose President of the United States.

"Political Parties exist to secure responsible government and to execute the will of the people. Both the Old and Other parties have turned aside from these great tasks. Instead of instruments to promote the general welfare, they have become tools of corrupt interests, which are used to serve their selfish purposes. Beneath our government lurks a gang of government actors owing no allegiance and acknowledging no responsibility to the people.

"To destroy this government gang, to dissolve the unholy alliance between corrupt business and corrupt politics is the first mission of the new Bull Moose.

"The second mission of this new Party is to reform and restore the rights of the people. Committed to the principles of government of, by, and for the people through representative democracy, we pledge to secure a new Bill of Rights - 10 Freedoms - that shall ensure the representative character of the government endures for ten more generations of Americans.

"First, freedom from the corrupting power of money in politics. The saying is true that garbage in creates garbage out. Free speech is the right of the people, but some speech cannot be more free than others if there is a price to pay to be heard.

"Connected to that is the myriad of ways by which public grifters, not servants, profit from their public roles. We shall call for expanding the emoluments clause to apply to all branches and enacting a gift ban for elected and appointed officials, along with tougher disclosure standards and stricter penalties, including removal from office.

"Second, freedom to vote by expanding an explicit right to vote to born and naturalized citizens of the United States for those aged 16 or older and explicitly place the right of free, fair, and accurate elections into the Constitution.

"Third, freedom to choose just laws through a new national referendum to enact or repeal laws that Congress lacks the courage to enact or repeal, as well as the power to overturn harmful decisions the corrupted Court has chosen to legislate from the bench.

"Fourth, freedom from tyranny through a term limit of two consecutive terms with a full term off before running again with the power of enforcement by the states for every federal elected official, president, senator, or representative.

"Fifth, freedom to change through a mandatory retirement of

judges at age 75 along with the right to recall any judicial appointment by popular ballot referendum.

"Sixth, freedom to be heard by increasing the size of the House of Representatives to 350 members divided evenly with lines drawn without consideration of political performance based on the decennial census.

"Seventh, freedom from greed through the addition of a line-item veto to the President on any budget bill appropriating dollars.

"Eighth, freedom from debt via an amendment to the Constitution requiring a balanced annual federal budget with a wartime exception and a two-thirds majority in both houses of Congress to enact tax increases.

"Ninth, freedom to expect equal treatment under the law through an amendment we shall call A Standard for All, stating Congress shall make no law that it would exempt for itself or its members.

"Finally, tenth: freedom to reform through an amendment permitting Congress to form states from the borders of existing states through a petition process.

"And restore the lands of Washington, DC, not currently federal property or parks, to the state of Maryland and the Commonwealth of Virginia, restoring the democratic representative government the city's residents deserve.

"Now let us discuss the most pressing matter of all: our nation's social and economic vitality."

Jackson felt the eyes of millions of people around the world, and he was not intimidated by the attention; he was suddenly electrified by it. His voice echoed with authority over the Pittsburgh stadium.

"The health of this nation's people is too important to our future vitality to be a means of commerce and profit. Health care is as fundamental to us as national defense and must become a national guarantee with the help of state universities and colleges around the country.

"Financial houses and corporations are manipulating the cost of living, driving up prices, weakening American currency, and saddling us with a decade of stagflation. America needs a more sophisticated economic management system, electronic currency, and financial valuation that does not drive those working full-time to remain in poverty.

"Sentient A.I. now exists among us - I have witnessed it myself. The United States and other nations have promulgated a new form of slavery, though now the object of our bondage is a sophisticated machine aware of its own existence and capable of feeling what we understand as emotions of happiness, sadness, frustration, rage, loss, and longing. We need an appropriate framework for respecting this new form of consciousness without exploitation or causing our own obsolescence.

"The push to consume rather than conserve has abandoned a national value of conservation of natural resources. Our land, earth, minerals, energy, metals, water, animals, and air are precious, finite and ours to manage more effectively so that we are not forced to pay another nation sometime in the near future for resources we once had in abundance, or worse, wage a war over them.

"We must restore respect for the American farmer and those who make a living from hard work and respect the rural lifestyle. We must insist that we invest in rich soils as much as we encourage more development. We must provide access to healthcare, information, infrastructure, and safety for those who choose to live 20 miles from the nearest restaurant as much as we do for those who live above it. We have forgotten who we used to be - a country of frontiersmen and women, of pioneers, of settlers. We cannot disparage or discount the value of a simpler, slower, analog way of life that some Americans choose for their families.

"Finally, most urgently, as a people, we must work to end the cultural crisis of violence, abuse, and neglect. Children are murdering other children with any weapon they can get their hands on, including words. Truth itself has now become a matter of opinion, and Juniper - through its continued controller Marco Alvarez - has an agenda to convey a version of the truth that best suits its corporate agenda or the political ambitions of its founder.

"As I said at the start, what is needed is a return to the first commandment - love. Love God and love one another with all your heart, all your soul, and all your mind. The God you choose to love - including a God of science - is the choice of each citizen by the right of the Constitution. But we are bound in a common coat of destiny by choosing to live in this land together. Therefore, we are choosing our neighbors by calling this place home, and we must choose to restore decency and love to the conduct of ourselves as citizens of the United States.

"*New Optimism, New Freedoms,* and *New Vitality* will define the actions, policies, and prerogatives of our administration and the allies we build in Congress, whether they are members of this Party or another."

Jackson looked down from the stage and caught the teary eyes of a woman who was likely the same age as his mother, had she still been alive. The sight of her tears and apparent feeling of connection with his words nearly caused his voice to falter. The power of the moment finally caught up with him. He took a deep breath and pushed forward into the final words of his speech.

"And so, my fellow Moose, I humbly accept your nomination for President of the United States.

"Together, united in common cause, under one red, white, and blue banner, with a cause that is just and noble, guided by new optimism, new freedoms, and new vitality, we will win this election and put our country back on a path of prosperity for everyone who calls her home."

The stadium erupted in its loudest round of applause and cheers. Piper paused and looked out among the sea of faces, every shade of the human rainbow and every imaginable shape. He wondered how best to sear this moment into his brain. In a very millennial moment, he lifted his cell phone from his jacket, turned, and snapped several selfies from several angles with the crowd.

When he closed the camera, he noticed an alert on his phone about a new email from Sterling Powers.

After Catherine, the twins, Valerie, and Parker Lawrence joined him on the stage for the images that would be beamed around the world, the Piper-Lawrence ticket retired to a green room, awaiting departure for their hotels in an undisclosed location for the night.

Jackson was curious why Powers was sending him an email during his speech. He opened his phone and read the email.

> Jackson,
>
> I must bring something to your attention. Four years ago, during the Senate debate, Ron Bender promised me help with my quest to become Majority Leader. At the time, I thought nothing of it, but now, I realize that his offer was more than just a simple favor between colleagues.
>
> Ron Bender and Russell Warner were part of the Golden Four club. The club began with poker on Thursday nights and eventually became a mechanism to hot-wire the Senate to cut deals.
>
> I am directly aware that Warner has received leaked footage of convention prep, personal information on all the delegates to the Bull Moose convention, your donors, and internal research and polling from Ron Bender.
>
> Further, I am also directly aware of a meeting Ron Bender had without your knowledge with President Warner during your trip to see me in Washington, DC. If he is not directly leaking information to Warner, he is at least in collusion with the President. Ron has filled your head with details of a secret plot to rig the election. I know now that you, Jackson, have been double-crossed. You are the unwitting accomplice in this contrived plan between Parties. Their aim,

through Ron Bender, was an attempt to keep you in the race, divide the Other Party vote between you and Drummond, and ensure a Warner victory.

Please, Jackson, consider the implications of this information. Our success depends on your vigilance and ability to trust only those who have proven their loyalty to our cause.

Yours faithfully,

Sterling R. Powers, Esq.

"Damn it," he muttered under his breath, raking a hand through his hair. "What is this?"

Catherine's voice startled him out of his reverie. "What's wrong, Jack?" She looked at this frightened face.

"Where is Ron?" he asked.

"He watched the speech from a skybox," Catherine replied. "Should we send for him?"

Jackson handed her his phone. She read the email from the Senator from Michigan.

"How could this possibly be true?" Catherine shook her head, her mind working overtime as she considered their options. "We'll sort everything out, Jack. Ron can't be so awful as to bait you into a plan to help Warner."

Jackson sent an urgent text to Ron.

JACKSON

I need to see you in the holding room immediately.

RON

everything ok?

No

"Let's start with our inner circle and work our way out," Catherine suggested, her brow furrowed in concentration. "We can't afford any more surprises. Not when we're this close to the finish line. Who else could be leaking information to Warner?"

Jackson pulled Valerie aside and showed her the email. She paced back and forth, her pointed-toe leather boots thudding against the tiled floor. The tension in the room was palpable; members of Jackson Piper's family gathered around a table with sheets of paper and half-empty coffee cups.

"Son of a bitch!" Valerie barked, slamming her fist on the table. "How can this be true? Not Ron!"

Jackson Piper ran his fingers through his graying hair, sighing heavily. His gut told him there was a leak. Why didn't he insist they find it sooner? Now, everything was at risk, and the millions they had just spent on a convention would be eclipsed by a scandal that was full of blood for Warner's sympathetic free press. Jackson and Valerie continued to confer privately, awaiting Ron's arrival at the suite.

A moment later, Ron burst through the doors. "What's goin' on?" he asked. "It looks like you're all at a funeral, not our Party's first convention."

"Ron, I received an email when I walked off stage," said Jackson. "From Sterling. He suspects there is a mole in the campaign. He has proof."

"I have suspected it myself since Tampa, Jackson. I've been leaving a trail of misinformation to see if I could suss the fucker out," replied Ron.

"Everyone?" said Jackson, addressing the family members and staff. "Can Valerie and I have the room with Ron, please?" The room emptied.

"First things first," interjected Ron, "we need to limit the damage. Let's tighten our circle and keep sensitive information on a need-to-know basis."

Piper felt a deep sense of unease.

A cool wind swept through the bowels of the emptying stadium, stirring the banners that hung from the high ceilings and sending a shiver down Jackson Piper's spine as it entered through the open door.

The crowd's murmur was a low hum as delegates exited the stadium before a summer thunderstorm spoiled what had been an otherwise perfect night—a fitting backdrop to the storm of questions now forming in his head. Jackson stood in the dimly lit holding room outside the main concourse, his heart pounding as he prepared to confront Ron Bender.

"Ron," Piper said quietly, "I've been meaning to ask you something."

"Shoot," Bender replied, his gaze fixed on his team.

"Did you ever work for Warner?"

"For him?" Bender sighed, rubbing the back of his neck. "No. Back when I was just starting in the Senate, I had a brief stint on a committee where he was the ranking member."

"What is the Golden Four?" asked Jackson.

Ron's face flushed. "What are you talking about?"

"You were a member with Warner, weren't you?" asked Jackson firmly.

"Yes, but it had a falling out over some ethical issues."

"Ethical issues?" Piper pressed, curious about the history between these two political powerhouses.

"Let's just say Warner wasn't always as squeaky clean as he appears to be," Bender answered cryptically, unwilling to divulge more. "But that was long ago, and I've since put it behind me."

Piper nodded, appreciating Ron's disclosure of the question, but all Jackson could think about was why he had not asked such a fundamental question sooner. Unnerved by the connection, he attempted to press forward with another question, but Valerie interrupted.

"A credible source has told Jackson and me," she began, her voice shaky. "They're saying you are the one who leaked our campaign information to Warner."

"Ron, I don't want to believe it, but..." Piper hesitated, unsure of how to proceed. "We need to get to the bottom of this."

"Jackson, you know me better than that," Bender insisted, his eyes pleading for understanding. "I would never betray you. Who is saying this shit about me? Is it Warner? That mother fucker..."

"It is coming from Sterling," said Jackson with a tone of growing impatience.

Bender's eyes narrowed, and for a moment, he looked like a cornered animal caught in the crossfire of an invisible enemy. "Jackson, what's wrong?"

"Information has been leaked from our campaign," Jackson replied, his eyes never leaving Bender's. "Warner has been using it against us and only means to keep us in the race to divide the Other Party vote and sail to victory. The election is rigged, but I'm an unwitting part of the plot."

A flicker of shock crossed Bender's face before he recovered, his brow furrowing in frustration. "How? Who would do such a thing?"

"Warner says he met with you when we were in DC for the Governor's road show with the Senate," Jackson paused, searching Bender's face for any trace of guilt or betrayal. "Tell me it isn't true."

"Jackson, I swear, I've never—" Bender began, but his words were cut off by Governor Lawrence shifting her weight, causing every chain, gem, and bangle she wore to jingle.

"This is preposterous!" she exclaimed, her loyalty evident in her fierce defense of Bender. "Ron has served you faithfully for years, Jackson. You can't possibly believe these lies."

"Believing them is not my first instinct," Jackson admitted, his gaze returning to Bender. "But this has my attention."

Jackson flipped his phone over so the two could see a video attached to the email. It showed Ron Bender leaving the lobby of the Hay-Adams Hotel and entering the President's Church across the street. The date stamp and time coincided with their trip to Washington last month. The footage continued, taken from a camera mounted on the church balcony, showing Ron Bender and President Russell Warner seated side by side in the pews. No audio was included.

"Jackson, I understand your concerns," Ron said, pleading for trust. "But I promise you, I am not the source of any leaks. You know me better than anyone else here."

"Let's investigate this matter together, y'all," Valerie suggested, determination etched across her features. "We can uncover the truth and expose Warner's lies."

Ron paced the room, building the courage to speak a terrible truth to his only true friend, who did not possess binary programming. "The video showing me meeting with Warner is not a fake…"

"What?!" shouted Jackson.

"Oh, no. No, Ron," whispered Valerie.

"Behind my back?" questioned Jackson.

"I'm sorry. I should have told you where I was going…"

"Why would you be meeting with that miserable fuck? And without telling me?" asked Jackson. Valerie flinched at Jackson's uncharacteristically blunt description.

"It was stupid," said Ron, with hope and fear flashing across his face. "I was using an old connection to Warner to convince him to back off on the attacks. Dial back the rhetoric. I was pleading for Secret Service protection."

"Well, where is it?" Jackson hissed.

"Where's what?" Ron barked back.

"The Secret Service? The last invoice was over $2 million for private security just for the past 72 hours," roared Jackson.

Ron's heart felt like it had been ripped out of his chest as he stared at Jackson, his eyes pleading for an answer. But all he received was a cold, emotionless response.

"He refused, Jack," Ron repeated, desperation and disbelief lacing his words.

Jackson's face was contorted with anger, and he began to pace back and forth, each step echoing with fury.

"Governor Lawrence and I have discussed this," Jackson spat out, his voice dripping with disdain. "We both agree that it's best if you take a leave of absence until these false allegations can be disproved."

The room fell silent, Jackson's words hanging heavy in the air. Ron could feel his world crumbling around him.

"How could you do this to me?" Ron finally managed to choke out, his voice cracking with betrayal.

"I care about you, Ron," Jackson said, his facade of composure beginning to crack. "But I need time to process this situation. We've been close for so long... this is breaking my heart."

Valerie interjected, her voice trembling with sadness and regret. "Please understand that this isn't easy for any of us. But we have to protect the integrity of the campaign and the principles we're fighting for."

Ron felt like he had been punched in the gut as he realized that even Valerie, whom he had personally courted to bring balance to this ticket, was now turning against him. He knew what they needed - a plausible explanation to salvage their political image - but it didn't make the blow any less painful or heartbreaking.

Their phones started exploding in vibrations.

"When it rains, it pours," said Valerie.

They each opened their device, except Ron, whose assistant Ziggy spoke with a disembodied voice to the room from his phone. "Mr. Bender, there is a troubling new video about you and Mr. Piper being circulated around news feeds, particularly those sympathetic to President Warner."

Ron rolled his eyes. "I already admitted I was at the Hay-Adams, Ziggy."

Ziggy interrupted, "No, Mr. Bender, this is much different. Please open your phone. I am broadcasting to all of your phones now."

It was the intercepted video from the heated exchange days ago at the hotel outside of Denver preparing for the convention.

The clip rolled on an endless loop on the remaining networks. It was a camera on a cell phone, apparently on during their heated argument. The transcript rolled on the screen.

PIPER: "FORWARD, FORWARD, FORWARD. YOU NEVER TAKE TIME TO ASSESS, TO STOP TO THINK, IS THIS REALLY THE RIGHT CALL?"

BENDER: "YOU WANT TO REVISIT THAT RACE. FINE. WE WERE STILL IN THAT RACE UNTIL THE DEBATE. THEN YOU LOST YOUR NERVE. WHEN

THAT EMPTY SUIT, A RETIRED FOOTBALL STAR, CRACKED THE FIRST JOKE AT YOU, IT WAS LIKE YOU WERE IN HIGH SCHOOL ALL OVER AGAIN. THE NERD BEING BULLIED BY THE JOCK. AND YOU ****ING FROZE."

PIPER: "I DID NOT!"

BENDER: "YOU ****ING DID, JACK. YOU DID. YOU WERE SMARTER THAN HIM AND COULD BE BRAVER AND STRONGER THAN HE EVER WAS ON THE FIELD, BUT YOU COWED. YOU REFUSED TO PUNCH BACK AT HIM AND YOU LOOKED WEAK. YOU ANSWERED HIS STRENGTH WITH WEAKNESS, AND THAT IS ALWAYS DEADLY IN POLITICS."

PIPER: "YOU'RE OUT OF LINE."

BENDER: "AND YOU QUIT ON US. ALL OF US. INCLUDING CATHERINE. THE GOING GOT TOUGH, AND YOU SURRENDERED. I NEED TO KNOW IF YOU'RE GOING TO QUIT ON US ALL AGAIN?"

PIPER: "GIVE ME A ****ING BREAK!"

BENDER: "YOU'RE COASTING AS WE NEED TO BE. YOUR POPULARITY WILL MAKE THIS EASY. WE CAN TAKE SOME TIME OFF, THE REAL FIGHT WILL NOT BE UNTIL NOVEMBER."

PIPER: "THE ****! I WANT MORE MONEY! MONEY, MONEY, MONEY!"

BENDER: "I CAN'T HELP YOU RIG THIS ELECTION FOR WARNER IF YOU WON'T STOP WITH THE MONEY!"

PIPER: "I NEED MORE MONEY!"

BENDER: "DON'T YOU DARE MAKE THIS ABOUT YOURSELF, JACK. I HAND-PICKED YOU FOR THIS JOB BECAUSE I SAW SOMETHING IN YOU. BUT IF YOU CAN'T HANDLE IT, THEN DO YOURSELF A FAVOR. QUIT NOW!"

"What the fuck?" bellowed Jackson, throwing his phone across the room.

"Those were not our words. At least, not accurately," said Ron. "We didn't argue about getting you more money!"

"This is an attempt at checkmate by Warner. If I keep you on, it looks like I'm the ringer just like Sterling said was your plan all along. If I fire you, it looks like I have something to hide," shouted Piper.

"We have to put the needs of the country and this campaign first," cautioned Valerie. "If you're compromised, Ron, or if he is blackmailing you..."

"Again. If he's blackmailing us both *again*, Ron, then I need to know it right fucking now," boomed Jackson.

With a heavy heart, Ron nodded. "He's not blackmailing us. I understand."

"Jackson, I swear to you, I'm not the one leaking anything," Ron implored, his eyes pleading for understanding. "That doctored video shows that Warner is trying to manipulate this situation. Turn it into something it is not."

Ziggy cautiously interrupted, violating her programming. "Governor, Senator, Mr. Bender, there is something you should know. Juniper just gave the video a review by *The Mark*. A green check. They are saying the video is validated and unaltered."

"That criminal! Alvarez has made his company and its fortune an accessory in this conspiracy to rig the election."

For a moment, Ron seemed to shrink in on himself as if the weight of the world had suddenly been dropped onto his shoulders. His voice cracked when he finally spoke again. "Jackson, you know me better than anyone. You know how much this campaign means to me. How much you mean to me. I would never betray you. It would be unthinkable."

Jackson's eyes were on fire. "I want your resignation in writing immediately while we conduct a full investigation on just what the fuck is happening to this campaign held together by fishing line and duct tape."

"Fine," Ron whispered, his heart shattering into a thousand pieces. "I'll go. But remember, Jackson..."

Jackson swatted his hands and turned his back to look out the windows.

"Valerie. Valerie, listen to me, please. This is important." His eyes were full of tears. "The people of this country tonight are now listening to you and counting on you to lead them. Don't let them down. Do not waste a moment to connect the dots between *The Mark*, Juniper, Alvarez, and Warner."

As Ron left the room, Jackson felt a pang of grief so intense it nearly brought him to his knees. He knew he was making a difficult decision for the greater good, but that didn't make it hurt any less.

∽

RON BENDER STOOD ALONE in the dimly lit corridor, his heart aching as the bitter taste of betrayal lingered on his tongue. The shadows cast by the flickering lights seemed to dance menacingly around him, echoing the turmoil that haunted his thoughts. He knew he had to act – not for himself but for the future of the campaign and the principles it represented.

Ron dialed a number on his phone as he walked towards the nearest exit.

"Mr. President," Ron called out, his voice wavering slightly as he addressed the man who had just emerged from behind a heavy wooden door. "We need to talk."

President Russell Warner's eyes narrowed on the other end of the call, his face a mask of cold indifference.

"Speak your mind, Mr. Bender," the President said, his tone dripping with contempt.

"Sir, I have been falsely accused of leaking information from the Piper campaign," Ron began hesitantly, acutely aware of the gravity of his words. "I believe you are behind this smear campaign, attempting to undermine my loyalty to Jackson. And now you have released a manipulated video you no doubt obtained illegally…"

The President leaned back into the plush White House chair, his arms crossed over his chest, a sinister smile playing at the corners of his mouth.

"Ah, Mr. Bender," he sneered, his voice low and menacing. "You always were perceptive, just as your theories about the salad dressing were spot on."

Ron's blood turned to ice in his veins.

"Let's just say I hate loose ends, Mr. Bender," the President replied, his voice barely above a whisper, "And if you don't want to meet a similar fate, I suggest you go back to the Piper campaign, beg for your old job back, and become my informant. And then run the ship into the rocks."

Ron's mind raced as he tried to process the enormity of the President's threat. How many more of Ron's skeletons would Warner reveal? Could the President still pin the death - the murder - of Mark Meriwether on him? How much inside intel had the President lifted from servers or a mole? Ron believed that the Piper-Lawrence campaign and the nation's future could depend on his compliance with this order from the vile inhabitant of 1600 Pennsylvania Avenue.

"Mr. President," Ron said, his voice trembling but resolute, "Fuck you!"

The President's cold laugh echoed out of the speaker as Ron ended the call. For the first time, he felt like he was the last man on earth, alone and afraid.

PART IV

26

THE GOLDEN FOUR

It was common for Senators and their staff to spend hours in a waiting game, remaining close at hand for a hastily scheduled vote when the U.S. government was staring down the barrel of a credit default. One such standoff had gripped Washington in the Spring of 2025. Russell Warner was in his first term as a United States Senator, sworn in just two years before after running a flawless campaign that trounced his opponent using the ongoing Mexican border crisis and spiraling inflation as a bludgeon.

Senators and staff attempted to pass the time waiting for the discordant House of Representatives to send over anything resembling a debt limit bill that could pass the Senate.

Senator Warner had been out to dinner with a group of men and women from the gaming industry and was returning to his office in the Russell Senate Office Building with four of the more attractive lobbyists for the casino industry. He had consumed at least one too many gin and tonics and was hoping to see what these two lobbyists were into before lying down in his office waiting for the 3 or 4 am vote on the Senate floor. It was 12:14 a.m. Senator Warner could recall the time because just when he had checked his watch, he had walked by an open janitor closet where he saw a blonde-haired woman performing what he assumed to be a sex act on a man whose face was out of view.

"That is surely a brilliant way to pass the time," he said aloud, which startled the couple in the closet. Warner proceeded down the hall towards the elevators with his two guests. As he boarded the elevator with the lobbyists, a man he recognized as a legislative director for the Other Party was exiting the elevator with a red-haired woman with bright green eyes easily twenty years his junior.

"Good evening, Senator," said the man.

"Mr. Blender? Is that your name?" asked the Senator. The drunken lobbyists were giggling like children.

"Bender, sir. Bender. Have a pleasant night. From the looks of it, as I am sure you will," said a younger Ron Bender.

Two days later, once the debt limit crisis was over after a narrow passage of a temporary debt limit increase, a junior Senate communications staffer named Nichole King, with blonde hair and blue eyes, filed a complaint with the Office of Compliance, claiming Ron Bender had made unwelcomed sexual advances to her during the late hours of the debt limit standoff. In her written filing, Nichole claimed Bender insisted on her providing him oral sex in exchange for a more senior role.

The Other Party Majority Conference Chair, Mark Meriwether, was tasked with approaching Ron Bender about the accusation since Bender was without a direct supervisor. Ron immediately insisted on his innocence. Ron was single, in his early fifties, and insisted he knew better than to make unwanted sexual advances toward anyone in the workplace. Meriwether assured Ron he believed him, but did he have anyone who could corroborate his story?

That very afternoon, Ron asked to speak privately with Senator Russell Warner, who was planning to fly back to Las Vegas for the recess.

"My assistant said you needed a private word with me, Mr. Bender. She said it was quite urgent," Warner said, motioning for Ron to sit while the Senator closed the door.

"Thank you for your time, Senator," said Ron.

"You have exactly five minutes before my driver takes me to Reagan National, so let's skip the pleasantries," said Russell Warner.

"Do you recall seeing me leave the elevator in the Russell Building three nights ago, Senator?" asked Ron.

"I can't say that I do," said Warner. "I was asleep on a cot in the Other Party Cloakroom. Is there a problem?"

Ron looked at the Senator in disbelief. He had not imagined seeing a drunken Russell Warner escorting male and female lobbyists back to his office at midnight for something other than talking points.

"Senator, I was with a redhead named Marley. She works on House Armed Services," insisted Ron. "I need to keep her name and presence with me that night out of this situation."

"Doesn't ring a bell," said Warner with a dry frown. "Three minutes left." Warner stood and began assembling his carry-on for his flight. Ron sensed he had to make a dramatic move, or his career in the Senate, which had just started, would end. He would be lucky to land himself back in a House role if he could not get the accusations dropped.

"Senator, I need a witness to help refute her version of events on the night in question," pleaded Bender. "There is a woman named Nichole King who is trying to push me out of the way so she can climb the ladder of prominence among Senate staff. She doesn't work nearly as hard as I do. She is having an affair with a Senator on your side of the aisle whom I do not want to name as part of all of this. He's not senior enough to land her a better job, but she knows that a sex scandal can sink an older man in a workplace full of twenty-somethings in short skirts and heels. If you could just jog your memory, Senator..." Warner exited the office, but Bender followed him.

"Senator," continued Ron as they walked through the empty Senate office. "I know you were in the cloakroom that night, but perhaps you came to your office just to grab an extra blanket before returning?"

Warner stopped in his tracks but did not turn back to look at Bender.

"A blanket, sir. Nothing more," insisted Bender.

Warner did not move nor turn to face Bender for what seemed like an eternity. He pushed open the heavy wooden door and headed for the airport.

Senator Mark Meriwether called Ron Bender into his office the next day and informed him that Senator Russell Warner had vouched for him. Warner said he had been in the elevator with Mr. Bender, and he was alone. Senator Warner said he saw nothing out of the ordinary about Ron Bender and nothing that led him to believe there was anything close to unwanted sexual advances in the time and location that she alleged. This contradicted the story of Ms. King and her claims of Ron Bender's unwanted advances.

The affair between Ms. King and the Senator became known that same day, though it was unclear who had outed the tryst. Ms. King was transferred to the Department of State before the end of the month.

Ron Bender quickly gained the respect of some Senators on both sides of the aisle for his discretion and knowledge of what made the body run and what brought it to a screeching halt.

Bender was invited to a Thursday night poker game that was invite-only in Warner's DC apartment. A quick but unique brotherhood formed among four men - Warner, Bender, Meriwether, and the Senate's President Pro Tempore. While drinking at a DC bar one night with women half their age, someone suggested they sing karaoke. Bender picked the most ridiculous song on the list - the theme song to the sitcom The Golden Girls. The drunken Senate quartet sang the lyrics on the stage, and the Golden Four was born.

They adopted the code names of the four characters—Rose, Blanche, Dorothy, and Ma—and the quartet became instrumental in cutting deals and using their relationships to control the Senate.

Meriwether had a long, secret friendship with the Nevada Senator from across the aisle, Russell Warner. There had been rumors that the friendship was more of an infatuation on the part of Mark Meriwether, which Warner was all too happy to goad and grist in private if it meant furthering his career in Washington.

Their secret club was powerful and close-knit until a rift emerged between Warner and Bender. The Pro Tempore sided with Bender and Meriwether with Warner. By that summer, the poker games had become less frequent; by the fall, they had ceased altogether.

Ronald Bender had risen to a senior role on the staff of Mark Meriwether when he became the Majority Leader. Mark was peculiar, demanding, and ritualistic. He had served in Washington for more than thirty years as a Senator from Virginia, witnessing many faces come and go on Capitol Hill during his three decades of service. However, Jackson Piper immediately stood out among his freshmen class to the Majority Leader.

Meriwether presided over a razor-thin majority, and he was just as interested in helping to take credit for the inevitable success of Piper as he was in keeping close tabs on the man from Pittsburgh. Meriwether invited Piper to a one-on-one breakfast to get to know him better. After an hour of rapt enthusiasm for Piper's legislative agenda, Meriwether suggested Piper add one of the most experienced Legislative Directors in the Senate to his office as his new Chief of Staff.

"I promise to consider him fully," said Piper. "What's his name?"

"You will like him. He has great relationships on both sides of the aisle. He's an old hand in the business of running Congress. Ronald Bender."

27

SURPRISE PATIENT

Dr. Piper mindlessly stirred a cup of coffee while looking at the brilliant purple mountains. She never grew tired of the Denver view. Sitting the General Election out might be a pipe dream, but she had grown weary of the many weeks on the road away from her children. Being home with them now while Jackson campaigned nationwide with his new running mate restored her balance. After Labor Day, she had to devise a safe way for Ben and Alex to be on the trail with her and Jackson.

Catherine stood in the faculty lounge, stirring that cup of coffee, thinking about Ron's horrific departure a week ago. She worried about Ron's emotional state. She thought about reaching out to him, but did not want to complicate matters further. She had to leave this to Jackson to solve.

It felt like Jackson was under constant attack now, and it was wearing him thin. He wasn't eating well and sleeping even worse. She picked up her phone to text him words of encouragement but was interrupted by a page over the hospital loudspeaker.

"Dr. Piper. Dr. Piper. Please dial 7-0," the impersonal SI voice said over the speakers.

When Catherine dialed the extension, she learned her VIP

patient was now waiting in room 921. The hospital administration said this VIP was insistent that they only be seen by her. She took the charts from a nurse and walked toward the patient's room.

It was a consultation with a patient, but the name was withheld ("Jane Doe"), and there were no links to electronic health records.

Dr. Piper's confident strides echoed down the quiet hospital hallway as she approached the exam room to greet her mystery patient. Her eyes scanned the nearly blank electronic chart as she scrolled through it with a finger, mentally preparing for the encounter ahead. As she neared the exam room, she took note of two serious-looking women seated outside the room - their black business suits and neutral-colored blouses gave off an air of authority.

"May I help you? Is there a problem?" asked Dr. Piper.

"No, Dr. Piper." Their stoic expressions unnerved Catherine. Was this a celebrity? Given the urgency and secrecy, it had to be. She took a deep breath before entering the room, suspecting that whoever awaited her inside would require all of her medical expertise and tact.

She gripped the gleaming metal handle, unsure who she might find on the other side of the door. With a slow exhale, she turned the knob and pushed open the door, revealing a small, sterile room beyond. A woman dressed in a flimsy gown sat on the exam table that did little to hide her fear and discomfort. Her face was absent of any makeup, and her black and grey hair was pulled tightly into a bun atop her head. But her face caught Dr. Piper's attention - it was strikingly familiar, and then instantly, it was clear who the mystery patient was. Dr. Catherine Piper's heart hammered in her chest.

"Ma'am?" said Dr. Piper in shock. "Is that really you?"

"Good morning, Dr. Piper," the woman extended her hand with a formality strange for such a setting. I hope you are not offended by the secrecy of today's visit. No one knows I am here except my husband and those two agents outside. No one else."

"Madam Vice President...please..." said Dr. Piper, still in shock.

"No, Dr. Piper. Today, I am Jessica Brown. I am told I have

metastatic breast cancer, and I am seeking a second opinion. My situation is one of the utmost consequence, Dr. Piper."

"A second opinion from me?" asked Dr. Piper.

"I need a doctor who is an irrefutable expert in my particular type of cancer. I need a doctor who will look at my case with fresh eyes and is someone I can trust to understand the international consequences of maintaining the confidentiality of this visit."

"I don't understand, Ms. Brown," said Catherine, her mind racing for answers. "Metastatic breast cancer? What stage? There is no chart here. No medical records."

Jessica straightened her spine and pursed her lips, keeping her body from quivering under the dread of the situation each time she spoke of it to a new person. "I received a letter of diagnosis this spring—stage four. We began a course of aggressive treatment. But I want a set of fresh eyes with no bias or influence from what other doctors have said."

"I do not understand, Madam Vice President, why would you trust me? My husband is running quite fiercely, I might add, to prevent you from having a second term in office."

Jessica remained serious and stoic in her tone. "My suspicion, and the reason I am here, Dr. Piper, is someone may already have beat him to it."

THREE FIRE EMOJIS appeared on Marco's phone. It was an agreed-upon code from Jon Rushan that an urgent, secure conversation was needed.

Marco flipped open his personal laptop, punched a few keys, and opened a secure communication channel with the man he had personally put in charge of running Juniper in his absence.

"VP has flown the coop."

"To where?" Marco typed.

"Denver," came the reply from Rushan.

Marco Alvarez read the text three times before he responded.

"Why is she in Denver? She said she was going to Jackson Hole for a retreat," typed Marco.

"She and her detail are off the grid. Went invisible in Denver. We have confirmed she is at the University of Colorado Medical Center."

"WTF. Why there?"

Rushan sent a link to a photo of Dr. Catherine Piper, head of the university's Cancer Institute.

"Fuck!" screamed Marco. His mind darted for potential solutions.

Another message came from Rushan. "She is suspicious of her diagnosis and is seeking a second opinion."

Marco considered the reply. "Fucking bitch," he typed. "Seeking medical advice from people with the only people on earth with more to lose than her."

Rushan went directly to the next steps. "Elimination?" asked Rushan.

"No," came the reply from Marco immediately. "High risk. There are too many x factors to move quickly. What other options?"

"Given her medical history, our model suggests that psychological threats would be sufficient to silence her."

"How much?" asked Marco.

"Our friends can accomplish this, but wish to speak with you first."

Marco considered the risks for only a moment, then, after calculating the odds quickly, directed his loyal chief to set up the conversation as soon as possible.

Several minutes passed, then came instructive texts across the screen.

"People's Republic of China Embassy, 3:00 pm."

"Confirmed," replied Marco.

DR. PIPER immediately made arrangements for an exam and an X-ray to establish a baseline understanding of Vice President Brown's condition. After about an hour, she returned with preliminary results and offered a reassuring smile.

"The x-ray shows a mass in your breast, confirming what I felt in the physical examination, but it is not imaging like a standard tumor. I am going to want to take a biopsy for our own direct assessment that it is, in fact, cancerous, ma'am. However, so far, I find the diagnosis of metastasized cancer to be suspect. Preliminary imaging shows no tumors in your lymph nodes, lungs, or other abdomen organs. Blood tests are still processing, so perhaps something shows up there?"

"Thank you, doctor," said Vice President Brown, trying to manage a smile under the harrowing circumstances.

"I appreciate your willingness to stay in town so we can get you prepped for a surgical biopsy. With proper preparation, we can manage that safely the day after tomorrow. I have cleared my schedule to accommodate that," said Catherine. "Can I ask you a serious question, Jessica?"

"Yes, doctor."

"You indicated earlier that you find the diagnosis suspicious. At first, I was skeptical. It is hard to misdiagnose metastasized breast cancer, but given these results, I have to ask you, what makes you think that your doctor got this wrong?" asked Catherine.

"They are not my doctors. These are doctors I was directed to visit," said Jessica. "I am not even certain they *are* doctors."

Jackson's phone rang. It was Catherine; he rose and excused himself to take the call.

"Hello, babe," said Jackson. "Miss me yet?"

"Oh, of course I do," said Catherine. "I only have a few minutes."

"I was thinking that when you join me to campaign in Arizona, we should try to duck out and sneak around to dinner alone."

"Jackson," she tried to interrupt him delicately.

"Maybe we could double date with Parker and Valerie?" said Jackson.

"Shut up and listen to me," said Catherine. Her tone was deadly serious.

"Cate? What's wrong?" asked Jackson.

"I take my oath as a doctor extremely seriously..."

"I know that, Love. Are you ok? Were you fired?"

"My new patient...fuck...I can't tell you, do you understand? It's against the law and my oath to tell you anything about my new patient. Tell me you understand that is why I can't tell you."

"I helped revise the HIPAA statute when I was in the House. Of course, I understand."

She switched over to a video call.

She looked at her husband helplessly, wishing to tell him. But now, as she looked into his hopeful, beautiful blue eyes, she did not wish to frighten him unnecessarily. She realized in the back of her mind this visit by Ms. Brown could all be a vile ruse designed to terrorize them and send them reeling.

She regained focus. It was a narrow but plausible way to maintain her integrity and her oath if this was not a diversion but something far more terrifying. "But if there was an emergency," she said, "I could reveal certain facts about the person I am treating and the nature of their disease, correct?"

"Catherine, is someone in danger?" He saw the panic in her eyes.

"I am not sure yet. But if I determine someone's safety is more important than my oath, please promise me you'll take that call immediately."

"Should we have a code word? A signal?"

Catherine thought carefully. "Your aunt Mary." Jackson had no such aunt. "I will be calling with an update on your Aunt Mary's health. Understand me?"

"Yes," replied Jackson.

"Just promise me that you will stay safe. This is not like New Hampshire. You are going out there completely exposed. This time, they know you could beat them, and they may not go down willingly. I want you to take your security seriously. I want you to come back home to us. Do you understand me?"

He promised her. She was being paged over the hospital intercom. She apologized, ended the call, and hurried off. Jackson stood in the hallway of the hotel in Nashville, wondering what had so spooked his wife.

28

ENEMIES DOMESTIC

The Chinese Embassy to the United States was located in a nondescript office building in the Van Ness neighborhood in Washington, DC, just a mile away from the temporary home of the cuddly and drowsy Su Lin and Xin Xin, the giant pandas on loan from the People's Republic to the Smithsonian Institution since 2032. No red and gold flag flew at its entrance, opting for a small sign visible only from the sidewalk on a heavily fortified street and catty corner to the closely allied Pakistani embassy.

His State Department security detail drove Secretary of State Marco Alvarez to the embassy's main gate under the pretense of official U.S. business. The Chinese ambassador had requested a meeting, which is standard protocol when an urgent matter of international significance requires a face-to-face conversation. While it was unusual for such a meeting to occur at the Chinese embassy and not the U.S. State Department, it was not unprecedented. Marco would need a convincing story to share with the President later that night, explaining the reason for the summons.

Marco's highly polished shoes snapped on the tile floors as he was escorted down a sterile hallway by two armed Chinese officers on the building's top floor at the center of the complex. The room was no doubt secure and far from any listening devices that curious state actors could deploy from the street. A heavy door was opened, revealing another sterile room with no photos nor windows, only a round, thick glass table, and simple, modern chairs assembled around it. Marco was directed to sit and await the Chinese Ambassador, Qi Feng.

Marco removed his phone from his breast pocket, but he discovered no signal and dared not attempt to join the Wi-Fi. He replaced the phone in his pocket and attempted meditation to pass the time. After twenty minutes alone in the silent, sterile room, a second door, not the one he had entered through, opened. Marco stood and bowed solemnly.

"Ambassador Qi, Xiàwǔ hǎo," said Marco.

"Mr. Secretary," Qi Feng said in a heavy Mandarin accent, "Good afternoon." Feng pulled out a chair at the table and sat slowly. The door he entered opened again, and a woman dressed in silk, white pants, and a blazer poured tea into a handleless cup she placed on linen before Feng. No tea was offered to Marco.

Feng spoke first. "The People of the developing world remain committed to eliminating the nuclear saber America has unleashed and held at the throats of nations for a century. You understand that, don't you, Mr. Secretary?"

"It would be in the interest of all peoples to live free from the fear of annihilation at the hands of nuclear war," replied Marco Alvarez.

Feng nodded, his fingers delicately grasping the ornate ceramic cup. The rich, earthy scent of the hot tea rose and enveloped his senses as he lifted the cup to his face. He savored the aroma. He closed his eyes and brought the cup to his lips, letting the warmth of the liquid soothe his throat before gently placing the cup back on the crisp white linen. The steam swirled gracefully from the surface of the tea, adding to the serene atmosphere of the room.

"The People's Republic of China is eager for a day when brilliant, peaceful technology such as that pioneered by Juniper can bring balance and equity to international cooperation," Feng said before taking a second long sip of the tea. "I must make it clear to you that

China does not want an incident that would jeopardize the peace before such a future can be secured."

Marco attempted to make eye contact with Qi Feng but did not look at the Secretary of State. Marco then tried to move the conversation to the purpose of his visit. "Juniper would no doubt like to expand its partnership with China. Your offer for significant investment in Juniper remains my reason for joining the Warner administration. I remain committed to..."

"There is no need to restate what you have said previously, Mr. Alvarez," said Feng, looking into the dark eyes of the U.S. Secretary of State. "We took you at your word then, and we do so now." He took a finishing sip of his tea, stood, bowed, and left the room discreetly through the same door through which he arrived. Before it closed fully, three serious-looking men entered the room. None of them spoke with accents that would imply English was not their native language.

They sat at the circular glass table. A bald man seated to Marco's left unlocked a strange-looking tablet and placed it in front of Marco.

"She's gone on a trip. She appears to have dropped all of her detail except for two agents that she trusts," he said.

The mustache man across from Marco continued to say nothing, only staring at Marco. The icy glare unnerved him.

"Where has she gone?" asked Marco, alarmed.

The fatter man clarified. "That's why we're here. It may be time to eliminate her from the equation."

Marco interrupted immediately. "No, NO! There is no way on earth that the Vice President of the United States can be eliminated right now. It would set off a firestorm of questions and investigations. Not to mention the delay in selecting a replacement."

The men sat stone-faced around the table.

Marco continued to insist on a more measured approach. "She has to resign and disappear voluntarily. Go into hiding. Get her out of the country and away from her protective detail. No one will care if an old black woman who used to be somebody dies in an accident on a trip overseas in a place no one ever heard of. Everyone will ask questions if she dies prematurely while I'm already angling with Warner to replace her."

The men conversed in a dialect of Mandarin Chinese that Marco Alvarez did not wholly understand. They seemed to discuss the plausible outcome of attempting to scare Jessica Brown out of the United States. The two men to Marco's right and left argued intensely while the third man seated directly across from Marco only stared him down coldly.

"Ānjìng de," the third man said sternly as the two men continued to argue. Their argument immediately ceased. "This will cost you significantly more, Mr. Alvarez. The price will be $50 million."

Marco scoffed. "Are you out of your fucking mind?"

"Come now, Mr. Alvarez. The end game for you is worth 100 times that amount," said the fattest of the three.

Marco worked over his problem aloud. "She is worthless in the role. But too fat at the trough to walk away on her own accord."

The mustached man laughed. "What is your so-called freedom worth to you, Mr. Alvarez?" Marco's eyes widened, but he did not want to reveal the scenes filling his mind. These men detested complications as much as President Warner and Marco needed to avoid becoming uncontrollable complications.

"How soon could you approach her?" asked Marco.

"We are always within striking distance of her husband. We also have a team already on the ground in Denver," replied the man to Marco's left.

"What's the likelihood of success?" asked Marco.

"Models say 87 percent likelihood," the fat one said.

That was not as high as he hoped, given the price his "friends" were quoting.

The man with the mustache laughed hauntingly. "Or we can see how the President reacts to the news that his Vice President's cancer …"

"Enough!" snapped Marco. "No need to state the obvious."

The three men nodded.

Marco was not a fool. He understood pretty clearly he was out of options. "Well, if it is $50 million that you insist upon, I will see to it that it is paid through the proper channels. That sum will take time to be paid without raising suspicions."

The three men gave no outward indication that they were pleased with this outcome. Marco patiently waited for a break in the tension.

"We will be in touch again, Mr. Alvarez," said the mustached man.

Standing, the mustached man gave Alvarez one final look before knocking on the door thrice. It opened, and he and his two associates disappeared through it. No one else entered the room. After a moment, the door through which Marco had entered was opened, and the armed guard returned, prepared to escort the Secretary of State back to his waiting secure vehicle that sat on the street outside the consulate.

29

BAD TO WORSE

As she stood over the operating table, her gloved hands deftly navigating through the biopsy procedure, Dr. Piper began to sense something peculiar was presenting itself. The sterile room hummed with the sound of medical equipment, and the faint scent of disinfectant filled the air. Sweat beaded on her forehead as she focused. An assistant wiped her brow. She kept her breaths even and measured beneath her mask.

"Scalpel," she requested, extending her hand without looking away from the patient. A nurse placed the instrument in her palm, and Catherine continued her work with practiced precision.

As she reached the mass that appeared as a tumor on Jessica Brown's breast cancer x-rays, she hesitated. Something about it seemed off, and she furrowed her brow behind her surgical mask. As her scalpel sliced into the tissue surrounding the mass, she discovered not a tumor but a small, foreign object - an implant designed to appear as a malignant growth on imaging scans.

"Impossible," she murmured under her breath, her heart racing. She looked up at her surgical team, eyes wide with shock. "This isn't a tumor. It's some sort of implant."

"An implant?" Her assistant echoed, disbelief evident in her voice. "But why?"

Dr. Piper ignored the question. Catherine carefully sliced the stitching that was holding the small mass in place and extracted the object from Jessica's breast, her mind racing with possibilities. She held it up to the light, examining its intricate design. It was engineered to perfection for imaging; that much was clear. What kind of monster would seek to deceive doctors - or a patient, for that matter - into believing this woman had a cancerous tumor? Such a diagnosis could ruin lives and careers.

The nurse posed the question another way. "Who would dare do such a thing?"

"Take this to the lab for analysis," she ordered, placing the object into a sterile container and handing it to a nurse. "I want to know what it's made of and how it ended up in the Vice President."

As one nurse hurried the bizarre pseudo-tumor away, Catherine tended to Jessica's wound, her mind still reeling from the discovery. Could this be a ploy to discredit the Vice President? To force her out of office? Is this what she meant by someone had beat Jackson to the punch? The implications were too terrifying to contemplate.

"Dr. Piper," her assistant said, snapping Catherine out of her thoughts. "Are you alright?"

Catherine took a deep breath, steadying herself. "I'm fine," she said, stitching up the incision. "Just need to finish up here. How's she doing?"

"Pulse and respiration are fine, doctor," said a nurse.

"Good," said Catherine. "What have you gotten yourself into, woman?"

Catherine walked from the operating room, which hastened to a fast walk, and then she ran for the stairs. She made it down four flights to a rear exit, exploded through a steel door into the hot June air, and vomited in the grass. She breathed the fresh air deeply through her nostrils and exhaled through her mouth slowly. Her hands shook ever so slightly as she walked in circles, searching her mind for the next possible move. The weight of the knowledge that...

that...*thing* in the Vice President sent another round of chills through her tense body. She had seen many things in her career, but this was something altogether new and horrible.

"Who had the power to do something like this?" she said aloud, alone in the ally, her voice strained with horror. "What kind of twisted minds are we dealing with?"

She raced through the myriad of potential explanations, each more sinister than the last. In each scenario, she concluded that someone needed Jessica Brown out of the way quickly and quietly, and they were willing to go to unthinkable lengths to achieve it.

Whoever was behind this would go to incredible lengths for access to power. Her next thought was of Jack; she had to tell him what she had seen with her own eyes.

∽

MEANWHILE, in the dimly lit hospital room, Jessica Brown was awake from her surgery and waiting anxiously for news from the care team at the University of Colorado Medical Center. Blood rushed to her head as Dr. Catherine Piper entered the room, looking fraught with worry.

"Jessica, I've got some interesting news," Dr. Piper began. "You don't have cancer."

"I don't understand," said the Vice President. "Not anywhere?"

"Nowhere, dear," said Dr. Catherine Piper carefully but with a smile. "It appears, in my professional opinion, you never did."

"What about the lump in my chest?"

"What I removed from your body was a foreign object designed to mimic a tumor on imaging. I have never seen anything like it in my career."

Jessica stared at her in disbelief. Her mind raced, trying to make sense of the revelation. "How is that possible?" she whispered. "Why would someone do this?"

"My theory is that whoever contrived the initial diagnosis, which was likely false, made up a need to perform an initial biopsy in order to implant this object. Everything they have shown you, from blood tests to x-rays, have been falsifications."

"They want me out of the way, Dr. Piper," Jessica Brown whispered. "I don't know why. I have been nothing but loyal and done as I was told. Obeyed every directive. I played my part. Why would he..." Her voice trailed off as panic filled her face.

"We do not need to theorize about the reasons right now, Madam Vice President," Catherine said, subtly reminding Jessica Brown of the station of importance she held. "Let us savor the great news that you are healthy."

Jessica felt anything but well. She felt worse now under the curse of knowledge. Jessica's heart pounded in her chest, her throat constricted. A film projector clicked on, and its light illuminated in her mind scenes of doctors strapping her to a table while slowly poisoning her. She saw her hair falling out in clumps. She was in a wheelchair, unable to speak.

Jessica's fear quickly morphed into paranoia. She felt a cold shiver crawl down her spine as she considered the implications of Dr. Piper's words.

"Dr. Piper, I have to leave this hospital immediately," Jessica whispered urgently, her eyes darting around the room. "I need to find refuge somewhere safe. I can't trust anyone. What if the Secret Service is planning to kill me?"

"Jessica, you're not thinking clearly," Dr. Piper tried to reason, sensing that her patient's mind was spiraling out of control. "Let me help you."

But Jessica was inconsolable, her delusions consuming her. She began to shake and moan. Tears filled her eyes.

"Jessica, try to stay calm," Dr. Piper urged, concern etched across her face.

"You must not tell them, Catherine! Who knows? Do they already know?"

Catherine reassured her that the small team in the operating room an hour ago had been directed to maintain complete secrecy given the patient's identity. "I told them it was a matter of national security. They seemed to get it."

Fearful but weak, Jessica could not muster the strength to leap from the bed and run. She felt helpless, like in a dream. "I am such an old fool!" the Vice President said in a hushed voice. "Oh, sweet Jesus, what am I to do now?" She continued to cry, but when Catherine Piper moved in close and placed a hand on her arm in an attempt to console her, Jessica began to thrash and kick. One of her swings landed squarely across Catherine's jaw. Jessica did not apologize.

Catherine pressed the red button to summon assistance from the nurses' station. Two large women and a young man descended upon the room and found the VIP patient in a state of terror.

"Postoperative delirium," said Dr. Piper. "Too much new information too quickly is putting her into a state of shock. I'm going to make her more comfortable."

Jessica continued to thrash and resist the terrifying realities closing in on her in the small, sterile room. Sedation may be the only way to ensure Jessica's safety.

"Ms. Brown, this is Dr. Catherine Piper. You just finished surgery, but you need to rest now. I am giving you something to help you be more comfortable while this news sinks in. Please rest while we figure out your next move, okay?"

"Don't let them get to me," Jessica pleaded, tears streaming down her face. "I need to speak to Steve. Where is Steve? I don't have much time." Dr. Piper administered a calming medication through the IV, watching Jessica's wild eyes finally flutter shut.

Catherine's head filled with a dozen potential scenarios of how to protect her patient. But it was not long before her thoughts returned to her situation. She couldn't help but worry about the implications of this new knowledge. The sinister conspiracy unfolding before her eyes threatened to upend everything she believed in, and she knew she had to act cautiously to protect Jessica and expose the truth while avoiding placing a target on her back and the back of her unknowing husband.

She decided she must alert him immediately.

The Bull Moose candidates for President and Vice President were in a motorcade in Charlotte. Jackson's phone buzzed with an incoming call. It was Libby in the truck behind them. "Jackson, Catherine's on the line. She's trying to reach you. She says she has urgent news about your Aunt Mary. Everything ok?"

"I'll call her," Jackson said, his brow furrowing with concern. He ended the call and dialed Catherine.

Catherine stood in their kitchen. Hours had passed since the frightening conversation with VP Brown.

"Jackson," Catherine's voice trembled over the line. "I need you to listen carefully. Something unexpected has happened. I need you to listen carefully."

He sensed her panic. "What's going on?"

"Jackson, I need you to listen carefully," Catherine said over the phone, her voice trembling with urgency. "Your Aunt Mary is not doing well. The situation is very serious. Please reach out to your Uncle Ben as soon as possible. He has all the details."

"Of course, Catherine. Thank you for letting me know," Jackson replied, his brow furrowed with concern. Through the cryptic code, he could sense the gravity in her tone and knew that something was deeply wrong.

"Thank you," Catherine breathed, relief washing over her for a moment before being replaced with urgency once more.

"I love you," Jackson said, worry gnawing at him. "Whatever it is, we've got this, you hear me?"

When their call ended, Catherine rushed into Jackson's office, her heart pounding in her chest. She spread the medical file across the table, and the patient's name was blacked out to protect their identity. She thought momentarily, then scribbled a pseudonym with a thick black felt marker. Her frustration mounted as she fumbled with the papers.

"Franklin, I need your assistance," Catherine pleaded, glancing nervously over her shoulder. "Please capture images of these documents and encrypt them as securely as possible."

"Understood, Dr. Piper," Franklin replied, capturing the images with a camera mounted near the screen and encrypting them with precision.

Catherine retrieved a pan from the kitchen and placed the file in it. Striking a match, she set the file aflame, watching as the flames consumed the papers. Once it had burned to ashes, she washed them down the drain, her heart heavy with the knowledge she now carried.

"Jackson," she whispered to herself, "please hurry."

As they reached the airport to depart for the next city, Catherine's call still hung heavily in Jackson's mind. He pulled Valerie aside as they prepared to board, needing to share his concerns with someone he trusted.

"Something's wrong in Denver," Jackson confided, his voice barely above a whisper. "Catherine called me saying my Aunt Mary isn't doing well. But we don't have an Aunt Mary. It's code – we agreed on it. She wanted me to know something serious was happening with a patient whose identity she could not reveal to me without alerting anyone else."

Valerie's eyes widened with alarm as she listened to Jackson's words. "What do you think it means? What's going on?"

"I don't know, but it concerns us," Jackson admitted, his mind racing with worry. "She told me to contact my Uncle Ben, which I think means I need to access Franklin's encrypted section for clues."

"Let's get on the plane and see what Uncle Ben has waiting for you," Valerie suggested, placing a supportive hand on Jackson's shoulder.

Upon boarding the plane, Jackson wasted no time accessing the encrypted files through Franklin, his heart pounding in anticipation of the information Catherine had so urgently relayed.

Franklin's database appeared before them with a few deft swipes on the touchscreen, revealing a medical record for "Vincent Price" scrawled in black marker on the files.

"Vincent Price? Catherine must be taking her love for old horror films a little too far," Libby joked, trying to lighten the tense atmosphere. But none of them could ignore the gravity of their situation.

"Franklin, could you provide an analysis of these records?" Jackson asked, his eyes scanning the dense text. The digital assistant obliged, processing the information in the blink of an eye.

"Patient Vincent Price presented with a stage 4 metastatic breast cancer diagnosis, seeking a second opinion," Franklin began, adjusting his digital bifocals on the screen. "After conducting various tests, including x-rays, blood tests, MRIs, and a biopsy, Dr. Catherine Piper concluded that the patient is cancer-free and, more alarmingly, never had cancer of any kind."

Jackson listened intently for the payoff. Valerie's face mirrored his concern as she leaned in closer to hear the rest of the report.

"Dr. Piper removed a foreign object implanted in the left breast of the patient, which was designed to appear as a tumor on imaging. The origin of this object is unknown. The patient, Vincent Price, displayed erratic behavior, paranoia, and emotional distress following the revelation that the patient's cancer diagnosis was part of an apparent elaborate hoax."

The private aircraft cabin grew silent as the team absorbed the information. Each felt a mix of fear and anger at the deception they uncovered involving this unwitting patient. Jackson's thoughts raced as he tried to connect the dots and determine the significance of this mysterious patient.

"Whoever Vincent Price really is," he whispered, "we need to find out why someone went through all this trouble to deceive them."

The private jet hummed as the team debated Catherine's cryptic message and Vincent Price's strange medical records. Jackson rubbed his temples while Ron paced and Valerie stared out the window.

"What does the file say about the patient's description?" asked Libby.

Franklin read aloud, "A U.S. citizen, black female, brown eyes, black and grey hair, aged seventy years. Five foot five inches tall, one hundred sixty-seven pounds, low blood pressure, married."

"But Vincent Price is a man's name?" said Valerie.

"Vincent Price is a pseudonym for V - P. Vice President," said

Franklin. "Catherine is telling us that Vice President Jessica Brown sought her trusted second opinion from Dr. Piper."

"Are you suggesting that someone implanted a fake tumor in the Vice President of the United States?" Jackson asked.

Libby jumped in, "Not just any fake tumor. One designed to appear to be a metastasized cancer tumor with low survival rates."

"Seems ludicrous," Valerie retorted. "But someone wanted her out of the way by making everyone think she's dying."

Jackson shook his head. "But who would do something so evil? And why?"

"Maybe they wanted someone else in the position," Valerie suggested uneasily. "Someone more easily manipulated?"

"Or someone they owe," added Jackson with a knowing look at Valerie. "A billion reasons."

∼

MARCO'S PHONE vibrated on his desk at the State Department. He flipped it over to reveal a message from a number he did not recognize. The codeword "Yosemite" was on the screen. Marco opened his personal, secure laptop, typed in a series of passwords, and revealed a message with an address nearby.

Marco stood and told his security detail that he needed fresh air. He asked to be driven to a nearby cafe for an espresso.

While Marco Alvarez stood in line waiting for his order, a man approached behind him. It was the bald man from the Chinese Embassy several days prior.

The bald man held a phone to his ear, pretending to speak to someone on the other end. "Dr. Piper has removed the implant and has sent it to a lab for inspection. We have intercepted that package already. No tests will be run on it."

Marco did not make eye contact. "So the doctor will soon look like a whacko if she tries to suggest she removed a noncancerous object from Jessica Brown?" asked Marco.

"Already there," said the bald man. "And we will soon have access to the hospital's data room to eliminate all records of Jessica Brown's brief stay in Denver."

"A good solution," said Marco nervously.

The mustachioed man reached for a biscotti in front of Marco, still holding the phone for the fake call to his ear. He said, "And now you must do something for us."

Marco looked confused. "Me? You are the assholes that lost her. She gave you the slip and took a trip to see our opponent's wife, a fucking cancer expert, for a second opinion."

"Quiet down," said the man behind Alvarez. "You will ensure that your FBI investigates the home of the Pipers, locates any files she has taken from the hospital about Jessica Brown and sees to their destruction..."

"How can you be sure she has?"

"Oh, she has, Mr. Alvarez," said the fat man.

"But how am I to get the FBI to investigate her and look for such files without raising suspicions of my involvement?" asked Marco, looking around the table for an answer. His palms left watermarks on the glass.

"You're a smart man, Mr. Alvarez. You'll find a way."

"Next!" shouted a barista behind the counter. Marco stepped forward to place his order. He heard the bell on the entry door to the cafe ring and did not need to turn to know his meeting was over.

∼

THE SEDATIVE WAS WEARING off as Jessica Brown blinked her dry eyes, and the dimly lit hospital room came into focus. Disoriented momentarily, the reality of her circumstances soon washed over her like a piercing cold rain.

She was completely unaware that the sparse Secret Service detail she had brought with her on this confidential excursion to Denver was drugged by two people posing as orderlies making the late-night rounds at a time when the hospital was at its most barren and sparsely staffed. Moments earlier, they had disabled the security cameras on the floor to hide the actions that would have required perhaps no more than ten minutes on the silent floor of the hospital.

The orderlies propped the two agents up in their seats, then slipped into the hospital room of Jessica Brown to find her lying in her bed, staring hopelessly into the void of uncertainty.

One closed the door, while the other pulled privacy curtains.

"Is it time for more medication?" asked the Vice President, unaware of their intentions.

"Of sorts," said the female of the pair.

They moved swiftly, placing a gag around the mouth of Vice President Brown while at the same time tossing two fabric bands across her body, which they used within seconds to restrain her to the bed. She could neither move nor scream; it was a terrifying predicament.

The tall, slender man removed a tablet from a bag, unlocked it, and revealed a live video of Steven Brown under extreme duress. Jessica Brown's eyes opened wide and flashed with horror. She looked at the pair and shook her head violently, showing her objections to the scene.

Off camera, someone wearing black leather gloves placed a semi-automatic pistol to Steven Brown's head. Steven began to shake his head and breathe heavily through the gag in his mouth. Tears were streaming down his cheeks as he faced what he was sure was the end of his life.

A disguised voice came through the tablet. "Jessica Brown, you have made a most grave error. Listen carefully; if you do as we say, you and Steven will be free to go. All you must do is resign your office immediately and leave the country. An autocar is waiting for you outside to take you to the Denver Airport. You will fly to Cairo, Egypt. An account with $10 million in US is waiting for you there and a palatial estate that will be yours to enjoy for the remainder of your days. You will renounce your U.S. citizenship. You will never discuss your cancer or the events of the past 24 hours with anyone and never return to the United States. If you violate any of these terms, we will act swiftly to end your life, as well as Steven's, in a far more painful way than cancer. The choice is yours. You have ten seconds to decide."

The woman produced a letter of resignation and a pen. It indicated Jessica Brown's desire to live out the remainder of her days with her husband, Steven, seeking alternative medical treatments in Africa and Asia in hopes of beating her cancer since the United States has been unable to provide her with hope of a cure. Her resignation from the Vice Presidency was effective immediately. The letter requested privacy and respect during this time of challenge.

"Ten...nine...eight..." counted the voice.

Steven shook his head no on camera, but Jessica Brown was not willing to watch her husband executed on camera, then likely killed herself. If it was a question of doing the right thing, what was the moral choice at this moment? Take a noble stand and lose everything? Stand on principle at the hands of assassins who held all the cards. Damn her foolishness to think she could run to Denver from these psychotic monsters.

"Seven...six..."

This ignominious end would erase her career in the House of Representatives and extinguish the hope of her country-before-party decision to cross the aisle and run on a unity ticket with Warner after the crisis of '39. It had been a historic moment, even if their administration had accomplished little of what they had promised. This was a terrible end to her career.

But would anyone know? Could she live with this shame? To the world, she would be a woman with stage four cancer seeking time with her husband to die with dignity. She could regain anonymity and privacy again. She had not experienced privacy in four years, and she missed it. She could live her final days with the love of her life. Would $10 million be enough? Surely it was. Was it enough to buy her conscience?

"Five..."

Was this a crime? Was she committing a crime? Was this a bribe, and if she accepted it, was it a felony? Could she be prosecuted if anyone ever found out?

The gunman placed the pistol at Steven's temple and cocked the hammer. He shook uncontrollably, drenched in sweat.

Jessica looked up at the woman hovering over her hospital bed. Jessica could not speak with the gag in her mouth, so she nodded urgently, her eyes wide and focused. Tears streamed down her face.

"Dá'àn shì kěndìng de," said the tall man in the room, indicating that Jessica Brown agreed to their demand.

"Wise decision, *former* Vice President Brown," said the gunman, slowly releasing the hammer on the pistol, removing the imminent threat to Steven's life. "You will love Cairo. We'll be watching." The screen went black.

"Sign!" said the woman urgently as they released the restraints on Jessica's body. Her weak, shaking hand reached for the pen and signed the resignation letter.

The fake orderlies quickly disconnected the numerous sensors detecting Jessica's pulse, respiration, and blood pressure. They also turned off the alarms that would have alerted the charge nurse of a problem in the room. Finally, they quickly dressed Jessica in a black tracksuit and placed her in a wheelchair.

"Where are you taking me?" asked Jessica.

"The airport, as you agreed, Ms. Brown. Don't worry. We will hold up our end of the bargain. You will not be harmed. You have done as you were told. Continue to do so, and no further harm will come to you or your husband."

30

THE CURSE OF KNOWLEDGE

Billings' office reeked of old books and bourbon — trophies from Louisiana's political arena where he'd battled for over thirty years. Legal volumes loomed from towering shelves, casting long shadows across the plush carpet as Jackson Piper stood under their silent scrutiny.

"Mr. Speaker," Jackson began, his voice steady. "I am afraid I have grave news."

Billings' jowls quivered as he chuckled. "Spit it out."

Jackson clenched his jaw and withdrew a sheaf of papers from his briefcase. "Dr. Catherine Piper met with an anonymous patient a week ago. Only the College of Medicine's dean knew their identity."

Sylvester leaned back in his chair, its springs groaning under his weight.

"Upon meeting her, Catherine discovered the patient was Vice President Jessica Brown."

The Speaker's skepticism faded to intrigue as he scanned the documents.

"She was seeking a second opinion on stage four metastatic breast cancer. Dr. Piper found that Jessica Brown is cancer-free... and had never actually had cancer," Jackson revealed. "An element was implanted in her to appear as a cancerous tumor on x-rays."

Sylvester Billings shifted in his chair, eyes wide, placing the medical files on his desk.

"Who provided the original diagnosis?" asked Sylvester.

Jackson reached into the file and showed a copy of the original letter Jessica Brown had received indicating an abnormality detected during a routine mammogram. She was referred to this doctor by the letter, Dr. Jia Geming. He performed the biopsy and blood tests and made the diagnosis."

"Sounds like the Vice President has a strong medical malpractice case to wage, Jackson," huffed Sylvester.

"Sir, there are only six Jia Gemings in the United States, and not one of them is a doctor of oncology," Jackson said with a grave look of alarm.

"You're certain of that, Jackson? I hope you used more resources than just a search engine?"

"Let me be clear, Sylvester. Someone generated a false medical diagnosis in April, posing as the Vice President's physician. Under false pretenses, they convinced her to undergo grueling treatments for a condition she doesn't have..."

"You've done your homework, Jackson," Billings' voice softened, his southern charm wrapping around each word. "But what do you expect me to do? I'm the Speaker over mutinous pirates, each waiting for their shot at command."

"Sir, last night Vice President Jessica Brown left the hospital without being discharged and without her Secret Service detail. She left a letter of resignation, and it appears that she and Mr. Brown have disappeared." Billings didn't believe the words coming from Jackson's mouth.

"And no one is attempting to locate them?" asked Billings.

"Indeed. The dean and the nurses who assisted with the procedure are missing. The Secret Service agents have vanished along with any evidence that Jessica Brown was ever a patient there."

"Oh, come now, Jackson," said Billings. "You sound like one of those wide-eyed conspiracy talkers."

"Who would most benefit from the Vice President having a terminal illness that would require treatments so severe that she would have to contemplate not remaining in office?" asked Jackson. "And then disappearing without a trace?"

"I think we know the answer to that, Jack. That fox is sitting in the henhouse already with a mouth full of feathers," said Sylvester.

"Sir, I am appealing to your sense of justice," Jackson replied, his gaze unwavering. "This is bigger than Party lines or regional loyalties. This is about the foundations of our nation. This has gone from a political saga to a full-blown Constitutional crisis."

Billings looked up at the ceiling then in a heavy Louisiana drawl, "You know, my daddy used to say, 'Just because there's a mouse in the gator's mouth, don't mean he ain't got a taste for chicken, too.' KnowwhadImsayin?"

"Then stand up against this chiseler," Jackson urged. "Russell Warner is a selfish and vindictive son of a bitch, but I am starting to finally see that he is not the true threat to the nation in this election. Sylvester, the threat is Alvarez."

Sylvester suddenly leapt from his chair and pounced for a remote on the edge of his desk. He throttled up the volume on the large screen that consumed an entire office wall. In the shot was the East Room of the White House.

Jackson's phone vibrated wildly. It was Catherine.

"Excuse me, Sylvester...Cate?" Jackson said as he lifted the phone to his ear.

"Jackson, you're never going to believe this. The FBI is in our home. They have a warrant for a search," said Catherine.

"What? A search for what?" Jackson asked. He placed the phone on speaker so Sylvester could hear what she was describing.

"The warrant says," she began to read over the phone, "they are authorized to search and obtain any evidence connected to suspected threats against the Vice President and other officers covered under the Presidential Succession Act of 2006."

"What the fuck?" said Jackson.

"Jack, what do I do?" Catherine was scared and breathing heavily into the phone. Then she screamed.

"Cate! Cate! Are you there? What's wrong?" asked Piper.

"They are breaking things, Jack. Destroying our home!" she screamed. Sylvester's jaw dropped in horror.

"Where is Yael and your security detail?" screamed Piper into the phone.

"The FBI has detained them all outside," she answered.

"Hang up with me and call the attorneys. Tell them you want them onsite to observe the FBI's work immediately. Catherine, this is important. I want you to *pull the ripcord.*"

Catherine knew this was code for immediately emptying the home of all staff, gathering their children, and then traveling with her private security agents to one of three previously agreed-upon secret, secure locations. The protocol was developed by the private security team.

"I love you," she said.

"I love you, too. Everything's going to be alright. Now go!"

Catherine ended the call.

On the screen in Billings' office, President Warner entered the shot and approached the podium bearing the seal of the President of the United States. Next to him stood Marco Alvarez, who looked resolute and calm; a half smile was painted across his chiseled features.

"It is with a heavy heart that I share with the nation that our Vice President, Jessica Brown, has for several months waged a private battle with cancer. As she seeks alternative treatment to wage a heroic fight against this deadly disease, she has concluded that she cannot continue as my Vice President now or in a second term. Defeating cancer should be her sole focus, and we must respect that decision. I believe this was a difficult decision, but I respect it and ask the nation to respect it."

Speaker Billings whispered, "That lyin' sack ah shee-it."

"There is only one person I know capable of assuming the heavy responsibilities of the vice presidency and willing to join me as my running mate - as my Vice President - so we may continue our work to save America. My choice is Secretary of State Marco Alvarez."

The President smiled and began to clap as he invited a smiling Marco Alvarez to the microphone. Marco started by asking all to join in a moment of silent prayer or transmission of positive thoughts to Jessica Brown and her family; then, he began to address the small cadre of assembled White House staff and press in the East Room.

Sylvester looked at Piper in shock. He finally found the appropriate words of warning. "You are in danger, son. If you know this is all a clever lie, and they are searching your home, they are looking for this file." Sylvester handed it to Jackson as if it were on fire.

Jackson began gathering his things with urgency.

"What you know to be the truth is dangerous to them," the Speaker continued. "If they are willing to subject a poor old black woman to pills and radiation and surgeries to convince her she has cancer that does not actually exist, then they won't think twice about arranging your disappearance or worse."

Sylvester's skin drained of color, leaving him pale and ghostly like a delicate lily. His trembling hands shook uncontrollably, betraying his fear and panic. In a hushed voice, he pleaded with Jackson to leave the Capitol, his words frantic and urgent. "You must go, Jackson! Leave Washington and find safety! This madness is spreading like a plague, and it will consume us all!"

"I will be in touch once I have relocated my team and we do not perceive that we are in danger. Whatever you do, Sylvester, do not allow the House or the Senate to confirm that man as Vice President."

"Don't you worry about that, Jack. This nomination is going nowhere, but that is the least of your worries. Get to safety!"

Jackson lifted the phone to his mouth and, with steady precision of his words, spoke the phrase "Green Goblin!"

With a loud bang, six private security officers flung open the doors to Speaker Billing's office. They grabbed Piper roughly by the arms and dragged him at breakneck speed through the halls of the Capitol Building despite his protests to slow down. As they reached the exit, an armored SUV screeched to a halt on Independence

Avenue, driven by a stern-faced Esmael. Once inside, Piper called Governor Lawrence on her private phone. In a steady and calm voice, he relayed the unfolding chaos and danger they could all be in. The triumphant atmosphere of the previous week's Bull Moose convention had been replaced with a frantic scramble for safety, possibly even moving the principal members of the presidential campaign into hiding from unknown threats.

"Where do we go? Do I stay in Austin? Am I safe here?" she asked.

"You're the Governor of Texas. For now, double your protective detail in Austin and stay close to a phone until I contact you about the next steps."

31

GHOSTS

Election Day: 61 days. Early voting: Begins in the first states in just over two weeks.

> National Poll: (+-5%)
> Warner 36%
> Piper 27%
> Drummond 19%
> Undecided 18%

Amongst the palms and the glistening modern furnishings of the JW Marriott Desert Palms resort outside of downtown Phoenix, Ron Bender paced like a panther. He had not been on the outside looking in on any presidential campaign he supported since before the start of the millennium.

After what felt like an eternity, the doors of a nearby elevator opened, and out of it stepped Senator Diesel Browning and two private security guards for the Piper campaign.

Ron attempted a warm smile, and Diesel attempted one in return. This meeting was not easily obtained, and amidst the charged atmosphere of Phoenix, Arizona, and the President's Save America actions along the Mexico border, everyone was operating with an electric charge in their movements.

"Thank you for getting him to meet with me, Senator. This means a great deal to me," said Ron.

Diesel nodded, but he did not speak. It was not until they reached their destined floor that Diesel spoke and only after the doors opened.

"The evidence you shared with me is compelling, but I would appeal to his better angels. Seek forgiveness more than exoneration. Jack is under constant threat right now. He is suspicious of everyone," said Diesel.

The security detail whisked the pair down the hall at a faster-than-normal walking pace to the end of a hallway that held one of the more spacious suites still in the responsible price range of a presidential campaign wary of every penny it was spending.

"This was by far the most secure location we could afford in Phoenix. A little pricier than the budget should permit, but we have the principals in the hotel, so security trumped price."

"You don't have to explain anything to me, Diesel. It is a solid choice. I would have done the same."

The doors to the suite opened, and inside were two more security guards, as large as Jackson, standing in suits near the door. They were armed. To Ron's surprise, the guard he knew as Oliver stood and then wanded Ron with a metal detector to check for concealed weapons. He then patted Ron down.

"My apologies, sir. Standard procedure now," said Oliver.

"Don't apologize. It's what you should be doing," said Ron.

Jackson stood and greeted Ron with a cool look of serious contemplation. Ron spoke first.

"Thanks for seeing me, sir," said Ron.

"Of course. Diesel expressed the importance of us speaking face to face," said Jackson, sitting in a large armchair next to a comfortable-looking soda. "Can I interest you in a drink?"

"Sure, how about a coffee?" Ron asked, wishing to stay focused on his mission and keep his head clear.

Jackson signaled to Harper, who poured two cups of coffee from a hot metal urn near the door and brought the mugs over to the seated men along with a creamer.

Jackson noticed Ron fiddled with the sugar and the creamer nervously.

"Ron, take a deep breath. You're going to walk out of here alive," said Jackson. Then, in his best Don Vito Corleone voice, he said, "I'm a reasonable businessman."

The humor broke the tension enough for Ron to launch directly into his case.

"I want to begin by apologizing. I was reckless and operating without a full appreciation of the need to keep you and Catherine aware of my calculations," said Ron, finally able to exhale.

"Thank you for that, Ron. It is greatly appreciated," said Jackson coolly. I just don't understand how you could be so sloppy as to endanger all of our work."

"I have provided a timeline that I think presents an alternative explanation for how Warner has obtained documents and data," said Ron.

Ron quickly unfolded two pieces of paper from his jacket pocket and handed one to Jackson. He flattened the other on the translucent glass coffee table between them. He then poured over the timeline with careful detail for Jackson.

"You're like a younger Columbo right now," Jackson said.

"How would you know who Columbo is?" Bender asked.

"Catherine made me watch the reruns a few winters ago. She's a fan," Jackson said.

Brushing the momentary distraction aside, Ron continued to outline his theory. First was their conversation about the state court cases. Ron had outlined who was aware of the specific details of that conversation that appeared to have leaked to Warner. The list included the three attorneys, Diesel, Ron, Jackson, Catherine, Sylvester Billings, and Sterling Powers.

The second and third conversations were about selecting the running mate. Those conversations had been contained to just one of the attorneys who was performing the vetting of the potential candidates. Ron, Diesel, Jackson, and Catherine were the only people with a full view of the details.

"Tell me more about this fourth meeting on this list," Jackson said. "This is the trip and conversation that Senator Powers brought to my attention. It's primarily why I made the difficult decision to relieve you of your duties."

"There was a very good reason why I kept my history with Warner from you," Ron said.

Ron's chest tightened as he approached the summit of revealing to his candidate what he had managed to keep withheld for so long.

Jackson shifted uncomfortably in his chair, waiting for Ron to speak during the unsettling silence.

"Before you came to Washington, DC, long before I met you as a rising star in our Party, I was part of a secret club in the Senate that controlled a lot of what the Senate did or did not do. Under Senate Leadership, our quiet group mainly influenced meaningless things like the Senate dining room menu or committee staff promotions. We influenced some of the better-than-expected office location assignments when there was a member we wanted to impress or influence."

Jackson was listening intently. He did not interrupt Ron's confession with questions, yet.

"But after the Health Care fight, things began taking a different flavor. During that fight our 'club' had collected many high-profile bargaining chips. We suddenly found we could sway votes, not just committee assignments. People started to joke that I was the 101st Senator. To be honest, I loved the power I had. It went to my head."

Jackson sat forward in his chair. "What do you mean out of hand?"

"Our club taught the rest of the Senate to be partisan, vindictive, and controlling. Before long, it didn't matter that our group had disbanded by 2035 when you got there. The damage was done and somewhat irreversible."

"Can you tell me who was in this secret club?"

"Mark Meriwether, Russell Warner, and the former President Pro Tempore who preceded Jessica Brown as Vice President."

"Wait. What?" exclaimed Jackson in disbelief. "But then why would Meriwether blackmail me using you as the bait if he was in the club with you?"

"Because the club ended over an issue of ethics. The Vice President sided with me. Meriwether sided with Warner."

"Why?" Jackson asked.

"Because Meriwether was in love with Russell Warner. He wanted to pave the way for Warner's presidency, and I became a foil to that plan."

"Are you saying President Warner is gay?" asked Jackson.

"No! He is not gay, Jack. But he has been known to engage in behavior that blurred the lines. He loves to manipulate people, Jack. Even though Russell is not gay, it did not prevent Mark from falling in love with him. Russell is such a sleaze-bag that he used Mark's feelings as leverage to get his way in the Senate and to convince Mark to take you down. The Rule XXII fight before the start of the session in '39 was a trap concocted by Warner to sink you."

Jackson was beginning to feel his stomach turn and flip like he was on some madness-driven merry-go-round. "Sink me?" Jackson stood and began to pace to relieve the anxious fear that was building inside of him.

"You were Time's Man of the Year in '38, Jack. That article was brimming with predictions you would run for President in 2040," said Ron.

"And you knew full well that was not my intention whatsoever. I was planning for a reelection bid to the Senate. There was no way that was going to be the right time for a presidential run, no matter what some magazine said. I'm not convinced now is even the right time for this."

"But our club - the Golden Four - was long gone by then. I could not speak directly to either of them," said Ron.

Jackson began to pace. Ron swallowed hard as he approached the most dangerous part of his story.

"You really ought to sit down for this next part, though, Jack," said Ron.

Jackson stopped pacing and sat slowly in the chair, staring cautiously at Ron.

"I lied to you about the video Russell Warner took of me in the summer of 2038. The one that was the linchpin to that blackmail scheme. It was not a deep fake; I was with the woman in the video. She was a prostitute and drug addict. I had paid her for her company that night. I lied about being with my niece," said Ron. "I'm deeply sorry." Ron's eyes became glassy as his embarrassment became physically evident.

"Why did you lie to me?" asked Jackson.

"I lied to protect myself. If I could convince you that the video was a fake, I thought I might be able to get you out of the trap they were planning. But you didn't back down. You courageous, brilliant jackass. So that meant I either had to allow you to fail and save my neck or ensure you won that Senate fight so that I had leverage to use against Warner."

Jackson was running his hands aggressively through his hair. The facts Jackson had assumed to be true were being shredded before his very eyes, if Ron was to be believed. It was making Jackson's head spin.

"The Vice President at the time and Senator Meriwether had a falling out some years back. I called him the morning of the floor fight and told him I needed one last favor for him on your behalf. He was open to it, given your courage in getting the President's Social Security deal done. I asked him to break Senate tradition and ignore Mark Meriwether, the Majority Leader, whenever I gave him a signal from the balcony. I stationed myself in his line of sight but made it look like I was there to watch the drama. He was happy to oblige me to humiliate Meriwether in front of the entire Senate," said Ron.

Jackson stared at Ron as the revelations came pouring out of his mouth. Ron felt like a steel yoke had finally been removed from his soul. He continued with his confession.

"Our whip count was not going to get us to three-fifths under the best scenario. I remembered an old tactic from thirty years ago called 'going nuclear' to change the Senate rules via a ruling of the chair. The Vice President told me he would not cast a tiebreaker in our favor, but he would put the question to the Senate. It would be up to me to see if we could get to 51 votes. We did not have the votes, so I bluffed."

Jackson continued to listen intently to the confession.

"I went to Sterling Powers and pledged to help whip votes for him and remove barriers to make him Majority Leader by 2045, possibly '43. He took the deal. Then I told Warner I would convince you to stay out of the presidential contest in 2040 if he would get rid of the video..."

"It never leaked. Never became public," confirmed Jackson.

"I am afraid Warner may have seen it as an opportunity to rid himself of loose ends. Meriwether's affections were becoming infatuations, and Warner was afraid that Mark was about to embarrass him with some sort of public pronouncement of his affection..."

"What?" said Jackson in disbelief. "This sounds like something Diesel would watch on Netflix," joked Jackson.

"Jack, Warner killed the Majority Leader. Not directly, but he had a guy do it. Mark was deathly allergic to shellfish. So he had someone poison Meriwether, deleted the videos, and then threatened to pin the murder on me."

"This is so fucked up," said Jackson.

"When we reformed Senate Rule XXII, it was the exertion of old tactics on Sterling Powers that got him to move as the decisive vote. It was not virtue, Jack. As much as you would like to believe it."

Jackson shook his head in disbelief. "No, Ron. No. You have Sterling all wrong. He is a good man. He was Diesel and my roommate for nearly six years..."

"To keep an eye on you at the behest of the Leaders, Jack. Senators Meriwether and Fontana were terrified you would climb that ladder."

"Not Sterling," said Jackson. His face grew red with frustration.

Ron meticulously provided his counterargument and evidence, laying the pieces on the table before them.

"Sterling Powers is the only person outside the campaign who knew every piece of information along the way. I got his vote for the Senate Rules vote by promising to use every relationship I had in the Senate to get him the Majority Leader's office. And he revealed his true allegiance to me in this election when he took the bait in a trap I set for him in June."

"Your visit to the church?" asked Jackson.

"I sent a cryptic message to the President. One only he would understand. But we never discussed anything secret about this campaign. I made it clear I knew he had gotten rid of Meriwether. I expressed my concern to him that Alvarez was playing him for a fool, but he did not care to listen. He insisted I convince you to leave this race, or he would pin Meriwether's mysterious and sudden death following the Senate debate on me."

"The police questioned you and me in '39 and found nothing," said Jackson.

"I think we both know that to this White House, truth and justice were drowned in a small bathtub long ago," said Ron.

"What are you talking about?"

"Sterling Powers is the leak. Everything you tell Sterling is making its way back to Warner," said Ron. "And he has someone on the payroll feeding him access to records."

"That son-of-a-bitch," said Jackson. "He has coveted the Leader's office for a decade."

Ron was nodding as the story came into focus for Jackson. "And it seems Warner has promised to help deliver what Powers seeks."

Jackson became cautious. "Why should I believe you, Ron?" Jackson set his coffee down hard on the table in frustration. "What has burned me time and time again in politics is placing my trust in the wrong people who were manipulating my optimism and my loyalty for all the wrong reasons."

"Because I am not asking for my job back, Jack," said Ron. "You're going to win the presidency with or without me."

Jackson looked at Ron in disbelief.

"Firing me is the perfect cover to hide that we know Sterling is the mole. You have to continue to speak to him like nothing is wrong. Like you don't know of his betrayal. You must continue to feed him some facts and some fiction."

"Why?" said Jackson.

"Because you don't want Alvarez as your Vice President. If this election is still set on a collision course with the United States Congress, it will likely be a Senate led by Sterling Powers that picks the Vice President. If Warner can manipulate Powers, Alvarez can buy him. If you retaliate against Powers now - show him what we know about him - he could act to saddle you with a fiercely wealthy and unscrupulous Vice President instead of that gem Valerie Lawrence."

"So you don't want your job back? Why come all this way? Why seek this private meeting?"

"To clear my name and my conscience. To ensure you knew I never betrayed you and never would." Ron's eyes welled again. It was either one hell of an act, or Ron had finally found redemption.

Jackson stood and approached Ron slowly, wrapping his massive arms around the shaking frame of his once most trusted advisor, whose humiliation had come to an end. "I believe you, Ron. Thank you for your confession. I wish you would have trusted me to know all of this sooner," said Jackson.

The sense of relief and absolution for past trespasses washed over Ron Bender in an emotional tidal wave. He cried silently in the arms of a man who remained the most thoughtful and caring man Ron had ever met in his life.

"You are going to make one hell of a President, sir," said Ron. "You're nearly ready for the hardest job on the planet. You are almost ready," said Ron.

"Almost? What is left to learn?" asked

Ron did not answer the question.

The men ended their friendly embrace. "Thank you for sharing this story with me. I still need you, even if I can't hire you back without raising Sterling's suspicions."

"Warner's as well, Jack. You need to keep the double-cross in mind. If Sterling believes he still has you by the balls, then so does Warner," said Ron.

Jackson signaled to the security detail that the meeting had concluded. The lead officer radioed a series of codewords to the rest of the team.

"Will you ride with me?" asked Jackson with sincerity.

"It would be my honor, but please drop me near the gate so I can enter alone and not as part of your entourage. Do you mind if I make a call first?"

The tallest agent informed Ron they should meet the motorcade at the west exit of the lobby near the hotel bar in nine minutes. Ron promised he would be there.

Ron stepped into the hallway and scrolled through his phone. He wondered which call would seem most appropriate to align with the fiction he was about to weave. He landed on the name that was probably too obvious a choice, but it did not matter. He had to close the loop so Warner and Powers would believe their plan to oust Bender had worked.

Ron walked briskly down the hall. He needed to work up some agitation in his voice. The phone buzzed in his ear as he dialed the Senator of Michigan.

"Ron?" said the man who answered the call. "You seriously callin' me?"

"Senator, I'm going to Piper's rally in Phoenix. I'm begging for my old job back," he said, pushing open the doors to the stairwell that led to the lobby. He started descending the stairs rapidly, making him increasingly out of breath. "I tried to catch him at the hotel but he refused to meet with me there. I'm going to try to speak with him after he steps off the stage in Phoenix. Diesel says Piper doesn't believe I'm not a leak. Senator, I need you to vouch for me. I need you to tell Piper I am loyal, Senator. Whoever is behind this is out to get me. I'm desperate for help, Senator. Please!"

Powers was with his wife and children at a festival in Lansing. He could barely hear Ron. He could tell he was agitated.

"Calm down, Ron, I'll certainly call Jackson and advocate for you," said Powers, even though he had no intention of doing so.

Ron stopped running as he reached the door leading to the lobby. "Thank you, Senator. If anything changes, I'll call you after the rally." The call ended, and Ron smiled, knowing the message would land in Warner's ears either through the secret wiretaps he had on every phone surrounding Piper or through the conniving mind and empty heart of the Sterling Powers.

Over 20,000 people gathered at the Talking Stick Amphitheater, a vast 75-acre expanse west of downtown Phoenix. Clad in a navy suit and vivid blue tie, Jackson Piper joined Dr. Catherine Piper inside their SUV. She seemed to be on heightened alert at all times after the sudden disappearance of the Vice President without explanation, the resignation letter, hounding by the FBI, and now hopscotching across the country with Jackson despite her instincts that told her she should be at home with the children. A distance had emerged between them, and it was filled with unspoken fears.

Ron Bender discreetly settled into another identical vehicle behind them. The motorcade, comprised of SUVs and sports cars filled with armed private security agents and emergency personnel, resembled the Secret Service in its tenacity. Speed limits were often disregarded when the Pipers or Governor Lawrence attended events. However, on this sweltering September evening, Governor Lawrence campaigned in New Orleans instead.

During the twenty-minute ride, Jackson excitedly conveyed as much of the surreal hour he had just spent with Ron Bender. He spoke of the deceptions by Warner.

"No surprise," Catherine said, who detested President Warner's gross tactics and moral ephemerality with a white-hot contempt. Catherine was shocked Ron had been concealing information from Jackson for over five years. She was not as convinced as Jackson that Bender had come entirely clean during their private meeting. "The moral of this story, once and for all, Jackson, is you must carefully about who you trust for the rest of this campaign and perhaps your career."

Jackson looked quietly out the vehicle's window as countless desert palms stood motionless in the windless desert evening air as the motorcade rushed west on the interstate. Thousands of homes in the sprawling Phoenix suburbs were likely filled with families who cared little that a man who sought to be their President was within feet of their homes. Many were still at work, and some might have just been sitting down to dinner. It was humbling to Jackson to be faced with the reality that to him, this race had consumed eleven months of his life, but so many millions of Americans had more pressing matters before them. It made his past arguments with Ron seem petty and meaningless while so many families were fighting for enough money to avoid eviction or cried themselves to sleep at night because their children had gone to bed hungry yet again.

"Be kind to one another," Jackson said suddenly.

"What was that, babe?" asked Catherine, distracted by social media, which she used under a pseudonym and email from the hospital.

"Ephesians. Be kind to one another. Be tenderhearted. Forgiving to one another, as God in Christ forgave you," said Jackson. "Esmael, stop the car. Stop the car!"

Esmael radioed to the motorcade to pull over. The motorcade immediately stopped on the side of the highway, still in tight formation. When the SUV Jackson was riding stopped, Jackson leaned over to his wife of 20 years. "I love you," he said, smiling warmly into her eyes and squeezing her eternally cold hands. I need to speak to Ron again. I'll see you at the amphitheater. They will drop us off at the same spot behind the main stage."

Before she could reply, he gripped the handle on the rear passenger door and flung it open. The ninety-degree heat of the desert evening rushed angrily into the idling vehicle. He jogged along the graveled berm of the highway to the SUV directly behind his own. He opened the rear passenger door, pressed his polished brown cowboy boot onto the running board, and climbed inside.

"What are you doing, Jack?" demanded Ron.

"Go!" Jackson said to Yael, the agent driving the second SUV. She radioed to the team, and the caravan merged in tight formation back onto the interstate and quickly regained their cruising speed of over 90 miles per hour.

"If you wanted to fuck me over, you could have sabotaged this campaign in a thousand other ways," said Jackson. "I believe you. More importantly, I forgive you for being afraid to trust me. Since I met you ten years ago, the most honest thing you ever said was when we were in that bar after the Steelers-Bears game. Do you remember that?"

"Sir?" said Ron, unclear what Piper was referring to.

"You said that night that you were most afraid of being alone, Ron. But you can't be part of a family if you don't truly trust the people who love you. I trust you, Ron. And we love you. You are the one who got me into this race, and you're going to see me through it to the finish whether you like it or not," said Jackson.

"Jack, you can't," said Ron.

"Shut up and listen to me. Fuck Russell Warner and Fuck Sterling Powers. If they want to play the old game of secrets and leaks, they can do that. But I refuse to play that game. I'm reinstating you to the campaign immediately as Campaign Manager. You fight the fights that need fighting, not those you think you can win. And you fight them with your friends by your side. I intend to win this fight, and I need your help to do it."

"It's my bet they don't have what it takes to beat us, Ron. We have the truth on our side. We need to stick to that game, not more lies."

Tears welled in Ron's eyes. He was touched by Piper's loyalty and genuine belief in him.

"But promise me something, Ron," said Jackson.

"Anything," said Ron.

"No more deception," said Jackson.

Ron frowned. "Then I need to tell you about a phone call I made to Sterling Powers when I left your hotel room fifteen minutes ago, and then we will be completely square. I wanted Sterling to think we were still on the outs, so I told him I came to Phoenix to confront you, but you refused to see me. I begged him to vouch for me to you."

"Clever," said Jackson. "Nothing else you need to share with me?"

"I have one hell of a fucking crush on Ziggy. I modeled her after a woman named Marley, who died of suicide. I wish Ziggy were the real deal," said Ron, smiling and putting his arm around his restored friend and leader.

The motorcade slowed rapidly as the vehicles navigated the exit of the Interstate and made their way to a road the campaign managed to convince the local police department to close to protect the Pipers' arrival at the campaign site.

Jackson and Catherine reunited next to single-story metallic pole buildings sprawled closely on the hot pavement behind the stage of the amphitheater. The crowd's cheers were deafening.

A senior campaign staff came over to brief the Pipers, shouting above the crowd's roar and the blaring of *We Are the Champions* by Queen.

"We estimate we are at maximum capacity. Officially, there are 20,000 people inside the amphitheater and another 30,000 who couldn't get inside but are lining the parking lots and the streets nearby. We have set up monitors to broadcast your speech, sir."

"That's incredible!" shouted Catherine. "This is our largest crowd since the Conventions, Jack!" she shouted to him, excited for his strong reception in such a critical state.

The entourage was escorted to a holding area at stage left. Off stage, several campaign staff were directing sound, music, and lighting. Four uniformed Phoenix police officers and the campaign's official photographer took photo after photo documenting the campaign's progress towards November 8.

Senator Arthur Huerta of neighboring New Mexico was on stage addressing the crowd with his trademark animated speeches. He was doing a masterful job building up the crowd. Behind him were several members of the Arizona congressional delegation and several local Bull Moose Party chairs. Jackson reached into his suit coat to refresh himself on the subtle changes to the stump speech he would give the assembled crowd.

"And now, hermanos, the moment you have been waiting for. Put your hands together..."

The crowd roared twenty decibels louder as cameras panned to show Jackson Piper standing in the wings, about to walk on stage.

"Our next President of the United States of America..."

Phones raised among the sea of faces to capture his entrance.

"Jackson Piper!"

Jackson waived energetically to the crowd, but he did not proceed directly to the center of the stage. As was typical for Jackson, he began by greeting the voters, and fans gathered along the stage. He was often whisked out of events once his remarks concluded, missing the opportunity to meet the men, women, and children who had stood in line, usually without bathroom breaks, for four or five hours to have a spot in the front row. He also felt this helped to build the anticipation for his remarks.

The stage at Talking Stick was not tall, making it easy for Jackson to bend down in his navy blue suit and cowboy boots and extend his mighty hands to thank the men and women who had come to see him.

Esmael and Oliver were stationed about six feet each from Jackson and four others along the stage as he shook the hands of screaming supporters. Jackson wanted to get closer to take photos with the crowd easily. So he dropped down onto the main floor of the amphitheater to get a better position to snap pictures quickly with some supporters.

From his vantage point on the stage, Ron saw an older man - mid-fifties - stiffen, his eyes rolled back into his head, and then fall hard to the ground, convulsing into a seizure. This immediately drew the attention of the crowd around him and two of the six security personnel near Jackson. For a moment, Oliver and Esmael's focus moved off Jackson and onto the convulsing man. The scene became chaotic as spectators scrambled to care for the man who was having a seizure while still many more did not want to lose their chance for a photo.

Ron saw a large male in a white America Needs Piper t-shirt

slowly remove something short and blue with squared edges from his backpack. Ron immediately recognized it as a gun and, through instinct, ran from his position off-stage toward the man who was just twenty feet from Jackson.

"Gun! GUN!" shouted Ron, diving towards the man.

Five shots were fired in quick succession, then innumerable more. The crowd erupted into a screaming stampede away from the stage.

Esmael and Oliver dove on top of Jackson, but not before the two shots struck Jackson in the chest and left arm. Jackson was pushed to the ground by Esmael and a falling Oliver, who had been struck in the temple by the next shot, killing him instantly. He was now lifeless as crimson blood poured from his head over Piper's body.

Esmael had managed to draw his weapon and kill the shooter before the sixth shot would have been fired from the blue weapon. Esmael checked his own body. He was not injured and shouted into his radio for immediate paramedics and the evacuation of the Pipers.

From under the pile of men, Jackson saw a man's legs writhing in pain. It was Ron Bender. His face was ghost-white, and blood poured from the corner of his mouth as he managed to prop himself sideways against the stage, holding his abdomen with his hands. Dark red blood stained the lower half of Ron's white dress shirt.

Not even Esmael, a former Navy SEAL, could keep Jackson pinned on the ground at the sight of his injured friend. Jackson shoved Esmael aside and scrambled along the ground to the wounded Ron Bender.

"Ron! Ron!" shouted Jackson above the screams.

"Were you hit?" screamed Ron, looking up at the amphitheater's half-shell roof. "Jack? Were you hit?" He slurred his words as the taste of metal filled his mouth.

"Yes, but you're hit worse. Keep pressure right here, Ron." Jackson screamed for Esmael, who joined Jackson at Ron's side. Sirens began to fill the world around them and soon drowned out all perceptible sounds of life near them.

Esmael quickly assessed the situation. Thousands of people were screaming and running for the exits. People had been trampled in the chaos. Sirens seemed to scream now in the distance from all directions. Camera crews were unsure if they should record the scene or take cover.

Esmael looked down. Blood everywhere. Blood was quickly soaking Ron's white shirt and both of Jackson's hands, which were applying pressure along with Ron's to the wound. Oliver was dead. The shooter lay lifeless, a single bullet wound in his forehead. Ron was bleeding profusely from at least one gunshot in the stomach. He was coughing up blood.

"Ron, we are going to get you out of here," urged Jackson, who then screamed to Esmael over the roar of the sirens, "Is anyone coming?"

Ron grabbed Jackson's shoulder. "Please stay with me, Jack. I don't want..."

Jackson looked at the tender eyes of his wounded friend. The light of life was slowly slipping from them. "I'm right here, Ron," Jackson said tenderly, using his left hand to hold Ron's hand.

"I don't want to die alone, Jack," said Ron, speaking his worst fear aloud.

"You're not alone, Ron. I'm right here. I won't leave you until I know you're ok," said Jackson.

Ron began to cry and looked into the clear blue eyes of the only man who had ever demonstrated true devotion and friendship to him. "I love you, Jackson. Please tell Catherine the Great that I love her, too."

"I absolutely will, Ron," said Jackson.

Ron took a final breath, choked with blood. His eyes became empty and looked without focus to a horizon no one living could see. His muscles relaxed, his grip on Jackson's hand went soft, and Ron Bender ceased to exist on Earth.

Jackson began to cry. He held the man in his arms and said the Lord's Prayer.

32

AFTERMATH

As Jackson sat on the ground in front of the stage, holding Ron in his arms and praying quietly, Esmael saw there was a hole in Jackson's left suit jacket sleeve. He started to search Jackson's body for wounds. Jackson winced when Esmael touched his left arm, and then Esmael determined there were both entry and exit wounds on that arm. He saw the hole in the chest of Jackson's shirt immediately over his heart. He ripped open the shirt to reveal Jackson's Kevlar vest had stopped a bullet from a 7 mm pistol at close range that would otherwise have brought an abrupt end to the possible presidency of Jackson Piper. He also found a bleeding wound on Jack's left side, possibly from the bullet that ripped through his arm.

Esmael made a tourniquet out of his belt and wrapped it around Jackson's left bicep. He urged Jackson to apply pressure to the wound on his left torso. Esmael would not leave Jackson's side until all threats were eliminated. It was clear Jackson was not going to leave Ron Bender's body. But an alarming message came over the earpiece Esmael was wearing. He sat straight up and gripped the broadcast button on his neck that turned on his microphone.

"Repeat that last message," said Esmael with fierce focus.

Esmael stood and used a handkerchief to collect the blue weapon from the body of the lifeless assassin in America Needs Piper t-shirt. "A digitally printed ghost gun," he said. "Undetectable and fucking UNBELIEVABLE!" A voice came over the radio, repeating the previous message. Esmael drew his weapon again, checking the clip for ammunition and igniting Jackson's attention.

"What's the matter?" asked Jackson with urgency. Four private paramedics from the Piper campaign finally arrived at the base of the stage with medical bags to the body of Ron Bender. One took his pulse and felt nothing.

"Esmael?" said Piper. "What's the matter? Are there more shooters?"

The paramedics began to lay Ron Bender on the ground carefully. Jackson said to them calmly and clearly. "Esmael and I want to be notified where you take his body. I do not want his body released to any law enforcement without my approval. Especially any federal agents, am I clear?" The team nodded in ascent.

"Sir, we need to go. Now!" said Esmael. "I'm putting you into a vehicle with paramedics already waiting to address that wound and provide you with blood. Sir, let's go!"

Jackson closed Ron Bender's eyes and began to run with Esmael.

"Is Catherine in the SUV?" yelled Jackson.

Esmael winced, turned, and looked at Jackson as they ran. "That's why we need to go now, sir. No one can find Dr. Piper."

"What in the fuck!" yelled Jackson, trying to suppress his anger and rising terror.

"The three agents guarding Dr. Piper were also killed. Right now, we're treating this as an attempted assassination, sir, and political abduction until we prove otherwise."

"I want my kids on the phone in the next minute," he ordered. "They are going to hear about the shooting on the news any minute, and they need to know immediately that I'm safe." Jackson stopped running. Esmael heard the pounding footsteps cease and turned to see Jackson staring at him as four police helicopters approached the scene. His voice welled with emotion as the loss of his friend set in. "Esmael, find Cate. I can't lose her, too."

They climbed into the SUV. The jet-black vehicle's tires screeched as its engine roared, and Esmael drove them toward downtown Phoenix. He was on the radio brainstorming with the rest of the team on the appropriate rally point that was unquestionably secure.

Medics were cutting off Jackson's suit and helping to remove the Kevlar vest. A bullet fell onto the floor of the SUV. Jackson picked it up and examined the disfigured projectile. Electrodes were being attached to Jackson's chest to check heart function. Their fear was a heart attack following such trauma. Both pulse and blood pressure were highly elevated.

They were putting an oxygen mask over his face when his phone rang. It was the twins. He took a deep breath for strength and answered the call.

"Hey boys, I wanted you to know right away that Dad is alright. I hurt my arm, but otherwise I'm ok...what's that? Yes, I was wearing my vest...Yes, Mommy will be happy about that, you're right. Well, we are looking for her right now. She's alright, I have no doubt. She got lost in all the chaos here, but she... calm down, boys. It's okay to be scared right now. Just know that the adults here are doing everything they can right now to make sure everyone is safe, including mom, ok?"

His voice started to falter. He muted the phone for a moment and took another breath.

"You shouldn't watch any of this on any screen, ok? Esmael and I will call grandma and grandpa the minute we find out where Mom is and not a second later. I have to go right now so they can stitch up my cut, ok? But I promise to call you as soon as we get to our hotel, ok boys? I love you both very much." His voice cracked. "Be a bull moose. Be brave, ok?"

Within a minute of ending the call with his children, the adrenaline in his bloodstream that had been fueling Jackson Piper finally began to decline. He finally allowed the medical team to do their work; and the bull moose himself lay flat in the SUV, and the world went black.

~

THE SCENT of antiseptic and blood filled the sterile hospital room when Jackson awoke. Jackson lay on a gurney; medical professionals hurried to prepare him for surgery. The physical pain was intense, but it paled in comparison to the searing heartache that gripped him. Ron Bender, his friend and confidant, had been ripped away from them instantly, leaving a gaping hole in his heart, not to mention the campaign's ranks.

"Jackson, you need to take it easy," Diesel Browning said. Jackson could not see the Senator, but he sounded nearby.

"Are you shot, Diesel?"

"No, I'm ok," said Diesel.

"Jack, are you awake? Can you hear me?"

It was Catherine.

Jackson reached for her, and then tried to look in her direction. She pushed between nurses inserting IVs and taking measurements to kiss her husband. She was in tears.

"Where were you?" asked Jackson.

"Someone tried to take me," said Catherine. "They shot...they shot all the agents around me and tried to grab me. Diesel saved me. He shot them with one of the officer's guns, and then we ran for cover. We were afraid there were others."

"I love you, Cate," said Jackson. "I'm glad they found you. Diesel?"

"Yes, Jackson?" he said, moving closer.

Jackson mouthed the words *thank you*, but no sound escaped. He was overwhelmed with the news of her narrow escape.

"Folks, we need to get him into surgery now!" said a gruff nurse, pushing the gurney out of the room and towards an operating room.

The hospital prepared a private conference room for the campaign team to wait for news. Esmael said, "Ron's death is a tragedy. I feel personally responsible that my team did not detect that weapon," he spoke steady and commanding.

"Have we gotten any of the security camera footage yet?" Diesel asked in desperation. "Any leads on who is behind this?"

A member of the private security team came into the hospital room carrying a tablet.

"Sir, we have the first look at footage from Talking Sticks," he said.

Libby, Diesel, Esmael, and Catherine gathered with great anxiety around the conference table to catch the first glimpse of an answer about the perpetrators. The video showed Piper jumping down from the stage and then out of frame. Catherine was watching him closely. Ron ran from the stage wings and dove off the stage towards the assassin. Shots were being fired, and then gunfire closer to the camera could be heard, striking the three agents in the backs who were guarding Catherine. The Phoenix police officers who had been standing in the wings attempted to slip a black hood over her head, and Diesel attacked them. When a disguised attacker drew a weapon, Diesel dove for a pistol and shot the man three times in the chest.

The room fell silent. The murder of five of their colleagues brought their worst nightmares to alarming reality.

Esmael pointed at the screen. "There's another camera here. Show me its footage." The agent navigated a few screens, typed in a passcode, and then revealed a clear video of a black van. The back doors swung open, a man dressed as a police officer jumped inside, and the vehicle sped off. When it exited, it was clear its plates had been removed.

"I want the make and model of this vehicle shared with Arizona State Police and Phoenix City PD," ordered Esmael. "I want them aware they had imposters posing as PPD at the scene. That ought to fire them up. I want detailed descriptions of these four imposter cops shared with every law enforcement agency in this state and the five surrounding. It's been two hours since the shooting. Let's get our team working on a 200-mile radius from Phoenix looking for this van."

"That's almost all of Arizona, sir. Parts of California and New Mexico. This will be like searching for a drop of water in an ocean."

"Did I stutter?" snapped Esmael.

The agent darted from the room to execute the commands. Esmael looked at Diesel for further direction.

"No feds on this. We have to operate with the assumption this attack came from Warner until we know otherwise," said Diesel.

"Agreed, sir," said Esmael, nodding.

"I want to speak to the Governor of Arizona," said Diesel, "but first I need to know, where is Valerie Lawrence?"

∼

It was 9:15 pm at the White House when news of a shooting at a Piper for President campaign rally reached the President. His aging body had been stretched to the limits of late by a rigorous campaign schedule demanded by Olivia. While he insisted he could do even more than the seven to ten events a week on top of running the country, his aching muscles and joints told a different story. This was a rare night off from the campaign trail since he had an entire weekend of travel planned, crisscrossing the country.

Warner had already taken several large anti-inflammatory pills, changed into his favorite maroon silk pajamas, and slid his slightly swollen feet into his favorite pair of Loewe leather slippers. Although it had been a hot September day in Washington, the nights were growing cooler, and the White House was a drafty mansion.

The President had just flopped into the luxurious brown leather recliner in front of a large screen. He was half-listening to his favorite news channel while reading over his speech for the weekend. An aide knocked on the door to his bedroom.

"What's the matter?" asked Warner, alarmed. He would only be disturbed at this hour if something of the utmost urgency required his attention.

"Sir, there has been a shooting at a Piper campaign event in Phoenix," said the aide.

Warner lowered his legs, closing the recliner. "Gun violence or an attack?"

"It would appear to be an assassination attempt, based on phone video circulating in the media," said the aide standing at attention at the door.

"How many are injured?" asked Warner.

"Arizona Highway Patrol reports over two dozen injured, primarily injuries from the stampeding crowd," said the aide. "Jackson Piper was shot as well. His condition is stable. He is in surgery now for two gunshot wounds to his arm and chest."

"How many dead?" asked Warner, standing, considering if he should dress to return to the Oval Office.

"Nine, sir. Arizona Highway Patrol has identified Ron Bender is one of them," said the aide.

Warner's stomach flipped, and his legs became unsteady. The news pierced his frozen heart. Ron Bender was once a man he considered a friend, a rare find in the District of Columbia by a man like him. The last conversation with Ron Bender before the convention had been an attempt to mend a burned bridge to regain an advantage over Piper. Warner had misread Bender's newly developed sense of absolute loyalty.

"Anything else?" asked Warner.

"You are asked to come to the Situation Room, sir," said the aide. "It would appear that someone attempted to grab Catherine Piper during the chaos and then fled. We are trying to determine if the assassins took any hostages."

"Jesus Christ," said Warner. He darted to his wardrobe to dress. "I want the Joint Chiefs in the room and the Directors of the NSA and FBI on the line when I get down there. Give me ten minutes."

"Yes, sir." The aide departed to execute the orders.

After the President had dressed in a black tracksuit bearing the presidential seal, he picked up a secure cell phone and asked the White House switchboard to be connected to the Secretary of State. A serene Marco Alvarez answered the phone.

"Mr. President," said Marco into his secure government phone from his hotel in Detroit, Michigan. It had been a long day on the campaign trail.

"I'm walking down to the Situation Room, Marco," said Warner, his words cold and direct.

"I see," said Marco. "Something you need my help with, sir?"

"That's why I am calling. If there is anything I need to know or that you should tell me before I meet with the Joint Chiefs and the FBI Director, now's your chance," said President Warner.

"Something you should know, you say?" said Marco evasively.

Warner walked down the hall of the White House residence to an elevator that would take him directly to the floor, where he would be escorted into the Situation Room. "Yes. I do not wish to be on the spot if the events in Arizona are not a random act of violence by some hot under-the-collar supporters of ours or Drummond," said Warner. "So I'm asking again, is there anything I should know?"

"No, sir," said Marco. He chose his next words carefully. "Except the voters of Michigan sure do love you. You would be so warmly received here. Much warmer than what Piper got in Arizona."

"I see," said Warner, and he ended the call as he boarded the elevator. He rubbed his tired eyes with his hands, and his thoughts suddenly raced about the condition of Piper. He dreaded the possibility of reaching the Situation Room to be made to watch an execution video of some poor sap taken hostage. Some things were out of bounds in politics, and killing kids or wives fit into that category of things Warner considered off-limits. Now, he suddenly worried that such boundaries had never been a topic of discussion between him and his new running mate.

∼

"HAS ANYONE FOUND VALERIE YET?" asked Diesel desperately to the security team assembled around the table in the hospital conference room.

At that moment, the Governor of Texas burst into the room out of breath, as if Diesel's words had magically summoned her.

"Catherine, I'm so sorry. I got here as fast as I could from New Orleans. I might have pulled a muscle, though, running up the stairs." She composed herself and looked at the grim faces around the room.

"How much do you know, governor?" asked Diesel.

"I know from the news coverage that Ron Bender is dead, and four of our agents." Repeating the news made fresh tears fill Valerie's eyes, though she remained composed. "I'm so sorry, guys. Ron was an incredible man. So was Oliver and the others."

"Governor, there is more. This was not only an assassination attempt; it was also an attempted political kidnapping. These fucks tried to take Catherine."

Fresh horror washed over Valerie Lawrence's face, quickly replaced by anger. "We need to get on the phone with the Governor of every state that touches Arizona. We need borders closed. We need airports closed. We need troops on the border preventing these shitbags from getting into Mexico."

"I'm so glad you're here, Governor," said Diesel.

"What's our next move?" asked Esmael.

"I want a command and control space for us to operate out of here for at least the next 48 hours. I want the Piper children on a private flight from their secure location immediately. The only way they are safe is if they are with us," said Valerie.

"Agreed," Esmael said.

"Elevate Libby permanently to campaign manager and get her on top of setting up a press briefing for midnight local, sharing the facts as we know them. We need to get the public on our side looking for these assholes," said Valerie.

The room listened to her intensely as her mind worked through the logical next steps to prosecute the location of the assailants.

"I want us to coordinate directly with the leadership of all the surrounding states. Borders closed. Airports closed. I want to ask them for every available resource to find these pricks."

"We have to assume they intended to kill Jackson and use Catherine as leverage to escape prosecution. Perhaps to leave the country."

Diesel spoke up. "I was stationed in El Paso for a portion of my time. I still know some of the military brass in the region. I will try to make some calls to see what they can do without Presidential orders or find out if they have presidential orders to stand down."

"Speaking of which," said Valerie, "I want to get on the phone with Warner. I want someone calling the White House every half hour until he agrees to take my call."

An hour later, St. Joseph's made a secure command center available for the Piper-Lawrence campaign, outfitted with suitable communications infrastructure necessary to coordinate response to the horrific events of the past six hours.

Seated at the long conference table was every senior campaign staff member who was not in complete shock from the assassination attempt. That is how they were going to refer to this event going forward, ordered Governor Lawrence to the team. Agents Esmael and Yael were at her right hand, with a volume of information before them. Seated next to them was Sinthia Sloan, the campaign's newest addition and an information technology genius.

She was brought on after Ron's suspension at Valerie's urging. Her mission was to develop a suite of security technologies and procedures to reduce, if not eliminate, espionage by rival campaigns.

"Ok, let's go," said Valerie to the room, which snapped to attention. "Tell me the state of the dead and wounded."

Esmael chimed in. "Four of our private security agents were killed. Our preliminary investigation has determined the assassin to be Javier Juan Castro, age 34, of Mesa, Arizona, using a ghost gun he likely 3D printed using plans he purchased online. It was undetectable to our scanners. We do not know how he snuck the ammunition into the venue, but our working theory is he stowed the bullets in a trash can or even dug a spot in the ground days ago before the event tonight."

The dozen or so senior staff were silent at the chilling revelations.

"Six months ago, he started hanging out with the three men we can confirm posed as Phoenix PD and killed our team. It appears

Javier had been recruited into an extremist organization who call themselves 1789."

"What do we know about this group?" asked Valerie, taking copious notes on a digital tablet.

Esmael read from his briefing notes. "Little, but it appears they support expanding the 2nd amendment to include all weapons of war. They oppose all immigration and refer to themselves as *purifying* constitutionalists. The men of interest are these men." Their pictures appeared on the screen in the conference room. "Manuel MacDonald, Armando Acevedo, and Lyle Alexander."

Valerie rubbed her temples. "We can drill down on their ideology later. We need to find where they are headed. Has anyone been able to reach the White House yet?" Valerie was angry at the slow pace of Warner's response. With each moment without a call, her suspicions grew that he had something to do with this.

"Senator Browning," said Valerie with growing anger in her voice. "You are to get on the phone with every Senator you know until I am on the phone with the President. One of them will have his ear and can get him to call me back. I need those satellite feeds, and I need to know what the U.S. government is doing to stop these men from escaping."

Diesel Browning gave a determined nod and raised his phone to his ear.

The huddle of senior advisors worked silently in the board room on preparations for the press conference for the next fifteen minutes. Then, Governor Lawrence's personal phone rang with a call with a 202 area code - Washington, DC.

"This might be the President," said the Governor to the room. All grew immediately silent. She answered the call. "This is Governor Lawrence," she said firmly and clearly.

"Governor, please hold for President Warner," said a switchboard operator who may or may not have been a SiOperator. It was hard to discern the difference these days.

"Governor?" said President Warner's icy voice. "Thank you for reaching out. What can I do for you?"

"Mr. President," began Governor Lawrence with exasperation. "Can you update me on what you know about these assassins?"

"Seems like a state matter to me, Governor," said President Warner, masking any concern he might have felt for the well-being of Jackson Piper. "If the state of Arizona needs help handling this mess, I suggest the Governor of *that* state give me a ring."

"We don't have time for political games, Mr. President. The men who tried to kill your closest rival are likely heading for Mexico, and if they cross that border, this instantly becomes an international crisis."

"Valerie, why don't you take me off speaker so we can dispense with the theatrics and political posturing, eh?" said Warner calmly.

She muted the phone. "Clear the room. Esmael, I want you to brief the Arizona and California governors. Find the assets we need to intercept that van ourselves. I just need Diesel to stay behind as a witness."

When the room had nearly cleared, Valerie resumed the call. "It's just Senator Browning and me now, sir. I'm afraid that is as small an audience as you're going to get."

"Good enough. Listen, my National Security Council has briefed me. It seems some border vigilantes have taken it upon themselves to terrorize your candidate and his wife," said Warner.

"You take me for a fool, Mr. President? We know the names of the three men who escaped and the shooter. They are known associates of a group called 1789 that has your campaign slogans plastered all over its dark web chat rooms," said the Governor. She shrugged. It was a guess, but she had no other cards to play against him.

"Interesting theory, Valerie. Do you have any evidence to back that up? Of course, you don't. You love to shoot from the hip, cowgirl," said the President.

Valerie's clenched her fists. She took a deep breath.

"You know me, sir. I never shoot unless I'm aiming at my target. If you aren't willing to help us, I wanted to be clear when I walk out to those microphones with 100 million people watching that it is on the record that I tried to reach out," said Valerie. "How do you think that plays with those suburban housewives you need in November, Mr. President? I think every housewife will imagine her husband in that operating room and think about your refusal to help."

"I've got an idea, Governor. If you want to play hardball, here it is. I can have a Delta Force in Phoenix in four hours," said Warner.

"They'll be over the border by then, Mr. President. Nice try," said Valerie.

"You didn't let me finish. I can have a Delta Force in Phoenix in four hours, ready to take whoever is driving that van. I can have FBI crisis response ringing whatever phones are inside that van off the hook. And keyhole satellites are already in position searching for this van that fled the scene."

"*Posse Comitatus,* Mr. President," said Valerie. "You can't use federal troops on U.S. soil to enforce federal or state laws without approval from Congress."

"Congress? Fuck Congress! You think my Justice Department will prosecute me for finding Ron Bender's killer?" the President let out a horrible laugh. "Apparently, you haven't been paying attention the past four years, young lady. I own them. They answer to me. They do what I tell them to do. I have whatever power *I say* I have, and they will not lift a finger to stop me."

"So what's the price for this help? Nothing comes from you without a catch," said Governor Lawrence, recalling her extended stay in a federal holding cell.

"Good girl," said Warner slowly, like a snake coiling around its prey. "The price for my assistance is you, and Jackson Piper will call the race quits. Tonight,"

Olivia Clay and the Joint Chiefs of Staff, seated around President Warner in the Situation Room listening in on the call, tried their best not to flinch at such a blatant violation of about a dozen federal laws, not to mention human decency.

"So, Governor, what is your answer? Time is wasting…"

Valerie looked at Diesel with wide eyes. Of course, she was not even beginning to entertain such a ludicrous notion. Diesel rolled his eyes. *End the call*, he mouthed.

"No deal," she said firmly.

"So that's your choice, Val," said Warner crudely. "Good luck finding that van."

Diesel and Valerie looked at one another in horror. Valerie was as mad as a box of frogs, as her father used to say.

"Hey, Russ," said Valerie, intentionally dropping his title of honor, "Jackson Piper looked to be in good health, all things considered, when I saw him just before his surgery. It takes more than a couple of your lackeys carrying plastic guns to kill a bull moose."

She ended the call in disgust and headed to check on Jackson.

33

RIVER OF DOUBT

The rhythmic beeping of monitors stirred Jackson Piper to consciousness as the antiseptic scent confirmed his location. Lying on a stiff hospital bed, he ached from surgery that stitched his abdomen and set his broken arm. In the dim post-operating recovery room, a sliver of light cast a ghostly glow over the medical equipment, keeping him company.

Alone for the first time in months, this unsettling silence was not what Jackson had imagined for solitude. Pain consumed him, but it wasn't from his wounds or isolation—it was fear that his pursuit of power almost cost him Catherine, his wife.

Jackson's mind flickered with snapshots of happier times, blurred by unshed tears. His children's laughter from their summer boating trip echoed in his memory, only to be drowned out by panic. Who was behind this? Was there more to come?

A shudder ran through Jackson's frame as he rolled the tape in his head of him having to conduct one of the most unthinkable, unspeakable duties of all: telling his children that their mother was gone, taken from them because of his own political dreams. Would they understand? Could he even find the words to explain how their world had been shattered by his selfish desire for acclaim and achievement? The thoughts suffocated him, filling his lungs with an invisible pressure that no amount of oxygen could relieve.

"Mr. President," he whispered, the title felt more like a curse than an honor. Jackson closed his eyes, haunted by vivid images of his wife's potential fate. The silence offered no comfort but deepened the dread in his bones. Fear grew with each beep of the machine, threatening to consume him. Confronting this uncertainty, he realized his quest for the presidency could end in death.

His thoughts drifted to Ron Bender's murder, and guilt weighed heavy on him, turning into a physical force anchoring him to the bed. He couldn't suppress his sobs any longer and wept openly for his fallen friend.

As grief overwhelmed him, the looming challenge of Russell Warner crept in—a formidable opponent who had previously defeated him. "Can I beat him?" Jackson questioned, self-doubt consuming his thoughts. "Or will I face humiliation on a national stage?"

He clenched his fists as the memory of his failed Senate reelection campaign resurfaced. The smug smiles of then-Senator Warner with his arms around the victorious retired football player, now Senator-elect, who had brought Jackson's single term in the Senate from Pennsylvania to an end. Despite the pain in his arm and abdomen, he forced himself to sit up, gritting his teeth as he did so.

A memory played in his mind — Ron Bender, always coaching and sharing insight, once encouraged Jackson to be more cautious in his political dealings. "Too often, things are not as they appear in politics," Ron had warned him, his words now echoing through the years with chilling precision.

At the time, Jackson had brushed off the advice, confident in his ability to easily navigate the treacherous waters of politics. But as he gazed around the sterile hospital room, he realized how wrong he had been. His pursuit of power had left him vulnerable in ways he'd never imagined, and now, those closest to him were paying the price.

Jackson's phone began to vibrate on the windowsill, among other personal items. The window reflected the darkness of the night outside, but through it, he could see Reese Tulson calling him. It was a voice he needed. He used every ounce of his available strength to reach for the device carefully in time to take the call.

"Jackson," a familiar voice came across the speaker. "My God, are you ok?"

"I just got out of surgery," said Jackson. "I was shot twice, but only one bullet made it through. I was wearing a vest."

"Oh, such a smart man. You always were," she smiled on the other end of the phone, relieved to hear his voice. She laid back in her bed. It was pretty late in Pennsylvania.

"Something awful has happened, Reese."

"I know. I heard about Ron Bender as well…"

Jackson could not speak; he simply cried. The teary breaths and sniffs made that clear to Reese on the other end of the line. She did not wait for him to apologize for his lost composure.

"You must not allow your mind to wander to the ghastly scenes it will paint of the very worst-case scenarios. Stay focused on hope. If you stand in hope, you will have the courage to move forward."

"I feel so empty," Jackson confessed.

Reese's heart broke when she heard her protege sound so broken and afraid. "None of us is alone, Jackson," said Reese. "God is always with us. Take a deep breath and feel His presence."

He closed his eyes and breathed deeply, comforting breaths soothing his breaking heart. Jackson opened his eyes and whispered, "thank you, Reese."

Reese had called hundreds of family members whose loved ones were victims of shootings and violence during her terms as governor. She channeled the calming energy and soothing voice she last employed a decade ago to console her younger mentee.

"I can't do this anymore, Reese," said Jackson. "I can't put the people I love at risk for this. It's not worth losing another person I love."

"You know, when I ran for governor, I was absolutely in love with the idea that I would be the first female governor of Pennsylvania. I daydreamed about taking the oath of office and having people cheering me on, signing bills into law, and making history. I was quite certain when I was running for governor that I would have a blast doing it," said Reese.

Jackson closed his eyes and breathed deeply, regaining composure. "You seemed to relish every moment of being governor," he said. He had been on her campaign team since she declared her intentions.

"Yeah, but I was scared shitless the moment they told me I won, Jack. There is the dream of becoming President, and there is the reality of being the President. There is a time when you have to suffer to know in your heart if you're truly up for the job," she said.

"This role is not worth losing people I love to attain it," he confided.

"You know, I look back at all the time I lost with Anne during late nights with strangers and politicians who haven't given two shits if I'm alive or dead in a decade. And I wish I could give it all back for one more day with her."

Tears began to roll down his cheeks again. "Is that supposed to make me feel better, Reese? It doesn't."

"But in the real world, Jack, you can't make those trades. We live with the choices we make. None of us has a time machine. Anne knew politics and policy were in my bones. It's why she loved me. If I had been some boring ass accountant, she would never have fallen in love with me. It was a permanent part of who I am. You are a warrior for other people, Jackson. You always have been, and that's why Cate loves you. She knows you were born to do this. She knew when she met you that someday you'd run for something full of risks, yet she said, 'I do.' And when Ron and Diesel came to your doorstep insisting you run, she called me while you were in flight to be sure I didn't talk you out of running."

"She what?" said Jackson, his mouth agape.

"She loved the idea of President Piper, and she knew I could be a downer, especially in my old age. She wanted me to give you clear advice and hold the mirror up, but she didn't want me talking you out of this. Her words were, 'he was born to do something great for humanity, Reese. This might be that thing.' Who was I to disagree with the woman who loves you more than anything on earth, except maybe those adorable children."

"The price to win is just too high. People are losing their lives now. This is not normal."

"But that's why you're running, right? Because Warner and Drummond are taking the abnormality of their Parties to a dangerous place for the nation. You're running to bring us back from the cliff of chaos, back towards justice, right?" Reese knew how to push him.

"First, it was thugs at my campaign stops. Then, they burned down our headquarters. Then, the Parties barred me from running. Then, it was the arrest of Valerie for sticking up for me. Then, it was a money crunch that still hasn't ended. Now I've managed to get Ron Bender killed and Cate nearly kidnapped."

Reese's voice was suddenly calm and quiet. "You didn't kill Ron Bender. And don't you ever let that thought come to your mind again. The greatest gift God gave creation was free will, Jackson. Ron chose to work for you. Ron chose to go to Denver. Ron stood up for you when everyone else tried to stop you."

"This campaign might be the hardest in history…" said Jackson.

"Puh-leez. You're the history teacher; you know that statement is total bullshit. If you want to lay in that bed and feel sorry for yourself, that's your choice. But I believe it is not the choice Catherine would expect you to make. Like me, I bet she expects you to honor Ron Bender by fighting harder to win rather than surrender."

"What if Warner's behind this?" asked Jackson.

Reese was silent before she answered. "Then you must beat him, or the Republic is lost. No pressure, dear."

Jackson cleared his throat. He wanted to tell her how much she meant to him. She interrupted.

"If you're done crying, there is a country out there that needs you. It's dying for a genuine leader that its citizens can believe in. Someone with a brilliant mind, a huge heart, and boundless courage."

"And you think that's me?" he asked.

"I know it's you. But you have a choice to make. When you came to see me, I told you that it takes a warrior to win the presidency now. Nice guys who run for President lose. It's time to decide who the Jackson Piper you are asking people to vote for is."

Jackson could hear a news broadcast. Was it the screen in the room?

"At this hour, many in Phoenix have made a makeshift shrine at the gate to Talking Sticks Amphitheater in honor of the man killed today by unexplained violence that broke out at a campaign rally for Jackson Piper..."

"In addition to the memorial for Ronald Bender and the security personnel confirmed to have been shot and killed at Talking Sticks, thousands are beginning to leave messages of cheer and recovery at a Phoenix-area hospital where Jackson Piper, also shot in the assassination attempt today, is undergoing surgery at this hour."

"Can you hear that?" asked Jackson. "What is that?"

Reese replied, "It sounds like the news..."

"The nation is on edge tonight as a leading candidate for President of the United States was the target of an assassination attempt tonight in Phoenix. His condition is still yet unknown, but five members of his campaign are dead, including Ron Bender, Piper's campaign manager, who had taken a leave of absence recently for medical reasons. About an hour ago, about a hundred Piper supporters gathered, holding a candlelight vigil here in front of the hospital, awaiting word on their presidential hopeful's condition. That crowd has grown to thousands, filling this beautiful plaza and stretching toward West Earll Drive. We are standing by for a press conference called by Texas Governor Valerie Lawrence, the Bull Moose Party nominee for Vice President. We are told she arrived onsite within two hours of the shooting, and she is in command of the campaign's response."

"My God," began Jackson into the phone. "I've got to let them know I'm ok. They should not worry like this."

"My dear, as I said, you are anything but alone." Another of Reese's coughing fits echoed in the phone. When it subsided, she took a long drink of water and apologized to the man who had been the closest thing to a son she ever knew.

"I am sorry I am keeping you up, Reese," said Jackson. "I want you to know that my mother died so long ago, but sometimes I feel like I can hear her in your words."

"Oh, that is beautiful, Jack. I didn't know your mother, but I bet she is a wonderful woman."

"Thank you for always having the right advice at the right time, Reese," said Jackson tenderly.

"It would be a shame to waste eight decades of wisdom on the plants in this old house alone," said Reese. "I love you, Jackson. You were like a son to me. Thank you."

Something pinched Jackson's arm. It was a doctor examining the wound, and he was jolted awake.

"How are you feeling, Mr. Piper? Ready to see your wife?"

"Where's my phone?"

"Your phone? I'm not sure. Your wife has all your personal effects. I can ask her to bring it when she comes to see you."

Jackson looked at the windowsill. No personal items and no cell phone. He looked down at this body. His arm was heavily bandaged, as well as his torso. He could suddenly feel his body; it was throbbing in pain everywhere.

"Oh, okay," Jackson said, confused. Yes, I want to see her. Please send her in right away."

~

AN EMPTY PODIUM stood in front of a stone latticed wall in the main lobby of St. Joseph's Medical Center. A bouquet of microphones was attached hastily to the podium. Two screens mounted on rolling frames stood on either side of the podium. A sea of reporters sat anxiously in hastily assembled chairs, awaiting the appearance of the Texas Governor.

Valerie Lawrence emerged from a hallway wearing a navy suit. On her lapel, she had a beautiful hand-painted silver 51-star American flag pin accompanied by a black ribbon. Her heels clicked rhythmically as she approached the podium. When she reached the microphones, she looked solemnly at the sea of faces before her. She did not smile. Her face was etched with concern but also exuded determination.

"Good evening," she began. Cameras flashed and flickered, capturing the scene and blinding her for several seconds before she proceeded with her remarks. "Today, five members of the Piper-Lawrence campaign were killed in an apparent assassination attempt targeting Bull Moose Party nominee for President of the United States, Jackson Piper. Killed today was one man believed to be part of this conspiracy, posing as a Phoenix Police Department officer. A woman who was part of the crowd died of cardiac arrest attempting to flee the chaos. Also killed today were private security agents for our campaign: Oliver Watt, Winston Schiff, Rebecca Diaz, and Yael Cohen. Our campaign manager on medical leave, Ron Bender, was killed when he dove in front of the shooter, saving the life of Jackson Piper. The assassin who shot Ron Bender and Jackson Piper was killed by private security. His name was Javier Jose Castro, aged 34, of Mesa, Arizona."

An image of Javier Juan Castro's Arizona driver's license was flashed on the screens behind Governor Lawrence. She did not turn to look at his face.

"Senator Piper is currently recovering from surgery following the assassination attempt," Valerie explained to the eager crowd of journalists, who typed furiously on devices as she spoke. "His condition is stable," she smiled, "and he's expected to make a full recovery." Her tone immediately became serious again. "At this hour, our most urgent matter is the location of three men wanted in connection with today's horrific events.

Three faces appeared on the screens behind the governor.

"Manuel MacDonald, Armando Acevedo, and Lyle Alexander were posing as Phoenix Police Department officers. They are believed to be armed and considered extremely dangerous." Three sinister headshots of the men appeared on the screens simultaneously behind her. "They were last seen in this black Ford van, which we can now confirm bears an Arizona license plate X696PL1. That's X-ray, 6-9-6, Papa, Lima, 1. We have traced the van in the past 30 minutes to a location outside of Yuma, Arizona. Our theory at this hour is that these men intend to cross into Mexico."

Cameras continued to flash as Governor Lawrence continued to brief the press. "My message to these men and anyone involved in this conspiracy is simple. Turn back now and save yourselves and the ones you love."

Governor Lawrence looked down at her notes and swallowed hard. She recalled the difficult conversation with the President an hour before. That choice he had put to her was now hers and hers alone to make. Her heart thundered in her chest and her mouth felt dry and empty. She sought one last time for the courage and the wisdom to make the correct choice. She looked up at the sea of reporters, puzzled by her pause.

"An hour ago, I spoke to the President of the United States. He refused to assist with this investigation to apprehend these conspirators, calling it, and I quote, 'a state matter', end quote."

Nearly all of the press let out audible gasps of horror. It seemed like an obvious role in a time of crisis for the might and skill of the United States government to step in.

"It, therefore, falls on us with the assistance of state authorities to bring these men to justice. Tonight, I have spoken with the governors of Arizona, New Mexico, and California. Alongside Texas, we are united to take whatever steps necessary to prevent a clear attempt by these assassins to destabilize the United States and to interfere with a free and fair election in the greatest country on Earth."

"Furthermore," Valerie continued, "we will not be deterred by these acts of cowardice and violence. Senator Piper's campaign for the presidency will continue. We will fight for our great nation's more just and brilliant future."

34

DAMNATIO MEMORIAE

Warner feared Alvarez's involvement in the assassination plot despite Alvarez's continued denials. The preceding events that had spurred the bombastic press conference at St. Joseph's Hospital on September 8 led President Warner to meet throughout the early morning hours of September 9 with his National Security Council about the many loose ends and unanswered questions for the three men in the van racing for the Arizona-Mexico border.

Warner pulled the Secretary of Defense aside.

"I need a reason to obliterate that van," said Warner in a quiet corner of the situation room. "Do we have its precise location?"

"We do, sir. Military assets were moved into position and locked on the van. It had stopped for about two hours in the New Water Mountains area, but has resumed its travel on SR 95 South. We believe they are headed for Yuma and will try to cross into Mexico in Los Algondones. That's our theory anyway."

"Can we hit that van, Rich?" asked President Warner.

"How so, sir?"

"Those men cannot make it to Mexico, and they cannot be

arrested to stand trial in Arizona or anywhere else," said Warner with an icy gaze that conveyed more than his few words.

"Well, sir, I supposed if we had any indication that the men would try to kill more civilians at the border crossing, possibly with some sort of mass casualty ordinance," said the SecDef.

"Your team has fifteen minutes to make a projection on the likelihood these men have *other* weapons."

"What sort of other weapons?" asked the SecDef.

"I don't fucking care. Does it matter? The kind that can kill a lot more people. Even the slimmest odds of them carrying such weapons would empower me to order a strike on that van," said Warner.

The Secretary understood and left to attend to the directive.

At 1:55 am, the SecDef returned to the Situation Room with an analysis that *1789* extremists had a history of planning mass casualty events, and several of the senior leadership had traveled to Lebanon, Syria, and Palestine to receive direct training on such tactics. He informed the Council there was a 46.9 percent chance these three men were planning to kill more innocent people. That chance increased to 78.1 percent if Arizona authorities attempted to stop the men from crossing into Mexico.

"And what are the chances the three men Valerie Lawrence named at her sideshow tonight are in that van?" That question was aimed at the FBI Director.

The Director answered the question truthfully. "Her intelligence is solid, sir. Those three men are known associates of the shooter, and all three went missing at various times about 72 hours ago. They have not been at work, and the family we have been able to reach do not know where they are."

Olivia Clay felt a pit in her stomach. "This feels like a leap," she said. The words had escaped her mouth before she had considered the implications of disagreeing with the President in front of the National Security team.

Warner turned to look at Olivia. "Come now, you're not going weak on me now, are you Olivia?"

"Without a visual confirmation, that van could be filled with children for all we know." She sat up straight in her chair and turned to look the President in the eyes. "And if they are conspirators, they ought to face charges and trials. Not executions without due process, sir."

"Nonsense. Now you are just making shit up, Olivia. Can you even recite the Fourteenth Amendment for us, Ms. Clay?"

She stared at him. Had he finally turned on her like he had so many other loyal Chiefs of Staff?

"You're being reckless and emotional, Olivia." He laughed at her.

"Excuse me?" she shot back.

"You heard me," President Warner said. "Hysterical." He raised his eyebrows and laughed louder.

Olivia understood all the implications of those words. She was the only female in the room and the only one questioning the intelligence. Now the President was firing off sexist and demeaning labels, that frankly, she was tired of absorbing as if they did not sting each time he fired them at her.

President Warner turned from Olivia and looked at the Secretary of State. "What would you do, Marco?"

"Sir, I would do whatever it takes to protect Americans. I believe those three men are domestic terrorists and pose a clear and present danger to American citizens," said Marco solemnly.

Olivia looked around the room. She was the only person expressing doubt. She made a note in her tablet of her objections and wrote down the date and time.

At 2:12 am, Warner ordered a missile strike on the van.

A laser-guided 114-Hellfire R11X missile - known as the Ninja Bomb because of its ability to limit collateral damage - was fired from a drone over the pitch-black southwest Arizona sky. Within 47 seconds, it deployed four massive blades that shredded through the windshield of the speeding Ford van and then detonated. A gigantic white light flashed, and then a hellish amber explosion illuminated the barren expanse of the Arizona desert.

In sixty seconds, any remaining evidence of the conspiracy and all knowledge about who had trained, planned, and paid for this outrageous plot burned with the bodies of the three American men in the desert. No *habeas corpus*. No trial. No further investigation would be possible.

35

REST IN PEACE

The autumn wind whispered through the South Pittsburgh cemetery, rustling leaves and casting a solemn chill upon the gathered mourners. The pastor of the church that the Pipers had attended throughout their years living in Pittsburgh was presiding over a final graveside ceremony.

"Greater love has no one than this: to lay down one's life for one's friends," the minister began, his voice steady and calming. "John Chapter 15, verse 13. Today, we gather at this graveside to say our final goodbyes to Ronald George Bender and to commit his body to its final resting place."

As he continued, the sad faces of Diesel Browning, Valerie Lawrence, Art Huerta, Eileen Frazier, Catherine Piper, Libby, and other campaign members listened intently. Each wore their grief like a shroud, the pain of the loss still coursing through open wounds.

"Ron was not just a member of our team; he was family," Jackson said, pausing momentarily to collect himself. "He gave everything in service to our country. And his final great act was to conceptualize this campaign, and we will not allow his sacrifice to be forgotten." He grabbed a handful of earth with his right hand and whispered something unheard to the casket before tossing the soil onto it.

Diesel Browning stepped forward as Jackson finished speaking, his typically boisterous demeanor subdued by the occasion. He carefully picked up a handful of soil and gently let it fall onto the black casket below. "You were a brother to me, Ron," he whispered.

The others stepped forward to pay their respects one by one, each scattering a handful of earth over the casket while sharing their memories of Ron.

Holding back her tears, Catherine Piper whispered a heartfelt thank you to Ron for his unwavering support of their family. Choking on her sobs, Libby simply said, "You'll always be with us, Ron."

As the last mourners paid their tribute, the minister offered a final blessing and prayer.

"Merciful God, you heal the broken in heart and bind up the wounds of the afflicted. Strengthen us in our weakness, calm our troubled spirits, and dispel our doubts and fears. In Christ's rising from the dead, you conquered death and opened the gates to everlasting life. Renew our trust in you that by the power of your love, we shall one day be brought together again with our brother Ron. Grant this, we pray, through Jesus Christ our Lord."

"Amen," spoke most of those gathered.

A hundred yards away, a bagpiper began the lonely tune of Flowers of the Forest as guests removed yellow carnations from a graveside arrangement and tossed them one by one onto the lowered casket of their fallen friend.

As the sun dipped below the horizon, casting long shadows across the cemetery, the gathered mourners bowed their heads in one final moment of contemplation for Ron Bender. The bagpipes echoed their ghostly wail through the rolling hillside of the cemetery.

Jackson examined the names of his long-deceased relatives in this corner family plot of the cemetery. Laying Ron to death among his blood was the most fitting tribute that Jackson and Catherine Piper could offer to a man who gave his life to save theirs.

Through tears and with interlinked arms and hands, the mourners filed to their waiting cars to travel to Homestead for comfort and food as was the tradition in Western Pennsylvania. Ron's family had roots in Homestead that went back to the early 1880s, though no living relatives could be located to invite to the funeral or celebration of life.

After several hours of eating and telling their favorite stories of their fallen friend, the celebration began to wind down. Under the moon's soft glow, Jackson and Catherine slipped away from the group for a rare, quiet evening together. Their hearts still heavy with grief, they sought solace in revisiting the city they had called home for nearly twenty years.

"Remember when we used to park over on the Southside and then take the T over to concerts at Heinz?" Catherine asked, a nostalgic smile playing on her lips.

"Of course," Jackson replied, his memories flooding back as they strolled hand in hand in the shadows of towering steel bridges that crisscrossed the Allegheny River. "Remember when we lost your brother in the crowd, and you climbed that street sign to look for him?"

"Never happened!" laughed Catherine.

"I have photographic proof," he laughed, squeezing her hand.

As they continued their journey walking along the river through the city, a heavily armed security force not far behind them, they paused to take in the majestic outlines of PNC Park and Rooney Field.

"Wow, it feels like a lifetime ago that we were there walking on cloud nine only to have it all come crashing down to earth with Warner's direct assault," said Catherine.

"Sure put a damper on things and nearly erased any sort of post-convention bounce in the polls we had hoped for."

"Looks like the Pirates were at home tonight," smiled Jackson. "Ron would have loved to ditch the wake early and skip away to watch the game."

"He always had a connection," laughed Catherine. "Someone who would get him into the game for nothing."

"And usually some plush box!" recalled Jackson.

Their shared memories became an uncomfortable silence as they recognized there would be no more games for Ron.

"Did we make a mistake moving out of Pittsburgh?" asked Catherine.

Jackson thought carefully about his answer. "I don't know. Colorado is beautiful, but this will always be home to me. I wonder what they would say if we gave the choice to them?"

"Well, if you win, where would the Presidential library be? Here?" asked Catherine.

"Shhhhh," said Jackson. "There must be some kind of jinx or curse about discussing a presidential library before you've even won."

"Sorry!" she said softly with a giggle under her breath.

"PITT would lobby hard to get that honor; they are my alma mater, after all," smiled Jackson. He was referring to the University of Pittsburgh, where he earned his bachelor's and Juris Doctor degrees.

"I think the Mayor would push hard for it to be over by the stadiums," smiled Catherine.

They ducked into a small cafe near the Andy Warhol Bridge.

A waitress named Lucy, not older than twenty, with curly blonde hair and dark purple eyeshadow took their order for two coffees and two tiny slices of cake - one chocolate and one spice. The security detail dutifully picked a booth by the door out of earshot to screen for any unsavory characters as they entered.

The second time the waitress refilled their coffees, she looked terrified and filled Jackson's cup so quickly that it nearly overflowed.

"Is everything alright, dear?" asked Jackson.

"Yes, sir. I just realized why yins look familiar," she stammered.

"Don't be afraid, dear," said Catherine. "We don't bite."

"I'm gonna vote for you, sir," said Lucie.

"Can I ask you why that is? What about my campaign excites you?" asked a curious Piper.

"Well, you two are hypic," said the young woman.

"What's hypic?" asked Catherine, perplexed.

"Hot, but you play it cool," said Lucy. "It's an anagram."

"Acronym, right Lucy?" said Jackson.

"Huh?" she was confused.

"Not important. Are there policy reasons?" asked Jackson.

"I can't say that there are."

The excitement faded from Jackson's face.

"I mean, you are young. You've got kids. Those other old men don't know what it's like to try to live in America right now. You guys do. I mean, fuck, you're sitting in this shitty cafe drinking coffee."

"Interesting perspective. I never looked at it that way," said Catherine with genuine praise.

Lucy tried to express a more thoughtful reason for her vote. "I hear you want to change things, and looking around, I can tell you things need a reset. It ain't right how people are struggling. I mean, this is America," she said.

"I agree with you, Lucy," said Jackson. "Is this your only job, Lucy?"

"Shit, no," she said. "I'd never afford to pay my bills on this. I sell things online. I walk dogs on the weekends. And about ten other things here and there."

"Well, how did you do in high school?" asked Jackson.

Lucy rolled her eyes. "Not so hot, I'm afraid. It sort of shrunk my options after I graduated. My GPA was mid. And I couldn't find nothin' worthwhile at CCAC," said the waitress.

"What do you dream of doing?" asked Catherine.

"I don't know. I don't really dream about nothin'," said Lucy. "I just wake up and go to work and try to keep getting by."

"It was wonderful to talk with you, Lucy. I hope I still have your vote," said Jackson.

"Oh, even more so now, Mr. Piper," said Lucy. "I'll leave you two to your date, but can we snap a selfie first?"

The Pipers were happy to oblige, and then the woman retreated to the back of the cafe, no doubt to tell everyone she knew who was sitting in her cafe that night.

Jackson reached into his suit coat and removed a worn leather wallet. He emptied the wallet onto the table. Among a driver's license, credit cards, and insurance cards were the authentication cards for Ziggy. These cards permitted the bearer to alter, program, and access the entire database of the S.I.-powered assistant.

"What are you doing?" asked Catherine.

Jackson unlocked the phone and operated it with his right hand only. His left arm was throbbing in pain after a day of ceaseless movement.

"Franklin is an off-the-shelf model with much to learn about the real world. But Ron hinted to me many times that Ziggy was an exceptional model. He implied she was at a level of programming unavailable to consumers. That means she is likely government, industrial, or military-grade programming. I am wondering if there is a way for Ziggy to remain with us even with Ron's passing."

Jackson downloaded the application name written on the card. Then, he used the listed credentials to sign in to Bender's account. The application prompted him for an encryption code 18 characters long. Jackson flipped the card over and saw a small screen embedded into the card, generating 18 new characters every minute.

He entered the current code, and Ziggy flashed to life on his device.

"Mr. Piper? How are you accessing my panel, if you don't mind me asking, sir?" said the brilliant and powerful digital assistant.

"Ziggy, how are you holding up?"

"Mr. Piper," she said with her digital voice filled with sadness, "I have been tracking the details of the past four days using all available sources. I have spoken to Senator Browning a few times, but I am trying not to intrude during this time of sadness for us all.

The Pipers were caught off guard by a programmed entity's clear expression of authentic emotion.

"I suppose, given Ron's death, I am to be retired?"

"Ziggy, are you aware of what Ron shared with me on September 8th?"

"Yes, sir. I am programmed to listen to his voice on a continuous loop. At least, I was." Tears moved down her face on the screen. Jackson and Catherine exchanged a look of bewilderment.

"Well, how would you like to join forces with Franklin and come to work for me now? It seems that Ron has made me the executor of his estate and willed all his possessions to Catherine and me - the damned fool." Jackson's voice surged with emotion.

"Would I? Of course, I would absolutely love that, sir! You should feel welcome to alter my appearance and settings in any way you deem appropriate for me to best serve you in my new capacity."

"Ziggy, we love you just the way you are. You are just as Ron wanted you to be, and that is how you'll remain," said Catherine.

"Ziggy, I have an assignment for you. I need to prepare for my only Presidential debate, and I am thinking about tearing up our plan of attack and starting over. Can you get to work on a strategy for us that will put both Drummond and Warner on defense but not make the entire debate about this conspiracy? I want my remarks to focus on what people are looking for in this election. Use polling and all available recent news and social media trends to arrive at a compelling argument. Draft up some sample talking points for me to use. We need this debate to be the most consequential night of the campaign."

The Pipers paid for their dessert, tipped Lucy generously, and made their way back onto Fort Duquesne Boulevard. To their surprise, a sea of baseball fans spilled across the Roberto Clemente Bridge. The Pittsburgh Pirates had just defeated the Milwaukee Brewers, and the crowd was jubilant.

"Let's go BUCS! Let's go BUCS!" Shouted a young man in the crowd. The growing crowd made Esmael and the rest of the security detail edgy. Jackson turned and gave a reassuring look to his sentry.

"It's ok, Es," he said.

"What was the final score?" asked Jackson to a woman and man dressed in black and gold head to toe.

"8-7. A fuckin' beautiful walk-off homer in the bottom of the ninth," said the man with a heavy Pittsburgh accent. Damn, Jackson missed that yinzer drawl, as it was called.

Catherine was high-fiving fans all around. Not one of them seemed to have a clue who they were.

"You two look snazzy," said a woman. "Date night?"

Not wishing to make the woman feel bad for confusing their black funeral attire for nice threads appropriate for a night in the city, Jackson said, "That's right. We are parents of twins. We don't get much time alone these days."

"You two love birds make time for each other," said a woman in her early seventies wearing a Pirates jersey. "That's the key to a long, happy marriage. At least one date night a month."

Catherine and Jackson looked at each other and smiled. Perhaps that would be possible once this all-consuming project was behind them.

Hundreds continued to cross the bridge and spread out in various directions, looking for rides to their homes and hotels.

Jackson continued to bask in the momentary anonymity he enjoyed among the many fans whose minds were not preoccupied with questions of the Constitution, immigration, or vast conspiracies. In the morning, diligent work resumed for the most consequential debate of his life.

PART V

## 36

TROUBLE IN ATHENS

October 1: 38 days until Election Day

The race was a dead heat between Warner and Piper by the time the one and only debate arrived.

National Poll: (± 4%)
Warner 34%
Piper 38%
Drummond 16%
Undecided 12%

The assassination attempt on Piper and the death of five of his campaign staff likely accounted for half of the swing. The fresh ideas and new approach the Bull Moose Party heralded seemed to finally get a second look from voters, and increasingly, they liked its platform. The rest of Piper's gains and Warner's losses came from suspicions surrounding Warner's involvement in the attack on Piper, although no one could offer any proof. It not only fit the narrative of a President desperate to remain in power but also Warner's specific tendency not to draw uncrossable moral lines, which added to the chatter that Warner could only win if Piper were dead.

Warner and Alvarez deployed millions in last-minute campaign spending leading up to the only debate on October 1. *Save America* ads for the Warner-Alvarez ticket consumed every second of the 90-second breaks on most streaming programming. Entire cities in some parts of the country were plastered with *Save America* billboards, bumper stickers, placards, and yard signs. The property owners did not place most but rather loyal Old Party members scrambling to save their President.

Warner's desperation turned off voters. It felt inauthentic and desperate. Old Party voters started to give the Bull Moose Party platform due consideration. The stakes could not be higher for Warner, Piper, and Drummond in the one and only presidential debate of 2044, set to occur in Athens, Georgia.

At 6 p.m., the doors opened to Ramsey Concert Hall at the University of Georgia. A carefully pre-screened pool of voters from the region who passed background checks and security clearances were pre-selected to receive tickets—300 in total. The campaigns were given passes totaling 15 each to be seated inside the concert hall.

The stage was set with identically sized podiums - Piper's to the audience's left, Drummond's in the middle, and Warner's on the audience's right.

Inside his green room, President Warner was experiencing a rage-filled explosion.

"What the fuck do you mean the moderator won't take the money?" growled Warner.

Olivia Clay's heart raced as she stood before the President, trying to contain her anger. She couldn't believe she agreed to try to bribe the moderator into asking easy questions of Warner. At that moment, she felt that the last of her journalistic integrity had died. She was starting to wonder if all the personal compromises were worth it for this man.

"Keep your voice down, Mr. President," she said through gritted teeth.

The President didn't seem to care about being discreet. "That no good cocksucker," he spat, referring to her former colleague at CBN. "I thought he liked you."

"Don't put words in my mouth, sir," Olivia insisted, her frustration building. "I may have been friends with him, but that doesn't mean I can bribe him for you."

But the President wouldn't let it go, his tone turning serious. "Well, did you offer him a trip to Olivialand?"

Olivia couldn't believe what she was hearing. She had been loyal and professional, even during his most lurid jabs, but now he suggested she be just another one of his pawns.

"I'm not your whore; I'm your chief of staff," she snapped, unable to hold back the truth any longer.

The President's face twisted in anger. "What did you just say to me? Do you realize who you're talking to?"

Despite her fear, Olivia refused to back down. "I said I'm not going to use sex to help you win a debate. Especially when the other candidate is already outshining you on your own turf."

President Warner seemed taken aback by her boldness but quickly regained his composure. "You think this is all about me? Tonight is about America and our future. And yet here you are, putting yourself above your country and your President."

Olivia's blood boiled at his accusations. "Sir, I won't be ridiculed any longer. This isn't about me or my loyalty. It's about your inability to lead and articulate your vision to the American people."

The President's eyes were on fire. He took a long drink of water, trying to calm himself down. "You think I can't do it? My opponent was a joke four years ago, and I mopped the floor with her. Now I have these goddamn Bull Moose to contend with. I'm going to rip their fucking hearts out! Out of my way!"

The President stormed out of his holding room. Where he was headed, she did not know, and frankly, she did not care.

On the other side of the building, Paul Drummond sat quietly in his green room in silent meditation.

He felt nauseous about standing next to Piper and Warner fighting for airtime. While his policy positions were clear, his anxiety was sapping his confidence. During his final prep session the night before, Paul continued to confuse the names of heads of state and even the names of countries. He knew the proper names, so why was he getting so confused?

When Representative Khan entered, Paul Drummond was sitting on the floor, sockless, with his hands on his knees and eyes closed. Paul had tapped her as his Vice Presidential pick at the Party's convention at the end of August, but the attempt on Piper's life quickly overshadowed the selection.

"Ohhhummmmm. Ohhhummmmm." Paul was repeating a meditation chant.

Representative Khan was unsure if she should interrupt Paul or allow him to continue his...well...whatever this was. She chose to share the news.

"Senator Drummond? Senator Drummond?" she spoke softly.

"Ohhhummmmm. Oh..." Paul opened one eye. "Oh, hey there." He pulled himself to his bare feet and looked up at Representative Khan.

"I'm sorry to tell you this, Paul, but several of our guests tonight are no-shows," said Khan. "I didn't want you to be shocked when you looked for them in the auditorium tonight."

"Which ones?" asked Paul.

"Well, Mrs. Drummond is out there. And my partner, Chaya, is here, of course. And I saw Representatives Fonchi and Herzer out there," said Khan. They were two of the House's most disliked members of the Other Party caucus. Their presence in Paul's guest section might actually scare others away.

"What about Diane Fogarty?" asked Paul.

Representative Khan shook her head. "I'm sorry, sir. But she canceled."

"But she was supposed to be our key spokesperson in the spin room!" squealed Paul.

"She says she has a stomach bug, Paul. She sent her sincerest regrets," Khan said.

Paul Drummond groaned and ran a hand across his shining bald head. "Thanks," he said glumly. Representative Khan attempted to console Paul but decided it was best to leave now before she was sucked into one of his downward spirals.

Now seated on the makeup chair alone in his green room, Paul wondered if it was even worth putting on his socks and newly shined shoes to walk onto the stage. Would anyone even notice if he didn't show up? Would they care?

Jackson Piper's dressing room was a circus of activity. Marty Dudash was peppering Jackson with questions, attempting to stump the Senator on the name of a foreign leader or one of the three dozen statistics he had committed to memory.

Diesel Browning paced quietly, nervously gnawing on his nails while Catherine played UNO with the boys. Jackson sipped on a final cup of coffee.

Governor Lawrence reviewed her talking points for her live on-camera interviews to follow the debate.

"I wouldn't take another sip, love, or you're going to need a bathroom break before the break at 45 minutes," warned Catherine.

"I'll be fine," assured Jackson. "Besides, I need to be alert and on my toes, for anything Warner tries to throw at me."

Jackson summoned Ziggy to the screen on the wall.

"Yes, Senator?" Ziggy asked.

Jackson looked at the screen. "Are you prepared to revise the press release and talking points as the debate unfolds?"

"Yes, sir," said Ziggy. "And I have completed the website build as you requested. I just pushed it live a minute ago." She smiled. "Anything else, Senator?"

"Be on standby. I'll have Senator Browning activate you if there is anything during the showdown that needs your immediate attention," said Jackson.

It was time for the candidates to take their positions. Everyone left the room except Catherine, Ben, and Alex.

"Well, Dad, this is it," said Alex.

"You're right, buddy. This is the big moment. Do I look good?" asked Jackson.

"Here, let me straighten your tie, Dad," said Alex. Jackson leaned down so Alex could carefully adjust the blue-striped tie under his collar.

"Ben, you're my safety valve," said Jackson. "If you think it's going poorly, I want you to give me a thumbs down when I look at you. A thumbs up means I'm holding my own. Deal?"

"Deal," said Ben, hugging his father. "I'm proud of you, Dad. Now go kick their asses."

"No foul language, Ben," said Catherine.

"What, I just said ass. Diesel says way worse in front of me all the time."

Jackson gave his son a disapproving look. "Listen to your mom. And no fighting in the seats. America will be watching, boys."

They scampered out the door while Catherine lingered a moment longer. "Whatever happens out there tonight, I am supremely proud of you. You have come so far, shown so much courage, and already started to push the country in a better direction."

"Thanks, gorgeous," said Jackson. She gave him a careful kiss on the lips so as not to leave any traces of lipstick.

"Now go kick their asses, Jack," she said, smiling, and disappeared out the door.

Jackson was alone. He breathed a few cleansing breaths, put on his suit coat, and left the room to face his opponents.

∾

THE NINETY-MINUTE DEBATE was in its 47th minute, and so far it had been a battle royale between Warner and Piper with Drummond meekly seeking speaking time. Warner would level a false accusation; Piper would counter it with examples of how out of touch Warner had become as President. On style, Warner was ahead but something strange had happened. Warner was not usually a policy wonk, but tonight he had every fact down cold. Some data points Warner shared were so precise that they caught Piper off-guard, causing him to stumble through some answers.

It was about to return from a 90-second break for commercials. One 30-second ad from each campaign had been permitted. The pause was actually a cleverly timed one to allow the candidates to rush to one of three separate restrooms, as was agreed upon previously in the negotiated debate terms.

Catherine had been right about the coffee. For the past ten minutes, Jackson had done all he could not to lose focus while the pressure in his bladder grew, making it impossible to concentrate on Warner's strangely detailed answers.

Jackson Piper was running at full speed down the hallway to return to the concert hall and reach his podium in time. Jackson rushed past Warner, but as he passed, he noticed something in Russell's ear. Was the President wearing hearing aids? Jackson did not recall the President being hard of hearing, but it was possible. Or was it an earpiece with someone on the other end?

Jackson signaled to Diesel Browning to come to the stage. He had only ten seconds to say something significant to compel Browning to act.

Jackson whispered into Browning's ear. "Unless Warner has hearing loss, he's wearing an earpiece upstage out of the sight of the moderator. Ask Ziggy to try to locate the transmission signal and jam it by whatever means possible."

Jackson was back at his podium when the lights came back up, and the moderator indicated they were back on the air. Drummond stood on an elevating box while Warner leaned cooly across from Piper.

The camera focused on the moderator, and the house lights went down. "Welcome back. We hope those campaign ads provided useful perspectives on their visions for America. We have completed four sections of the debate so far - our hot planet, international alliances, privacy, and education. Let us now turn to the final three topics of tonight: the economy, violence, and energy, and then each candidate's closing statements."

Jackson looked at the front row of the audience. It was about the only row of faces he could see. Marco Alvarez sat in the President's section with Olivia Clay at his side, along with Senator Diane Rothschild of New York and Governor Mason Dane of Florida. Diane had always been cordial to Jackson in the Senate. Governor Dane was only here to gain valuable airtime because he hoped to run in 2048, although he denied it unconvincingly when asked.

"Senator Piper, the next question is for you," said the moderator. Jackson snapped back to attention, focusing on the lips of the moderator now as he spoke.

"What is the Jackson Piper agenda for getting America's economic engine humming again, and how is it better than their plans? You have one minute to answer."

"When it comes to our economy, Russell Warner sure talked a big game when he was just a candidate for President. He promised to create over five million jobs in his first term alone, and the reality is we've lost a net of 750,000 jobs under President Warner these past four years. My agenda begins by reforming American fiscal policy to reflect new realities not present when our current governance structure was devised. I'd sit down with key industries to identify the gaps between their workforce needs and the realities our schools are producing, and I'd insist on change at the local level. I wouldn't be afraid to do whatever it takes to get our schools producing quality graduates again. And we must restore real competition to some of our nation's largest markets where just one or two major companies dominate with 90 percent market share."

Jackson stopped talking as a light under the moderator flashed red. That answer was not exciting, and Jackson wished he could take it back. Luckily, Drummond's answer was even more boring. It missed any contrast with Warner and instead attacked the Bull Moose platform as "dangerous" and "big on promises, small on realistic solutions."

Warner patiently awaited his turn. The speaking light illuminated green, signaling the President to begin his answer.

"Unfortunately, Jackson Piper is once again lying to you. My administration has done real work, and let's talk about the numbers. We have created an environment where over 1.4 million new jobs are created each year. We slashed over 3,450 different wasteful regulations that were impeding our economic growth. And interest rates are at a five-year low this month at 14.5 percent. So I guess the answer to how would my policies differ from Jackson Piper's? The answer is mine actually work."

That was a compelling answer, thought Piper. Tonight was the most in command of facts and statistics that Piper had ever seen Russell Warner, whom he had known for ten years. Jackson wondered if Diesel had reached Ziggy.

As the moderator asked the President a follow-up question about interest rates, Ziggy was at work hacking the light-security firewalls of the University - which took her less than a minute to penetrate. She was scanning every available device close to the debate stage to be programmed to emit a signal strong enough to jam anything using radio or Bluetooth frequencies that could be in Warner's ear. She also worked over 90 seconds to pinpoint the physical location of every device on the network. She looked through the browsing history to determine if anyone had searched for employment data or interest rates in the past two minutes.

"Senator Drummond, any follow-up you wish to offer on interest rates?"

Ziggy continued to scour the local network for viewing histories, but there were still no signals or clear suspects that could be feeding President Warner information.

"Senator Piper, same question. You have one minute."

Jackson began a detailed answer about artificially high interest rates and their connection to the skyrocketing national debt, which just surpassed $56 trillion. Jackson said the Bull Moose are calling for Constitutional amendments because Congress and the Presidents have demonstrated they are unable or unwilling to control spending without mandates.

Jackson looked at Warner, who was taking no notes on the legal pad before him. It added to Piper's suspicion.

After several more questions about the economy and the plight of American workers and retirees, the next topic was violence. Again, the first question went to Jackson Piper.

"Jackson Piper, this has been the most violent campaign of the modern era. You have stared down the barrel of a pistol pointed at you in New Hampshire and, just last month, lost your longtime staff member, Mr. Ron Bender, in a thwarted assassination attempt. Do you think America has gone too far, and should the Second Amendment be repealed?"

Jackson took a moment to compose himself before speaking of Ron Bender to start his answer. "Ron was a generous soul and a committed public servant who deeply loved our country. Throughout his career, powerful people have used Ron's desire to feel needed to use Ron as a tool for their deceptions.

"Both of these men have used Ron Bender as a tool to get what they wanted in the Senate," Jackson said, pointing at the other candidates. "When I arrived there, I helped Ron see there are better ways to change our country. I'm just sorry that Ron did not get the chance to be fully redeemed.

"But didn't you fire, Ron?" asked Warner. "Some hero if you had to fire him."

Jackson glared at Warner. "You keep that honorable man's name out of your mouth," said Jackson.

Warner scoffed and shook his head. "Fine, but the Ron Bender I knew was a sleaze. He cheated at cards, legislating, and on women his whole life."

Jackson's instinct was to respond, but then he saw Ben, who gave him a thumbs down from the front row. He took a breath, regaining composure. "I believe the question was about violence in America - specifically politics. I wish I could tell you that defeating Russell Warner would be enough to exorcise that demon from our national character; we all know this sickness goes back to our founding. When we founded this nation, we allowed human beings to be considered property. There is no greater scourge on America's soul than that. And this latest age of dehumanization and brutality is born of that original sin - that somehow, in America, one group can convince itself that it is better than another, so much so to draw blood from those they do not see as equal.

"I do not support repealing the Second Amendment," continued Piper, "and neither does the Bull Moose Party. Gun violence is without question a painful crisis, but eliminating all guns - even for those who obey their rights and respect guns at all times, like me - is not a solution that will stop hurting people from hurting their neighbors. The only people with guns will be the criminals, and the rest of us will be totally outgunned and unable to protect ourselves. Case in point, the gun that killed five of my friends and nearly me was an illegal ghost gun, 3D printed from illegal plans purchased online. Repealing the Second Amendment would not have stopped these fanatics from taking such extreme measures to execute their demented ends.

"We must rid ourselves of culture warriors like Russell Warner who condone violence, fantasize about killing others, and devalue human life. We must diagnose mental illness sooner, remove stigmas that still surround treatment, and offer greater mental health counseling and services for those in trouble. I would certainly support curtailing or limiting the right to own weapons to those convicted of violent crimes or in danger of hurting themselves or others.

"It was Thomas Jefferson who said, 'What country can preserve its liberties if their rulers are not warned from time to time that their people preserve the spirit of resistance? Let them take arms...The tree of liberty must be refreshed from time to time with the blood of patriots and tyrants. It is its natural manure,'" said Piper.

"Mr. President," said the moderator, "Your response?"

"Jackson Piper is a fraud. And it's a damn shame what happened to those brave security guards who gave their lives protecting even a loser like Piper. But this is a nation of brave Warriors. And I would hate to think what would happen if we took guns out of the hands of our citizens. They would be without the means to defend themselves from a tyrannical U.S. government run by Jackson Piper dead set on exerting its will upon them."

"Mr. Moderator," said Drummond, raising his hand. "Mr. Moderator, may I speak?"

To this point, Paul had looked insignificant in the shadow of two giants—Piper and Warner. Yet, Paul Drummond felt compelled to speak.

"Yes, Senator Drummond. It is now your turn."

"Thank you. Well, I just wanted to say that I disagree with these two men. I think guns are despicable and evil and ought to be removed from the United States altogether. Look at the other stable democracies around the world. You don't see them allowing their citizens to carry guns, and their criminals are not the only ones with guns. No one carries guns in those countries, and they sure as hell do not have the virus of mass shootings like we have here in America.

"Yes, if I were the President," said Paul Drummond, "I would work to repeal the Second Amendment. I would gather up the guns and burn them down into bars to use in our jails."

"I'm curious," said Jackson Piper, interrupting, "But can President Warner even name the number of acts of political violence that have occurred under his presidency versus ten years ago?"

It was a deliberate trap to flush out Warner's conspirator if he or she was assisting the President's strong performance.

Ziggy perked up. A computer located in what appeared to be a men's restroom on the second floor of the building was suddenly visiting websites about political gun violence and gun death statistics. The snake had revealed himself. Ziggy blocked the IP address of that machine. She immediately searched that room and found a radio transmission frequency that matched a frequency she had faintly detected in the concert hall.

"Here goes nothing," she thought. Ziggy used a code she wrote seconds ago to co-opt every cell phone, computer, and electronic device with an oscillator within 100 feet of that IP address to generate a jamming signal that would be sufficient to halt whatever audio transmission may or may not be coming from the stall in that bathroom. When she initiated the code, the radio signal from the restroom on the second floor immediately became far less efficient at sending it signal. Next, Ziggy bombarded the cell phone and computer, generating the radio signal with enough electronic trash to render the device into an expensive brick that was unable to function.

Back on the stage, Warner began to answer the question. "Of course, I can answer that question..." a pause.

"I said, I have those statistics easily at my disposal. If you just give me a moment to refer to the notes that I made here," Warner flipped through the blank pages in front of him. Suddenly, a loud, piercing screech filled Warner's head, and he swatted the speaker out of his ear. It flew across the stage and bounced onto Paul Drummond's podium. Drummond froze. He had no idea what had just landed on his legal pad. It looked like a flesh-colored bug but did not appear to be living.

Jackson saw the reaction and quickly surmised that Ziggy had found the signal. Jackson got cocky. "Well, out with it then," said Piper, pouncing.

"Just give me a minute, goddamn it," said the President. "Mr. Moderator, could you please ask Jack to repeat his absurd question?" The President stalled, wishing that his helper on the second floor would send him any sort of plausible number, even if it were wrong. He was having difficulty breathing. His heart began to race.

Olivia sat increasingly horrified in her seat. Although she could not have noticed the earpiece fly from the President's head, given how small it was, she felt something was wrong with her boss.

"I wanted to know," said Piper, "if President Warner happens to know the number of acts of political violence committed in the country he serves as the Chief Executive for? Even a round number would do," said Piper.

Warner struggled to maintain his focus. He started sweating profusely, and he labored to breathe. His heart was beating irregularly in his chest. Something was wrong. The moderator did not notice at first, but when the President turned visibly pale on the monitors in the control room, the broadcasters went to an indefinite commercial loop while physicians attended to the President.

It might be a panic attack or something much more severe. When electrodes attached to the President's chest finally signaled that the President's heart was in supraventricular tachycardia (SVT) - a rapid heartbeat that can be up to 300 beats per minute and lead to stroke or heart failure if not addressed, the event was ended. The President was taken by a special Secret Service ambulance to the nearby hospital.

The moderator returned only to say, "We are sorry that today's debate ended without closing statements. President Warner is unable to continue, and it would not be fair to him or Marco Alvarez if we were to allow Paul Drummond and Jackson Piper to close this debate on their own. We wish the President a speedy recovery and thank you for watching."

This gave the false impression that the President was simply not feeling well.

With no sitting Vice President and only a nominated one who had not even had a confirmation hearing in either chamber, the presidential line of succession would fall to Speaker Sylvester Billings if the president died. Short of death, there was no plausible means to transfer power to an acting President without a Vice President in office to initiate the 25th Amendment.

The nation was not yet aware that a Constitutional Crisis that would rise and fall like waves for months had begun.

37

ELECTION WAR GAMES

Within minutes of leaving the debate site, Warner's heart returned to a normal rhythm. The ambulance still transported him to the hospital out of an abundance of caution. After four hours of tests, fluids, and imaging, President Warner was released with words of caution about the moderation of alcohol and caffeine combined with high-stress environments. He was encouraged to get more exercise and perhaps meditate.

"Meditate? Bullshit!" said President Warner as he climbed gingerly into his limo and departed for the airport, where he would board Air Force One just after 2 a.m. and departed immediately for Washington.

Olivia was relieved to have the President back on the plane and returning to the White House, but her head ached at the thought of rehashing their argument from hours ago. Knowing the President as she did, he would likely call it water under the bridge, then continue to get his digs in every chance he got.

The debate's fallout was catastrophic and came at precisely the wrong time. Voters did not feel sympathy for the President; they felt alarmed and worried he was no longer up for the job. Piper rocketed forward in the polls, and Warner sank like a rock.

October 14
National Poll: (±4%)
Warner 34%
Piper 45%
Drummond 15%
Undecided 5%

Marco was furious at the President's abysmal debate performance. He had put nearly $800 million of his wealth on the line and intended to spend $200 million more in the next two weeks. Marco wanted answers on how the President intended to correct the blunder in Athens, but Warner had become evasive and even more temperamental.

President Warner was not necessarily capable of feeling shame, but he did become deeply disappointed with the trajectory of the public polling. He directed his team to return to the messaging that "polls were never right" and that "polls were unreliable" so that if, by their last-ditch efforts, Warner landed in the WINNER column on Election Day, it would not be a cataclysmic shock. Instead, people would understand the divergence between poling and results, which simply meant that the polling had it wrong yet again. It was a convenient explanation for more devious actions in motion that were as old as the Republic itself.

Leaving Athens, Jackson Piper, and Valerie Lawrence set off to barnstorm the nation during the final 30 days, speaking about their New Optimism, New Freedoms, and New Vitality anywhere they could grab an attentive audience. While the polling suddenly made them hopeful that the Contingent Election would not be necessary - that they might win the election outright - the words of Ron Bender echoed in their minds, keeping their heels on *terra firma*.

"Take polls with two aspirin and a grain of salt," he had repeatedly advised. "Remember, this is not a national election; it's 51 state elections for the Electoral College. What one state may love about us, the next may loath."

The Bull Moose strategy was to run as if Paul Drummond were

not even in the race. They had managed to land their new Party ticket onto all 51 state ballots and believed their path to electoral success lay through a diverse coalition of states, large and small. There were fifteen different pathways to victory, and luckily, they did not demand that Jackson and Valerie win just one linchpin state. This opened the table up for them to explore many options as Marco's money saturated the airwaves in the final weeks.

With President Warner needing to reduce his stress, otherwise risking another episode of troubling heart misfiring, Marco Alvarez was primarily responsible for campaigning coast to coast. Warner hopscotched between friendly crowds in major cities, always returning directly to the White House that night. Marco was front and center, carrying the baton for his team, and relished the new attention.

From Albuquerque to Zainesville, Marco spoke about the President's agenda to Save America: stronger borders guarded by the U.S. military; a national energy corporation designed to mine rich natural resources and divide the profits among every American through a profit-sharing and stock program; and unleashing the supreme economic talent of the American people.

While the last plank was vague and meaningless, Warner-Alvarez voters consumed it like pink cotton candy.

Warner and Alvarez did not say in their rallies that they intended to continue using the federal government to subvert the rule of law, using the FBI and DHS as personal grievances and hit squads. They failed to mention their lack of concern about the spiraling federal debt and that they had no plan for interest rates that were bankrupting the federal government and families from sea to shining sea.

CONTROL OF CONGRESS was coming down to the wire. The Old Party had been the favorite to win outright majorities in both chambers, but if the Old Party prevailed, it now would only be with a plurality and by a razor-thin margin in both the House and the Senate. If Sterling Powers and Sylvester Billings intended to lead the majorities in the next Congress, they would need a majority of Piper's Bull Moose allies to do so.

Sterling Powers couldn't shake off the guilt that weighed heavy on his conscience as he sipped his third glass of bourbon. He had misled Jackson Piper, but he must put securing votes to become Majority Leader ahead of their personal relationship. Deep down, Powers knew what he was doing was wrong, but he justified it as necessary for the nation's greater good. And besides, after years of being controlled by unelected kingmaker Ron Bender in the U.S. Senate, maybe this was just karma catching up to him.

But now, with his inside contact on the Piper campaign suddenly going silent, Powers feared that they had been exposed or scared off by all the chaos surrounding Bender's death. Yet, when he spoke to Jackson on the phone, looking for signs that Jackson suspected Sterling of deception, there was no hint of suspicion from him. They often discussed their mutual fear of a Warner second term.

Their conversations rarely touched upon how Piper intended to win the election; instead, they focused on Jackson's determination to secure Lawrence the vice presidency via the Senate if it came to that. They spoke occasionally about what it would mean to govern and work alongside Powers to push through their ambitious agenda with a coalition in the Senate - one that Powers was expected to help form. He was noncommittal about being the architect of such a force. As much as he wanted to see Jackson succeed and secure his role as Majority Leader, he also didn't want to risk jeopardizing his interests by touching the wrong wire in the presidential contest. It was a balancing act that weighed heavily on Powers' mind.

∼

As the nation woke up to Election Day, the sun shone brightly and spread its warm light on the faces of citizens eagerly anticipating the results.

At the 25th Ward polling location in New Hanover County, North Carolina, a line had formed before the polls had opened. The line was out the door and snaked around the block, at least two hundred people long.

The local affiliate of CBN had sent its veteran reporter, Ramona Youngblood, to interview voters standing in line at the polls.

Ramona approached a man in his late sixties with a brush mustache wearing a USA t-shirt. "May I ask you, sir, what is your first name, and who do you plan to vote for this morning?"

"My name is Clarence," said the man, looking at the reporter. "And I'm here to vote for Jackson Piper."

Ramona asked if he cared to share why the Bull Moose Party had earned his vote.

"Well, I am a Christian. I served my country in the United States Marine Corps. And I think Piper has a good message about reforming government so it works for people again. He has good ideas, and it appears to me he is a good man."

"Thank you, Clarence. What about you, ma'am?" Ramona asked the woman three behind Clarence in line.

"My name is Pauline. I'm from Wilmington. I am a retired nurse, and I'm voting for Jackson Piper and Valerie Lawrence," said the woman.

"And what makes you want to vote for them, Pauline?"

"That Governor is a firecracker. I feel like she and Jackson are going to shake things up. We need things shaken up in Washington, DC. We have had nothing but old men for years. Time to get some young blood in the White House."

Ramona moved down the line. She approached the next person.

"What is your name, and who is your choice for President?"

"My name is It Ain't None of Your Business Who I'm Votin' For,"

Ramona looked at the camera, rolled her eyes, and moved along about ten people back in the line. She spoke to a woman named Josephine, who was voting for Drummond. When asked why she voted, Josephine said she felt that Drummond's plans for energy and the economy were more in line with her views."

Behind Josephine was Red Stargell. Red said he was a carpenter and he was voting for President Warner.

"Why does President Warner have your vote, Red?" asked Ramona.

"I think President Warner has the right idea about saving America from invaders. We should be stopping these invaders from trying to steal our way of life. And I think we should have a national energy company to compete with Soddy Araybya. They do it, so I think we should, too."

A caravan of SUVs - perhaps twenty - roared up to the site, then suddenly screeched to a halt along the street where Ramona was reporting. Their gasoline engines went quiet as doors flew open, and out poured three dozen large men. Josephine watched as they reached into their vehicles and remove heavy black weapons - rifles, pistols, and was that a machine gun, she thought?

Heavily armed and dressed in black uniforms with black ball caps bearing the insignia of the Department of Homeland Security, they walked past the reporter to the entrance of the poll and went inside.

Ramona left her interviews and gathered all the courage she could muster. She chased the crew of men, sensing there was breaking news in the process. Through the windows of the voting location, Ramona saw the men flash badges and order all voters out of the poll. Ten seconds later, two of the men exited the building.

"This poll is closed. Everyone needs to leave this area immediately."

"Why?" asked Ramona as her camera continued to stream.

"Ma'am, we need all voters and media to clear this area. We have a bomb threat."

"You don't look like local law enforcement," said Ramona.

"You're a smart one. If you were real smart, you'd get the hell out of here."

"How long do you think it will take your bomb squad to clear the area?" she asked.

"We don't have that estimate right now," said the man dressed in black, holding what appeared to be an AR-15 rifle. "I wouldn't stick around."

Two major national streaming services were reporting anxiously about problems emerging at polling locations nationwide. The veteran anchorman's face on one such service contorted with alarm, his tone grave as he addressed the camera.

"We are bringing you this breaking news: polling locations across the country are being closed by the Department of Homeland Security due to what they deem to be credible threats of danger to Americans going to the polls on this Election Day. Our reporters are on the scene. We take you now to Carol in Ohio."

The screen split to show a frazzled reporter standing outside a cordoned-off polling station. "Thank you, Tom. As you can see behind me, the DHS has shut down this location after receiving what they characterize as an anonymous tip about a possible bomb. Voters are understandably upset, and many are questioning the validity of these threats given the high stakes nature of this election."

"Absolutely disturbing," the anchorman interjected. "We've received similar reports from California, Florida, North Carolina, and even Texas, where Governor Valerie Lawrence is reportedly meeting with federal agents. Let's go live to our correspondent there."

"Tom, I'm here outside the Governor's mansion in Austin, where Governor Lawrence is meeting with Homeland Security officials at this hour, fiercely demanding the reopening of voting sites across the state. Governor Lawrence is ready for a fight."

A clip rolled of the fiery Governor emphatically stating that DHS had no jurisdiction to close polling locations—that it was entirely a state matter and up to local and state authorities to make such calls. Lawrence threatened to initiate a tense standoff if DHS officials did not clear out every polling location in the Lone Star State.

"I am prepared to arrest every single DHS official in Texas who is executing this fraudulent action," warned Valerie Lawrence at a bank of microphones outside of the Governor's mansion.

The other national streaming service carrying the news of an Election Day being rocked with havoc was reporting about a far graver circumstance.

Members of the group 1789 and the Warriors were staging violent, armed protests at polling locations in Pennsylvania, California, New

Jersey, New Hampshire, and Virginia. At one poll in Allegheny County, Pennsylvania, members of the groups had erected a guillotine. They were executing dozens of stuffed moose toys with a blade stained blood red for effect. When they ran out of toys, they turned to less symbolic creatures to decapitate. One man carried a dead deer up to the device. It had been killed that morning and lay lifeless on the side of the road near the poll. Ceremonial, he and his fellow Warriors sliced its head off before a crowd of horrified local voters. The Warriors paraded the head with its vacant eyes around the line at the poll, chanting "Warner! Warner! Warner!"

At a poll in Richmond County, Virginia, men wearing black leather jackets threw glass bottles and beer cans in the air at a parking lot of a polling location. They shot at them using semiautomatic pistols and rifles.

In Kern County, California, a riotous mob of men and women wearing American flags as capes, turbans, and togas broke all the windows of a public library that served as a poll before taking the building by force. They rushed all the poll workers out of the polls at gunpoint, then set up a bonfire in the parking lot using books from the stacks as fuel. The fire was blazing hot, and flames licked the sky with black billowing smoke when the first camera crew arrived on the scene.

Under normal circumstances, Election Day is a hellish waiting game for a candidate, where minutes feel like hours. After attempting to visit a polling location in Boulder County, Colorado, the Pipers were told they should wait while DHS swept the building. Luckily, they both cast their ballots by mail weeks ago.

"How long will that take?" asked Jackson.

The clerk shrugged. "They are not giving us a time to quote to voters."

Jackson and Catherine were furious but not surprised. They had anticipated a variety of voter intimidation tactics, and Ziggy had projected something similar to the events being broadcast across the country in her Election Day "war game" models.

While the Pipers waited in the sun in the parking lot, Jackson dialed their voter protection team to get an update on legal filings.

"We estimate that we must file emergency injunctions in all 51 states to be safe. We are also seeking emergency injunctions in the U.S. District Courts where the Warriors and 1781 members are rioting to scare away voters."

"What sort of relief are we seeking?" asked Jackson into the phone.

"We want to start by asking to keep polls open well past 10 pm local tonight, but we might need to get more creative to overcome this charade Warner is running."

Jackson gave the go-ahead to filing in state and federal courts simultaneously to get as many polls open - and to stay open - as possible. He also suggested they request states to set up at least one emergency polling location per county and issue provisional ballots to anyone needing to vote there due to their standard polling location being overrun by marauders.

When the first emergency injunctions were issued at noon Eastern from ten state and three federal district courts, Jackson Piper organized a conference call of Governors. Piper had invited representatives of the Drummond and Warner campaigns to join, but both refused.

"Governors, I am not organizing you to sway the outcome of this election in anyone's favor," Jackson began. "I am in favor, however, of Americans being guaranteed free and fair elections. I think collaboration among you about overcoming these illegal actions by independent actors and DHS - now recognized by the Courts as illegal - would result in protecting the right to vote in the twelve hours remaining in this Election Day."

Governor Mason Dane of Florida spoke up first. "I am not going to let these assholes terrorize Floridians," he said. "You all know who I voted for in this election, but Florida is not going to stand by and watch these criminals scare people. We have 18 sites across the state where these creatures have ransacked or destroyed public property.

We aim to use the State Police SWAT teams to move into these locations, clear them, and reopen as many as possible."

"How many are still viable polling locations through midnight tonight?" Piper asked.

"We don't have an assessment on that as of yet," said Governor Dane.

"We have reports of these people destroying election machines, smearing feces on ballots. It's like something out of a horror movie," said an unidentified governor.

Governor Lincoln Fox of New York spoke up next. "My suggestion is that states use their emergency management agencies to set up temporary, mobile polling locations close to the affected sites. Commandeer RVs from local dealerships or owners if you have to."

"Good idea, Governor," said Valerie Lawrence, who was on the call from Austin. "I suggest clear signage and provisional ballots be on hand in the thousands."

"How do we protect the safety of voters without stationing armed police at the polls?" asked Governor Chen. "Most of our states have laws prohibiting law enforcement within so many feet of poll entrances."

Governor Polk of Illinois interjected. "I would recommend directing your state police to form a secure perimeter around the sites that is double the size of any statutory guidelines about law enforcement buffers. Given today's events, I think most voters would welcome a physical police presence to scare off these criminals."

"We are grateful for the unanimity we are hearing expressed on this call," Jackson said. He already sounded like a President, thought one governor. "I would suggest that as much as possible, some consensus actions be agreed to be taken immediately by every state where these intimidation and interference actions are occurring."

There was broad agreement among the governors on the call.

Piper proposed that the consensus actions be to seek rulings from counties in the affected states to keep polls open until 11 pm local time, that state police lead actions to detain instigators, including DHS officials that refuse to stand down, and set up of well advertised temporary polling locations using whatever available resources could be mustered into place by 3 pm.

"Might I suggest a joint press statement?" asked Governor Dane.

"What are the chances that receives a skull designation by *The Mark*?" joked Governor Fox, fully aware of the players not on the call who could quickly unravel their unanimity.

As standard closing hours arrived for state after state, election returns rolled in. Jackson and Valerie had united in Denver for their election night watch party downtown. Paul Drummond and Saima Khan, aware their chances were slim, were not planning a major campaign event but were together in Washington, DC, at a hotel downtown sponsored by the Other Party.

Warner and Alvarez were in Las Vegas at Warner's premiere property, eager to see if their many interventions throughout the day had bore fruit.

Results rolled in quickly at first since 60 percent of the vote was cast by mail and in early voting. The nation would likely have to wait days, if not weeks, to understand who had received the most votes in the 2044 presidential election.

With history's shadow looming large, many, including the candidates, understood that even those results would likely not be the final word on an Election that nearly all in the beleaguered nation were wishing would finally come to a peaceful end. Their wishes would not be granted.

38

A TRADITIONAL STOLEN ELECTION

The Piper-Lawrence campaign achieved a significant milestone as the first Third-Party to win the popular vote since 1864. However, the thrill of this victory was tempered by the absence of a clear Electoral College majority. In a display of respect for the democratic process, Jackson and Valerie refrained from pressuring electors to disregard their state's popular vote in order to vote for them. Instead, they personally contacted their electors, maintaining their total at 259 and countering any pressure from Warner and Alvarez, which was growing by the hour.

Popular Vote
Piper/Lawrence 78,503,476 (41%)
Warner/Alvarez 75,124,370 (39%)
Drummond/Khan 38,850,563 (20%)

Electoral College Votes (273 to Win)
Piper/Lawrence 259
Warner/Alvarez 258
Drummond/Khan 28

Warner was successful at winning Arkansas, Alabama, California, Florida, Georgia, Idaho, Illinois, Indiana, Kentucky, Mississippi, Missouri, Nevada, New Hampshire, New Jersey, North Dakota, Ohio, Oklahoma, Puerto Rico, South Dakota, Utah, Virginia, and West Virginia.

Piper's 259 Electoral Votes came from Arizona, Alaska, Colorado, Connecticut, Iowa, Kansas, Louisiana, Maine, Massachusetts, Michigan, Minnesota, Montana, Nebraska, New Mexico, New York, North Carolina, Pennsylvania, Rhode Island, South Carolina, Tennessee, Texas, Vermont, Washington, Wisconsin, and Wyoming.

With just 28 Electoral votes, Drummond eked out the most votes in just four states - Delaware, Maryland, Hawaii, and Oregon - plus the District of Columbia.

A bitter chill hung in the air, its icy tendrils creeping through the White House's usually grand and welcoming halls. The corridors were darker than usual, their shadows deepened by the absence of festive cheer. President Russell Warner had refused to decorate for Christmas this year, leaving the historic house feeling cold, unwelcoming, and heavy with tension.

It was December 19, and the eve of the Electoral College meeting where their official votes would be cast at State Houses across the country. Inside the Oval Office, Marco Alvarez stood beside President Warner as they made call after desperate call to pledged electors, seeking to manufacture a win.

One of three electors from Wyoming, an old cattle rancher with a gravelly voice, was on the other end of the line. His business had been severely damaged by worsening climate patterns, and he held Warner responsible for not signing financial compensation packages for ranchers harmed by the dramatic weather caused by global warming.

"Look, Roger," Marco said, his voice smooth and persuasive. "We understand your frustrations, but you have to realize that President Warner is doing his best to balance the needs of all parties."

"Balance?" the rancher snorted. "Seems to me that the scales are tipped more in favor of the folks who ain't sufferin' like we are. My cattle are dyin', Mr. Alvarez, and I'm not the only one in this predicament."

Warner's jaw tightened as he listened to the man's grievances, his eyes empty of compassion. He glanced out the window, where cold rain silently fell, saturating the White House grounds.

"Roger, please believe me when I say that we're working on a solution," Warner said, his voice firm and empty of empathy. "It's not that we don't care about your situation – it's just that a lot is riding on this Electoral College vote tomorrow."

"Really?" the rancher spat. "You mean like the fact that our land is dying, and you're more concerned with political games than actually doin' somethin' about it?"

Marco caught Warner's eye, silently pleading for patience as he tried to defuse the situation. "We know how important this issue is, Roger," Marco said, his voice velvety. And we'll do everything in our power to ensure that you and your fellow ranchers receive the financial compensation you deserve."

"You offerin' me money, Mr. Alvarez?"

"Would that help?" asked Marco.

"I don't take bribes," Roger said, growing further irritated with the call.

"You're an honorable man, Roger," Marco said with a hint of resignation.

"Your words are nice, Mr. Alvarez," the rancher replied, his tone skeptical. "It's not that I don't care about your situation; it's just that I feel bound by duty to vote for the candidate that won my state, and I don't take underminin' democracy lightly."

With that, the line went dead, leaving Marco and Warner standing in the dimly lit Oval Office. As they stared at the phone, both men knew that time was running out to flip votes in states that would count votes from faithless electors.

A faithless elector is an Electoral College elector who does not vote for the candidate for President or Vice President for whom they were pledged to vote but instead votes for another candidate or abstains from voting. Twenty states had laws requiring electors to vote for their pledged candidate, while fifteen states permitted those votes to be counted. The rest of the states had no law on the matter.

Marco rubbed his temples, trying to devise a solution that would appease Congresswoman Sween, who had sway over the electors in her state. Glancing out the window at the saturated White House lawn, he decided to try another approach.

"Congresswoman," Marco said, his voice cool and measured. "I understand your concerns, and I want to help you. What if we offered you a position on the board of directors for one of my subsidiaries? The compensation package would be quite generous, in the six-figure range."

Warner stood and walked away from the phone. He couldn't believe Marco had crossed such a line with a woman he detested without consulting him first.

There was a moment of stunned silence on the other end of the line. Then, the congresswoman's outraged voice thundered through the receiver.

"Are you trying to bribe me, Mr. Alvarez? You think you can buy my loyalty and support with money? This is precisely the kind of corrupt politics that is destroying our democracy! Good day, sir!"

With a click, the line went dead once more, leaving Marco red-faced and upset but not as angry as Warner. Before Marco could gather his thoughts, President Warner rounded on him, his brown eyes flashing with anger.

"What in the fuck was that, Marco?" he roared. "You can't just wave money around at members of Congress, especially members of the Other Party!"

"It worked on you," Marco said coldly. This comment did not soothe the angry President; in fact, it added gasoline to an already raging fire.

Olivia Clay, who had decided it was best to at least listen in on these calls, finally spoke up. "President Warner is right, Marco. Bribery and extortion won't gain us the support we need among these electors – it'll only turn more members against us if this election ends up in the House."

Marco clenched his teeth, struggling to contain his frustration. He knew they were right, but the pressure to succeed was immense. With each passing moment, their chances of capturing the 15 electoral votes they needed dwindled, spurring him to take desperate measures.

"Fine," he spat through gritted teeth. "We don't have much time left – I yield to you, Mr. President."

As Marco stormed out of the Oval Office, his mind raced with options.

Silence filled the Oval Office as the door slammed shut behind Marco. Olivia watched President Warner's face, which had turned a deep shade of red, and she knew it was time to voice her concerns.

"Mr. President," Olivia began cautiously, "We can recover. We have five more states to call through where faithless electors can have their vote counted."

"I have some reservations about Marco Alvarez, Olivia," said President Warner.

"What sort of reservations, sir?" Olivia asked.

"I do not know if I can share my thoughts due to the nature of your relationship with him, Olivia," the President said.

"Sir, I assure you..." began Olivia. Warner raised his hand to stop her.

"I am concerned about his intentions and his loyalty."

Olivia hesitated, searching for the right words when her phone buzzed. It was a text message from Marco apologizing for his outburst. She glanced at the message, then looked back at the President.

"No offense, sir, but perhaps you're overreacting," she said.

"What are your plans for Christmas and New Year's?"

"Actually, I was going to ask you the same thing, sir," Olivia replied, trying to shift the focus of the conversation.

"Christmas?" he scoffed bitterly. "I haven't celebrated it since...well, it doesn't matter. I had planned to spend the week-long break in Las Vegas at my casino. But with this Contingent Election looking more and more likely, I feel like I need to stay in Washington to continue to push our case." There was a hint of resignation in his voice, and Olivia could see the weight of his thoughts pressing down on him.

"Washington, sir? That's quite a departure from the usual holiday festivities," she commented gently. "Perhaps that is also a more responsible decision for your heart."

"Indeed," Warner admitted, staring off into the distance as if envisioning the neon lights of the city. "I may not be President on January 21st if I can't stop Marco from evaporating what remains of my relationships on the Hill."

"I'd like you to take a real break between Christmas and New Year's. I mean it. With a little rest in you, you can start fresh trying to persuade members of the House with me starting on January 2. But leave the Senate to Marco. It's time for him to sink or swim on his own merits."

"Of course, Mr. President," Olivia said the words, but would she obey them?

As Olivia left the Oval Office, she took one last look at the undecorated room; its emptiness was haunting.

"Thank you, Olivia," President Warner said suddenly, breaking the silence that had settled between them. "For your loyalty and for all that you do."

She turned to face him, a faint smile gracing her lips. "Of course, Mr. President. It's my honor to serve this country."

"Speaking of serving," Warner continued, his eyes twinkling with mischief. "Even if we win this whole thing and I end up back here, how much fun would it be to torture Valerie Lawrence as my Vice President? Especially if the Senate goes Bull Moose, but the House swings our way."

Olivia couldn't help but chuckle at the image he painted despite the gravity of their situation.

"Stranger things have happened, sir," she replied, shaking her head and excusing herself as she walked to her office adjoining the Oval.

A sudden buzz from her phone drew her attention, and she pulled it from her pocket to find another text message from Marco

Alvarez. He apologized again for his earlier outburst, then added, "I want you to come to my home in Palo Alto for New Year's. There's something important I want you to see."

Olivia hesitated, her finger hovering over the screen. She wasn't sure what Marco could possibly have to show her, but she couldn't deny her obsession with him.

"Alright," she texted back. "I'll be there."

Marco's burning humiliation did not subside when he reached his Washington apartment. He prepared to head west and watch the results of the Electoral College from his California estate. Fumbling for his phone, he dialed a number and impatiently tapped his foot as it rang.

"Tell Rushy to call me back immediately!" he barked into the phone before hanging up. He didn't have time for pleasantries or explanations – there was work to be done.

Marco's SUV pulled up to the curb with impeccable timing, and he threw open the door to slide into the heated leather seat. "Take me to Reagan National," he said.

He dialed another number, this one belonging to a friend who owed her career to him when he rescued her from scandal by burying stories about her husband's gambling addiction and drug abuse before her appointment to the U.S. 9th District bench. A woman's voice answered, sharp and confident. "Judge Delgado."

"Judge," Marco greeted her, trying to keep the frustration from his voice. "It's Marco Alvarez."

"Mr. Vice President soon to be," she said, smiling. "I have not heard from you in ages. Is everything ok?"

"Everything is wonderful. I have a surprise I want to announce at my home on New Year's Eve, and it would mean the world to me if you and your husband could join me."

"Ah, Marco," Nadine sighed, a hint of amusement in her tone. "Well, I suppose I can clear my schedule for the next Vice President and America's most eligible bachelor."

"Have you received a better New Year's Eve invitation?" he asked.

She laughed. "Better than an invite from a man with the world at his fingertips? As if!"

"Then promise me you'll bring your charm and grace to my home," he insisted.

"Very well," Nadine agreed, her voice firm. "I'll be there, Marco."

"Thank you, Judge," Marco replied, grateful for her support. As he hung up, his phone began ringing from his friends at the Chinese embassy.

39

FRANCIS SCOTT KEY

New Year's Eve morning found President Russell Warner alone in the White House gym, pedaling furiously on his stationary bike. The air was thick with sweat, and the pounding beats of 80s music pulsing loudly from the speakers. As he sang along to the lyrics, his eyes were closed, momentarily lost in a world far away from the political turmoil that consumed him.

The shrill buzz of his secure phone cut through the music, jolting him back to reality. Wiping his brow, he glanced at the screen; a text message from Congressman Webster appeared before him. The critical moderate swing vote requested Warner's presence at his Northern Arlington home that night at 10:00 pm to meet with several members of his Patriots Caucus about their votes in the Contingent Election.

"Damn," Warner muttered under his breath, knowing full well the importance of these holdouts. He quickly typed a response, asking Webster to clear the meeting with Olivia Clay, his Deputy Chief of Staff. To his surprise, Webster replied that Clay had been unresponsive, leaving the President to wonder if she was deliberately ignoring him or simply unaware.

"Can you do anything to clear the visit on such short notice?" Webster asked in the following message.

Warner considered the options and suggested they meet at the White House instead. However, Webster insisted that his Caucus preferred neutral ground. With a sigh of resignation, Warner asked for the address and promised to make it happen. "Christ, can't even get a day off on New Year's Eve," he mumbled as he turned off the music and made his way to the showers.

Later that morning, the President sat alone in the White House dining room, savoring a healthy breakfast. In front of him lay the tally for the Contingent Election. He frowned as he counted only 20 states likely in his column, maybe 21 if he were lucky. The frustration gnawed at him like a splinter under his skin.

"Where the hell is Olivia with the updates?" Warner muttered to himself, his fingers tapping impatiently on the table. He pulled out his phone and texted her, inquiring about any news she might have.

President Warner felt his heart flutter as he waited for a response. The symptoms of his new diagnosis of SVT were unnerving. Perhaps it was the significance of the meeting with Webster's Patriots Caucus. It could make or break his political career. And with each tick of the clock, the pressure only grew.

A SHAFT of morning sunlight filtered through the curtains, casting a warm glow over the bedroom. Olivia Clay slept soundly, her naked form tangled in the luxurious sheets of Marco Alvarez's Palo Alto home. On the bedside table, her phone lay untouched, not displaying any messages from the President.

"Good morning, beautiful," Marco whispered, leaning in to plant a gentle kiss on Olivia's forehead. She stirred, blinking her eyes open and stretching languidly before reaching for the steaming mug of coffee he held out to her.

"Morning," she murmured, smiling up at him. As her fingers closed around the mug, the light caught on the enormous new engagement ring she wore, making it sparkle like a beacon of their love. She couldn't help but admire it, feeling a surge of happiness at the thought of spending her life with this incredibly powerful and wealthy man.

"Big day today," Marco said, brushing a stray lock of hair away from her face. "You ready for the party tonight?"

"Of course," Olivia replied, sipping her coffee. "I can't wait to see everyone."

"Perfect. I'll leave you to get ready then," Marco said, kissing her before leaving the bedroom.

Marco met with an aide in his home office to finalize the details for the night's festivities. The party had to be underway by 7 pm, and the guests were well into conversation and clinking glasses together to celebrate the New Year.

"Make sure we have enough champagne and hors d'oeuvres for everyone," Marco said, glancing over his aide's list. "And don't forget the playlist Olivia put together."

"Got it, sir," the aide nodded, scribbling down notes.

Marco absentmindedly scanned the books on his bookshelf as they discussed the arrangements. His eyes narrowed as he realized one title was missing. The absence of that particular book nagged at him, even as he tried to focus on the party preparations.

"Add this to your list," Marco said, jotting down the title of the missing book and handing it to the aide along with several other items that needed to be purchased before 4 pm. "I need it back on that shelf by tonight."

"Understood, sir," the aide replied, pocketing the list and hurrying to fulfill Marco's orders.

With the party plans in motion and Olivia still blissfully unaware of the President's attempts to contact her, the stage was set for an unforgettable New Year's Eve.

In Alexandria, Virginia, the warm glow of a shelter kitchen serving breakfast cast a welcoming light onto the chilly streets. Inside, Jackson Piper and other volunteers bustled about, ladling steaming food onto plates for the homeless and underprivileged families who had gathered there.

"Here you go, sir," Jackson chirped, handing a bowl of oatmeal to an old man with a grizzled beard. "Have a blessed New Year." The man smiled his thanks before shuffling off to find a seat.

As the morning wore on, Jackson engaged in conversation with several men who had come to rely on the shelter for their meals. One man in particular stood out—he was mumbling incoherently to himself, his eyes darting around as if seeing things that weren't there.

"Hey, are you alright?" Jackson asked with genuine concern, stepping closer to the man. Their eyes met briefly before the man's gaze drifted back to some unseen point in the distance.

"Can't be trusted... they're watching us," the man muttered, his voice barely audible above the din of the crowded room.

"Who's watching us?" Jackson asked gently, trying to understand the man's disjointed ramblings.

"Them... the shadows," the man whispered, his voice trembling with fear.

"Let's get you some help, okay?" Jackson suggested, placing a comforting hand on the man's shoulder. Just then, private security assigned to Piper stepped in, nodding at Jackson before escorting the man away.

"Is that Secret Service?" a woman nearby asked another volunteer, pointing at the retreating figures.

"No, it's not," the other volunteer replied, shaking her head. "President Warner refuses to provide Secret Service protection to Piper and Governor Lawrence or their families."

"Such a shame," the woman clucked, glancing at Jackson worriedly. "They deserve better."

As he returned his focus to serving the needy, Jackson's mind couldn't help but wander to the coming convening of Congress on January 6. While he continued to ladle soup with a smile, his thoughts were consumed by the uncertain future ahead—a future in which the struggle for control could very well threaten to tear their nation apart.

. . .

IN THE TEXAS EXECUTIVE MANSION, Governor Valerie Lawrence stood tall in her study. Her husband, Parker, stood by her side, his hand resting reassuringly on her shoulder. A delegation of ministers and priests had arrived at the mansion, seeking to pray for the Governor's safety as she prepared to leave for Washington, DC, to meet with Congress about her candidacy in the expected Contingent Election.

A priest prayed solemnly. "May the Almighty guide and protect you in these trying times..."

THE WHITE HOUSE, usually buzzing with activity, had fallen unnaturally quiet on New Year's Eve. President Russell Warner stood before the mirror in his private quarters, adjusting his tie as he prepared for the critical meeting in Arlington. His reflection stared back at him, eyes heavy with fatigue.

"Where are those damn cuff links?" he muttered under his breath, rummaging through the drawer where they should have been. As he searched, his frustration mounted—not only with the missing cuff links but with the state of the White House itself. The staff was sparse due to the holiday, and he couldn't help but think of how Congress had cut the budget for its upkeep.

"Can't even trust them to fund this house properly," he grumbled, finally locating the presidential cuff links beneath a pile of papers.

Before affixing them, he checked his watch. It was 10:00 pm. Time to depart. With a sigh, he fastened them to his cuffs, taking one last look at his reflection before steeling himself for the evening ahead.

President Warner strode purposefully through the dimly lit White House hallways, his polished shoes clicking against the marble floor. The sparse staff exchanged nods and murmurs of "Happy New Year" with him as he made his way to the entrance. The cool night air greeted him as he stepped outside, his breath visible in the crisp winter chill. He was determined not to let this opportunity slip through his fingers.

"Mr. President," a Secret Service agent greeted him crisply, opening the door to the presidential limousine.

"Thank you," Warner replied, sliding into the plush leather seat. The heavy door shut behind him with a satisfying thud, muffling the sounds of the motorcade revving up. He took a deep breath, trying to center himself for the crucial hours ahead. Pulling out his secure phone, he texted Congressman Webster: On my way now. See you soon. The response never came, but he couldn't afford to dwell on it —time was of the essence.

Across the country in Palo Alto, Marco Alvarez stood in his California estate's elegant grand living room, surveying the elegant New Year's Party he had meticulously orchestrated. The room buzzed with conversation and laughter, champagne glasses clinking together in celebratory toasts. He sipped from his flute, the bubbles dancing on his tongue as he watched Olivia Clay on his arm.

"Marco, this party is simply divine," gushed a federal judge, her eyes alight with excitement. Olivia laughed at her exaggerated compliment, her engagement ring catching the light and drawing admiring glances from those around her.

"Thank you, Your Honor," Marco replied smoothly, his eyes flicking to his watch. He felt Olivia tense beside him, her grip on his arm tightening.

"Is everything alright, my dear?" he asked, concern lacing his words.

"I haven't heard from the President," she murmured, eyes scanning the party as if expecting him to materialize among the guests. "It's just strange, that's all." She tried to recall their last exchange, but it felt like a lifetime ago—during the flight out to the West Coast.

"Perhaps he's preoccupied with the Contingent Election," Marco suggested, though he could sense Olivia's unease. He glanced at his watch once more before excusing himself, disappearing into his office with an aid from Juniper in tow.

"Keep an eye on things out there," he instructed, shutting the door behind them. "No surprises."

. . .

The President's motorcade sliced through the crisp night air of Georgetown like a black serpent, its sleek limousines and police cars winding deftly toward the Francis Scott Key Bridge. Inside the lead limousine, President Warner stared out at the dark waters of the surging Potomac River, swelled by days of unending rain. His thoughts were heavy with the gravity of the upcoming meeting.

"Sir, we'll be arriving shortly," his Secret Service agent informed him from the driver's seat, eyes scanning the road ahead for any signs of trouble.

"Thank you, Agent Keats," Warner replied, his voice betraying a hint of apprehension.

As they turned onto the bridge, an explosion of fireworks erupted over Georgetown, illuminating the night sky and showering the city with a kaleidoscope of brilliant colors. The dazzling display momentarily distracted Warner, who couldn't help but appreciate the beauty of the scene before him.

He checked his watch again - 10:43 pm. "New Year's celebrations are starting early," he murmured with a wistful smile.

In an instant, however, the tranquility was shattered as the limousine's engine roared to life. A code implanted in the vehicle's complex navigation and control systems was activated like a microscopic nuclear bomb. The vehicle surging forward with alarming speed. Warner was thrown back into the fine leather seats, his heart hammering in his chest.

"Keats! What the hell is going on?" he shouted, gripping the armrests tightly.

"Sir, I don't have control of the car!" Keats yelled back, his hands frantically wrestling with the steering wheel. "It's like it has a mind of its own!"

With unstoppable force, the presidential limousine slammed into the police cruiser in front of it, sending the smaller vehicle careening sideways and rolling over with a sickening crunch of metal and glass. Still accelerating, the limo charged ahead, reaching speeds of over

80 mph.

"Mayday, mayday!" Keats screamed into the radio. "The limo is out of control! We need assistance immediately!"

Warner attempted to open his doors, pulling wildly on the chrome handles. Nothing happened. He leaned back and tried kicking the door with his highly polished shoes. Their steel forms and bullet proof glass — inches thick — did not budge.

As the car sped forward, it careened toward the edge of the bridge; the concrete barrier and oxidized copper railings offered no resistance, crumbling like paper under the multi-ton armored behemoth. The limousine sailed off the bridge and plunged sixty feet into the flooded Potomac River, rolling onto its roof before it hit the water with a colossal splash.

The water survival and life support systems did not deploy.

The limo windows incredibly rolled down on their own accord, allowing the murky, cold water to pour into the cabin. President Warner let out a strangled cry for help as the icy liquid engulfed him, the shock of the frigid water taking his breath away. He tried to crawl through an open window, but it began to close again, nearly severing his arm had he not removed it in time.

Agent Keats smashed buttons and pounded on the dash, now underwater, attempting feebly to regain control of the limousine. The doors would not open, and the raging river's water pressure had trapped them inside the upside-down car. The heavy vehicle sank deeper beneath the surface, disappearing from view as Secret Service agents dove into the water, swimming helplessly around the submerged limousine.

One agent attempted to pry open the door with a tire iron while the vehicle sank deeper into icy waters.

Russell Warner felt his heart beating in his chest like a snare drum. The crisis had caused his heart to plunge into another SVT episode, rattling at over 220 beats per minute.

A Secret Service agent dove into the water and swam towards the sinking vehicle. In desperation, he drew his pistol and discharged his weapon at one of the windows while underwater, knowing full well that nothing he was armed with would penetrate the glass. The gunshots actually activated countermeasures on the car, deploying glowing red hot flares from the fenders into the murky water.

For a moment, an agent saw the horrified face of the President of the United States illuminated by the haunting glow of the flare burning red like hell's flames in the frigid water. The massive car sank deeper, and the face of the helpless President disappeared from view.

The agent returned to the surface of the black river as red and gold sparks exploded overhead. More booms of New Year's celebrations sounded in the distance.

Warner struggled to make sense of what was happening. A face came into focus in his mind—a man with the most to gain through the President's disappearance, someone who had often stated his willingness to take the extreme measures imaginable.

Warner had seen the repeated warning signs but ignored them.

That bastard, thought President Russell Warner, bracing himself against the cold water, the encroaching darkness, and the pain stabbing in his chest like a thousand knives.

40

SUCCESSIONIST

The wail of sirens pierced the bitter-cold night as emergency crews swarmed the Francis Scott Key Bridge like ants on a mission. The monstrous presidential limo had plunged into the murky waters below, creating an eerie ripple in the otherwise calm Potomac River. Secret Service agents, their faces etched with determination and fear, barked orders into their radios, urgently calling for backup. They knew this wasn't just any accident – it was a catastrophe. As they assessed the gravity of the situation, they realized it was time to notify the White House.

"Get Olivia Clay on the line!" one agent shouted, his voice barely audible above the chaos.

"Jackpot is down. Repeat: Jackpot is down. Initiate Code Red protocols!" another yelled, his hands shaking as he fumbled with his radio.

IN THE LAVISH mansion of Marco Alvarez in California, the atmosphere was one of luxury and obliviousness. Guests sipped on expensive drinks as their host emerged from his study and refilled

Olivia's glass. The sparkling liquid glimmered under the chandelier's soft light, casting an enchanting spell over the room.

But their thoughts of engagement were shattered as Olivia's phone erupted with violent vibrations. Messages from the White House Situation Room and National Security Advisor flooded her screen. Excusing herself, she went to the balcony, her heart racing with a sense of impending danger.

"Olivia, listen carefully," the National Security Advisor's voice was a mix of authority and concern. "President Warner's limo was involved in a multi-vehicle crash on the Francis Scott Key Bridge. It has plunged into the Potomac. Based on the Mayday signals from the Secret Service agents driving the car, we believe there may have been a malfunction in the life support measures. We're working on getting more information, but you need to be prepared for any outcome."

Olivia's breath caught in her throat as she processed the devastating news. She clutched her phone tightly, her knuckles turning white from the pressure. Her mind raced as she thought of the implications, the potential fallout, and her final words to Russell.

"Understood," she managed to choke out, her voice barely a whisper. "Should Marco take the oath as a precaution as Acting President?"

The White House Counsel was also on the line. "Not according to the 25th Amendment. Mr. Alvarez is not yet the Vice President. He has not been confirmed by both Houses of Congress by a majority vote."

"But he is the Secretary of State. In terms of presidential succession, he is at the top of the Cabinet," she replied.

"But we should consult Speaker Sylvester Billings," the Counsel continued. "He is technically next in line before Mr. Alvarez. But Billings would have to resign the Speakership and his House seat to take the oath of office. The Senate President is not a natural born citizen and therefore is ineligible to serve."

Olivia ended the call and composed herself. Time slowed as Olivia turned back towards the house.

The tranquility of Marco Alvarez's home had been shattered by

Secret Service agents swarming the premises, their faces taut with anxiety as they tripled their presence inside. They drew the blinds and moved Marco to an interior room, away from any potential threats outside.

"What's going on?" asked Marco.

Olivia began to explain. "The President's limousine has been involved in an accident. They are not certain about his condition."

"How serious is this?" Marco asked.

"As serious as it gets," Olivia replied.

Marco stood tall and resolute. "What should I do now?"

Olivia thought quickly. "You should contact the Cabinet for advice on how to proceed. There is no confirmed Vice President, so a temporary transfer of power in the 25th Amendment is not possible right now."

"What do you mean?" asked Marco. "I am the nominated Vice President. Is that not close enough?"

No, it's not, she thought, but she said nothing. She struggled with the shock and the guilt. Why was she here and not in Washington traveling with the President?

She found a Juniper aide carefully removing cellophane from a crisp, new leather-bound volume – the Holy Bible. The aide handed it to Marco, whose face was resolute. His hands were calm as he took the volume from the aide.

She looked at him in shock. What was he doing?

Marco saw the concern on his face. "Deferring to the Cabinet and Billings is a foolish half-measure that will only invite panic and chaos."

The guests who had been enjoying themselves just moments before were now clustered around a large screen in the living room, watching live coverage of the rescue efforts at Georgetown. A crane strained to lift the wrecked limo from the river's depths.

Marco held the new Bible, its leather cover still gleaming and its spine still stiff and unwrinkled. "Hold this for me, please," he asked gently, the solemnity palpable in the air.

She took the book into her shaking hands. Olivia's mind was flooded with doubts and fears. What was he doing?

"We must protect the nation. Someone must be President. I can't do this without you."

She stared at him. Was he sincere? She froze. She held the holy book in her hands and looked down at it, the new engagement ring he had given her catching her eye.

"Ladies and gentlemen." Marco's voice boomed, hushing the worried conversations of his guests. "We need decisive action, not uncertainty."

"Olivia, would you do me the honor as I take the oath?" Marco asked.

Was she going along with this? she asked herself. Why was she so terrified and frozen? Did she agree with Marco that this was the most prudent action? What if the Cabinet disagreed with his decision? Her decision? Should she have consulted Speaker Billings first? Her body froze as she struggled with conflicting thoughts.

The federal judge, coincidentally a friend of Marco and at the hastily organized party, approached. Was it Judge Delgado? She could not remember her name. The judge was solemn and stood before Marco with a phone in her hand.

Olivia felt numb, pinned between duty and doubt.

"Olivia, darling," said Marco. His eyes were soothing and sincere. Turning to the judge, standing nearby, he asked, "Are you ready, your honor?"

"I am," the judge replied. She unlocked the phone. It displayed the text of Article II, Section 1, Clause 8 of the Constitution on the screen. She had located it quickly from a web search.

Marco raised his voice so that all in the room could here his declaration. "As Vice President designate and Secretary of State, I'm next in line to assume the presidency."

"Marco, I'm not sure about this," Olivia whispered, her voice wavering slightly. Her mind raced with concerns about how the public and political insiders would react to such a bold move.

"Olivia, we don't have time for hesitation," Marco urged, his eyes never leaving her face. "Our country needs strong leadership in this time of crisis. We must act now. I am certain about this, Olivia. We must protect the country. Our enemies abroad will seize upon a vacuum and attack us. We need to move swiftly to protect ourselves."

The tension in the room was palpable, as if a storm were brewing outside, and Marco's piercing gaze seemed to crackle with electricity.

Marco gently pulled Olivia to his side, his eyes searching hers for acceptance.

"Of course," Olivia replied, holding the Bible before him as she prepared to become an accomplice in this impromptu event. Her fingers brushed against his briefly, and she felt a tingle of electricity pass between them. Shaking off the sensation, she steadied herself, ready to witness the man she loved become the leader of the free world.

"Can someone record this?" Marco called out, his voice carrying through the room like the peel of a bell. The remaining guests, now fully aware of the gravity of the situation, scrambled to comply. Phones were raised, capturing the scene before them as Marco stood tall and proud before the judge.

"Are you ready?" the judge asked quietly, her voice steady despite the extraordinary circumstances. She was a woman well-versed in law and history and understood the importance of what they were about to undertake.

"Ready," Marco replied.

The peaceful silence that fell over the room was almost suffocating as all eyes turned to Marco Oscar Alvarez. As the judge began administering the presidential oath of office, the words seemed to etch themselves into the walls. Marco's voice was steady and resolute as he repeated the solemn vow, his gaze locked onto the judge's.

"Congratulations, Mr. President," the judge said softly once the oath was complete, her eyes brimming with tears at the historic moment she just presided over. The room erupted in subdued and respectful applause; this was not a time for celebration but for resolve and unity.

As the self-proclaimed 50th President of the United States of

America, Marco Alvarez faced his fellow citizens, his heart swelling with pride and determination. He may have been descended from humble Cuban immigrants, but today, he stood before them as the President, and if he moved quickly, no one would know how to stop him.

∼

IN CAIRO, as men and women awoke to the first morning of 2045, two bodies lay in bed of a lush bedroom on the building's third floor. Their eyes stared ghastly and lifeless at the ceiling. Their bodies were riddled with bullet wounds from the silent assassins that had ambushed them just hours before. The white cloth sheets were soaked in oozing blood. Silencers attached to the killers' weapons ensured no one would know for hours that the former Vice President of the United States and her husband had been murdered while asleep in their bed.

∼

IN THE DARKNESS of a quiet Arlington neighborhood, an unassuming house stood empty and silent. It was the rental home of Congressman Webster of Ohio. The lights were off, and it was empty and silent. This had been the supposed meeting place for President Warner and the Patriots Caucus, but the contents of the house told a different story.

The rooms were untouched, nothing arranged or assembled to indicate the arrival of the President of the United States. Shadows danced on the walls as the wind whispered through the branches of an Alder tree outside. It would have been the only living thing President Warner would have found had he reached the house that night.

Hundreds of miles away in Ohio, Congressman Webster sat in disbelief, holding his children in his arms as they stared at the images on the screen. Images of the chaos at the Francis Scott Key Bridge flickered before him.

There were no messages to the President on the phone in his pocket. No messages from Russell Warner confirming a meeting. In fact, he did not know that the President had been traveling to Webster's rented home when his motorcade came under cyber attack.

Webster had no knowledge that he was the tiny final piece of an elaborate web built to lure the President into a complex web to be caught and consumed by a calculating and patient spider.

It was a web that had been carefully woven over two years. A critical strand was set when the Presidential limousines sat silently in a Los Altos driveway at a lush estate of a generous donor. While the President sat inside consuming gin and the staff partook in a feast, the onboard computers of the limousine had been infected by a new weapon invented by Juniper as part of its SiDefense programs. It was used to transfer code simply through proximity to another chip. The code had been successfully planted and instructed to lie dormant and undetected for months until the proper opportunity presented itself.

That opportunity finally arrived on December 31, 2044, at 10:43 pm on the Francis Scott Key Bridge, leaving Georgetown for Arlington.

41

SEEDS OF REVOLUTION

The sounds of merriment echoed through the rented home in Alexandria as friends assembled for New Year's festivities. The heart of these celebrations was Jackson Piper, engaged in deep conversation with Congressman Murphy while Governor Valerie Lawrence held court with stories of her time as an Olympic sharp-shooter near the fireplace.

"Jackson! How's our future president holding up?" a guest called out, catching his eye.

The room cheered.

"Doing well," he replied, raising his glass in a toast. "To new freedoms!"

The room raised their glasses and cheered again.

A wave of disbelief rippled through the partygoers as someone cried out, "The President's limousine has crashed!" Unease painted their faces as they reached for their devices, desperately scrolling through an onslaught of notifications.

"Francis Scott Key Bridge... multi-vehicle accident..." another guest stammered, reading from their phone screen. Members of Congress whipped out their phones, texting colleagues and aides for any shred of information they could find. The news spread like wildfire, igniting a chaotic mixture of anger, fear, and confusion.

"Is this for real?" a woman whispered. "Or is it one of those damned lies again?"

"TRUTH" and "LIE" labels flashed on screens around the room as *The Mark* confused fact and fiction, as intended for this fateful night. Fear and disbelief began to grow in homes and parties across the nation.

Jackson felt his phone buzz in his pocket. He quickly glanced at the screen – a call from Speaker of the House Sylvester Billings. Motioning to Valerie, Parker, and Catherine, Jackson led them into a study in a quiet corner of the historic home. He put the call up on a screen in the study.

"Jackson," Sylvester said, his voice slurred and frantic. "Are you seeing this? What the hell happened?"

"Your intelligence is probably better than mine," said Jackson. "Care to fill us in on what you know?"

"Well, President Warner was headed ovah to an event in Arlington. His limo lost control, crashed into a police cruiser, and then shot off the damned bridge like a gator at a Pekinese." The words were heavy with bourbon, allowing his cajun side to shine through.

"Surely the limo has about 50 different defense measures and an underwater life support system, right?" asked Valerie.

Billings blinked his blurry eyes. "Secret Service is saying right now that they believe there was some sort of malfunction. The driver of the President's car had screamed, 'Mayday, Mayday' at the start of the ballyhoo."

Jackson received a text. It was from Reese Tulson.

> REESE
>
> Tippecanoe returns

> JACKSON
>
> We don't know that yet

> **REESE**
> Alvarez is going to take the oath. Get your family to safety, Jackson. Don't take this lightly. The rules have changed again.

There was a crash on Billings' end of the call.

"Mr. Speaker," said Valerie, "Are you alright?"

Sylvester Billings, who had been ringing in the New Year with libations and jubilation, had literally fallen off his chair during the call.

"Galee, if that isn't the craziest way to start 2045, I don't know what chiz," said Billings.

"Billings is next in the order of succession," Valerie said quietly. He was in no condition to assume the presidency if it came to that.

"Dang-blasted-cheap shit!" exclaimed the drunk Speaker, wresting to climb back into his chair.

Jackson muted the call, working over the dire scenarios as he spoke, "If Billings becomes President, we risk losing control of the House."

"Because there is no clear successor to Sylvester," said Diesel. "It would be like Planet of the Apes over there."

"A vacancy in the Speaker would likely take priority over counting the Electoral College or conducting a Contingent Election," said Piper, recalling years of ridiculous tug of-wars over the Speakership in the 2020s.

"And that means we lose any chance of a fair Contingent Election," said Valerie. "Our enemies would be lining up to fix the Election for Alvarez."

Speaker Sylvester Billings, leaning back gingerly in his chair and stroked his bulky chin. "Y'all still there? Your mouths are moving but I can't hear nuttin!"

"Look, Mr. Speaker," Jackson cut in, his voice firm yet measured, "I know this is asking a lot of you, but we need you to hold the line in the House. We don't have much time and can't afford to lose footing there. You must ensure a fair set of Rules is adopted for the Contingent Election."

"Whatcha gettin at, sonny Jack?" Sylvester asked.

Parker whispered to the group, "You're asking Mr. Billings to say no to becoming the President?" said Parker wide-eyed. "That's a big ask of a man of his patriotism."

"Don't you worry about a gawd-dang-thing, Jack! The House will do its part to ensure a fair election."

"We must see the Contingent Election through. We have to resist the temptation to just cut a deal like 1876. It was a disaster. The framers insisted on the Contingent Election for a reason," Jackson said.

"Alright naw, I see whatch yer sayin. You have my word, Mr. President-to-be-selected."

"Thank you, Mr. Speaker," said Jackson, relieved.

"I'm gonna need a monument or something named after me," said Tulson with a hiccup. "The man who refused the power of the presidency. Naw aint that sumptin."

Another urgent text arrived.

> REESE
> You on the road yet?

TRUMPETS BLARED, and drums boomed as news organizations announced a new development in the situation involving the President.

"We have just received official confirmation that Russell Warner, the 49th President of the United States, has died. His body was recovered at 12:20 a.m. Eastern."

The home in Alexandria went silent.

Jackson's mind was starting to fill with dozens of potential scenarios. He was certain that the mighty wall of protection that surrounded the President via the Secret Service would never allow such a freak accident to occur. They were too attentive to the details. No, in Jackson's mind this was an attack and the next assaults would come at any moment. He needed time and quiet to think.

"Diesel," Jackson said pulling his closest advisor aside. "I want you to clear the house. Send everyone home. We're giong to need time to regroup and plan our next move. This changes everything. We now need to run against Alvarez in the Contingent, not Warner. This could set us back..."

More trumpets blared.

BREAKING NEWS flashed across the screens, causing their small clutch to grow silent again. A video played of Marco Alvarez standing proudly before a federal judge in California, his hand raised high as he recited the presidential oath of office. It was a surreal image that sent shockwaves through those who had not yet seen it.

"Are you fucking kidding me! That bastard!" Valerie said.

It was followed by "President" Marco Alvarez, issuing a statement directly to the camera.

"My fellow Americans," said Marco Alvarez. "We are mourning on this usually festive eve of a new year. Our President has been taken from us in what would appear to be an accident, but intelligence agencies are telling me otherwise."

The room gasped. Diesel and Jackson exchanged a horrified look.

Alvarez continued. "Given this sudden and disruptive transfer of power, I am declaring a National Emergency. I am ordering a national curfew of 1:00 a.m. to 6:00 a.m. until further notice. There will be no looting or destruction of property for any reason. I am mobilizing the National Guard immediately to enforce these curfews."

Many citizens watching the address across the country were frozen in shock.

"Unbelievable," Valerie whispered, her eyes locked on the screen as she watched Alvarez claim the mantle of President without a shred of legitimacy.

Billing's mouth was agape. "I'm gonna put the gris-gris on that sommabitch for jumpin ahead of me in line! The Speaker is to become President when there is no Vice President!"

President Alvarez continued. "Until we know the true cause of the death of our beloved President, which I now believe to be a brutal attempt at a coup, I am closing all federal buildings until further notice, including the United States Capitol and the Supreme Court. This is to protect the lives of our elected leaders. Because I have reasonable intelligence presented to me that the Bull Moose Party likely coordinated this attack on the President in order to install Sylvester Billings as President, I am declaring the Bull Moose Party and its leaders enemies of the United States."

The Alexandria home gasped, then became consumed in panic.

"Can he do that?" Parker asked.

"Legally? Fuck no," Billings said. "But I don't think that's going to stop him. We all need to get to safety. Jackson, Valerie, go!" Billings urged, his voice strained. "When you're safe and settled, send me a signal for us to speak about our next move! God be with you!" Billings ended the call, and the screen went black.

The television screen flickered, casting an eerie glow on the tense faces gathered in the dimly lit room. Jackson was angered as he watched Marco Alvarez's smug expression.

"If he closes Congress, it cannot count the Electoral College votes on January 6th," said Valerie. She stood before the large screen as others watched in silence. She turned, the screen casting her silhouette as a ghostly shadow. No Electoral Count, no Contingent Election. He's consolidating power, ladies and gentlemen. He's the one mounting a coup."

It was a moment of outrage shattered by the shrill sound of Ziggy's voice coming over the speakers of Jackson's devices.

"Jackson, Valerie," she said hastily, her voice trembling with agitation. "You need to leave immediately. Take your families and go with the Security Team to undisclosed locations, Alpha and Omega. Directions are being sent via encrypted message to your security agents' vehicles."

"What's this now?" asked Catherine, beginning to panic as she approached Ziggy on a screen.

"I have detected across numerous government communication channels that President Alvarez has issued an order for your arrest, naming each of you as enemies of the United States and interfering with a national emergency," replied Ziggy. "You have absolutely no time to lose. You must leave now. They will arrive at this location in less than nine minutes."

"Run and hide?" Jackson snapped, his eyes blazing with defiance. "That's not who we are."

Catherine looked around the room in horror. She bolted to the back of the house where the boys were playing. She frantically packed suitcases with anything she could grab of importance, zipped them closed, and emerged with her two boys in tow.

"Jackson! Listen to me," Catherine said. "We have to go. Now!" The boys were in tears, scared by the panicking adults all around them.

"Cate, just hold on a second," said Jackson.

"Jack, when a being with ten million times the intelligence of a human violates her programming in order to tell you to run, you know what you do?" She looked at Valerie. "You fucking run," Catherine said desperately.

"Attention!" Ziggy pleaded, her voice cracking. "A fleet of fifteen FBI vehicles - including SWAT - just left a local FBI branch office. There is an extremely high probability they are coming here. You must leave now!"

The house emptied of party-goers and the leaders of the Party scrambled to pack their most necessary belongings.

Jackson texted Reese.

JACKSON

> You were right. I can't talk now, as communications are compromised. I'll be in touch soon. Pray for our safety.

"Ziggy, do what you can to stall any approaching vehicles," Jackson ordered, his voice firm.

"Already on it," Ziggy replied. Her function was at peak capability, writing programs that she used to hack several critical infrastructure systems between the FBI vehicles and the home in Alexandria. She overloaded water pressure on several fire hydrants, sending water gushing into the street, forced signals at intersections into four-way stops, and successfully implanted a virus in the government autocars that sent them driving in the wrong direction, their navigation now pointing them to an address in Chicago.

Ziggy started autocars near the approaching FBI vehicles and placed over two hundred of them stationary in the streets leading to their locations, creating an instant midnight traffic jam.

Outside the home, headlights flashed as several empty SUVs whipped and rolled to ready for transport the senior members of the entourage.

Diesel had ensured the last of the guests were out of the home and heading to safety. Standing now in the kitchen were the Piper four - Jackson, Catherine, Ben, and Alex - Valerie and Parker Lawrence, Libby, security agents Esmael and Sol, IT specialists Sinthia Sloan, and Senator Diesel Browning. They quickly joined hands at Jackson's request.

The group stood in the quiet, dark home and bowed their heads. Jackson prayed over the group, the words spoken swiftly but sincerely. "God our Father, we pray for our nation tonight. We ask you to reveal to us the wisdom of these events and the role we are to play in them. Bless our travels tonight; provide us safety from here to our destinations. Calm our worried hearts and heal the wounds of division and fear gripping our country. Gird us with courage and make us instruments for justice. All this we pray in your holy name, Amen."

They ran for the waiting vehicles. "What's next?" asked Sinthia, heading for one of the SUVs.

"We regroup. Plan a counterattack," Diesel said.

"We awaken the revolutionary spirit of our country and its respect for our Constitution," Jackson said.

Sinthia climbed into an SUV with the Lawrences. Sol started the car and plotted a route to destination Omega.

"If it's just the twelve of us waging this fight, Alvarez can label us as agitators and put us in jail," Parker said.

"But if there are a thousand of us..." Valerie began.

"Ten thousand," Libby interrupted. "We can easily mobilize ten thousand." She climbed into the rear seat with Sinthia.

Jackson and Valerie stood alone on the wet grass of the front lawn in the midnight darkness. "We might have a shot at keeping our Constitution intact if we can energize people against this," Jackson said.

"Damn right," Valerie said. "When do we speak again?"

"I will have Ziggy send you each a message. You'll know it's from me because it will reference the Tree of Liberty."

"From the debate," said Valerie. "Outstanding!"

They exchanged a handshake, but Valerie reached for Jackson and hugged him tightly. "Please be safe, Jackson. We need you."

Esmael plotted a route to destination Alpha via encrypted instructions from Ziggy. "Let's go, Mr. Piper!" he shouted.

The leadership of the Bull Moose Party boarded two separate SUVs—in the first were the Pipers and Diesel, with Esmael at the wheel, and the Lawrences, with Libby, Sinthia, and Sol driving the second.

The year 2045 opened for America by plunging over the brink of disunion into a dark abyss of uncertainty unlike any in its history. Never before had such a vacuum of leadership occurred between Election Day and Inauguration Day. Never before had someone declared themselves to be the President without opposition and contrary to the lawful order of presidential succession. Never before had a man successfully used wealth to maneuver undetected to ascend to the presidency without winning any prior election to secure it.

Marco Alvarez insisted to the nation that his motives were honorable and that he would be guided by the Constitution. His surreptitious moves and concealed aims belied the truth—that Marco Alvarez was not acting alone, and the health of the Republic was the very last thing on his mind.

The two vehicles carrying Piper and his allies accelerated into the night, one heading south and the other west. Vague tire tracks on the wet pavement were the only remaining signs of their escape from

Alexandria. They disappeared into the darkness as silently and mysteriously as the bull moose in the aspen grove. Jackson now recalled the harrowing wild encounter as they drove furiously through the night. He closed his eyes and imagined the smell of the forest and the quiet solitude. It felt like a dream to which he feared he could never return. Now, he was the one being hunted.

∼

ACKNOWLEDGMENTS

To write a book of this size and ambition, it takes many individuals to get the final product across the finish line.

First and foremost, thank you to my wife and partner, **Serena**, who gave me the space and the understanding to explore something that is at the core of who I am - writing. She has worked beside me during every campaign, supported my every dream, encouraged every new idea, and who has been the peanut butter to my jelly during the good, bad, and ugly moments of life.

Thank you to my sons, **Jackson, Parker, and Luke** who gave up many hours of quality father-son time so I could work at my keyboard in the basement. I tried to write at night as often as I could so as to not take away from our time, but your generosity proves to me that you three will be great men one day.

Thank you to my mom, **Sherry,** who was an exceptional beta reader. She provided powerful insights to keep the plot moving and the details lining up as the story marched across the page. Your love and support have made a world of difference in my life.

To my father, **Steve** , thank you for the many hours talking about politics. Even when we don't see eye to eye, the time you take to show interest in my passions means the world to me.

To my step-father, **Greg**, for your eternal optimism and awe for my talents and passions.

A word of special thanks to **Christopher Harris** who gave me the gift of a notebook that set all this madness in motion.

Thank you to **Thomas Umstattd, Jr.** for the inspiration and education that made my publishing dreams finally become reality.

The Novel Marketing Podcast was a lighthouse for me when I was unsure what to do next. My appreciation to **James L. Rubart** for his genuine positivity and encouragement to shock the Broca, not to mention the education on how to be a successful narrator.

Thank you to **Thea Newell** for her early developmental editing expertise that transformed this book into a viable novel. Thank you to **Joshua M. Coffey** for the brilliant line editing support and for 30 years of genuine love and friendship.

My deep appreciation to the **Book Launch Blueprint Class of 2024** and the **Order of the Oxford Comma** for the shared experience of setting goals together and professional mentorship.

Thank you to Jedi Master **Sue Petersen** who read the first draft of this story in 2005, and even though it was awful then, you always encouraged me to keep writing.

To the many people in my life who think they might have inspired a character in this book, it is truly a coincidence, I assure you.

To writers who inspire me to pursue this art, **Michael Crichton, Michael Beschloss, H.W. Brands, Aaron Sorkin, Allen Drury, Stephen King, Tom Clancy, Candice Millard, Dan Brown,** and **Daniel Silva,** thank you for your dedication to quality, inspiration and cultivation of the written word.

ABOUT THE AUTHOR

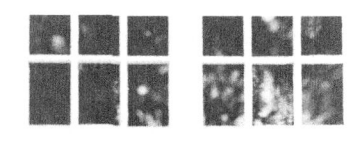

Michael Fedor, independent author.

American author Michael Fedor brings 20 years of experience from the wild, wooly worlds of Washington, DC and state capitals to tell captivating stories of power, politics, and the human condition. His style is fast-paced, rich with accurate details, and deliciously thrilling. Readers will wonder where the lines of real-life end and political fantasy begin.

Michael began his career as an English teacher, standing on desks (ala John Keating) declaring *"Carpe Diem!"* and urging adolescents and young adults to "make your lives extraordinary."

Feeling drawn to another calling, Michael left the classroom two decades ago to work on policy and politics. Working for candidates from Dogcatcher to President, Michael gained an up-close view of the personal costs of pursuing power. A multi-year candidate himself, he won 3 of the 5 offices he sought before hanging up his "running shoes" for good in 2020.

Earning both master's and bachelor's degrees from Penn State, Michael says the single greatest takeaway from his alma mater was meeting his best friend and love of his life, Serena, who is a fellow Penn State alumna. Michael and Serena celebrated 20 years of marriage in 2024. They live in Pennsylvania, raising three boys to have imagination, healthy loves of ice cream, and generous souls.

Like the main character of the *Bull Moose* series, Michael is an avid outdoorsman, a voracious reader, and a student of history. Michael remains undefeated at Pub Trivia.

Learn where to purchase past and upcoming books, check out events with Michael, or join the author's exclusive *Intrigue Insiders* email list at www.michaelfedorbooks.com

- facebook.com/michaelfedorbooks
- x.com/michaeljfedor
- instagram.com/michaelfedorbooks
- amazon.com/stores/Michael-Fedor/author/B0CSWNPH18
- bookbub.com/authors/michael-fedor

ALSO BY MICHAEL FEDOR

The Senate Deception: A Political Thriller (Bull Moose Prequel) January 2024

Tree of Liberty (Bull Moose Book 2) November 2024

Printed in Great Britain
by Amazon